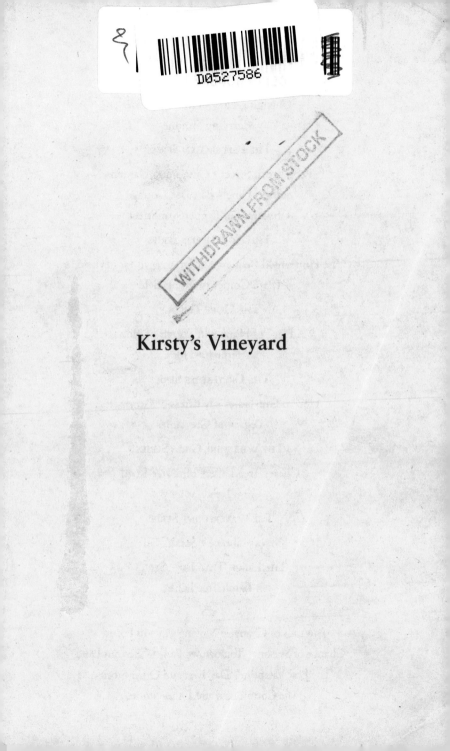

Kirsty's Vineyard

By Anna Jacobs

THE PENNY LAKE SERIES

Changing Lara • Finding Cassie
Marrying Simone

THE PEPPERCORN SERIES

Peppercorn Street • Cinnamon Gardens
Saffron Lane • Bay Tree Cottage
Christmas in Peppercorn Street

THE HONEYFIELD SERIES

The Honeyfield Bequest • A Stranger in Honeyfield
Peace Comes to Honeyfield

THE HOPE TRILOGY

A Place of Hope • In Search of Hope
A Time for Hope

THE GREYLADIES SERIES

Heir to Greyladies • Mistress of Greyladies
Legacy of Greyladies

THE WILTSHIRE GIRLS SERIES

Cherry Tree Lane • Elm Tree Road
Yew Tree Gardens

THE WATERFRONT SERIES

Mara's Choice • Sarah's Gift

THE LARCH TREE LANE SERIES

Larch Tree Lane

❧

Winds of Change • Moving On • In Focus
Change of Season • Tomorrow's Path • Chestnut Lane
The Best Valentine's Day Ever and Other Stories
The Cotton Lass and Other Stories

Kirsty's Vineyard

ANNA JACOBS

Allison & Busby Limited
11 Wardour Mews
London W1F 8AN
allisonandbusby.com

Previously published in 2008.

This paperback edition published in Great Britain by Allison & Busby in 2022.

Copyright © 2008 by ANNA JACOBS

A CIP catalogue record for this book is available from
the British Library.

10 9 8 7 6 5 4 3 2 1

ISBN 978-0-7490-2863-3

Typeset in 10.5/15.5 pt Sabon LT Pro by
Allison & Busby Ltd

Printed and bound by
CPI Group (UK) Ltd, Croydon, CR0 4YY

Prologue

Lancashire, England

Kirsty took a lot of care choosing a new dress, bright red and, she thought, very flattering. At least, Mike's eyes said so when he saw it. It was their eighth wedding anniversary and they'd booked a table at their favourite restaurant, going there by taxi because they wanted to share a bottle of champagne. She reached out for Mike's hand, smiling at him. He gave it three squeezes, their secret signal for 'I love you' and she responded in kind.

Sirens suddenly wailed and a blue light flashed ahead of them. The driver cursed and yelled, 'Hold tight!' He braked hard, trying to avoid a speeding car that was coming round the corner on the wrong side of the road.

As tyres screeched, Kirsty was flung against the seat belt and the car side-swiped the taxi. The world seemed to explode around her as they rolled over. Everything happened so fast it was over before she do more than scream.

It took her a few seconds to work out that she was upside down and something warm was trickling along her face. She tried to move and moaned as pain sliced through her arm, so fierce, so all-consuming she felt sick. After that one attempt to free herself, she kept perfectly still.

'Mike? How are you?'

There was no answer, but his warm body was pressed against hers. He must be unconscious. She prayed he wasn't badly hurt.

She found it hard to concentrate. Lights flickered and blurred around her, voices told her to lie still and she did. She wished desperately for Mike to regain consciousness.

After what seemed a very long time, someone got the car door open and put a collar round her neck.

'Don't touch my left arm!' she gasped.

The man muttered something to the person behind him, then said gently, 'We'll have to strap it, love. Can't give you anything for the pain yet. I'm sorry. What's your name?'

She told him, then gasped. It hurt so much she couldn't hold back her moans.

'Nearly there now,' that soothing voice said. 'We're cutting you free, then we'll ease you out.'

'See to my husband first. He's unconscious.'

'We'll look after him, love, don't worry. We need to get you out of the way so that we can reach him.'

That made sense, if anything did tonight. She tried not to whimper as they laid her on a stretcher trolley and wheeled her through a barrage of blinding lights into an ambulance.

When they shut the rear door, someone started up the engine and she pleaded with them to wait for Mike.

'There's another ambulance for him, love,' a female paramedic told her.

At the hospital they wheeled her straight through the emergency department to a cubicle at the rear, where a doctor was waiting.

'You've broken your arm, Mrs Miller. We'll have to operate. When did you last eat?'

She had trouble working it out. 'It was – I can't – oh, yes, at lunchtime. We were on our way to the restaurant when the crash happened.' Tears filled her eyes. 'It's our wedding anniversary today.'

'Tough luck, eh? Now, let's get you prepped. You'll feel a lot more comfortable when they've sorted out that arm of yours and given you some proper painkillers.'

'What about my husband? How is he? Surely they've brought him in by now?'

'Not arrived yet.'

'Can't I wait, see him first?'

'He wouldn't want you to lie there in pain, now would he?'

When Kirsty woke it was still dark and she couldn't think where she was. Her eyelids felt so heavy she let them close and didn't wake again until daylight.

Her sister was sitting by her bed. She'd been crying.

'Sue?'

'Kirsty. How do you feel?'

'Dopey. And thirsty.'

'I'll fetch a nurse.'

They gave her something to drink and checked her arm, which was now in plaster, then the nurse looked at Sue, who nodded.

Kirsty watched the nurse leave then looked at her sister. 'How's Mike?'

Sue took her hand. 'He didn't make it, darling.'

Kirsty couldn't think what she meant for a minute, didn't want to understand those words, then stared at her sister in horror as the meaning sank in. 'No.'

'I'm so sorry.'

'No.' Someone began to scream and only when the nurse came rushing in to help hold her still did Kirsty realised it was herself screaming. Only she couldn't stop. They gave her an injection and she drifted away.

Her last thought was that this was a nightmare and she'd wake up soon.

It was the worst nightmare she'd ever had.

She was alone when she woke up. She looked round to see a hospital room. It wasn't a dream, then. She really was here.

A shadow fell across the bed and she looked up to see her brother standing there, solemn-faced. She couldn't think what to say to him and to her relief, he simply sat down beside her without speaking.

'What about the taxi driver?' she asked.

'He died too. That side of the car got the worst of it.'

'Poor man.' She swallowed hard, trying not to burst into tears. 'I can't believe Mike's dead.'

'No. Sorry. It's – bad.'

A nurse looked in and immediately came to stand by the bed and take her pulse. 'Do you want another sedative, Mrs Miller?'

'No.' It would only postpone things.

'Call me if you need anything.'

When the nurse had gone, silence fell. Kirsty had never been so thankful that Rod was a man of few words. It was comforting to have him there, but she didn't want to talk. What was there to say? She reached out for his hand.

Two days later they said she could go home if she had someone to help her.

'I don't want to go home,' she told her brother, who was spending another mainly silent hour by her bedside. 'I can't bear the thought of that flat without Mike. I just – can't.'

'You can come to my place if you like. I've got a spare bedroom.'

'Thanks. That'd be . . . better.'

A few tears escaped but she was getting used to ignoring them, hadn't given in again to the urge to howl aloud in sheer misery. It'd not do any good. Mike was dead and nothing would ever bring him back.

A month passed and she was still at Rod's house. He'd fetched her clothes and books, but she hadn't gone back to the flat.

'Why don't you live here permanently?' he suggested one evening after tea. 'We can share expenses.'

She stared at him for a moment. 'I thought you liked living alone.'

He shook his head. 'I don't. But no one else wants to live with me.'

She could understand that. Her brother had a communications disorder, which affected his interpersonal skills. He was brilliant with numbers, so had found a job without too much trouble, but had no idea how to deal with people. He understood this, but could do little about it.

He'd learned to be quiet sometimes, but mostly he said the first thing that came into his head. She got on all right with him, though.

'OK. Thanks.' She'd be glad to economise. Mike had let his life insurance slip and the funeral expenses had been hefty. They'd been saving to buy a house, but hadn't got very far. People who worked in libraries weren't well paid and Mike had always said life was too short to live meanly. She was glad now about that, but wished they'd done more together before she lost him.

She realised Rod was beaming at her but couldn't manage a smile in return, didn't feel as if she'd ever smile again.

Chapter One

October, four years later

Kirsty escorted this month's speaker to the side area of the library, casting a quick glance over the audience, assessing it. Enough people to make a respectable showing, thank goodness. She introduced the elegant older woman and sat down at the front, not at all interested in the topic, which was 'Getting the Best out of Life'. But it was her turn to babysit the speaker today, so she tried to look interested.

It was quite a coup to have Catherine Kintley. They'd booked her to speak six months ago, but since then her second book had hit the bestseller charts and she'd appeared on television, been featured in articles in women's magazines, had become a celebrity, as people called it these days.

In spite of her reservations about motivational speakers, Kirsty was quickly caught up in what the woman was saying. Catherine had lost her husband when she was thirty-two, just as Kirsty had, and at forty had been diagnosed with ovarian cancer. At sixty, Catherine was vibrant with life and enthusiasm, and communicated it so well the audience sat up straighter, smiled, laughed, nodded – putty in her hands.

Afterwards they queued up to buy Catherine's book. She took the time to speak to everyone and make them feel special.

When it was all over, Kirsty picked up a copy of the book and surprised herself. 'I'd like to buy one as well.'

While the bookseller took the money, Catherine signed the book then smiled at her. 'I hope it helps. You look rather quiet and sad.'

'Do I?'

'Yes. Just when you relax your guard. I saw it happen a couple of times during my talk. You're too young to have such a guarded expression.'

'I lost my husband too,' Kirsty admitted.

'Recently?'

'No, four years ago.'

Catherine held Kirsty's hand in both hers. 'You've not really moved on, dear. I can see it in the way you hold yourself; quiet, tight, shut away. Sorry. I shouldn't be so personal, but I hate to see lives wasted, when there's a big world out there full of exciting things to do. I hope my book helps you.'

The warmth of Catherine's smile lingered long after Kirsty had waved goodbye to her at the library door.

She looked at the book and wondered what had got into her. She never read this sort of thing, preferring gentle romances or family stories. Nothing violent, nothing miserable or extreme.

And she had moved on, of course she had. She'd made a whole new life for herself with Rod and it was very . . . pleasant. She had friends, family she loved, good books to read, didn't need or expect any more than that from life now.

But Catherine's words lingered in her mind all day.

When she got home, Kirsty found Rod in a much more cheerful mood than usual. 'There's a new job advertised at work,' he announced before she'd even got her coat off. 'It'd be a promotion for me and I could do the work standing on my head.'

She made all the appropriate noises, but he went on and on, so in the end she escaped to her computer. But she spent more time staring blindly at the screen than she did answering emails or getting on with her genealogical research into their family history.

At sixty, Catherine Kintley had been glowing with life. Kirsty's eyes went inevitably to the photo she kept on her desk: her and Mike on their wedding day. In it, they both radiated happiness. She stared across her bedroom at the mirror. From a distance she might have been a well-preserved fifty, not thirty-six. The woman in the mirror was . . . she searched for a word and came back reluctantly with 'colourless'. Why had she never noticed that before?

Oh, she was being silly! And she might have been stupid enough to buy the book, but she wasn't going to read it.

She did, though, and couldn't put it down. Every word seemed meant for her.

But how did you do it? How did you break out of your comfort zone? Catherine said it would be a different way for each person and you had to find your own route – and that was the challenge.

Kirsty truly enjoyed her job, loved helping people, hearing how much they'd enjoyed a book she'd recommended. She certainly didn't intend to change that.

And she didn't fancy going out on the hunt for a new guy, either, whatever her friend Neris said.

So what could she do to change things? She racked her brain, but came up with nothing.

Two weeks later Kirsty parked her car and began walking towards the library. Her shift didn't start for half hour but she always liked to arrive early. As she turned the corner, she saw an old man stagger and sag against the wall for a moment or two. He looked so like her beloved grandfather, it stopped her in her tracks. She still missed Pops dreadfully, ten years after his death.

She hurried across to help the stranger to a nearby bench.

He gave her a faint smile as he eased himself down. 'Sorry to trouble you. Came over dizzy for a minute or two. It must be the new medication.'

'If you like, I'll stay with you till you feel better, in case you need help.'

'That's very kind of you. Are you sure I'm not keeping you?'

'I'm on my way to work at the library but I'm early.' She sat down beside him. 'Is there anything I can get you?'

'No, thanks. I just need a minute or two to pull myself together then I'll call a taxi. I've got one of those mobile phones, but it's fiddly to use and the keys are too small for these.' He held out a hand whose fingers were gnarled with arthritis.

The way he spoke was strange, basically northern like hers, but with a hint of something else as well. 'I was just trying to place your accent.'

'I was born round here, all my family were, but I've been living in Australia for the past sixty years.'

'Oh, so you're visiting.'

'No, I'm here to stay this time. I've an urge to hear the sounds of my childhood, see the places where I was young. It's a sentimental journey, I suppose, but I've only myself to please now because my wife's dead.' He shook his head as if baffled. 'Can't believe I'm nearly ninety. I still feel like a lad inside my head sometimes.'

His colour was improving but he still looked frail, and that resemblance to Pops kept her by his side. 'Do you want me to call you a taxi?'

'Yes, please.' He fumbled in his pocket and held the little phone out to her. 'Show me how you do it again. To tell you the truth, I've not quite got the hang of it. I didn't need one of these at home in Australia, you see.'

So she showed him, but turned off the phone as soon as it rang. Then she made him turn it on himself and dial for a taxi, to reinforce the lesson. 'There. You did it.'

'You explain it better than that uppity young fellow in the shop.'

She smiled. She was used to explaining things to elderly people at the library and really enjoyed their company.

The taxi arrived five minutes later and she helped him into it. He held the door open and looked up at her. 'My name's Ed James, what's yours?'

'Kirsty Miller.'

He offered his hand, looked down at hers, then glanced at her left hand. 'Thanks for your help, lass. Your husband's a lucky man.'

She didn't spoil the moment by telling him she was a widow. She didn't know why she continued to wear the wedding ring. Habit, probably. After watching the taxi drive away she thrust her hands into her pockets and walked briskly across the car park to work. The weather was getting chilly now, soon be winter. She was going to miss the warmer weather.

It turned out to be the sort of day that brought one minor crisis and irritation after another.

And when she got home, there was a crisis of another sort – Rod. One look at his face and she knew he'd not got the promotion.

'What do they want from me?' he demanded, thumping the table. 'I couldn't have worked harder. What do they want? This is the third time I've been passed over for promotion.'

Kirsty tried to listen patiently because she knew how bitterly disappointed he was. She could have told him exactly why he hadn't got the job in management – because he wasn't good with people and was so pernickety about details he drove people mad. He irritated her too sometimes. She'd have found a flat of her own by now, only she knew how much that'd upset him. He had no friends, no one to socialise with except her.

Most of the time they rubbed along together quite well, but lately she'd been feeling restless. It was partly the fault of that book.

She sighed. There must be more to life than this placid existence, only what? How to find it?

Two days later, the old man she'd helped walked slowly into the library. He looked a lot better today, but was leaning heavily on the stick. He saw her and smiled, such a warm smile she murmured to her friend Neris, 'Can I deal with this customer? I know him slightly.'

'Sure.'

He took a chair at the queries desk. 'Hello again, Kirsty Miller. I'd like to join your library, please.'

'And we'd love to have you, Mr James.'

'Ed. We don't go mistering people in Australia.'

By the time she'd helped him fill in the forms and choose some books, it was her lunch break. The sun was shining, so she ate her sandwiches quickly and went for a walk in the park. Ed was sitting there in a sheltered spot, face turned up to the weak wintry sunlight, both hands resting on his walking stick. His expression was so sad, she couldn't help stopping.

'Hello again. Want some company?'

'I'd love some, but what's a pretty girl like you doing with an old fogey like me? Why aren't you meeting that husband of yours?'

'Mike was killed four years ago.'

'Ah. That explains the sadness in your eyes. I lost my wife ten years ago. You never stop missing them, do you?'

Why did people keep telling her she looked sad? She wasn't – well, not more than any other widow.

They sat for a minute or two in a companionable silence, then he harrumphed and pulled his scarf more tightly round his neck. 'There's a nice little café on the corner. It's warmer there. Have you time for a cup of tea?'

'Yes.' She'd make time.

When they were sitting with steaming cups in front of them, she said, 'Will you tell me about Australia? I've always wanted to go there.' She'd read several travel books about it.

She was late getting back to work, but no one worried because it was give and take, and she often worked more than her set hours if they had a rush on. She'd thoroughly enjoyed her chat. Ed's body might be frail, but there was nothing wrong with his mind and he had a way of describing things that brought them to vivid life. He seemed a lot like Pops in nature as well as appearance.

After that he came into the library regularly, borrowing only novels, largely romances, which he said reminded him of his wife. If Kirsty wasn't free, he'd wait to be attended to by her and have a quick chat. Once or twice they went out for a coffee in her lunch break and one Sunday she drove him out to a little village where he'd lived as a lad and he bought her lunch at a pub. She was worried he couldn't afford this and tried to pay her share.

He placed his hand over hers, stopping her opening her purse. 'I can well afford it, Kirsty. I'm not on the old age pension.'

'Oh. Well, all right, then.'

Another day, the wind was raw and he looked chilled to the bone. She looked at him in concern. 'Surely you'd have been better staying in the Aussie sun until our summer started, Ed? The weather's awful at this time of year.'

He hesitated, then gave a little shrug. 'I shan't be here then. Got cancer. They can't help me any more.'

She didn't know what to say, feeling tears well in her eyes. It seemed as if she no sooner grew fond of someone than she lost them.

He patted her hand. 'Don't grieve for me, Kirsty. I've had a good life, longer than most, and I don't want to linger on till someone has to change my nappies.'

'How can you face it so cheerfully?'

'Sometimes you get no choice about what you face, only about how you face it.'

That was so true, she thought.

Of course, her brother didn't approve of her new friendship and complained bitterly that she was always out these days. Rod had become very short-tempered since failing to get that promotion.

Kirsty sometimes popped in at Ed's flat after work for a coffee and chat. It was small but comfortable, with a pleasant view over a public garden, and he had all sorts of services to make his life easier.

But she couldn't help noticing that he was looking even frailer these days, with that translucent, other-worldly look to his eyes that people sometimes got towards the end of their lives.

So she made the most of their time together and ignored Rod's complaints that she was never home.

Ed answered the door and sighed when he saw his great-nephew, Noel, standing there. His sister's grandson – and as unlike Ed's sister as any direct descendant ever could be.

'Aren't you going to invite me in, Uncle Edward?'

With a sigh, Ed held the door open. 'How did you find me?'

'It isn't hard to track someone down with a computer and the Internet. I knew you'd be somewhere round here because it's where you and Gran came from. I was worried about you.'

'I don't know why you should be.'

'You're ninety and living on your own. How could I not worry? You should have come to stay with us, as I suggested when you phoned from Australia, so that my wife and I could look after you properly.'

Ed went across to his chair and sat down, shaking off the too-firm grasp on his arm. 'I don't need looking after and I value my privacy.'

'I'm concerned that you're still holding what my dad did against me.'

Ed was fed up of being polite to his great-nephew. 'What you're really worried about is that I won't leave you anything.'

'I am the last surviving member of your family, so it'd be a fair thing to expect, surely? And I'm prepared to help you as much as I can while you're . . . ill.'

'Dying, you mean.' Ed smiled. 'You're in the will, Noel, but only if the main beneficiary rejects my terms.'

'What the hell do you mean by that? Who else is there to leave your money to?'

'Friends.' Suddenly he was a little afraid of the ugly look on Noel's face. The fellow's father had been a bad 'un and the son was just like him, only not as clever.

'Look, uncle—'

There was a knock on the door and Ed yelled, 'Come in!'

His cleaner used her key to enter. 'Oh? Are you busy, Mr James? Shall I come back later?'

Noel glared at her. 'Yes. We're having a private discussion.'

Ed looked at her pleadingly. 'No. Please don't leave, Dorothy. Just show my great-nephew out and then get on with your work as usual.'

Noel breathed in deeply then stepped back. 'We'll talk another day, uncle.'

When he'd gone, Ed said, 'Would you lock the door, please? I don't want him coming back in.'

Dorothy came to stand beside him. 'You look upset. Are you all right?'

'If you'd just get me one of the pills in the blue bottle, I'll be all right in a minute or two. I'm going to change my will. That fellow isn't going to have a chance to inherit a thing.'

He waved a hand in dismissal. 'I'll just have a little rest, then I'll ring my lawyer. You get on with your work.'

Dorothy came back a few minutes later and found him slumped in his chair. She bent to feel for a pulse but found only a faint, irregular fluttering. With tears in her eyes, she picked up the phone and called an ambulance, then got the piece of paper out of the kitchen drawer and called the lawyer.

Ed had made certain things clear when she came to work here.

Chapter Two

January, Australia

Sam Brady picked up the phone and wished he hadn't when he heard his ex-wife's voice at the other end. He knew what to expect and sure enough, after the most cursory of enquiries as to how he was, out she came with it.

'Tina needs some more money for living expenses. She can't manage at university on what you give her.'

'I told you last time, I don't have any more to spare, Lorraine.'

'You would if you got yourself a proper job. It's disgusting, a forty-four-year-old man living like a hippie.'

He breathed in deeply, trying to control his anger.

Lorraine didn't wait for him to speak. 'Your only child needs at least fifty dollars a week more. It's your duty to help her.'

'I don't have it. Tina will have to get a part-time job. Most students do.'

'If you're going to be unreasonable, I'll ask my lawyer about this.'

'Ask who the hell you want. I don't have even ten dollars a week to spare at the moment.'

'Tell her yourself that you're going to let her down, then.'

There was some fumbling and the phone was passed to his daughter.

'Dad?'

'Yes?'

'I don't want to be a pest, but I really can't manage on what you give me. I'm not being extravagant or anything, but you know how much it costs to run a car.'

'Tina, they put up your tuition fees this year and that wiped me right out. If I didn't grow my own vegetables, I'd be scratching for something to eat, that's how short of money I am at the moment.'

'But Mum says you've got lots of land and could easily sell some.'

It hurt to hear his daughter talking like that, as if she was prepared to strip him of the main thing he had left. She was old enough to understand that money didn't grow on trees – or anywhere else convenient, either. It had to be worked for.

'I'm not allowed to subdivide my block and if I sold it, I'd lose my home. Would you be comfortable with that?' He didn't think Lorraine would have any legal grounds for getting more money out of him, but it was the sort of threat she made sometimes.

'Things can't be that bad, surely, Dad.'

'They are. Have I ever lied to you?'

Silence, then an aggrieved sigh.

'If you'd come to visit me after Christmas, you'd have seen for yourself that I'm not exactly living in luxury.'

'I had a chance to go to Bali with friends and—'

This was the first he'd heard of it. 'How did you pay for that?'

Silence, then, 'I had some money saved from last year and Mum helped out a bit.'

That only made him more certain it was time to pull back from supporting his spoiled brat of a daughter. Going off on overseas holidays then claiming she was short of money! At twenty, she should be budgeting properly and standing on her own feet. 'Well, you'll have to find a part-time job now to make up for the holiday. I do not have any money to spare.'

The phone was passed back without a word of farewell and he heard a murmur of voices.

Then Lorraine came back on, her tone sharp and vicious. 'I think emotional blackmail is a very low thing to do, Sam Brady. Lose your home, indeed! It wouldn't kill you to give her another fifty dollars a week.'

'That's more than I have to live on at the moment.'

'Which just goes to show what a fool you are. You used to earn really good money – and could again.'

'And the stress of that job nearly destroyed me.'

'Well, you've had a couple of years now to do your own thing so it's clear your painting isn't going anywhere. It's just a pity your daughter has to suffer for your laziness. I can't imagine what gave you the idea that you were an artist. I reckon you simply wanted an excuse to get out of working.' She hung up.

Sam put his phone down carefully because he couldn't afford to replace it if he slammed it down and broke it. Then he went outside, took his sledgehammer and smashed up a couple of rocks. Only when they were crushed to tiny pieces did he stop and put the sledgehammer away.

The activity might have taken the edge off his anger, but it didn't get rid of the feeling of unfairness. After he and Lorraine had split up, he'd been generous in what he let her take from their marriage and had continued working at a job he hated to pay Tina's private school fees until she got into university. He'd saved hard and could still remember the utter joy when he had enough to cover the cost of three years' university fees for his daughter and could resign from his job. He'd sold his flat and bought this tumble-down shack on a small country property.

And he loved living here. He felt so much happier, and his health and energy had improved by leaps and bounds. No, he could never, ever go back to the stress of corporate life. If lack of money forced him to get a job, then he'd find something that didn't exhaust him mentally and physically, something that still left him time and energy to paint. There was plenty of casual work in the Margaret River district in the holiday season and he didn't have expensive tastes.

Knowing that in this mood he'd be no good at painting, Sam strolled up the track to his neighbour's property. He was caretaking Whitegums for a modest weekly sum while Ed was overseas. The garden needed watering and he liked to check regularly that the house was all right.

He smiled as he passed the little vineyard Ed had planted many years ago on a sunny slope. It was only an acre or so, not big enough for commercial production, but provided generously for its owner by producing a nice Cabernet Merlot style of red. Sam liked to see the neat rows of vines and had shared many a bottle with Ed and their neighbours.

As Ed had grown older and frailer, Franco, who owned the next property, had taken over the management of the vineyard, making wine every year for Ed and himself. Franco had proved to be as much of an enthusiast as the old man.

Sam always helped with the harvest and received a couple of crates of wine afterwards.

The bunches of grapes were showing now but wouldn't be ready for harvesting until March, probably late March, but Franco would judge exactly when.

Sam reached the house and unlocked the front door. Caretaking Whitegums provided his main source of income at the moment and was a godsend, but the old homestead didn't seem the same without its owner and it always felt a bit sad to go there. He really missed the old man, who'd been like an honorary grandfather to all who knew him.

One cold, rainy evening in late January, Kirsty popped round after work to make sure Ed was all right. He usually came to the library every day or two, but hadn't been in for over a week, nor had he answered his mobile phone. There hadn't been anyone at the flat on her last visit, which was unusual, because Ed got very tired by teatime and rarely went out in the evening.

The previous week he'd insisted on taking her out for a lavish dinner, but had eaten almost nothing himself. Come to think of it, he'd thanked her for her friendship too.

Was he . . . getting worse? In hospital again? Had he known that and been using the dinner as a way of saying farewell?

There was no answer at his flat, no lights on inside either. She hesitated, then knocked on the next door and asked if anyone had seen him during the past week. But the elegant woman who answered it said she didn't believe in living in neighbours' pockets and shut the door. When Kirsty got home, even more worried now, her brother greeted her with, 'We were supposed to be going to the movies tonight.'

'That was tomorrow, surely?'

'It was tonight, but it'll be too late by the time you've had your tea and you know how I hate rushing.'

She stifled a sigh with great difficulty. It was harder to deal with Rod when you were feeling a bit down yourself. 'Sorry. I was late leaving work, then I called in to see Ed on my way home. But no one was there and he's not answering his phone, which isn't like him. I've been wondering if I should ring the police, ask them to check on him. What do you think?'

'I think you're a fool to fuss over him like that. The closer you get to him, the more grief you're building up for yourself when he dies.'

She bit back a sharp reply and got their tea ready.

Rod started on the washing up afterwards, but she couldn't settle to watching TV, so in the end went upstairs to play on her computer, something which would put her even deeper in her brother's black books. She wished he had friends and a social life of his own. That dependence on her made things very difficult at times.

Her sister Sue said she was crazy living with him. Perhaps she was right. Sue had no patience with Rod. But he did his best, poor love, didn't mean to upset anyone.

* * *

At work the next day Kirsty tried to discuss her worries with Neris, but all her friend said was, 'Ed's probably gone into hospital again for a short stay, like he did just before Christmas. He'll have forgotten to tell you, that's all.'

'But what if he's—'

'Honestly, Kirsty, you should be getting out and meeting guys your own age not spending your time with that weird brother of yours and an old man. I keep telling you to join a dating website. I met this great guy on one last week. We've emailed every day since and I'm thinking of meeting him in person.'

'No, thanks. I've no desire to marry again.'

It was her stock answer, but after Neris had moved away she frowned. Catherine's book told you to be honest with yourself. Since reading that book, Kirsty had admitted to herself that she would like to marry again. Only she couldn't face going on an Internet manhunt – or any other sort of manhunt, either.

If fate didn't bring her a man, she'd do without.

The next morning, Kirsty rang the local hospital before she left the house. They hadn't had a Mr James admitted in any area. She didn't know who Ed's doctor was, so she called in at the police station on her way to work and explained the situation.

'We'll send someone round to check, Mrs Miller. Have you a phone number where we can contact you?'

She received a phone call from the police at work that afternoon.

'Mr James no longer resides at the flat.'

'Did you find out where he went?'

'Yes, but he left instructions with his lawyer that no one was to be informed where he was. That's all we can tell you, I'm afraid. We've made quite sure nothing untoward has happened to him so I hope that sets your mind at rest, madam.'

She put the phone down but didn't move. Suddenly she was quite sure that Ed was dying. He'd said once that he intended to do that in private. He'd probably gone back to Australia, where he had close friends.

But she wished she could see him just one more time to say a proper goodbye.

Rod remained scornful. 'That man was just using you, Kirsty, and now he doesn't need anyone to do his shopping or bake him cakes, he's up and left without a word of thanks. You're too gullible and soft-hearted. It's a good thing you've got me to look after you. He'll have gone back to Australia.'

'Yes, I suppose so.'

One day Sam's daughter turned up with a friend. He hugged her and gestured to the veranda.

'What are you doing down here?'

'Oh, we were out for a drive and I thought I'd visit you, Dad.'

'Bring your friend to join us. I'll get you a drink. It'll have to be coffee. I don't have any tea.'

She beckoned to her friend and stayed where she was, studying the shack. 'I don't know how you can stand living in a hovel like this, Dad, after the sort of home we used to have.'

'I like it here. It's very peaceful.'

'Have you done any more paintings?'

'Yes.'

'Can I see them?'

He hesitated, puzzled by this. 'You don't have to pretend you're interested.'

'No, I want to see them, really. And Darren does too. He's an art lecturer, so he knows about paintings.'

Sam stared at her in surprise. When she shifted uncomfortably, he grew suspicious. 'What's this visit really about, Tina?'

She turned to her companion, who was looking distinctly embarrassed. 'I need to talk to Dad privately, Darren. Would you mind waiting for me in the car?' When they were alone, she turned back to Sam. 'Mum said I should talk to you in person, try to make you see sense. And she said I should get an expert opinion on your paintings. She can't afford to give me any more money, because she's finding the mortgage repayments hard going. This is my final year, you know, Dad. My whole life may depend on my results. I don't need any hassles with jobs this year.'

'Tina, have you been listening to me? I don't have any money to spare. None.'

'You could get a job.'

'So could you.'

Tears filled her eyes. 'If I'm working, I won't be able to go out with the others. Darren might find himself another girl who's more available. I'm really keen on him, Dad. And it's my final year, so I need to study hard as well. I'm not a top student, you know that, never have been.'

'You've never really stretched yourself.'

'People have to have some leisure. Dad, surely there's something you can do to help me, take out a mortgage or – or . . . ?'

He tried to keep his voice calm, but it grew sharp in spite of his intentions. 'No chance.'

'You're so selfish! Parents are supposed to give their children a good start in life, not shirk their responsibilities.' She turned and stormed off back to the car, getting in and slamming the door without a word of farewell. Her mother had primed her to do this, Sam thought wearily. He stood listening to the noise of the engine throb away into the distance, feeling wretched, a failure as a parent. He and Lorraine had quarrelled several times over the years about the way she spoiled Tina, but the girl had chosen to live with her mother, so he'd been helpless to do much about it.

At first after they separated, he'd taken Tina out regularly, but the older his daughter grew, the shorter the time she was prepared to spend with him. Half the time Lorraine had rung up to say Tina didn't want to see him this week. He'd been surprised when his daughter got into university, given her lack of hard work at school. As for the English and fine arts degree, that seemed no way to find a job, unless she went into teaching and she didn't seem the sort to do that. He couldn't imagine her standing up to a class of stroppy teenagers.

He wandered into the freestanding metal garage which he used as a studio and stared at his latest painting, then shook his head and wandered out again, unable to settle.

He was going to have to toughen up about Tina or he'd never get any work done. But it hurt to be at odds with his only child. He should have spent more time with her when she was younger and they were sharing a home, and less time on his job.

He wondered if he'd see her again this year, even.

Cursing, he went out to work on his vegetable garden, yanking up the weeds with vicious twists.

Sam was sitting on his veranda drinking a beer in the cool of the evening when Penny from up the road dropped in. It was impossible to remain depressed when she was around, because she was always full of energy and happiness.

'We've got a glut of tomatoes and zucchini, Sam. Do you want any?'

'Yes, please. I never seem to have Franco's touch with tomatoes.'

'It's his Italian ancestry. They take one look at him and flourish.' She pulled a plastic bag out of the car and thrust it into his arms, then paused and stared at him, head on one side. 'Something wrong?'

'My daughter came to see me today and we quarrelled.'

'Tell me about it. I'm always quarrelling with my two. I'm glad they've gone to live with their father in Perth while they're studying. They're so selfish at that age.' She patted his arm. 'Your daughter will come round once she starts working and gets a few reality checks. Give her time.'

As Penny turned to leave, she hesitated. 'Why don't you come round for a barbecue tonight? Just a casual meal with me and Franco.'

'Thanks, but I've still got a lot to do today.' He hadn't, but he didn't want to take advantage of Penny's generosity. He'd accept a meal at their place every couple of weeks, especially if he had some spare produce or flowers from his garden to take as a gift. But that was all he'd accept. He wasn't a charity case yet, thank you very much.

She came back to kiss him on the cheek. 'You're too proud for your own good, you know that?'

'And you're very generous. Say hi to Franco for me.'

Sam waved as she drove away, then cheered up a little as he went back inside the studio to stare at the two paintings he had to deliver to a gallery in Margaret River the following day. The owner there loved his work and had recently sold a painting.

It was the most hopeful sign in a long time. He was running low on paint and canvases, really needed an injection of money to buy more.

Chapter Three

On a bleak day in February, Kirsty arrived at work for the afternoon and evening shift. The first person she saw was Neris, who was standing at the counter looking upset.

'Is something wrong?'

'We'll talk after you've seen Peter.'

Their manager came out of his office as soon as Kirsty went into the staff area at the rear. 'Have you got a minute?'

She followed him inside his office. From Neris's expression this wasn't going to be good news. With all the staffing cuts to libraries lately, they'd been wondering if they were going to be hit with the big axe.

Peter waved her to a chair, one popularly supposed to have been chosen for being so uncomfortable that no one would willingly sit on it for long. 'I won't beat about the bush, Kirsty. They have to make some staffing cuts to branch libraries and unfortunately, we'll be losing one member of staff. This—'

She couldn't stand the way he took ages to come to the point. 'Am I the one to be chucked out of my job?'

'There are three of you at the same level. I don't mind which one goes, so I suggest you discuss it among yourselves in the first instance and see if you can come to an agreement about who should look for other employment. I'd certainly not call it "chucking out".'

No, he'd use one of his euphemisms, but it amounted to the same thing. She couldn't help scowling at him.

'No use looking at me like that, Kirsty. It'd be much better to settle this amicably, democratically. If you three can't decide which one is to go, I'll simply draw lots. You're all – um, good workers and well qualified, but because of the cuts, there won't be any transfers available to other branches. There will, of course, be a redundancy payment.'

'Is a one-off payment supposed to make losing a job more palatable? We're none of us close to retirement and we all need to earn a living.' She looked at him angrily, and as he said nothing more, tossed at him, 'Is that the best you can do to protect us, as our manager?'

He spread his hands and tried to look sympathetic. Failed, as usual. The man was a po-faced robot.

'You've all got roughly the same years of experience, Kirsty, and you all need your wages.'

He was like that, Peter, avoiding anything that smacked of conflict or controversy. He was well in with the district manager and you could bet that his job would be safe.

'I suppose you didn't consider protesting, gathering evidence to show that we really do need three members of staff to run things properly here or—'

He held up one hand like a policeman stopping traffic. 'It'd make no difference. There have to be cuts across the board and that's it.'

'But services to the public will suffer.'

'We'll do our best to minimise that. Only the most peripheral services will need to be cut.'

She opened her mouth to argue then shut it again. You got nowhere arguing with Peter. He just gave you his bland, soapy smile and continued to toe the head office line.

'Right.' She walked out to have a word with Neris before getting ready to serve the public.

'He's told you, then?'

'Yes. We have to decide among ourselves who's going to lose their job or he'll draw lots. Isn't it great when your supervisor sees you all as interchangeable spare parts?'

They looked at one another unhappily.

'At least you won't lose your home for non-payment of the mortgage,' Neris said glumly. 'I might.'

'No, but I was thinking of getting a flat of my own. Now I won't dare to, even if I'm not the one who gets axed.' Kirsty sighed. 'I'd better go and tidy myself up. It's blowing a gale outside and my hair's a mess.'

Neris went with her, muttering, 'I don't care if the front desk is left unattended. I need a few minutes to myself. He told me out there, the rat, not even in private.' She stood back as Kirsty combed her hair. 'It looks better loose and fluffy, sexier. I don't know why you always pin it back.'

'Because it's more comfortable. And I don't care whether I look sexy or not.'

'Well, you should. You're only thirty-six. Anyone would think you were an old woman to hear you talk. And as for the way you always wear navy, well, it's visually boring.'

'I wear different-coloured accessories!'

Neris made a scornful noise in her throat.

Kirsty sighed and bent her head, pretending to search for something in her handbag, though at the moment she didn't give two hoots what she looked like. What she needed was time alone to come to terms with this blow. Fat chance of that here!

John Berringer went to his client's funeral, partly because he'd grown fond of Ed and partly to make sure everything was done properly. There wasn't a service but John held up one hand to stop the funeral attendants from sending the casket too swiftly on its way. He bowed his head and prayed, saying a personal farewell, then looked up in surprise as someone walked in late.

It was Ed's nephew. The fellow had come to see him to ask about the will the day after his great-uncle died. John's lips tightened as he watched Noel Porter bow his head very briefly, then flick one hand towards the attendant as if to say 'get on with it'.

John took great satisfaction in the enquiring look the attendant cast at him. He shook his head, looked down at his hands and held a mental conversation with Ed. You were right about that nephew. Just out for what he can get.

When five more minutes had passed, John raised his head and gave the signal to carry on. Then he turned and walked out. But of course he heard footsteps behind him, hurrying to catch up.

'Just a minute, Berringer.'

He turned to wait, not saying anything.

'I think you owe me an explanation now about the will. I'm the old man's last surviving relative and surely he's left things to me?'

'Ed said he'd already told you that you'd get nothing.'

'Not quite. He said I'd only get something if the principal legatee didn't agree to his conditions.'

'That's not likely to happen. And you're too distant a relative, not dependent on him, so you have no claim otherwise.'

'Who is the principal legatee?'

'I'm under no obligation to tell you that.'

'I'll find out and contest the will. My uncle had obviously lost his marbles towards the end.'

John smiled. 'I can find you several witnesses to prove that he hadn't. You'd be wasting your money.'

'At least I'd waste the legatee's money too.'

'No, you wouldn't. If you contest the will, I'll represent the legatee without charge because of my high regard for Ed. It'd be an open and shut case anyway.'

With a muttered curse, Noel spun on his heels and stormed off.

John watched him go, shaking his head. How that fellow could be related to a man like Ed was beyond his comprehension.

The three of them went round to the pub after the library closed to discuss the redundancy situation. But there was nothing to discuss as far as Kirsty was concerned. Yusef had a wife and family to support, and Neris lived on her own, with no family in a position to help her.

She looked at them unhappily, her stomach feeling hollow. She knew without asking that Rod would let her stay on rent-free, if necessary, and she'd have unemployment benefits till she found a new job. Surely she'd be able to find something quite quickly?

But she loved her present job, didn't want to do anything else, so it took her a while to pluck up the courage to say, 'I suppose it'd better be me who leaves.'

Yusef stared down into his orange juice, stirring the pieces of ice with his straw. Neris examined her nails.

Then they both looked up and the relief in their eyes was more than Kirsty could bear. She pushed her chair back. 'I'll tell Peter tomorrow.'

They both called, 'Thanks!' at the same time.

When she went outside to the parking area, she found that someone had vandalised her car, slashing the tyres and spray-painting the bodywork and windows with garish impartiality.

It was the last straw. Tears rolling down her cheeks, she went back inside.

Neris and Yusef came rushing across to her. 'What's happened?'

'It's my car.'

Her colleagues waited with her for the police to arrive. The landlord of the pub tried to offer her a brandy. Tears were welling up and overflowing, even though Kirsty kept telling herself it was only a car.

But the vandalism was the final straw in a horrible day.

The police were very polite but held out little hope of catching the culprits. They called a tow service and she took her bits and pieces out of the car and put them in Neris's, who gave her a lift.

They sat outside Rod's house for a few moments.

'It sucks,' Neris said at last.

'Everything sucks lately,' Kirsty agreed. 'I suppose I'd better go in. Thanks for the lift.'

As she walked along the path she saw her brother through the window. He was looking depressed, staring into space, had been doing a lot of that lately.

He made such a fuss about her car that she didn't tell him about the coming redundancies. She knew he'd be angry with her for volunteering to leave and would start off again about the lax way the country was run, so that people who worked hard and gave their all, weren't valued any more. It frightened her that she was beginning to agree with him.

Kirsty's shift at the library didn't start until later the following morning, so first she phoned up to find out how soon her car could be put to rights, then set about hiring a car for a few days, because she didn't fancy going home by bus after the late shifts. It took longer than she'd expected to arrange for a car, but why should she care if they had to manage without her at work today? It'd give them a foretaste of what the future would be like.

It was terrifying to think of having no job at all, no money coming in, being dependent on social security . . . Stop thinking like that, she told herself. You'll find something else. You've got a degree, years of experience.

In an area where job numbers were shrinking.

As she walked into the library past the main desk, Peter strolled out of a side area. 'Are you all right, Kirsty? Neris told me about your car.'

'I'm fine, thank you.'

He gave them both one of his tight smiles. 'Why don't you take your break now, Neris? I can watch the desk.'

Closing the staffroom door, Neris muttered, 'I don't know whether I dislike him most when he's being his own horrible little self or when he's playing at being a supportive and caring manager.'

'Don't look a gift horse in the mouth. It's given us a few minutes together. Another couple of weeks and we won't even have that.'

Neris gave her a quick hug, then went to switch the kettle on. Suddenly she slapped her hand to her forehead. 'I nearly forgot. This arrived for you earlier, delivered by courier, no less.' She picked up an envelope and held it out.

What next? Kirsty wondered as she took it. She examined the printing on the envelope. 'It's from a firm of lawyers, but I've had nothing to do with any lawyers. I wonder what it is. And why did it come to the library instead of my home address?'

Neris gave an exaggerated sigh. 'You'll never find out unless you open it, will you?'

'I suppose not.' She slit it open and read it quickly.

Dear Mrs Miller
We'd be grateful if you'd make an appointment to see
us at your earliest convenience concerning a bequest.
John Berringer

She blinked in surprise and read it again.

Neris nudged her. 'Well, what is it?'

Kirsty held out the letter, watching as her friend read it. 'This has to be a joke,' she said when Neris looked at her questioningly.

'It doesn't look like one. It's on proper headed notepaper. Give them a ring and make an appointment.'

'I'll do it later.'

'Aren't you curious?'

'Not very. I think it'll prove to be a case of mistaken identity. There's no one left in my family to leave me a bequest. The lawyer's rooms are just a few streets away, so I can walk that way at lunchtime and check that it's a bona fide business.'

'There's that old man you were friendly with.'

'He probably went back to Australia. And anyway, I only knew him for a few months. I don't think he would leave me anything.'

She didn't tell Neris, but she felt reluctant to deal with these lawyers. A bequest meant somebody had died. Who could it be? She'd have to ring her mother and find out if there were any old aunties unaccounted for.

Her friend gave her a sudden hug. 'You're not usually so negative. Are you feeling upset about losing your job? Maybe we should just have tossed for it. I feel awful about letting you volunteer to take a redundancy.'

Kirsty shrugged. 'It made sense and it's done now.' She watched Neris half-open her mouth then close it again. Shortly afterwards her friend started talking about the new guy, whom she'd met in person now and really liked.

It was a relief when a prolonged buzz from the front desk sent them both hurrying out to face a sudden rush of customers.

* * *

During her lunch break, Kirsty gave in to curiosity, not to mention Neris's nagging, and went to look for the solicitor's rooms. There was a gleaming brass plaque on the wall outside saying Limbrowner, Berringer and Parkerby. The whole place looked eminently respectable. So the letter wasn't a prank!

But she didn't go in, didn't feel up to facing any more unsettling news today.

Back at the library she rang to make an appointment for the following morning, then put the letter firmly out of her mind.

She couldn't put the thought of her future out of her mind as easily, however. What was she going to do with herself? Even if she was prepared to move to another town, most of the library jobs she'd seen advertised lately were for part-time work and that wouldn't pay for accommodation and living expenses.

She didn't want to retrain, didn't want an upheaval in her life. Oh, hell, she'd better snap out of this.

The words Ed had once said to her came into her mind suddenly. 'Sometimes you get no choice about what you face, only about how you face it.'

He was right. She could feel as sorry for herself as much she wanted, but it wouldn't change the situation. She didn't know what would, but she'd better snap out of the miseries and start looking for work.

That evening she rang her mother, who lived at the other end of the country now she was remarried, to ask about elderly relatives, but got only the answering service. Oh, well, she'd find out who the bequest was from the next day. It had to be a distant relative, who else would leave her anything?

* * *

When Kirsty arrived at the lawyer's office the following morning, Mr Berringer came out and introduced himself, then escorted her back to his elegant, high-ceilinged office. Once she was seated, he beamed at her across about an acre of desk.

'I expect you're wondering what this is all about?'

'I'm sure you're going to tell me.'

'Indeed I am. It's my pleasure to inform you, Mrs Miller, that you've been left a bequest by a client of mine. His full name is Charles Edward Finlay-James, but you knew him simply as Ed James.'

'Oh. I thought he'd moved away.'

'No, he collapsed and was rushed into hospital. He lingered for a day or two, then died. I had instructions which I was duty bound to follow that there was not to be anyone present as he was dying. He was very determined about guarding his privacy.'

'I'd have liked to attend the funeral, though.'

'He didn't want a fuss made, even for that. I was to attend and make sure everything was done correctly then have his ashes sent home to Australia and scattered in the same place as his wife's. Um – did you know Ed well?'

'Only for a few months. We used to chat sometimes at the library and we had meals together sometimes. He was so interesting to talk to, so young in spirit. What has he left me – his books? We shared a similar taste in novels, romances mainly. He said that was because they reminded him of his own happy marriage.'

The lawyer leaned forward and said in his rather plummy voice, 'Actually, Ed has left you nearly everything he owned: a property in Australia and quite a substantial amount of money. It's all carefully invested for maximum security and growth, and he told me he had great faith in his accountant, so I was to advise you to leave things in the man's hands. Ed was very shrewd where both money and people were concerned.'

She could only gape at him.

He smiled. 'You weren't expecting anything at all, were you?'

'Of course not. And surely his family are the ones who should have this money? Why did he leave it to me?'

'He only has a great-nephew left and I'm afraid he detested that branch of the family, used to say this man was a bad egg as well. I've met the nephew myself and was not, shall we say, impressed by him? We think it was a quarrel with the nephew that upset Ed. His cleaner interrupted them and the nephew tried to get her to leave, but she stayed. Ed told her he was about to change his will just before he collapsed.'

'Oh.'

'There are conditions attached to the bequest and if you don't accept them, you get nothing, in which case, half the money goes to the nephew and the rest to charity. I'd guess Ed wanted to change the reference to the nephew but if you accept, that won't matter.'

Kirsty was still trying to take all this in. It felt very unreal to think of herself suddenly possessing a lot of money. 'What are the conditions?'

He offered her an envelope. 'I don't think you'll find them unreasonable, but Ed wanted to tell you about them in his own words. We have a room down the corridor where you can read this in private.' He got up and gestured to the door, leading her to a pleasant little room overlooking a park.

'Read the letter and think about what Ed wished you to do, Mrs Miller. He asked that you make your decision within three hours of reading the letter. If you let my receptionist know when you're ready, you and I can discuss the practicalities. If you'd like a cup of tea at any time, just ask the receptionist. Three hours.' He looked at his wristwatch and took his leave.

When she was alone, Kirsty fingered the envelope, which was addressed to her in spiky, old-fashioned handwriting, with the address set very neatly in the centre of the envelope. Pops had always addressed envelopes with the same precision. Strange how she always linked Ed with her grandfather in her own mind.

She ran her fingertip over the words as if she could get closer to the writer that way. Why was she hesitating to open the envelope? Ed would never ask her to do anything wrong. Taking a deep breath, she tore open the flap and pulled out the pieces of paper it contained, her eyes misting with tears as she read the first paragraph.

My dear Kirsty
I would first like to thank you for your kindness over the past few months. Your company has meant a great deal to me. That's why I've left you all I own. I know you didn't befriend me in any expectation of receiving a bequest, but I do hope you'll accept this one as a gift from one friend to another.

I've imposed a couple of conditions on your inheritance and I hope you'll agree to them.

The first one is easy. Would you please scatter my ashes where I scattered my wife's, in the rose garden at my old home? Instructions for a small ceremony are with my lawyer in Australia.

The second condition is more complex and I've imposed it to try to help you. You see, I think it's time you moved on and made a new life for yourself. You seem to have been marking time since your husband died and you're far too young and pretty to do that. There's a big, interesting world out there and it would be a shame if you didn't kill a few dragons before you're too old to have adventures.

Please forgive my frank talking. It's because I care about you.

She stopped reading to blink away tears, not offended because Ed was quite right.

It suddenly struck her very forcibly that being redundant didn't matter any more. If she fulfilled Ed's conditions, she'd be secure for life, could do what she wanted. That was a wonderful thought.

My second and main condition is that in order to inherit, you must go and live in my house in Australia for at least a year, after which you'll be free to do whatever you wish with both house and money. If any of your relatives from England come to stay with you, those visits mustn't last longer than a month

*in total, and you mustn't return to England at all
during that time, unless you have a bereavement in
the family.*

*If you don't agree to my second condition, I'll be
disappointed that you haven't had the courage to do
as I'm asking. But I think you will agree, Kirsty. I
hope so, anyway.*

She gasped and re-read the last two paragraphs. No, she
hadn't made a mistake. He really did want her to go and
live in Australia.

On her own!

Her thoughts in a turmoil, she read on.

*I haven't imposed this condition lightly, believe me,
but have given it considerable thought. You need to
get away from that brother of yours and make a new
life for yourself.*

*Whether you make Whitegums your long-term home
or not, I believe you'll enjoy living in my house. It's
always been a happy place and the neighbours are
very friendly.*

*Oh, and there's a small vineyard, which produces a
rather nice red wine. My Italian neighbour, Franco,
manages that now and shares the produce. I hope
you'll continue to let him do that.*

Raise a glass to me when you get there.

She let the letter drop on to the desk and stared blindly
out of the window, seeing only a blur of cloudy sky. Go to

Australia. Live on her own in a strange country. Could she do that? She'd felt recently that it was time to get away from Rod, but not that far away. It'd mean a massive upheaval, a separation from everything and everyone she knew.

But if she didn't do it, the nephew Ed had quarrelled with would gain the money. She had no choice, really, for her own sake and for Ed's.

Inevitably, her thoughts turned to the last big upheaval in her life, the death of her husband. Mike would have told her to accept Ed's conditions, she knew he would. More than that, her husband would have relished the opportunity to visit Australia – and so would the lively Kirsty who'd married him.

Excitement beginning to stir in her, she picked up the second piece of paper and read on.

Finally, I have a request to make of you. This one isn't a condition, but I'd like you to give it serious consideration.

I have a neighbour in Australia who has been extremely kind to me. Sam Brady is a fine young chap. He's a little older than you, about forty-four to your thirty-six – or maybe you're thirty-seven now. Your birthday is in March, isn't it? I can see you smiling, but that seems young to me.

There's no way to dress this up, so I'll be blunt. I think Sam would make you an excellent husband.

You'll no doubt think this a strange thing for me to say, since you two have never even met, but I've facilitated several marriages over the years and I can sense such things. The marriages have always turned out happily, every single one.

The trouble is, you'd have to do the proposing, because Sam's far too proud to ask a woman with money to be his wife. I didn't leave him more than a token amount of money because he'd not have accepted it.

But dear Kirsty, if you've the courage to go to Australia, I'm sure you'll also have the courage to deal with Sam should things turn out as I expect between you.

Please accept the bequest and humour an old man's wishes. But have a happy life whatever you choose to do! And thank you once again for brightening my last few months.

Love,

Ed

P.S. When you and Sam are engaged, would you kindly inform my lawyer here in the UK. We've had a little bet on the outcome. He says I'm too sentimental. I say I'm a realist.

That final sentence made her laugh. So like Ed. She looked at the P.S. again. 'When', he'd said.

As if!

She re-read the whole letter slowly and carefully, then went to stand by the window. Small children were playing on the grass opposite, yelling and running, shoving one another, laughing – they looked to be bursting with life and energy. She couldn't remember the last time she'd run anywhere. Or laughed loudly.

Courage, Ed had said.

Oh, the sting of that word! She didn't feel at all courageous at the moment. She felt as if she was standing on quicksand.

Going back to the chair, she continued thinking in comfort. It took her quite a while, but eventually she got everything sorted out in her mind. She could do this, of course she could. Silly to have become so agitated, really.

Heavens, she'd never have to work again! How could something as wonderful as that happen to her? And she would own a vineyard. That seemed amazing. She loved a glass of red wine and now she'd be producing and drinking her own. With the neighbour's help, of course.

But what was most important of all was that Ed was right. She did need to make some major changes in her life – though she'd never have made such drastic ones without this nudge.

The only thing that really stuck in her gullet was the suggestion that she marry Ed's neighbour. What a ridiculous thing to suggest! And not only that, but to tell her that she would have to propose to this Sam Brady, who was too proud to marry a rich woman.

No way was that going to happen!

But it was only a request, not a condition, so she needn't do anything about it. And she wouldn't. Definitely not.

But she would accept Ed's challenge to go to Australia. Excitement ran more strongly through her as she stood up and caught sight of herself in the big, gold-framed mirror over the fireplace. Was it her imagination or were her cheeks pinker, her eyes sparkling with new life?

'Dare I?' she asked the neatly-dressed woman in the mirror.

The woman smiled back at her, mouthed the word 'yes' and nodded encouragingly.

Sam woke with a new artistic vision, one that had been growing in him for a while. Everything had come together suddenly in his mind and he knew exactly how his vision could be translated on to canvas. It was as if all the work he'd been doing during the past two years had prepared him to move in this direction. He slung on his clothes, tipped cereal into a bowl and gobbled it down as fast as he could, then went across to the studio to work.

At noon, he made a sandwich, begrudging every minute it took to eat it, then worked on, transferring his morning's sketch on to the canvas. It was a stinking hot day, with a forecast that the heat wave would continue for a few days yet. At times like this, he really missed having air conditioning. Sweat ran down his face and he went outside and switched on the hose, running the hot liquid that had been sitting in the plastic pipe in the heat of the sun back into the water tank, because water was a precious commodity. Then he sprayed himself with the cooler water, tying a piece of wet rag round his brow afterwards.

After that he forgot about the heat, forgot about everything except sketching out the painting. Joy hummed through him as he worked, a constant companion.

It wasn't until late in the afternoon that he stopped, took a few steps back and studied the canvas, nodding slowly.

The picture was plotted out now, with sample dabs of colour on another board. It was a large canvas, the biggest he'd ever owned, and he'd often wondered why he bought it. Now he knew.

His energy lasted till he'd put away his paints and cleaned his brushes, then he groaned and stretched his aching body before walking stiffly across to the house. He was deeply thirsty, so drank a glass of chilled water from the bottle in the fridge, then followed it with one of his carefully hoarded beers.

Feeling marginally better, he strolled back to the workshop to study the painting again, eyes narrowed as he imagined it finished. It was going to be the best thing he'd ever done – the very best – a riot of vivid flowers and foliage, hot colours like Gauguin's, plants thrusting towards you, curling around one another like Rousseau's jungles. Only, Sam's blooms would all be anatomically correct, not primitive or impressionistic, and would be arranged on the canvas as carefully as a Japanese flower arrangement.

He'd loved and drawn flowers since he was a boy and had learned to defend that love with fists and words, till other lads no longer dared call him anything that questioned his manhood.

The painting that had sold recently had been of flowers, but much smaller, hadn't had the . . . he hesitated and could only think of the word 'power' – yes, power that this big one would have.

Doubt shook him for a moment. Could he do it, paint what he'd visualised? Would people like it? Did he even care? Not really. He was driven by a force that would have had him working again if there had still been a few more hours of daylight.

He went back outside. No sign of an afternoon sea breeze today. The sun was lower now, but heat still shimmered around him, distorting the air. With a grin, he took off all his clothes. As soon as the water ran cool, he attached the hose to the sprinkler in his vegetable garden and stood beside it with a sigh of relief, letting the cool drops drench his hot skin.

When he and the vegetables had both had enough, he turned the tap off and ambled over to his house, taking another beer out of the fridge, because this was a special day. He sat on the veranda stark naked while he drank it. Who was there to see him? Or care? Anyway, he'd hear a car coming long before it got to the house.

This was his favourite way to end a hot day. The coolness of his bare skin in the late evening sunshine made him feel great. 'You're turning into an eccentric, Brady,' he told himself with a grin. 'Talking to yourself, too. You're a sad case.'

When the shadows began to lengthen, the mosquitoes came out to dive bomb the tender parts of his anatomy, so he went inside to pull on a pair of jeans and a long-sleeved shirt, and spray any skin still on view with insect repellent. One day he'd enclose that veranda in fly screen mesh, then he could sit out there all evening in the nude if he wanted to. But at the moment he couldn't afford to enclose it. He was so short of spare cash that during the winter he'd had to scavenge at the rubbish tip to find a piece of corrugated iron to mend a leak in the roof.

Only the studio was new, a free-standing metal garage set up for his needs, with transparent panels in the roof and some walls to give him adequate light, while still shielding him from the heavy rains of winter and the burning sun of summer. He'd spent the last of his money on that, rather than renovating the house he lived in.

As the sun began to dip below the horizon, he used the brief Australian twilight to wander down to the letterbox at the end of his three hundred metre long drive and pick up his mail. He usually left the letters on the table for a few days until he could face business matters, but the foreign stamp and airmail sticker on one of them caught his eye. An English stamp. Usually such letters came from Ed, but this was typed and came from some firm of lawyers.

He guessed what it'd say even before he opened it. Tears thickened his throat and filled his eyes as he read that his former neighbour had died. He'd been expecting this for a while because the doctors had given Ed only six months to live – and that had been nine months ago. But it hurt to hear that such a dear friend had passed away.

When he resumed reading again, he found that Ed had left him enough money to live on for a year, 'to help you on your way as an artist', and also the four-wheel drive that had been standing idle in Ed's garage for the past few months, except when Sam took it out for a drive, as per instructions, to keep the battery charged.

'Thanks, mate.' His grief overflowed at the thoughtfulness of the bequests and he had to wipe the tears away with his sleeve before continuing.

The modest legacy would make a huge difference to him, give him time to explore this latest style of painting, buy some even bigger canvases and lots more paint. The car was quite frankly a godsend, because his old rattle-heap wasn't up to much these days. Every time he had to go to Perth, he went with his fingers mentally crossed that it wouldn't break down.

He wasn't going to spend the inheritance on his daughter, though. He'd been very disappointed in Tina's attitude towards money. She had to learn to work for what she wanted from now on, not expect life to give her everything on a silver platter. She could be a sweet kid, as well as a total bitch. Surely she'd work things out and become friends with him again? He couldn't bear to think of losing her completely, remembered sometimes the little child who'd fallen asleep on his lap or come running to him when her toys were broken or when she'd fallen over.

Something made him read the lawyer's letter a second time and he discovered that he'd missed a final page of the thin notepaper. Would he please continue to look after Ed's house until the new owner, a Mrs Kirsty Miller, arrived? The same rates of payment were offered and he should continue to send monthly invoices to the accountant in Perth, who would also see to the legalities of the vehicle changeover.

Who the hell was this Kirsty Miller? The only close family Ed had was a nephew he disliked. He certainly hadn't mentioned a female acquaintance called Miller.

A terrible thought suddenly occurred to Sam: what if Ed had been taken for a ride by some old harpy who'd soft-soaped him into leaving her everything? It didn't bear thinking of, but he knew it happened sometimes.

A letter from Ed was enclosed with the lawyer's letter. Sam fingered it, but couldn't face reading it tonight.

Tomorrow, when the sun was just rising and the world was fresh and new, he'd walk up the road to Ed's house, do the watering and read it there.

Chapter Four

As she strolled back to the library after leaving the lawyer's rooms, Kirsty couldn't stop thinking about Ed's letter. It was particularly annoying that the part which stuck in her mind was the one about her marrying his neighbour – not just marrying, but doing the proposing.

'You shouldn't have suggested that, Ed,' she said aloud and could have sworn she heard gentle, rusty laughter from somewhere behind her.

But if this Brady person was a neighbour in Australia, she'd be bound to meet him and . . . Not that she was thinking of doing anything about the request, of course she wasn't! It was just – well, she had to admit to feeling rather curious about why Ed had been trying to bring them together, why he'd thought they would suit well enough to marry.

Oh, get over it, Kirsty Miller! she told herself. You're being ridiculous! It's not a condition of inheriting. You need never even speak to the man if you don't want to.

She'd committed herself to moving overseas for a whole year. The idea of that was enough to set butterflies dancing in her stomach. The English lawyer had instructions from Ed to expedite her preparations for departure so that she could leave as soon as possible. The Australian lawyer had already started sorting out probate so she'd have money waiting for her. He'd be faxing forms through for her to sign.

She was both terrified and excited about going to live there. To be alone in a foreign country – well, that wouldn't be easy for anyone, would it? It was normal to feel nervous about it. But she could join things, make friends, surely? Aussies were noted for being friendly and relaxed. She hoped that was true.

As she walked into the library, her friend Neris pounced on her. 'Well? What was the bequest? Are you rich now? If so, don't forget that I'm your very best friend and I don't mind you taking me on a luxury world tour and . . . Kirsty? Speak to me!'

She could feel herself blushing. 'Well, um, I am going to be rather comfortable, as it happens. The bequest was from Ed James and he's left me quite a lot of money – I don't know how much exactly yet, but quite a bit – a house and a vineyard. Isn't that marvellous?'

'That old man who used to come into the library, the one who reminded you of your granddad?'

'Yes.'

Neris screeched so loudly everyone turned to look at them.

'Shh! I don't want to tell the others yet.'

'But we should be celebrating.'

'I'm shocked rigid, if you must know.'

Neris looked at her, smile slipping a little. 'The redundancy won't matter now, will it? But oh, Kirsty, I'm going to miss you like hell. Yusef's nice enough to work with, but you're a friend.'

'We'll stay in touch.'

Neris nodded, then got that determined look on her face. 'You're not getting away without a celebration, my girl. We shut at eight tonight. At one minute past I'm opening a bottle of champagne. I'm not going to allow you to slip away quietly. We're going to party all the way.'

Before Kirsty could stop her, Neris went to tell the others what had happened. Even Peter got excited, though mainly at the thought of the money, the amount of which he tried in vain to dig out of Kirsty.

Later, she and Neris nipped out, with his blessing, to buy wine, fruit juice and a few nibbles for the celebration. Neris had phoned some colleagues working in other libraries and wondered if Kirsty wanted to invite her brother. She didn't. Rod was going to throw a fit when she told him about the conditions and she'd rather he did that in private.

It was frosty outside, making their breath cloud the air and Neris's high heels ring on the hard ground as they tramped along to the nearby supermarket. They linked arms to keep warm, as they had done many times before.

'Aren't you getting excited now?'

'I'm still more numb than anything else.'

'What did Rod say?'

'I haven't told him yet. It's – um, not all that straightforward. There are conditions attached.'

'What?' Neris stopped walking. 'You never said. Tell me this minute.'

'I have to go and live in Australia for a year.'

Neris hooted loudly and made a fist of triumph. 'Your benefactor was a genius. I can't believe you're getting away from Rod at last.'

'That's a rotten thing to say.'

'Well, you know what I mean. Your brother is well-meaning, I grant you, but he's a bit of a plonker.' She hesitated, then asked, 'You aren't going to let him spoil this, are you?'

'What do you mean?'

'Rod runs your whole life. He'll want to come with you and control your new life, too.'

'He does not run my life!'

'This is me, remember? I've known you since university.' Her voice became more gentle. 'And seen you curl up into your shell after Mike died. If you don't take this opportunity to break free of him, you'll be lumbered with Rod for the rest of your life and you'll never find another husband. You should have gone to share a flat with your sister in Manchester when she invited you.'

'I wasn't ready to leave town then.'

Neris waggled a finger under her nose. 'Stop wool-gathering and listen to me, Kirsty Miller. Promise me you'll go out to Australia without Rod and not let him come to visit till you're well settled in. Your Mr James should have said no visitors at all for the first year.' She planted herself in the gateway that led to the supermarket car park. 'You'll have to fight to get past me to buy that champagne if you don't swear a solemn oath.'

Kirsty chuckled and tried to pass, but Neris raised her fists and took up a mock boxing stance. After a minute or two of pushing and shoving, they both dissolved into giggles. Kirsty found herself promising to be more independent from now on – and she meant it, too.

On the way back, they moved their cars and left them in the library delivery area, where they could be locked safely away.

Kirsty enjoyed the champagne and it was lovely to see the old friends who'd managed to make it to her impromptu celebration. Everything seemed a bit surreal, but in a happy way.

All the way home excitement welled up inside her like the bubbles in the champagne she'd drunk. It was a long time since she'd felt so happy.

But when the taxi stopped outside her home, the euphoria vanished abruptly.

Now she had to tell Rod.

Sam did as he'd planned and sat down on Ed's veranda the following morning to open the letter from his old friend. 'I should have phoned you more often,' he muttered as he ripped the envelope open. 'I'm sorry about that.'

Dear Sam
I'm nearly there now, feeling pretty weak and ready to let go, but I'm very glad I came back to England. It's suited me to live quietly and revisit some of the places I loved in my childhood.
I've a final request to make of you, my dear young friend. Since you were so adamant that you didn't want my fortune, I'm leaving you only a small gift,

which I hope you won't spurn, and my car. You wouldn't accept it when I left but I hope you will now. The rest is going to a young woman I've grown very fond of. She's like the granddaughter I never had.

She's had a hard time during the past few years and has retreated into herself, living so quietly she hardly makes a ripple as she passes by.

Ha! Trust old Ed to see only good in people.

Her rather selfish brother bullies her shamefully, so I've made it a condition of the will that she live at Whitegums for a year before she's free to dispose of the house. That should get her away from him, but it won't necessarily bring her happiness. For that I'm relying on you.

Sam stopped reading for a moment to stare suspiciously at the page. Relying on him! What was Ed up to now? How could Sam bring happiness to a complete stranger?

As you know I have a gift for matchmaking, and all 'my' marriages have turned out well.

Sam knew what was coming now. He'd heard Ed boast about bringing together several couples in the neighbourhood over the years, including Penny and Franco, who had both been marrying for the second time. And yes, Ed's marriages did all seem to have turned out well, but Sam didn't want or need that sort of help, thank you very much. He'd told Ed so, and he'd meant it, too. One marriage had been more than enough for him. He didn't intend to put on the golden shackles again. 'No, way, Ed!'

It came to me one day how well you and Kirsty would suit. I can see you scowling and saying, 'No way!' as you read this.

This drew a reluctant laugh from Sam.

But dear boy, for the sake of our friendship, and because it's the very last thing I'll ever ask of you, get to know her, at least. See how you feel then.
Wherever I am, I'll be watching, because I very much want for you and Kirsty to be happy, preferably together.
Farewell, my dear boy! I've enjoyed knowing you and I'm sure your paintings will do well once you've found a style you can make your own.
Ed

After he'd finished reading the letter a second time, Sam blinked furiously and ran a fingertip over the words, handwritten, not produced on a computer, even though Ed had been good with computers. The letter was so like Ed it was as if his old friend was standing next to him speaking to him.

So he shook his head again, smiling as he repeated, 'No way, Ed!'

Anyway, this woman would probably be horrified once she saw how isolated Ed's home was. The Australian bush wasn't everyone's cup of tea. Mrs Miller would no doubt stay for the requisite year, then sell up and go straight back to England, having got what she wanted – Ed's money.

Sam couldn't now imagine living anywhere else but here, a place where he'd found peace after turmoil and where he'd started doing what he truly wanted with his life. Just to walk out of his little house and hear birds singing gave him enormous pleasure. His twenty acres of mainly virgin bush contained many treasures, both flora and fauna, and were going to be left more or less untouched, except for the paths he'd cleared through them. He'd discussed that with the local conservation society first. Only the land near the house had been fully cleared and better soil brought in so that he could grow his own food as much as possible.

It was paradise here, as far as he was concerned, even if his house was rather primitive.

Ed's money and car would be a boon, though. He'd be able to buy more art supplies and put fly screens round the veranda. He'd sell his old car and put the money from that aside for later.

Folding up the letter carefully, he put it in his pocket, muttering, 'And whatever you thought of this female, I bet she did suck up to you.'

A kookaburra startled him by laughing loudly in a tree nearby. You'd almost think it was Ed refuting what he'd said.

Hell, he was getting too fanciful for his own good, Sam decided. He'd just check the automatic watering system up here then drive his new car back and get on with the painting. It would take a week or more to finish it. He loved doing that, making flowers look as realistic as he could, so that you wanted to pick an armful from the canvas.

When Kirsty got home from the party, she found Rod sitting in his favourite armchair. He hadn't switched on the television, the newspaper was lying unheeded on the table and he was staring blindly at the carpet. He looked unhappy, poor thing. If she could think of a way to help him, she would, but although he was a lot more respectful now than he had been as a child, he'd never turn into a tactful, sensitive human being.

And yet he could be so kind and protective, had supported her in her darkest hour and ever since had tried to look after her in every way he could.

He greeted her with, 'You're not usually so late on a Wednesday. I was getting worried but when I rang your mobile there was no answer.'

She looked in her bag. She was sure she'd left it switched on, but now it was turned off. Neris must have done that. The trouble with old friends was they knew you too well. If Rod had rung, she'd have invited him to join them at the party, and his presence would have cast a cloud over everything because he considered office parties a total waste of time. She'd not have dared drink so much champagne with him there, either. Because alcohol didn't agree with him, he didn't see the point of drinking.

'Sorry. We had an impromptu party.'

He went across to draw the curtains and glanced out at the street. 'Where's your hired car? You haven't had an accident, have you?'

'Of course not. I drank too much to drive so I left it at work and came back by taxi.' She waited for him to ask who the party was for, but he didn't. She felt a prickle of irritation and opened her mouth to tell him her news, get it over with. But he interrupted.

'Well, come and sit down. I'll make you some drinking chocolate.'

'No, thank you. Not on top of champagne.'

His eyes narrowed. 'Champagne? What exactly were you celebrating?'

She saw the exact moment when the probable reason dawned on him.

'Did you go to see that lawyer today?'

'Yes.' She fumbled for a way to tell him about the legacy and conditions, but couldn't think clearly, was a bit sloshed if truth be told.

'Well?' he prompted.

'It was the old man I got friendly with last year. He's died and – and he's left me his house.'

There was dead silence then Rod beamed at her. 'A house? You've been left a house? Where is it? How much is it worth?'

'I don't know how much because it's in Australia. Um, there's some money as well. Oh, and a small vineyard. That sounds so romantic, don't you think, a vineyard?'

'To be left a house is wonderful! I'm really glad for you, Kirsty.'

'There's a condition, though.' She had to take another deep breath before she could continue. 'I have to live in the house, in Australia, for a whole year before I can sell it or return to England.'

Rod's smile faded. 'Are you sure you understood the lawyer properly?'

'Very sure.'

'But that's ridiculous! Why should you have to leave your home and family like that? The old fellow's wits must have been addled. We'll contest the will.'

'I wouldn't dream of doing that. If Ed wants me to live in his house for a year, then it's exactly what I'm going to do.'

'You can't just drop everything and go to Australia! How will you earn your living there?'

'I won't need to. The money is . . .' she took a deep breath before she said it, still wasn't quite used to the idea herself, '. . . enough to live on in comfort for the rest of my life.'

He opened and shut his mouth, then said faintly, 'How much exactly?'

'I don't know yet.'

'But the lawyer did say enough to live on for the rest of your life?'

She nodded. With every hour that passed the excitement was building up. It was as if the bequest had already started to transform her, to send blood flowing more vigorously through her veins.

There was a long silence, then Rod said, 'Well, I suppose you'll have to do as the old man asked. I'll go out there with you and help you settle in.'

'Thanks, but I'd rather go on my own.'

'Nonsense. You're so dreamy, always with your head in a book, you're not fit to fend for yourself in a foreign country. Besides, you'll need me to sort out the financial side of things. After all, I am an accountant, and a good one, too.'

'They do speak the same language as us in Australia and Ed already has an accountant there, as well as a lawyer. Oh, Rod, I've read so much about Australia. I've always wanted to travel, you know I have. I even suggested we have a holiday there when I saw that special offer last year.'

'It'd have been a waste of money and I didn't intend to pay a fortune to go camping, even to see Ayer's Rock. Living in tents is my idea of hardship, not pleasure. But I wouldn't dream of letting you go out there on your own, Kirsty. I shall take a month's leave and come with you. I won't have any trouble getting leave at this time of year.'

'Rod, I want to do this on my own. You can come and visit me later and—'

But nothing she said would deter him. He was like a steam roller once he got his mind fixed on something.

She was tired, so decided to have another go at him the following day, when she was stone cold sober and could think up better arguments.

John Berringer got into work the next morning to find the place in chaos and the police already there. 'What's happened?'

His clerk, partner and receptionist all tried to speak at once. 'We've been burgled.'

It took several hours to work out that nothing had been taken except for the petty cash.

'I think this was someone with a grudge against you, sir,' the forensic officer said. 'They've gone for damage. Look at the way they've simply pulled the files out and scattered them, and sprayed paint on the walls. Can you think of anyone who'd like to get back at you for something?'

'Quite a few. If the law doesn't act as people think it should, they blame the intermediaries.'

'Could you get me a list of those with most reason to want to trash the place?'

'I suppose so. But it'll be mere guesswork.'

He went to his office and sat down, staring at the mess, unable to believe someone could be so vindictive. As to why, who knew what got into these people?

They'd probably just been unlucky.

Then it occurred to him that whoever it was had bypassed the security system and he went out for another word with the detective, after which he rang the company who had installed it.

The system was supposed to be state of the art, and monitored. Why had it not worked? Whoever had broken in must have skills in that area. But why bother? There had been nothing of real value here. It was crazy.

He couldn't think of any client or former client who'd be angry enough to do such a thing. Perhaps one of his partners would have an idea, when they'd all had time to think about it. Only it was his office that had copped the heavy damage. Theirs had hardly been touched.

* * *

The following evening when Kirsty got home, she found Rod back early.

He beamed at her. 'I've got my leave arranged and I've booked our tickets to Australia.'

That took her breath away and for a minute or two, she couldn't even form a protest.

'We're leaving in three weeks. I've even found a hotel in Perth for when we arrive, because this house of yours is in the country. I looked it up on the Internet at work today.'

'How could you book the tickets without asking me?'

'Well, you have to go in and confirm yours, show them your passport and all that, but I've paid the deposit for us both.' He looked at her, his smile fading as she said nothing. 'What?'

She hadn't seen him so lively for a long time, couldn't bear to spoil things for him. After all, he was only playing the big brother, trying to look after her. 'You took my breath away.'

His smile returned.

Later on, she went up to her bedroom and rang Sue on her mobile, wanting to be able to speak freely to her sister. When Kirsty told her the news, she had to hold the phone away from her ear because Sue's shrieks of joy nearly deafened her.

'That's brilliant, just abso-bloody-lutely brilliant! Have you told Mum? When are you going out to inspect your house? You are going, aren't you?'

'Yes. I'm flying out to Australia quite soon, actually. And I'm going to ring Mum after I finish talking to you. I can't do just as I want, though.' Kirsty explained the conditions of the will.

'Oh, goody. That'll get you away from Rod at last. I've been in despair about you, my girl. You've given up on life and settled down under his thumb. Our dear brother always was a bossy sod. Everything has to be just so for him and he's made you conform to his ways. After you've gone, he can rot away quietly in front of the TV, which is all he ever wants to do in the evenings.'

'You're too hard on him. He can't help how he is. Um . . .' Kirsty hesitated, not knowing how to say it, then finished in a rush. 'Actually, he's coming with me.'

'What? Oh, Kirsty, no!'

'He's only coming to help me settle in. He's not allowed to stay more than a month during the year, by the terms of the will.'

'Kirsty, how could you? Now you'll never escape. He'll set things up to suit himself and he'll be out there again sponging off you as soon as the year's up. Tell him you've changed your mind.'

'He's already paid the deposits for our fares.'

'You can still stop him going if you really want to.'

Kirsty sighed. 'I can't bear to hurt him. He's so excited. He's been really miserable lately because of not getting that promotion.'

'He'll never get a promotion and you know it. Oh, Kirsty, he's ruining your life and you're just letting him!'

'He gets more upset about things than you realise.'

'I give up! You're scared to strike out on your own. You'll never find another man while you've got Rod!' She hung up.

Kirsty stared in astonishment at her phone. Her sister had scolded her many a time since Mike's death about not making a life for herself, but Sue had never hung up on her before. Never given up on her, either. And unless Kirsty was mistaken, Sue had been in tears.

But how could she have stopped Rod from booking their plane tickets? How could she take the happy look from his face?

Her mother said much the same as Sue had, but said it more gently.

'It's all settled now. What about you? Are you all right, Mum?'

'I'm fine as long as I take things easy. They've cleared up all the cancer so you've no need to worry about me. Besides, Francis takes excellent care of me.'

'I'm glad you met him.'

'It's about time you met somebody, darling. It's dreadful to lose a husband, as we both know, but that shouldn't stop you living a full life, especially at your age.'

'I know, Mum.'

'You always say that but you never do anything about it.'

'Well, who knows what will happen in Australia?'

When she went to bed that night, Kirsty admitted to herself that she was a bit disappointed not to be going on her own – or rather, to be going with Rod.

The next day she nerved herself up to suggest maybe they rethink and he come out to see her later. Only he came home excited about the purchase of two new wheelie suitcases at a bargain price, one for him, one for her. The words of protest died in her throat.

Anyway, he'd only be there for a month, after which she'd be free to do as she pleased for eleven months. A lot could happen in a year.

Coward! whispered a little voice inside her head and she closed her eyes for a minute, trying to drive it away.

It wasn't cowardly to avoid hurting someone.

Was it?

Neris was even more upset than Sue had been and was still trying to persuade Kirsty to stop Rod going to Australia when they went out for a final meal together at the little Indian restaurant near the library.

'You've caved in again! You always do. What are you, a woman or a mouse?'

'A mouse.' Kirsty wiggled her nose and tried to make a joke of it but the accusation had upset her and Neris didn't even crack a smile. 'Look, Rod has a job here in England, one with an excellent pension. He's not intending to give that up, just take a month's leave to help me settle in.'

'You don't get it, do you? He'll leave his mark on things out there and they'll never fully belong to you. He doesn't tread lightly as he passes, even I know that. I've seen him stop you doing want you want quite a few times. Oh, I give up.'

After that, the evening fizzled out. Neris sipped her wine and they chatted about other things, but the accusation hung between them.

When Kirsty got back, Rod was waiting for her with sheets of figures. 'You'll be able to save quite a bit of money this year if you're careful. You shouldn't spend too freely till you know exactly how you stand financially. We can work out our long-term plans during my month in Australia – I can't tell you how much I'm looking forward to a break from that office. The woman who got the promotion will be starting while I'm away.'

Kirsty couldn't think what to say to this, he looked so energised and happy.

'Of course you'll sell the house eventually, even if you decide to stay on in Australia. It's not everyone's cup of tea, living in the country and you've always lived in a town. Now that you've got all that money, you'll want to be near theatres and places where there's plenty to do.'

He was looking at her with a hopeful, expectant expression on his face, had clearly put a lot of effort into the figures. She realised with a shock that Sue was right and he did expect her to offer to keep him as well from now on – in return for which he'd no doubt manage her accounts. Well, she wasn't going to do it. That would be going too far.

Before the end of her year in Australia, she'd write to Rod and tell him what she was going to do, and it wouldn't include living with him. She'd hint at it beforehand and let him down gently, of course. She did so hate to upset people who meant well.

But first, she'd have to find out what it was she *did* want to do with herself. All she could think of at the moment was resting and maybe getting a bit fitter.

Her old life was over, but what would her new one bring?

Two days before they were due to leave for Australia the phone rang. Kirsty picked it up, her mind on which clothes to take with her and which to send out, because it was summer still in Australia.

'Is that Kirsty Miller?'

'Yes?'

'I'm calling from Valley Green Hospital. I'm afraid your brother Rodney's had an accident. He fell down some stairs and—'

'He's not dead?' Memories of the day when her husband had been killed set Kirsty fumbling for a chair and collapsing on to it.

'No, no. He's just broken his leg, quite a nasty break, though. He's in surgery now. Could you bring in some clothes and things for him? I'm afraid he'll be in here for a day or two, after which he'll need looking after.'

'I'll be there within the hour.'

'Make it three hours, middle of the afternoon. He'll still be groggy, even so, but he'll be more comfortable with his own things.'

It was a minute or two before Kirsty could pull herself together. She hated hospitals, absolutely hated them. The memories they roused were still as sharp as daggers.

She went into Rod's bedroom, something she rarely did, because he always cleaned it himself. She felt like an intruder as she opened his immaculately-neat drawers and took out pyjamas and other necessities, taking care not to disturb the arrangement of items because he was pernickety about that. Afterwards she chose a couple of books from her own discards pile and his latest model cars magazine, which had arrived in the post today.

She'd have to postpone the trip to Australia to look after him. And she'd do it, of course she would, but she'd been so looking forward to it.

Rod was very groggy when she went into his room. He smiled at her then drifted in and out of sleep, so after a while, Kirsty left him to it.

When she got home, she phoned Sue and told her the news. 'I'll have to cancel our arrangements as soon as the travel agency opens in the morning.'

'No, don't! This is your big chance!' her sister said at once.

'What?'

'Don't you see? This is your chance to escape.'

'I can't leave Rod on his own. He'll not be able to walk properly for ages. I'll have to postpone my flight. I'm sure the lawyer will understand.'

There was a loud sigh from the other end of the line. 'I'm going to regret this, but I'll take some leave and look after him once he comes out till he can manage on his own. You go to Australia as planned.'

Kirsty sat for a minute frozen in shock. 'I can't just leave him.'

'Oh yes you can. What's more, if you don't do it, I'll never speak to you again. I mean that. I've been in despair about you for years. Oh, Kirsty love, you have to get a life of your own again. Let me help you this time, please?'

'I'll . . . phone you back in the morning.'

'No. Agree now or my offer's withdrawn. You're supposed to leave the day after tomorrow, aren't you?'

'Yes.'

'I'll sort things out with my boss and drive up after work tomorrow.'

Kirsty took a deep breath. 'All right. I accept. And thanks, Sue.'

'You won't change your mind on me? Promise!'

'I promise.'

Sam picked up the phone and winced as he recognised the voice.

'Lorraine. Um – how are things?'

'I'm fine. It's Tina I'm worried about.'

He bit back a sharp response. 'Look, I'm in the middle of a painting and I don't want the paintbrushes to dry out. Hurry up and tell me why you're ringing.'

'I just wanted to let you know that your daughter will be waitressing in a café three nights a week from now on, and I hope you're satisfied with what you've done to her!'

'It'll do her good.'

'If she fails her degree, I'll hold you personally responsible, Sam Brady.'

'Oh, no. If she fails, it'll be her own fault. Is that why you rang? If so—'

'No. I've got the chance to go away for a couple of weeks at Easter and I want to know if Tina can come down and stay with you while I'm gone? The art lecturer has finished with her and I don't like the looks of a new guy she's hanging about with. I don't want him given free rein in either my house or her bed.'

He stifled a comment. If Lorraine thought she could stop their daughter sleeping with whoever she chose, she was fooling herself. At twenty, Tina would make her own decisions about sexual partners, and ought to do so. 'Will she want to come and stay with me?'

'She'll have no choice. I'm having the house decorated.'

That should put Tina in a really good mood for the visit. 'If she agrees, then of course she's welcome. I can bunk down in the workshop while she's here.'

'Well, make sure you clean up that hovel before Easter. I'll let you know the exact date and drive her down myself.'

The phone cut off abruptly and he listened to it beeping for a few seconds, wondering how Lorraine would force Tina to come here.

He went back to his painting. It was nearly finished now and all the early promise had been fulfilled. At last he'd found his way, he knew it with a certainty that gave him immense satisfaction. It was the best thing he'd ever done, but was far too big for a home. It should hang in a foyer or a boardroom and that was what he was aiming at: corporate art.

He studied it again, frowning. What he didn't know, what no one knew for certain, was whether this sort of painting would find favour with the public and the company bosses.

Only – the sort of people who bought that type of painting didn't go to normal galleries. They got their pieces of art through the interior designers who did business interiors.

That thought made him sit down and have a good think. Perhaps it was time to call in a few favours and try his own path to selling big time?

When he'd come to a decision and before he lost courage, he picked up the phone and rang an old colleague.

Chapter Five

Kirsty arrived in Western Australia early in the morning, local time. It was already hot because February was the height of summer here. She was close enough to a window in the plane to see that the land near the airport looked beige and dusty, not nearly as attractive as she'd expected.

People in the terminal were complaining about the heat, but after the northern English winter, Kirsty welcomed the warmth. She stood in the taxi queue smiling like an idiot and holding her face up to the sun. Then someone behind her said, 'Excuse me,' and she realised she'd not moved along with the queue.

Murmuring an apology she closed the gap, looking forward now to getting to the hotel because underneath the excitement she was exhausted by over twenty hours of travelling. She hadn't been able to sleep on the plane, should have booked business class – she could have afforded it now. But Rod had only booked tourist class fares and she'd been in too much of a hurry in the end to try to change that.

She still felt guilty at how disappointed he'd been about not going with her when she visited him in hospital and how brusquely Sue had treated him. But it was too late to do anything about that now. The die was cast. Whatever her new home was like, Kirsty had to stay there for a year – in a country where she didn't know a single person. That was a very scary thought. What if she broke her leg? There'd be no one to take care of her.

The taxi took her in to the city. Perth stood near a broad river with a wide grassy area between the skyscrapers of the city block and the water itself.

She was disappointed in the hotel, which was small and rather shabby. It wasn't even close to the centre, let alone within walking distance of the Swan River. Why on earth had Rod chosen it? That was a no-brainer. It was cheap. It even looked cheap. Her room was poky, furnished in depressing beiges and browns, not the sorts of colours to cheer you up.

She unpacked her toiletries, looking down at her bare ring finger. After much consideration, she'd decided to take off her wedding ring from now on, but her hand still felt strange. After taking a quick shower, she fell into bed, letting sleep whisk her away almost as soon as her head touched the pillow.

When the phone woke her, she felt groggy and couldn't for a minute think where she was. There was enough light coming round the sides of the curtains for her to see the phone and pick it up. 'Mmm?'

Rod's voice boomed in her ear. 'Why didn't you ring to let me know you'd arrived, Kirsty? That was very selfish of you. I've been worried sick.'

'I was asleep, Rod. What did you think could happen to me on a flight? No planes have crashed, have they?' She heard her own sharp tone and bit back further sarcastic comments, which would be wasted on Rod anyway. 'Look, I'll ring you tomorrow.' She hung up, then picked up the hotel phone and called reception. 'Please hold all phone calls until further notice. I need to sleep.'

Rod would be furious at her for hanging up on him. Well, she wasn't too pleased with him for waking her up, either. Even he should have realised she'd be tired after such a long flight.

According to the bedside clock, it was late afternoon when she woke. A piece of paper had been pushed under the door and she found a note, dictated by her brother.

> *Please ring as soon as you wake up.*
> *Never mind the time differences. Very worried about you.*
> *Rod*

Screwing up the note, she threw the piece of paper across the room, letting it lie where it had fallen. Why would he be worried about her? This wasn't a war zone.

Drawing back the curtains, she grimaced at what she saw outside, the backs of buildings and untidy car parks. Kirsty liked this place even less now she was fully awake. She was able to make herself a cup of tea and there was a complimentary packet of two plain biscuits, but even after devouring them, she was still ravenous.

Picking up the amenities information folder, she found there wasn't a café in the hotel, so decided to go out for a walk and pick up something to eat.

She grabbed a few tourist brochures from the rack in the foyer, consulted the receptionist about the distance into the city, and took a taxi. The driver suggested dropping her at King's Park, which overlooked the city block and from where she could easily walk into town. She stood at the lookout there, staring down at the city, the tall buildings on the south side casting reflections across the water. It was so beautiful. Rod should have got them hotel rooms looking out on to this.

Her irritation and tiredness dropped away and she began to stroll down the hill into town. When she got there, she went into the first café that appealed to her for a meal, then continued her walk, checking her progress with the tourist map so that she could learn her way about. It was a long time since she'd been anywhere new on her own, and she was enjoying herself.

She passed a hotel that looked out on to the river, gave in to impulse and went inside, booking a luxury spa room for the following day. Then she continued her exploration, enjoying a glass of red wine at an outdoor table in the last of the evening sun. She smiled down at it, wondering what her own wine would taste like.

Long shadows slanted across the pavements now, but it was still warm enough for short sleeves. Such bliss after the dull grey light and chill of an English winter!

For once, she could afford to do whatever she wanted. She'd never been in that happy situation before. It made her feel different, relaxed and free – younger, somehow.

She didn't even feel guilty at how glad she was not to have Rod with her.

* * *

Sam fidgeted around, waiting for his former colleague to arrive. He hated asking favours, absolutely hated it, but whenever he looked at the new painting, he knew he was right to target this particular market. The painting cried out for a large space to set it off and was perfect for the foyer of his old company.

There was the sound of a car in the distance and he jumped up. He was wearing clean jeans, hadn't been able to face finding anything smarter that was fit to wear. But he'd ironed them and was wearing a short-sleeved shirt instead of his usual paint-streaked T-shirt. This was as smart as he got nowadays.

The car was a Merc, naturally. Geoff was a high-flyer. Taking a deep breath, Sam stepped forward, hand outstretched.

Geoff shook it, but only absent-mindedly because he was gaping at the house. 'Hell, Sam, you're not living in that heap of rusty tin, are you?'

'I like living here and anyway, I spend more time in my studio than in the house.' He waved a hand towards the shed.

Geoff's expression said most eloquently that he didn't consider a metal garage much better. 'You should have worked another year or two and bought yourself a decent place.'

'I needed to paint, couldn't bear to wait any longer. Anyway, it's great to see you. I'm really grateful to you for coming down.'

'Oh, I had plenty of time in lieu owed and felt like a drive out. Besides, I'm curious to see these paintings of yours.'

'I still make a good cup of coffee, if you're interested in having one of those first.'

'Now you're talking.'

They sat on the veranda and chatted, or rather, Sam let Geoff tell him who was doing what in the company these days. It all seemed rather unreal and only reinforced his feeling that whatever happened, he could never go back to such a frenetic life.

When he judged he'd played the interested listener for long enough, he said, 'Let me show you why I called.'

At the door to the big metal garage he stopped and switched on all the lights. He'd worked hard to clear the place up and had draped sheets at each side, to hide the clutter and show the huge painting to its best advantage. 'As I said on the phone, I'm into corporate art.'

Geoff put out one hand to stop him talking and moved forward, looking at the painting.

The silence continued for a while so Sam leaned against the doorpost and waited for his friend to speak. Surely this was a positive sign?

Geoff walked slowly up and down in front of the huge canvas. 'I didn't know you were this good.'

Sam closed his eyes for a minute in sheer relief.

'You're right. This is the sort of thing people hang in foyers and reception areas, or even in boardrooms. Only it's more cheerful than most.' Geoff eyed the painting, then chewed the corner of his mouth. 'It's not really my remit, though, interior design.'

'I know. But I hoped you could have a word with whoever's in charge of that these days.'

'I'd be happy to. You know,' he sounded surprised, 'it'd brighten up my day to see that painting.' Another silence, then, 'Could we take it on loan, perhaps, to see how people react to it? That might be the best way to go.'

'Of course.' Sam hid his elation. He'd expected this reaction.

Geoff walked up and down in front of the painting again. 'Damn, I really like that, but it's too large for our house. Could you do me another flower painting, smaller but just as vivid? I'll have to send you the exact dimensions we need. Lara's doing up the formal areas of our house again. She's into stark modern stuff usually, but I think I could persuade her to have just one accent painting.'

Sam winced at the phrase 'accent painting', but hoped he'd concealed it. If that's what it took to keep Geoff on his side, he'd do a dozen accent paintings, if necessary. 'You'd need to tell me the main colours of the new decor. If I remember correctly, Lara has very definite ideas about colour schemes.'

'I'll have to ask her. But I'm sure she'll want one when she's seen this, especially if she knows she's in the forefront of a new trend. I'll arrange to have it picked up.' He smiled, his eyes still on the painting. 'It'll all take time, though. You know how things go.'

'I know. But if we can start planting a few seeds . . .'

'Can do. How much do you want for this?'

'I don't know. I thought maybe Lara would advise me.'

'I'm sure she will.' Geoff snapped his fingers. 'She's been asked to help arrange a fundraising function for cancer research. How would you feel about donating a painting?'

Before he'd heard about Ed's legacy, he couldn't even have afforded the canvas for it. Thank you, Ed. 'I'd be happy to do that. It's the sort of charity I support myself. Is Lara still handling those sculptors?'

'Yes.'

Sam crossed his fingers behind his back. 'Do you think she might take me on as a client?'

Geoff pursed his lips. 'She does her own thing there, but I'll ask her. In the meantime, you should do some market research, Sam. Always know your sales targets.'

Sam shrugged. 'There aren't enough hours in the day to paint, let alone start researching markets. I really, really need an agent.'

'Not good to turn into a recluse if you want to make a success of your new career. You should be in Perth. You need to network.'

'I work better here. And I've needed a learning period. But I can nip up to Perth and chat up the punters every now and then, if necessary.'

'No woman in the frame these days?'

'No. I'm not in the mood for more complications after Lorraine.'

'Saw her in town the other week with a younger man. Tall, thin fellow with a straggly beard. They were all lovey-dovey.'

Sam frowned. It sounded like the guy who'd come down with Tina. Surely even Lorraine wouldn't pinch her own daughter's boyfriend? Then he remembered how keen Lorraine was to get rid of Tina for the holidays and his heart sank. He hoped his guess was wrong. He didn't want his daughter to be hurt.

After a last regretful glance at the big, vibrant painting, Geoff said, 'Let me buy you lunch somewhere decent.'

'That'd be great. We'll go to one of the local vineyards. They have some great restaurants.'

But as Sam slid into the luxurious car, air conditioning whispered past his nostrils and tinted windows dulled the colours outside. These days he preferred fresh air, scented by gum trees or by the old-fashioned roses in Ed's garden, or else tangy salt air as you walked along a beach on a windy day. And he was into bold colours after years in dark suits.

The lunch was excellent and Geoff was a long-time ally, as close to a friend as you got in a big company, so they chatted easily. The outcome today had been everything Sam had hoped for, but he didn't dare relax his guard. This was too important.

As he waved goodbye and saw the car vanish down the track, he let the smile slip from his face. It had been true friendship with Ed, as it still was with Penny and Franco. He still missed Ed so much and had been a little lonely lately – in more ways than one.

But though his body needed a woman, kept him awake at night sometimes because of it, he wasn't ready for another relationship. And he'd never been into casual encounters.

Besides, he couldn't afford to do anything about his shack and what woman would live with him there in the state it was in? No, he'd go on as he was until he'd sorted out his life and work.

The next day Kirsty woke to more messages from Rod. Feeling stubborn, she rang her sister's mobile instead.

'Are you all right?' Sue asked. 'Rod's really worried about you. He's impossible to live with when he's like this. I don't know how you've put up with him all these years.'

'I used to go to my bedroom when he was in one of his moods. Look, next time you see him, assure him I'm fine, will you?'

'So what's it like down under?'

'Warm and sunny. I'm about to change to a nicer hotel, though. Rod booked us into an el cheapo and it's ghastly.'

Sue chuckled. 'Sounds like him. Don't tell us where you are for a day or two. It'll do him good to realise you're not on call for him any more.'

'Can you cope?'

'For a while. At least it's a break from work. Rod comes home from hospital today. I'll hang around for a few days to make sure he can manage then make my escape. Social services said they can arrange temporary household and shopping help for him after that. You'll owe me big time for doing this, my girl.'

'I know. But Sue – be kind to him.'

'Sometimes, Kirsty, it's better to be a bit unkind and make someone stand on their own feet, instead of letting them stand on yours. Look, this call must be costing you a fortune. Ring us again in a day or two and in the meantime go out and enjoy yourself.'

Kirsty put the phone down, feeling both guilty and relieved as she got ready to change hotels.

The new one was like a different world. Smiling staff, light airy spaces, a coffee bar just off the foyer, a stylish restaurant with a menu that made her mouth water. And her room was a dream, with a window overlooking the Swan River. She wondered if butterflies felt like this when they emerged from their chrysalises.

That afternoon she went to keep her appointment with Ed's Australian lawyer. Jason Grieves was younger than she'd expected, not much older than her. He looked at her in surprise as the receptionist showed her into his office.

'Do take a seat. Pardon me staring, but I'd expected you to be older, Mrs Miller. Had you known Ed for long?'

'Just a few months.'

'Great old bloke, wasn't he?'

She smiled involuntarily. 'Yes.'

'Now, let's get down to business. I've sorted out the probate for you, pushed it through quickly. So all I have to do is turn the estate over to you formally. The accountant's away on holiday at the moment, he's my cousin, actually. I felt you ought to know that. But he's good at what he does, so I'd advise you to let him continue to oversee the finances. But of course you can choose another accountant if you wish.'

'If Ed trusted your cousin, then so do I, Mr Grieves. And I hope you'll continue to act as my lawyer here.'

'I'd be happy to.' He smiled 'But call me Jason. We're pretty informal here.'

When he told her exactly how much there was at present in her new Australian bank account, not to mention the value of her share portfolio, she couldn't speak for shock.

'Didn't the English lawyer tell you how much Ed had left you?'

'He said there was enough to keep me in comfort for the rest of my life if I wasn't too extravagant, but that's far more than I'd expected.' She felt quite faint to think of all that money.

'Well, Ed didn't have expensive tastes, so the money kept mounting up year by year. Presumably he didn't tell the English lawyer the exact details. He never really cared about how much there was himself, just that the money was safe. He wasn't into risk taking.' Jason gave her a sympathetic smile and pushed across a big folder. 'My cousin left the details for you to peruse at your leisure and as soon as he gets back you can ask him any questions you like.'

She took the folder, glanced at the summary on the first page and gulped. She hadn't expected that much. 'I don't think I have expensive tastes, either.'

'Well, you'll have a few major expenses as you settle in. For a start, you'll need to buy a car. Your property is in the country and there's no public transport at all, not even a deli within walking distance.'

'Deli?'

'Corner shop, I think you'd call it.'

'Oh. I didn't realise Whitegums was quite so . . . remote. I thought maybe it was in a village or something.'

'We don't really have villages in Western Australia. Even tiny places with less than a hundred population are called towns here, country towns usually. I've been down to Whitegums a few times. Ed was a hospitable old guy. It's a lovely old house on about ten acres, with a small vineyard for his own use, just an acre or so.' He smiled. 'Produces good wine. He usually sent me a case at Christmas.' He frowned. 'What else? Oh yes, the surroundings. There are a couple of other properties of a similar size off Gulliver Road, both within walking distance. There are a few more within driving distance. It's definitely not urban land round there. Ed got on well with his neighbours. We've been paying one of them, Sam Brady, to look after the house and garden, see everything's watered, that sort of thing. We can ask him to keep doing the garden for the time being, if you like?'

'Yes, please. I lived in a terraced house in an industrial town in England and we didn't even have a garden, so I don't know much about gardening at all, except for house plants.'

'I'm sure Sam would be happy to do that. Ed's other close neighbour, Franco Callione, was an unofficial partner in the vineyard, did most of the work in recent years and took half the wine.' He looked at her questioningly.

'I hope he'll continue to do that. I know nothing at all about vineyards.' Though she intended to learn.

'OK. I'll contact Sam and Franco, then. We kept the electricity on in case Ed came back unexpectedly and I've put everything in your name now. If you call in at the bank – it's just across the road from here – you can finalise the transfer of Ed's money from his old account to yours. Now that probate is sorted out, everything is waiting for you to turn up with your passport for identification.'

'You and the accountant have been very efficient. Thank you.' She looked down at the sheets of figures he'd given her, shaking her head, unable to take it in that this much money belonged to her. When she looked up again, she realised he was smiling at her.

'Still in shock?' he asked sympathetically.

'Definitely. I didn't expect Ed to leave me anything. I didn't know he was rich, he lived so simply. But to leave me so much—'

Jason smiled, then looked at the clock. 'Sorry, I've got another client to see, so I need to press on. I'll have Ed's ashes sent to Whitegums. He wanted very much to have them scattered where his wife's are. He's left instructions for a small ceremony, which will include Sam Brady and the Calliones. I'd like to attend, too, if that's all right with you. My wife and I can make a weekend of it if it's on a Saturday or Sunday.' He passed her a small packet. 'You're to open it when his ashes arrive.'

'All right. I'll let you know when I've arranged something and I'll definitely make it a weekend affair.'

'Thanks.'

She went to the bank then walked back to the hotel, studying the cars parked on the streets and wondering which would be a sensible buy. They seemed to be bigger than English cars, on the whole.

She was so lost in thought she bumped into someone in the foyer and then found they were sitting at adjoining tables in the café, each on their own.

The woman smiled across at her. 'Lovely day, isn't it?' She had an American accent.

'Beautiful.'

An elderly woman with an even stronger American accent came across to the other. 'Aren't you coming on the city coach tour, Marlene?'

'No, honey. I've been to Perth before. I'll just have a nice quiet day wandering round the shops.'

'Well, don't forget the Chinese banquet tonight.'

When the woman had gone, Marlene pulled a face at Kirsty. 'I'm on an eight-week world tour and sometimes it's good to get away from the others, though they're nice enough people. That accent of yours sounds British to me. Are you here on your own? Yes? Why don't you join me, then?'

The woman exuded such warm friendliness that Kirsty was happy to move to the next table and soon found herself explaining what had brought her here.

'And you're nervous now,' Marlene said shrewdly.

'A bit.'

'I don't want to poke my nose in, but if you'd like some company for a day or two, I'd be happy to show you around. I lived in Perth for a year in the nineties, when my late husband was working in Western Australia and I've visited it a couple of times since, so I know the city quite well. And to tell you the truth, I'd welcome some young company. My tour companions are all ancient, my age or even older.' She pulled a wry face, laughing at herself.

If Kirsty had expected a few quiet days pottering round the tourist attractions, she didn't get them. Marlene had more energy and enthusiasm than a woman half her age. She whisked Kirsty round the central shops, helping her choose some new summer clothes. 'Yours are too old for you, honey, and to tell the truth, they could be more flattering. I'd consider them too dull for myself, even, and I'm nearly seventy. Enjoy your youth while you can. You've got a lovely slender figure. You should show it off.'

As well as shopping, Kirsty took a couple of driving lessons to get used to the local traffic rules. She found that she'd only have to take a written test within three months to obtain a West Australian licence, which wasn't too daunting.

'Well?' Marlene asked as they came out of the licensing centre. 'Time to buy a car now, don't you think?'

Kirsty tried to concentrate on sensible sedans, but at the second car yard a silver BMW convertible parked at the front of the second-hand section caught her eye. She walked across to look at it, running her hand along the side.

Marlene nudged her. 'Go on! Have a sit in it, at least.'

'I can't afford a car like this.'

'From what you told me, you can. And you can certainly afford the time to see what it feels like, if nothing else.' She walked round to the other side and got into the passenger seat.

Kirsty hesitated then slid into the driving seat, which was very comfortable. She could just imagine herself driving along with the wind in her face.

'Why don't we ask for a trial run?'

'This car isn't practical.'

Marlene waved one hand dismissively. 'Practical, schmactical. You only live once and you're not short of money. Why not try being extravagant for a change?'

'I don't think I could. I'm too used to watching every penny.' Kirsty got out and went back to look at the other second-hand cars, sedans of various colours. But her eyes kept turning back towards the convertible.

A salesman appeared beside them. 'Can I help you, ladies?'

'She'd like a trial drive of the convertible,' Marlene said quickly.

Kirsty opened her mouth to protest, looked back at the car and was lost. A trial drive wouldn't cost her anything and would surely put her off buying it. The salesman squashed himself into the back seat, which wasn't designed for tall men, and when he found out she didn't know Perth, directed her where to turn.

The car drove like a dream and sitting in it, seeing the admiring stares it drew, made Kirsty feel like a princess in a fairytale.

Marlene sat beside her laughing as the wind blew her carefully styled pinkish-silver hair into a youthful tangle. At a set of traffic lights she leaned towards Kirsty and whispered, 'I dare you to buy it.'

Kirsty shot one look at her then concentrated on the road. As they drew to a halt in the car yard, she ran her fingers over the steering wheel. She should get out and find something more sensible.

But she wanted this car, really wanted it.

Just this one extravagance, she told herself and turned to the salesman. 'I'm interested in buying it, but—'

Marlene dug an elbow into her ribs. 'Only if you can do us a good price. You go into the office and we'll join you in a minute after we've done our sums.'

He looked from one to the other and nodded.

'Don't pay the asking price, honey. They're always open to negotiation. Barter him down. After all, you're paying cash.'

'I've never done that before. I wouldn't know how to start.'

'Then I'll bargain for you this once. After that, you're on your own.'

In the office, Marlene entered into a spirited session with the salesman, at one stage pulling Kirsty to her feet. 'Come on, honey. We can find you a better deal than this.'

'No, wait!' The man ran one hand through his hair, did some sums on his calculator, then sighed theatrically and threw his arms up in mock despair before naming a better price. 'And that's it. Rock bottom. I have to make some profit or I won't be able to pay my overheads.'

Marlene hesitated, looked at Kirsty, then shrugged. 'All right. But you have to deliver the car to her at the hotel.'

Once they'd signed the necessary forms and Kirsty had written out a cheque, she asked him to call her a taxi.

As they entered the hotel, she turned to Marlene. 'Thanks. You saved me more than I'd have believed possible. If you're free, dinner's on me tonight.'

'I'd love to have dinner with you. And you'll be able to save money yourself next time.'

'I don't think I was born with the bartering gene.'

'Of course you were. They can only say no, after all. And the more you practise, the better you'll get. You can start by ringing round the insurance companies for quotes. The one he's offering is bound to be more expensive because he'll be getting a kickback.'

When Kirsty got back to her room, she sank down on the bed, clasping one hand over her mouth. What had she done?

Rod would be horrified at the mere thought of buying a convertible, but Mike would have loved it. Only, they'd never have had the money for a car like that.

It was the thought of her husband, killed so young, that made Kirsty feel better about her purchase. You had to make the most of every opportunity. She hadn't been doing that. She would live more fully from now on, she vowed.

Thank you, Ed.

Chapter Six

Kirsty decided it was time to ring her brother again. She should have rung him before, but she'd been enjoying herself too much.

'Where the hell have you been, Kirsty Miller?' he roared, not bothering to greet her. 'Sue said you'd moved out. I've been worried sick about you.'

'You knew I'd arrived safely and you must have guessed I'd have a lot to do. I told Sue I was moving to a nicer hotel.'

'But you didn't let us know which one and it's been five days now since we've heard from you. Five days! Give me your number this minute!'

'There's no point. I'm driving down to my new home tomorrow.' She wasn't going for a day or two yet, but he'd never know that.

'Don't be stupid. Give me the hotel phone number at once. Sue will want to speak to you when she gets back from the shops. Damn! The home help has just arrived. Hold on.'

'Can't wait. I'm just going out. I'll phone you when I get down to Whitegums. Bye, Rod.' She put the phone down, pleased with herself for standing up to him.

* * *

It was Marlene's last evening and they'd arranged to meet in the foyer cocktail bar for a drink before her new friend went off to a show with her tour friends.

'I'm going to miss you,' Kirsty said.

'I'll miss you too, but you promised to come and visit me in LA next year, so don't forget that. I meant what I said. I'd love to show you round. And honey,' she hesitated, then said, 'there's a saying – "get a life"! If I were your age and had all that money, I'd be kicking my heels up all over the world. Make some plans, big ones. That pretty little car is only the start.' She leaned across to hug Kirsty. 'I've got your cell phone number and you've got mine. I'll ring you before I leave Australia.'

When Marlene had gone, Kirsty sat on in the bar to finish her drink, watching the other customers. Everyone else was part of a group and she felt conspicuously alone. It had been wonderful to meet Marlene and she'd rarely made friends with anyone as quickly, but it had been more than just a friendship. The older woman had been an inspiration, she was so full of vibrant life – like that library speaker, whose advice Kirsty hadn't taken. She wished now that she'd brought the book with her. She was sure she'd read it again with a new understanding.

Her eyes kept getting drawn back to a young couple in one corner. Every look, every gesture shouted to the world that they were in love. Kirsty sighed. It would be nice to be part of a twosome again. Maybe one day she'd meet someone . . . She realised where this was leading her and cut off the thought.

Get real! she scolded herself. Ed James wasn't a fairy godfather who could conjure up a suitable guy out of nowhere, just a kindly old man trying to interfere because he felt sorry for her. And this Sam Brady was probably as uninterested in her as she was in him. You couldn't force a relationship between two people. That certain spark had to be there first.

Before she went to bed, she rang the number the lawyer had given her to say that she'd be going down to Whitegums in two days' time. She felt nervous about contacting Sam and was relieved when she got an answering service and only had to leave a message.

If this Sam was so special, what was he doing on his own? Was he hiding from life as she'd been doing?

Sam watched the men carry out the huge painting and place it carefully in their truck. He could only wait to see how it went down with people at his old company.

Then he went out shopping, buying a few basic food items so that the new owner would be able to make herself a snack when she arrived. He looked round the kitchen at Whitegums as he stacked them in the fridge. He'd miss coming here, miss using Ed's computer, too. He'd better buy himself a new one, because his was very elderly in computer terms. He could afford one now.

What would he do if the year passed and the huge new paintings didn't sell? Would he continue to paint the smaller ones, living from month to month? Was he crazy enough to continue beating his head against a brick wall? He smiled in wry amusement. Yes, he was. Painting was as necessary to him now as oxygen. He wouldn't willingly stop doing it as long as there was breath in his body.

But he had been a high flyer in the corporate world and somehow, he wouldn't be content with being a nonentity in the art world.

He hadn't heard from Lorraine since her phone call, or from Tina.

Remembering the scornful way his daughter had looked at his shack – and at him – he was betting she'd find some way to wriggle out of coming down here for the Easter break. But if she did come, maybe they could use the time to draw closer. He hoped so.

While he was out at the shops, he bought some more beer and a bottle of Australian champagne that had won a gold medal. Penny had invited him round for a barbecue and this time he'd accepted, because now he could afford to contribute, wasn't just a charity case.

When he put the phone down, Rod sighed. He was not only worried about Kirsty, he missed her dreadfully. Sue wasn't nearly as understanding as their younger sister. She'd gone out this morning, leaving him on his own, saying she needed a break. He thought that pretty was selfish of her, because the cleaner was due this morning and how was he to keep an eye on the woman, stuck on the front room couch like this, only able to hobble round slowly on crutches?

'Are you in there, Mr Terrance?'

'Yes. Come in!'

A woman appeared in the doorway of the front room. She was younger than he'd expected, about Kirsty's age, with wildly curling hair in a deep auburn colour. He found it hard to tear his eyes away from it.

She came across, hand outstretched. 'I'm Belinda Ross, come to help you.'

He allowed her to pump his hand.

She stared at his plastered leg. 'Must have been a nasty accident. How did it happen?'

He explained and found her very sympathetic. But it pleased him that all the time she was chatting, she was straightening up the room, working automatically as if she was programmed to keep things tidy.

'Do you want a cup of tea before I start, Mr Terrance?'

'Yes, please.' He suddenly remembered the last human relations course they'd sent him on, which had urged sharing and friendly gestures. 'Um – get one for yourself as well. And – um, call me Rod.'

'I'm Linnie to my friends. Belinda's a bit old-fashioned, I always think.'

He was uncertain what to do next, but she didn't seem to need telling. She got the tea, then whisked round, singing at the top of her voice as she vacuumed and dusted. When she did the upstairs, she ran up and down at intervals, still singing away. In between, he had no trouble chatting to her, as he usually did with strangers, because she did most of the talking.

When she'd done her allotted two hours, she came in to see him. 'Can you sign my time sheet, please, Rod?'

He studied it carefully. Yes, she'd done the required two hours and a few minutes extra, actually. So he placed a tick and his signature at the bottom. Then, impelled by a memory from the same course about praising work well done, he wrote 'very hard worker' next to it.

She beamed at him. 'Thanks, love. The customers aren't all as appreciative as you.'

She didn't move away at once, just stood there, rolling her shoulders as if weary. 'You must be lonely lying there all day. Do you want me to get you some lunch before I go?'

'Well, er—'

'I won't charge you for it if you'll let me eat my sandwiches here and have another cup of your lovely tea. It's cold sitting in the car to eat on days like this and I can't afford to go to a café between jobs because I've got two kids to support – their father's always behind with his maintenance payments and you'd never believe how quickly they grow out of shoes. I've not tried that brand of tea before, but I think I'll buy it from now on. It's lovely.'

He brightened at the thought of help, because it wasn't possible to carry cups around while you were on crutches. 'That'd be great. And – um, you're welcome to stay.' He hauled himself to his feet and followed her into the kitchen. 'There's a plate of food for me in the fridge.'

She pulled out the sandwiches Sue had left for him. 'Do you want me to toast these? And if you have a tin of soup, I could open that to go with them.'

'Yes. And you could have a bowl, too, if you wanted.' He watched her anxiously in case this was the wrong thing to offer – he was always upsetting people when he didn't mean to.

'Are you sure? You don't need to give me any.'

'There's plenty for two in one of those tins. I usually share them with my younger sister, but she's in Australia at the moment.'

'Lucky her! I bet it's sunny there. I could do with a bit of sunshine, couldn't you?'

He watched Linnie get the food ready. She continued to work quickly and efficiently, talking away, hardly pausing for breath. He found her exuberance soothing because he didn't have to think what to say or do next. He was really sorry when she left, because then the house was all too quiet again.

Sue wasn't coming back till later and he had to be careful what he said to her, because she scolded him if she didn't like what he'd said.

He missed Kirsty so much. She hardly ever scolded him. He was worried that someone would be taking advantage of her.

He hoped he'd never break his leg again, because he was going mad from boredom and Sue wasn't in the least bit sympathetic.

He went upstairs and switched on his computer. He'd usually had enough of computers by the time he came home from work, but now, it'd give him something to do, even if he only played solitaire for a while.

Maybe Kirsty would be on email again soon, then they could exchange daily messages and he could advise her about the money. He was really good with money and figures. That always consoled him when he said the wrong thing to people.

The following morning Marlene sat on the plane and sighed. She'd enjoyed her stay in Perth, but this world tour was inexorable and she was now going on to Broome, on the north coast of Western Australia, whether she wanted to or not. She'd never fancied this part of the trip. The tropics were too hot and humid for her taste.

If her old friend in Perth hadn't died recently, she'd planned to skip Broome and stay with her. But old friends did that to you, usually suddenly. Old age was cruel. And Kirsty was too new a friend to impose upon for longer.

She wondered how Kirsty was coping. It had been like watching a fledgling leave the nest. She hadn't been sure Kirsty would really spread her wings until she'd bought the convertible. That had showed there was real hope for the girl.

Marlene grinned. If she'd been young, she'd have bought it, too.

That thought made her stop and wonder why she couldn't still indulge in one or two expensive whims. By hell, she was going to ride one of those camels along Cable Beach and buy herself a pearl ring in Broome.

Kirsty spent another two days in Perth, having her hair done in a new style, much shorter. It suited her and she thought it made her look younger – though perhaps she was fooling herself about that. It wasn't that she desperately wanted to look younger, but she now realised she'd been looking older than her age for a while.

She bought more new clothes, practical things for living in the country: jeans, T-shirts and trainers. She had enough elegant and casual clothes from her shopping with Marlene. She'd even been persuaded to buy a swimsuit, though when she was going to swim once she left the hotel, with its shimmering blue pool, she didn't know.

Then, with no more excuse for postponing her departure, she left Perth and headed south along the freeway, with the top of the car down and a headscarf protecting her new hairstyle. The sun was shining, making the water to the right of the freeway sparkle, and she caught occasional glimpses of groups of pelicans doing their ponderous ballet dances on the water. She'd watched them on her riverside walks and seen wild parrots flying around too, pink and grey galahs and flocks of noisy white corellas. Imagine that! She'd even bought a bird book so that she could learn to recognise the local ones.

It took her three and a half hours to reach her new home, which was near a small town called Margaret River. She'd pored over tourist brochures about the district, which was full of famous vineyards and golden beaches, apparently. She grinned. That was going to be so hard to take after an industrial town in Lancashire!

A year, she thought. It wouldn't be at all difficult to live here for a year, surely? After that she could do what she wanted. Return to England, settle here permanently, visit Marlene in America. For once in her life, she could afford to do whatever she wanted.

'Cinderella, move over!' she said aloud, experiencing a sudden sense of soaring freedom such as she had never felt in her whole life before. 'It's my turn to go to the ball.'

In England, Noel Porter conferred with his wife. 'What we need, Brenda, is to make that woman come running back to England. If she voids the conditions of the will, then we'll get our share of the money.'

She scowled. 'If you'd played your cards better, we'd have got our share in the first place.'

'I told you: it was my father, not me, who put the old man's back up. Stupid thing to do when Ed was the only one in the family with money.'

'You could have remedied that. We should have gone out to Australia to visit him years ago, just dropped in as we travelled round.'

'I couldn't have left my job for long enough, not the way things were.'

'Well, now you've lost that damned job anyway, so it's time you did something about your inheritance.'

'I broke into the lawyer's office, didn't I? Got the information we needed.'

'Yes, and it cost me a small fortune to hire a techno-wiz to stop the alarm system sounding off. And lower your voice. We don't want the kids hearing this.'

He breathed in deeply, not wanting to upset her. 'Do you suppose that lawyer told this female about me? I mean about the old man not liking my side of the family.'

'Bound to have. Part of the conditions she had to accept.'

'So it's no use us dropping in on her and pretending to be a long-lost cousin.'

'No, you idiot. You'll have to be a bit more ingenious than that. The only thing I can think of is for you to make sure she takes a dislike to your uncle's place.'

He frowned. 'Harass her, do you mean?'

'Of course I do. It's in the country, miles from anywhere, she's a female on her own. It should be easy to spook her.'

'I suppose.'

'Don't you chicken out on me, Noel Porter!'

'I did the other thing OK, didn't I?'

'Yes. And you'll have to do this one, too. I can't afford to take time off my job and anyway, who'd look after the kids? But you'd better not stuff things up, or I'm finished with you.'

He bit his tongue and tried not to show his anger at the way she was talking to him.

'We'll take some money out of our savings and you can go after the Miller woman. But there's to be no lavish spending while you're out there because we can't afford it. In fact, you should get yourself a casual job. There will be places that won't ask whether you have a work permit or not.' She sighed and gave him another of her scornful looks. 'You can leave for Australia as soon as you've worked your notice.'

'I've a good mind to leave work straight away.'

'You'll stay on and earn a bit more money while it's available. And remember, this is not, repeat *not*, a holiday.'

He sighed. When Brenda spoke like that, it paid to say yes. She was a bitch, but if he tried to leave her, he was quite sure she'd take him for all she could get. When children were involved, the courts took everything off the man.

He forced a smile to his face. 'All right, love, that's what I'll do.'

Kirsty found the directions the lawyer had given her excellent, until the very last part of the journey where she turned off the main road. There was a line of trees along both sides of this smaller road, which made it very attractive. She passed vineyards with signs at the end of their drives offering wine tasting.

Some of the side roads here didn't seem to have names and she was nervous that she'd miss the correct turn-off.

In the end she turned left on to a narrow sandy track a kilometre after a vineyard which had been given as a marker in the instructions. She could only hope this track was Gulliver Road.

A hundred yards along it, she saw a man standing near some gates and stopped to check. 'Excuse me.'

He turned to stare at her but he looked as if his thoughts were miles away. Then he blinked and looked at her properly, the sort of look of dawning interest a man gives a woman he finds attractive.

'Can I help you?'

She felt a little flustered by that appreciative gaze because he was quite good-looking, even though he was dressed in shabby, paint-stained clothes. He was tall and lean, his face deeply tanned and his wavy hair roughly hacked off, as if he'd done it himself with a pair of kitchen scissors. If she was on the right track, he must be one of her neighbours.

Then she suddenly realised. Neighbour! This couldn't be Sam Brady, surely?

The words she'd been going to say stuck in her throat and he had to repeat his question before she managed to pull herself together. 'Sorry. I'm Kirsty Miller. I'm looking for Whitegums and—'

His polite smile faded and he scowled at the car. 'Ed always was a sucker for a pretty face. Whitegums is at the end of this track, just after the vineyard on the right, your vineyard now. You can't miss the homestead. I've kept things in good order. Here! Go and take possession of your inheritance.' He fumbled in his pocket and tossed a key into the empty front seat.

'Oh. Well, er – you must be Sam Brady, then. Nice to m—'

But she was speaking to his back because he was already striding away down the dusty, rutted track behind the sagging gate. She sat in the car watching him, open-mouthed. 'Ed always was a sucker for a pretty face', he'd said. She could feel herself grow warm as she realised he could only mean he thought she'd conned the old man into leaving her his money. Talk about jumping to conclusions! And without knowing a thing about her!

That certainly put paid to Ed's matchmaking. In fact, if she never saw Sam Brady again, it'd be too soon. The cheek of it!

Almost immediately she saw the rows of vines and stopped the car again to stare at them, letting out a blissful sigh. There were bunches of grapes hanging there. She'd be in time for the vendange, or whatever they called the grape harvest here in Australia.

She started driving forward again and came to a left turn with a sign saying 'Callione'. Must be the Italian neighbours who looked after the vineyard.

Soon after that, some double gates barred the end of the track. On one of them was a sign saying 'Whitegums'. She got out of the car and opened them, pausing to look at the house.

Forgetting her anger with Sam Brady, she beamed at the old homestead. It was just like the photos Ed had shown her, one storey but quite a rambling structure. To the right of it was a free-standing garage made of white-painted wood. Beyond that were some huge sheds made out of corrugated metal. That must be where the wine was made.

She knew Whitegums stood on ten acres of land, but there were pretty white picket fences round the front garden, separating it from the bush. Along the side, between the house and garage, she could see part of the rear garden. White roses were blooming happily there. The path to the front door was bordered by petunias, in a myriad shades of pinks and purples.

Sam Brady had looked after Whitegums very well indeed, if the garden was anything to judge by.

She owned all this and a comfortable income. What more could anyone want?

The words drifted into her mind before she could stop them. A husband and children.

She was unable to lie to herself. She was normal enough to wish she had a family of her own, of course she was. Only she couldn't bear the thought of hawking herself on Internet dating sites, as Neris had, with a photo and cutesy particulars there for everyone and his dog to see. No, she simply couldn't bring herself to do that.

Pushing away those unwelcome thoughts, she studied the house again. It looked very Australian with its tin roof and verandas. Three huge gum trees stood at the far end of the house, as if to shade it from the sun, and she guessed they must be the white gums it was named after because they had pale trunks. Ed had once told her he'd planted the trees himself fifty years previously and had built the original, much smaller house for his beloved Mary with his own hands. Later, they'd extended it when they were more comfortable financially.

Why extend it? she wondered. They'd not had any children. Perhaps they'd had a lot of friends who came to visit? She remembered Ed once saying that all the friends of his youth were dead now. How sad!

As she went back towards the car, a kookaburra started shrieking with laughter from somewhere close by. She paused to listen, entranced, eyes half closed in pleasure. It was the first time she'd ever heard one in the wild. Not until the bird fell silent did she move on again.

She parked in front of the garage and went to unlock the front door of the house. There was an outer door made of metal mesh, then a wooden inner door. She felt like an intruder as she walked in.

'I'm here, Ed,' she called, and immediately a sense of welcome seemed to surround her. 'I'll look after your house, I promise,' she added quietly.

Inside, it was surprisingly cool. The entrance hall was about two metres wide, with coloured leadlight windows on either side of the wooden door. There were doorways off the hall to either side. The room on the right was full of bookcases and big leather armchairs, with one window looking out over the rose garden at the rear. She wandered into it and lingered for a moment or two, unable to resist reading some of the book titles and trying out the worn chair by the window. It looked out at a rose garden, full of red and pink and white bushes, all in full bloom.

That would be where she had to scatter Ed's ashes. Whatever his instructions about the ceremony were, she'd already decided that she was going to do it with due reverence, and with his friends there to say farewell to him, if possible. And they'd drink to him with his own wine.

Even that grumpy Sam Brady would be invited.

The room to the left of the hall was a formal sitting room, very old-fashioned looking. It felt as if it hadn't been used for a long time.

The hallway led to a kitchen at the rear. The entrance hall turned to the left, showing several doors to what she assumed would be bedrooms. She walked round the kitchen first. It was large enough to have a table and two chairs in one sunny corner without feeling crowded. Not only was the electricity switched on, but someone had stocked the fridge with basic necessities.

It could only have been Sam Brady. Why had he done a kind thing like that and then been so rude to her?

She examined the loaf and other foodstuffs, but could find no prices on them. She owed him money and was definitely going to pay him back because she didn't intend to be beholden to one of the rudest men she'd ever met.

She went along the corridor, investigating what lay behind each door: six bedrooms – six! Three bathrooms, one en suite, and a huge room at the far end with a full-size snooker table in it.

She was stunned. What on earth was she going to do with all this space? You could fit three or four houses like the one she'd been sharing with Rod into Whitegums.

Taking her time, feeling more relaxed now, she brought her cases and the bags containing her new clothes and other purchases inside. She chose the bedroom with the en suite bathroom for herself and opened the chest of drawers. To her horror, she found some of Ed's clothes still there.

Should she choose another bedroom?

Outside the kookaburra laughed again and she smiled involuntarily. No, of course she didn't need to choose another bedroom. If there was a ghost here, it'd be a very friendly one. But she would have to clear out Ed's things.

She went to get a cup of coffee and a piece of fruit cake, then began to empty the drawers methodically, putting their contents into one of the empty bedrooms until she could work out what to do with them. Most were too good to throw away. By the time she'd finished unpacking, dusk was falling and she was ravenous. She still hadn't gone to explore the huge sheds, but would leave that for another day.

She'd have cheese on toast, followed by an apple and a banana. And there were bottles of red wine with labels saying simply 'Whitegums Cabernet-Merlot' and the year. She must open one of those and sit outside on the veranda to eat, because it was still lovely and warm. Tomorrow she'd go shopping and stock up properly on food.

As she moved towards the refrigerator, she heard a car draw up outside and hurried along the corridor to peep out of the front window. It was a large, four-wheel drive vehicle. A plump woman who looked about fifty, wearing knee-length shorts and a bright red T-shirt, jumped out and opened the rear door to an extremely pregnant dog of uncertain parentage. It had a broad grin and a madly wagging tail.

The woman went back to pick up something wrapped in a tea towel from the front passenger seat and a plastic bag, then turned towards the house. She stopped to stare at the convertible, mouthing the word, 'Wow!' then came towards the front door.

Kirsty hurried to open it.

'Hi! You must be Kirsty Miller. I'm Penny Callione, your next-door neighbour. Sam said you were arriving today and I thought you might like a chicken casserole for tea. And these are some of our own vegetables. We've got a glut of tomatoes this year.'

'Oh, how kind! Do come in.'

'Just for a minute. I have to feed my husband soon or he'll get restless.' She walked through to the kitchen with the confidence of someone who'd been here many times and the dog pattered inside after her, going to lie down by the sliding door as if it had lain there many times before.

'You passed your other neighbour's house on your way in.'

'Yes. I met Mr Brady.'

Penny swung round. 'You don't sound impressed.'

'He was . . . rather rude, actually.'

'Only rather rude? He can be very rude sometimes, especially when his mind's on his paintings or his ex has phoned to nag him.' She looked at Kirsty and frowned. 'He really upset you, didn't he? Tell me.'

So she found herself describing her reception to Penny, who rolled her eyes. 'What a dumb thing to say. Sam's been under a bit of strain lately. He isn't usually as bad as that with strangers, I promise you. But he's been very short of money, scratching for enough to feed himself, so I suppose the sight of your new car upset him a bit. Just wait till I see him, though!'

'No, please! You mustn't mention that I told you. He'll think I was trying to cause trouble.'

'Hmm.' Penny tilted her head to one side, absent-mindedly stroking the dog with one sandaled foot as she considered this. 'All right. But on condition you agree to give him another chance. He's a lovely man, really.'

Kirsty bit back a sharp response. Lovely wasn't the word she would use to describe him.

Ten minutes later she watched wistfully as Penny drove off. The house seemed very quiet after her guest had left.

The food was delicious, especially the tomatoes. She'd never tasted any quite so flavoursome. By the time she'd washed up she was exhausted, so went straight to bed.

But she slept badly, waking with a start several times, not used to such a large house or the night noises of the Australian countryside. To add to her difficulties, the moon was nearly full and the faded curtains let in too much light.

A bird kept calling somewhere nearby, sounding like a cross between a cuckoo and an owl. Leaves rustled and branches rubbed against one another. And underneath it all was a chorus of sound that she couldn't place, almost like a faint, distant car race, or a spooky groaning. What on earth could that be?

She tossed and turned, worrying about how was she going to cope in such an alien environment. It was daunting. That was the only word for it: daunting. But she had no choice. Not only did she want to keep the money and the security it represented – who wouldn't? – but she needed to make a new life for herself.

Sam looked up when he heard the sound of a car engine and smiled as he saw Penny's diesel-guzzling monster chugging down his drive. She jumped down and ran across to give him some more tomatoes.

'I've just met our new neighbour. She's a bit reserved, typical Pom, but seems friendly enough. I'm going to have a barbecue and invite her so that she can meet a few people from hereabouts. It must be awful to be dumped in the middle of nowhere in a strange country. I'll let you know when.'

'Don't bother. I'll leave her to you.'

Penny gave him one of her penetrating looks. 'You've met her?'

He grunted and scowled.

'You didn't like her?'

He opened his mouth to say no, then bit back the words. 'I don't know her, do I?'

'But you obviously didn't take to her. How long did you spend with her?'

'A couple of minutes. She stopped to ask if this was Gulliver Road. We have to do something about getting a new sign at the main road.'

'And two minutes were enough to judge her? Wasn't that a bit hasty, Sam?'

As Penny stood waiting, head on one side, words tumbled out in spite of his resolve to stay non-committal, 'She's not wasted much time spending Ed's money, has she?

Did you see the convertible she was driving? Those things cost a fortune.'

'Well, who can blame her for having a little fling?'

He snorted. 'Little fling, indeed! I could live for a couple of years and buy my art materials with what she must have paid for the car.'

Penny threaded an arm through his. 'Money still tight? I must say I'm surprised Ed didn't leave something substantial to you. You did so much for him.'

'I told him not to, though actually, he did leave me enough money to last a year or so, which is an absolute lifesaver. And I heard just half an hour ago that the gallery in Margaret River has sold another of my flower paintings.'

'That's great news. So stop being grumpy and say you'll come to my barbecue and meet your new neighbour properly.'

He knew he had no choice. If Penny wanted you to do something, she simply wore you down till you agreed. 'I suppose.'

'And you'll play nice?'

'Don't I always?'

'No. Especially when you're in the middle of a painting.'

When Penny had gone, Sam wandered back into the house. His phone rang and he looked at it suspiciously. Lorraine's number showed on the screen. He didn't want to pick it up, but she'd keep ringing till he did, so he might as well get it over with.

'Dad?'

'Tina. Lovely to hear from you. How—'

'Mum just told me what you two have arranged for Easter.

I think it stinks! I could be working, earning money to buy some new clothes. With your stingy allowance, I've hardly a decent thing to wear. But oh, no! I have to come and spend Easter with you or I don't get my money from you for next term. Well, don't expect to enjoy my company. I'm not into sitting around in the middle of nowhere with no one to talk to.'

He didn't try to break into her flow of angry words. Tina never listened when she was in that mood. She was like her mother in some ways.

When she'd finished her tirade, she slammed the receiver down without a word of farewell. He hadn't threatened to cut off her allowance if she didn't come down. He was tempted to ring back later and tell his ex what he thought of her for making him the villain of the piece. But he didn't. Easter was a couple of months away, so Tina would have time to simmer down and he'd tell her then that the visit was her mother's idea, not his. He'd have to work out some things to do with her, so that it wasn't too boring. It was a tourist region, after all. He'd enlist Penny's help.

He went to get a beer and sat on the porch drinking it slowly. But as he began thinking through the events of the day, guilt crept in. Penny was right. He'd been rude to his new neighbour, jumping to conclusions because of the car. It was none of his business what she did with Ed's money or why he'd left it to her.

After a quick meal of bread, egg and tomatoes, he decided to make it a two-beer night, an extravagance for him. He sat there sipping, staring up at the darkening sky, letting the peace of this place seep into his soul.

Of course his mind went back to the encounter with his new neighbour. She had rather a nice face. He shouldn't have been so rude to her, let alone thrown the house key at her like that. She must think he was a boor. He'd apologise next time he saw her. And he'd go to Penny's barbecue and 'play nice' as his friend called it.

But in the meantime he had this idea for another big painting, based on a tangle of wisteria he'd seen when he was shopping – a huge vine, absolutely laden with the lilac-coloured blooms, nearly weighing down the old wooden veranda. He'd have to go back and photograph it. Thank goodness for digital cameras.

Chapter Seven

The next three days passed quickly for Kirsty. First she finished exploring her property, which meant, of course, looking at the wine-making sheds. She'd found some labelled keys in the desk, as the lawyer had told her, and when she unlocked the door of the shed, she felt excitement run through her. The place was carefully protected, with metal mesh across the windows and two locks on the door.

She stood for a moment, taking it in, seeing it as stripes of light and shade, from sunlight slanting in one of the windows.

Everything was immaculate. She breathed in, loving the rich smell. It was as if everything, even the concrete floor, was imbued with wine. The machinery was still carefully covered and a big vat rang empty when she rapped on it. To one side was another locked door and she used the third key to get inside, finding the air here cooler. She found the light switch and realised the place was full of racks of bottles. She pulled one or two out, hesitant about disturbing them, rubbing the dust from their labels and looking at the years marked on them.

When she got back to the house she rang her neighbour to ask if these were her bottles or Mr Callione's.

Penny's rich chuckle rang in her ear. 'Some are yours, some are ours. Ed always let us store ours there, as it's cooler in the insulated room, much better for the wine.'

'How do I know which are which?'

'I'll bring Franco over this evening, if you like, and he can tell you all about them – I warn you, he'll bore you to tears with details if you give him half a chance. But you should know which to drink first, at least, and which to save for special occasions.'

'That'd be lovely.'

After that, Kirsty found her way to Margaret River and enjoyed wandering up and down the main street. At the supermarket she stocked up on food staples, as well as fresh stuff, plus nibbles to offer her guests this evening. She stared at the menus in café windows and wished she had someone to dine out with.

New bed linen and heavier curtains for her bedroom were also on her shopping list and she found some pretty sheets in a rich burgundy colour. Then there was a potted plant which would look just right on the end of the kitchen counter. She also decided to order a new washing machine because Ed's old one leaked and was just about antique. But that was another thing she'd need to ask Penny about. She hadn't a clue which makes were good ones or what to look for, since most of the machines here were top loaders, unlike the ones in the UK.

Before she went home, she found the library and joined it, borrowing a history of the district and three romance novels. It felt strange to be on the customer's side of the counter, but to her surprise she had no desire to go back to her old job.

She might not know yet what she wanted to do with her life, but she did know it wasn't to go back to how she'd been living before.

Ed and Marlene would both have approved of that. It was going to upset Rod, though.

At the house, one simple pleasure drew her out again and again to the back veranda: birds fluttering in the circle of young trees at the edge of the garden. The ones she liked most were plump little things with upright tails about three inches long. She'd found a bird book on Ed's shelves and thought they were fairy wrens. She'd have to ask Penny. It was a pleasure to watch them bobbing in and out of the branches.

A couple of the tiny birds, braver than the others, came right on to the veranda, cocking their heads at her as if expecting something. When she threw them some crumbs they swooped in and, emboldened by this success, others darted in for a share of the feast.

There were parrots, too – fancy having parrots flying freely in your garden! – and all sorts of tiny honeyeaters, a whole cast of performers, in fact. She got immense pleasure from watching them.

And now that she knew the night chorus was frogs, she even enjoyed that. Fancy calling such creatures motorbike frogs! That wasn't what they sounded like to her, more like distant racing cars or, if she let her imagination run wild, a chorus of groaning ghosts.

It was so different and interesting here and would have been quite perfect if she'd only had someone to share it with.

She was surprised by the sudden realisation that Mike wouldn't have liked it here as much as she did, let alone considered it as a long-term way of life, because he was very much an urban creature. But she felt completely at home, for all her ignorance.

Penny brought her husband Franco round in the early evening as arranged and they took Kirsty through the wine-making shed, which was the larger of the two sheds. This time she found out exactly what the machinery was for. He poured out information about the local growing conditions as well, but most of it went over her head and after a while his wife stopped him with a joke about enthusiasts.

Kirsty stopped to stare at a machine with gleaming stainless-steel parts, which looked a bit like a giant food mixer.

'It's a grape crusher and destemmer,' Franco said. 'Only two years old. And that one over there's a hydraulic press.'

'No treading the grapes, then?' she joked.

The look he gave her was pained. 'Ed could afford the best, so he bought it.'

He led the way from the receiving area into the maturation room, closing the door carefully behind him. The fermentation vats were wooden and Franco patted them as if they were old friends. 'We keep the juice here for about three weeks, resting on the skins, then we press off the skins and put the wine into wooden barrels made of French oak. I do the blending myself now, but I learned a lot from Ed and from my uncle in Italy.'

She shivered and rubbed her arms. It was markedly cooler in here.

Franco moved across to a door on the far side. 'This is the main wine store. It's insulated, too and designed to keep the wine at an even temperature, so always close the door when you come in.'

It was another entrance into the area she'd visited earlier. Inside there were ceiling-high racks of bottles and not much room to move round.

Franco gestured. 'The racks on this side are Ed's, so you can take what you want from them. In fact, I hope you'll start drinking them. We're getting a bit tight for space. The racks with green markers are mine.'

There were fewer bottles in Franco's racks. Sad to think that Ed hadn't been able to drink his own wine for the last few months of his life. She listened to a short lecture on what was stored there, then let Franco select some bottles from different years for her to try.

As they carried them up to the house, she stopped for a moment. 'What's in the other shed?'

'The tractor and chemical spray unit, and various other pieces of equipment. Do you want to see them?'

'Another time, thanks.'

At the house, they stacked the bottles in Ed's nearly empty wine rack and Kirsty insisted they open one now. Franco selected a bottle which he said was a particularly good year.

She got the glasses out and even though it hadn't had time to breathe, sipped the wine carefully, closing her eyes to concentrate on the taste. 'Mmm.'

'You like it?' he asked.

'Yes, very much. I prefer red wine to white and cabernet merlot is my favourite blend.'

'It was Ed's, too. He started off with cabernet only, then later he added the merlot vines and started producing a blend, about 80 per cent cabernet to merlot. It works well, I think.' He sipped it and nodded appreciatively.

She'd wandered up and down the rows of vines, marvelling that they belonged to her now, stopping to inhale the rich scent given off by the ripening fruit.

'They're not quite ready yet. You – um – want me to go on organising things?'

'Gosh, yes! I wouldn't have the first idea about what to do.'

He beamed at her. 'Same terms as Ed? We split the wine fifty-fifty?'

'Yes. Who picks the grapes?'

'We all do.' Penny threaded her arm through Kirsty's. 'It's very hard work but so satisfying. Sam usually helps out, too. We get the merlot in first, then the cabernet, usually a week or so later.' As her husband went inside the house to open another bottle, she added in a low voice, 'Thanks for letting the partnership continue. You've made a friend for life. I think Franco loves that little vineyard almost as much as Ed did.'

When her glass had been filled again, Kirsty raised it and said quietly. 'To Ed.'

They both echoed her words and then everyone fell silent for a moment or two, thinking of their friend.

The next day a van drew up to the house, and a man brought a small parcel to the door.

'Mrs Miller? Special delivery.'

When she opened the box, she found an urn with a neat label saying EDWARD FINLAY-JAMES.

'You're back home, then,' she told him, stroking the label with one fingertip.

Setting the urn down, she went to the top drawer in his old-fashioned roll-top desk, which stood incongruously next to his computer desk. She'd put the package the lawyer had given her there and had waited to open it, as Ed had wished. She was following all his instructions carefully, in gratitude for what he'd given her. The money was wonderful, but best gift of all was a new and more exciting life.

Inside, she found another of his letters and some sheets of paper with notes on them. The sight of his handwriting brought tears to her eyes.

My dear Kirsty

If you're reading this, you've accepted my conditions and you're in Australia. The thought of that makes me very happy. Mind you, I was pretty sure you would.

I hope you settle in quickly at Whitegums. It's a big change for you, moving to Australia, but I'm sure you'll cope.

I've included instructions for a small wake, which will include you, Sam, Penny and Franco (my closest friends now that all the old ones are dead) and all four of you should scatter my ashes. I've made a list of the other people I'd like you to invite, with their phone numbers. If you can provide some simple refreshments and beer or wine, that'd be nice.

I like to think I'll be joining Mary again in the place where we were so happy together.

Ed

P.S. I wish you luck with Sam.

She could almost hear Ed saying the words. She smiled at the box, gave it another pat then sat down to read the instructions. He'd thought of every detail.

As she began to prepare for her small party the following morning, she remembered that she still owed Sam Brady for the food she'd found in her refrigerator. Penny had said he was extremely short of money, so it wouldn't be right to let him subsidise her. And however rude he was, however little she wanted to see him again, given his views of why Ed had left her the house, it was more than time she paid him back.

She rang Penny. 'Er – what time is Sam usually at home? I need to see him.'

'Are you in the mood for a quarrel, then? He's been in an unapproachable mood all week. I can't think what's got into him.'

Penny's voice was teasing, but Kirsty's heart sank. 'I try not to quarrel with people, but I owe him some money.'

'What on earth for?'

'He left a few basic necessities in my fridge for when I arrived.'

'Oh, there's no need to worry about that. He was just being neighbourly.'

'You said he was short of money. And anyway, I prefer to pay my debts.'

'Well, you'd be best going to see him in the late afternoon. He works in the mornings and hates being disturbed then. Usually refuses even to answer his phone.'

'All right. I'll do that. Oh, and Penny, Ed has left instructions for a small wake for when we scatter his ashes in the rose bed. Could you and Franco come over for it next Saturday afternoon? He wants it done at dusk.'

'We'd love to. What can I bring?'

'Bring?'

'Food.'

'No need to bring anything. I can do the catering.'

'We usually help one another out at parties. I'll bring some of my special herb rolls. I'm quite famous for my breadmaking.'

'Oh. Well, thank you.'

Kirsty went down the list, phoning people, introducing herself to them and inviting them to the wake. Every single one of them accepted, including Ed's lawyer, who would travel down from Perth specially.

It felt strange planning a party for a group of strangers, but no stranger than the things which had happened to her during the past month.

She'd been lucky catching people in and had only one more person to invite – Sam.

Before she went to see him Kirsty agonised over what to wear, not wanting to seem too well-dressed after his reaction to her car. In the end she chose a simple cornflower blue skirt and a white top, put on her new shady straw hat and strolled through the dappled shadows thrown by the gum trees along the sides of the track, turning up the drive to her bad-tempered neighbour's house.

She stopped to stare at it in surprise. It was tiny, made of corrugated iron and looking as if it was held together by wire and luck. But there was a fairly new four-wheel drive standing outside the house and a big metal shed to one side that looked brand new. People seemed to go for metal sheds here.

She went to knock on the front door before she lost her courage.

As she reached it, a voice behind her said, 'Good afternoon.'

Kirsty spun round. 'Oh! You made me jump!' He was wearing only a pair of worn denim shorts and his tanned chest glistened with drops of water. His hair was dripping wet.

He smiled – well, it was almost a smile, definitely an effort to be civil – and waved one hand towards the rear of the house. 'I was working on the vegetable garden. On hot days I cool myself down as well when I'm doing the watering. Did you want something?'

'I owe you for the food you left in my fridge, Mr Brady, so I came to pay you back.'

The scowl she remembered so well reappeared. 'You owe me nothing. And the name's Sam. We don't go much for that mister stuff here in Australia.'

People kept telling her that. She mustn't forget it again. 'Sam, then. And I'm Kirsty. How much do I owe you for the groceries you bought me?'

'It doesn't matter. It was only a few dollars.'

'I prefer to pay my debts, thank you very much, because that's the way we do things in Lancashire, where I was brought up. And if you don't tell me how much those groceries cost, I'll just leave what I think right on your veranda.'

To her puzzlement, a slow smile crept across his face, followed by a calculating expression.

'Are you any good at embroidery?'

'Pardon?'

'I need some embroidery fixing. We don't pay back cent for cent, but help each other out in different ways.'

'Well, yes, as it happens, I can embroider.'

'Come inside.' He took her agreement for granted and led the way indoors.

The tiny house was immaculately tidy and had a very homelike feel. Then she saw a flower painting on the far wall and forgot everything else. It was beautiful, unlike anything she'd ever seen before, a riot of lavish tropical blooms.

'Hello? Are you still with me?'

His voice jerked her back to attention. 'Sorry. It's that painting – so beautiful!'

He flushed slightly. 'Oh – well – I'm glad you like it.'

'Is it one of yours?'

He shrugged and tried unsuccessfully to look indifferent. 'Yes, as it happens.'

'It's gorgeous.' She went closer. 'The flowers look so real you feel you could pick them.' When she glanced at him, he was smiling again.

'That's exactly what I wanted people to feel.'

There was silence for a moment or two, a silence that seemed to hum between them.

'Anyway—' he held out a piece of material, 'this is the problem. It's fraying in one corner. It's an embroidery my great-grandmother did and I'd like to frame it properly. I can't ask Penny to mend it. She just throws things away when they get holes in them. Can you sew well enough to mend it – properly, mind? If you can't, you must say so. I don't want it spoiling.'

Kirsty picked up the embroidered scene. 'This is lovely, too. I can see where you got your artistic genes from.' She examined the back, admiring the small even stitches. 'Yes, I can mend it for you. I used to enjoy embroidery. I even studied fabric arts in college as an option.'

'Good. That'll be a lot more use to me than the money. Want a beer?'

She didn't normally drink beer, but she did want to get on better terms with him. Not for Ed's reasons, she hastily amended in her own mind, but simply because Sam was a neighbour. 'Um – yes. That would be very refreshing.'

He chuckled. 'Refreshing! Do you always talk like that? So formally?'

'I suppose I do. Aren't we English noted for it?'

He exaggerated his Australian accent. 'Right you are, mate.'

She couldn't help laughing.

He pulled two cans of beer out of the refrigerator, popped one of them and passed it to her. When he raised his own can to his lips, she realised he didn't mean to offer her a glass, so followed his example and discovered that a cold lager on a searing hot day was more than refreshing. It was sheer perfection!

'That's wonderful!' she said as she lowered the can and wiped her lips with the back of her hand.

'We'll make an Aussie of you yet.'

When she'd finished the beer she said goodbye, taking the embroidery with her and feeling sure things would be a little easier between them now. She turned at the gate and saw that he was still standing on the veranda, watching her. She wondered why.

* * *

Rod rang late that night, Australian time, to tell her Sue had gone home again. 'And it's a good thing she has, because I didn't want to quarrel with her after all she'd done for me, only she's not like you. She's very hard to live with, always trying to change things and pushing her opinions at me.'

Kirsty found it hard to concentrate on what he was saying. Her former life seemed so unreal now. How quickly that had happened!

'Kirsty! Are you listening to me?'

'Um – sorry. There's a lovely sunset here and I was looking at it.'

He clicked his tongue in exasperation. 'You're such a daydreamer. I can't imagine how you're managing without me.'

That stung her. 'I'm managing just fine, thank you. How's your leg? Is it healing well? Can you walk on it at all yet?'

'No, I can't. I've had to accept help from social services, someone to clean and shop for me. It's very inconvenient your being away just now.'

'What's your helper like?'

'Good at her job, if a bit of a gossip. But her heart's in the right place and she doesn't count every minute. I respect a hard worker.'

'That's good.

'Now, did you do as I asked and find out what the house is worth?'

'Um – no.'

'Why not?'

'Because I can't sell it for over a year, so why bother? And anyway, I like it here. I may stay on afterwards.'

Dead silence, then, 'Honeymoon period. Give you a few months and you'll be counting the days till you can come home to England again.'

She pulled a face at the telephone but didn't try to contradict him, wasn't in the mood for an argument.

'What about the vineyard? Is the wine sellable? Can you make money from it?'

'I'm still learning about that sort of thing from the neighbour who's managing it now.'

He sighed. 'You'd better keep an eye on the finances.'

'I don't need to keep an eye on Franco. He and his wife are delightful people. They'd not cheat Ed – or me.'

It was a relief when Rod said he had to go. She knew that was because he was timing the call. He was always very careful with money. She smiled at the thought of how he'd freak out when he saw her car. If he ever did. He'd already told her he couldn't get another month's leave for quite a while.

So she was safe for the moment. But safe to do what? Drift for a year? Continue drifting afterwards? No. She had to find something worthwhile to do with her life. She'd have to put Rod off coming out here until she'd sorted out her future in her own way. Sue was right. He did try to take people over.

During the night she dreamed about Sam Brady and woke up feeling very hot and bothered. It was as if her body and her physical needs, dormant since Mike's death, had suddenly exploded into life again. And she wasn't at all sure she wanted that. Sam made her feel. . . nervous.

Ed shouldn't have raised the idea of the two of them getting together. It made every encounter with her attractive neighbour a bit fraught.

And anyway, who'd want to marry a man who could be so rude, even if he was a brilliant painter? Not her.

As Rod put the phone down, he heard the front door knocker go. 'Come in!'

Linnie peered into the room. 'Hello again, Mr Terrance. You ready for me?'

'Yes. I was just ringing my sister in Australia.'

'I've never been abroad, because I married young and I was in the pudding club, had my Tommy before I could turn round, then Jem a couple of years later. Mind you, I wouldn't be without my lads, but it's been a bit hard going at times.'

He let her chatter on, finding it soothing. And as usual she stayed to eat her sandwiches with him. This time she'd brought a tin of soup to share, insisting she wasn't there to sponge off him. That touched him, he had to admit, when she was so short of money.

'What do you do with yourself for the rest of the day?' she asked.

He grimaced. 'Read. Watch TV. Go quietly mad.' It was one thing to have evenings for leisure activities, but to have nothing to do all day long was boring him to tears.

She hesitated. 'Me an' the boys could come round for an hour tonight. Well, I was going to ask you a favour, actually. My Tommy needs a computer to do his homework, only we haven't got one. I thought – if he was very careful – you might let him use yours? I know I'm being a bit cheeky and I'll understand if you say no, truly I will, but I don't want him to fall behind. He's trying ever so hard at school.'

Rod looked at her, thinking this over.

She watched him anxiously. 'I'm saving to buy a computer second-hand, but it's not easy.'

'If your son uses mine, I'd better sit with him to make sure he doesn't damage it.'

'But it's hard for you to get up and down those stairs.'

He shrugged. 'They're there, so I have to do it. I've got it down to a fine art now.' And he'd been intending to go up and use the computer anyway. You couldn't read and watch TV all the time. 'You bring young Tommy round tonight. I don't mind helping him.'

Her anxious look vanished. 'You're that kind to me, Rod. I shall be really sorry when I stop coming here.'

He hadn't thought that far ahead, seemed to have been in limbo since Kirsty left, but now realised that he didn't want Linnie to stop coming. 'If you could fit me in privately for a few hours a week afterwards, I'd be grateful. I'm no good at cleaning and that sort of thing.'

'I'd have to do it in the evening and bring the boys. I don't leave them alone after school, not for anything. Where we live, it's not a very nice area and I don't want them getting into bad company.'

'That'd be all right,' he said recklessly.

When the knocker sounded that evening, Linnie ushered in two lads who had hair almost as red and curly as hers. Their clothes were neat and their faces pink as if freshly scrubbed.

'This is Tommy, my eldest, and this young terror is Jem.'

They stared at him solemnly, were very polite and did as their mother told them without fuss.

Rod watched the way she touched them, little pats here, squeezes of the shoulder there. She seemed to like touching them. He frowned, trying to remember his own mother doing that, and couldn't. Surely she must have? Didn't all mothers do it?

He heaved himself to his feet. 'Tommy and I had better get upstairs. Why don't you watch the telly while you're waiting, Linnie?'

She smiled and settled down with the younger boy, pulling a piece of knitting out of her shopping bag. When Rod started to explain the TV remotes, she waved a hand at Jem. 'This one's the expert. I don't know what I'd do without him and Tommy to run my gadgets for me.'

Upstairs Tommy settled down in front of the computer, smiling cheerfully at Rod. 'It'll be a big help to be able to use this. Thank you very much, Mr Terrance.'

Rod watched carefully as the boy did his research and typed up the results. He didn't need much help with the Internet searches, so Rod mostly sat back and read a book, letting Tommy get on with it. When the information had been found, Tommy looked sideways at him.

'Do you have any computer games?'

'Only cards.'

'Oh. My friend's got all sorts of games on his computer.'

'Well, I haven't.'

'I didn't mean to be rude. If Mum's not ready to go yet, do you think I could play a few games of solitaire then? If I promise not to touch anything else?'

'Yes, why not? I'll go down to your mum now. You know how to switch it off.' Rod's leg was aching and he wanted to put it up again.

Linnie looked up as he swung himself into the living room, then jumped to her feet. 'You look tired. Here, sit down and I'll fetch you a cup of tea.'

He let her settle him on the couch with his foot up, sighing in relief.

'Where's Tommy?'

'I said he could play solitaire for a bit. I hope that was all right. He knows what he's doing with computers.'

She beamed at him. 'Thanks, Rod. You're that kind to us.'

'You could bring them round again, if you like.' He looked at Jem, who was now immersed in a book. 'They're no trouble.'

'I wouldn't let them be.'

All in all, it was a very pleasant evening. He listened to them drive off then locked the door for the night and picked up his own book again. But he couldn't settle. The house was too quiet. Far too quiet.

He'd got out of the habit of living alone. Still, a year would soon pass and then Kirsty would come back. She'd be tired of the novelty of living in Australia by then.

Surely she would?

Chapter Eight

The phone rang, which so surprised Kirsty that she stared at it for a moment before picking up. It was Penny's cheerful voice.

'Want to come round for a home made lemon squash and natter? We're not eating till later and in this heat I'm too lazy to do anything but chat.'

'I'd love to.'

'Bring your bathers. We might head for the nearest beach when the sun's gone down a bit more.'

'That'd be great.' She put the phone down, smiling. However determined you were to fill your time productively and not mope, when you'd not spoken to anyone but a shopkeeper and Sam Brady for a couple of days, the silence seemed to get heavier by the hour. In spite of the heat, she decided to walk round to Penny's, but even with a wide-brimmed hat, she was wishing she'd come by car well before she got there.

Penny appeared from the side of the veranda. 'You didn't walk across? Talk about mad dogs and Englishmen! No one walks around in this heat. That's what air conditioned cars are for. Come round this way. I'm trying to keep poor Ellie cool.'

Her dog was lying panting, belly heaving as the pups moved inside it. A fan was aimed at the poor thing and her fur was damp.

Penny bent to stroke Ellie's head then wipe it with a wet cloth. 'Won't be long now, girl, will it?' She stood up and gestured towards a chair. 'How about an iced tea?'

'Sounds lovely.' Kirsty took the chair indicated and sipped the drink. 'When are the pups due?'

'Any day now.'

'Will you be able to find homes for them?'

'We have to. I can't bear to think of killing them. Ellie's got such a lovely nature, though of course we don't know who the father is. We'll have her spayed afterwards but it's better if they have one litter first, so we were going to breed from her next time anyway. But madam here jumped the gun and chose her own lover. She vanished for a whole day and I was going frantic. Then she came back looking smug.' Penny leaned back in her chair and took a sip of her iced water. 'Now, tell me how you're going, Kirsty. What have you been doing to Whitegums?'

They were still chatting when there was the sound of a car pulling up on the other side of the house.

'That's Sam. I recognise the engine sound. It used to be Ed's car but he left it to Sam.' As a vehicle door slammed, she called, 'We're round the back.'

His voice preceded him. 'Fancy a swim, Penny? I'm driving down to the beach now that the sun's lower in the sky.'

She turned to Kirsty. 'You did bring your bathers, didn't you?'

'Yes, but I'm not a very good swimmer and,' she lowered her voice, 'I don't think Sam was inviting me.'

'Well, I'm inviting you.' Penny raised her voice. 'Kirsty's here. All right if she comes too?'

He'd rounded the corner by then and stopped to frown at Kirsty.

He clearly didn't want her to go with them, so she stood up. 'No need to worry about me, Penny. I've things to do.'

He barred her way. 'You're welcome to come. I was just worrying about your pale English skin getting sunburnt.'

'You're coming,' Penny said firmly, sounding so like Neris that tears came into Kirsty's eyes for a moment.

Sam and Penny both spoke at once. 'What's the matter?'

'You reminded me of a friend I'm missing very much. She used to order me around in just that tone.' She tried to smile and failed.

'It's a big step, leaving all your friends and family behind,' Penny said softly, hugging her. 'I'll give Franco a quick ring and tell him to meet us at the beach after he finishes work.'

The beach was fantastic, but the sand was burning hot underfoot and Kirsty was glad Penny had lent her a pair of flip-flops, only they were called thongs in Australia, it seemed. She stopped to gaze in delight at the long stretch of pale golden sand. The place was nearly empty, with only a few figures dotted about here and there, family groups mostly. It couldn't be more unlike the crowded beaches near the Spanish resort where she and her husband had once holidayed.

The sea was rougher than she was used to, however, so she stayed in the shallow water, not going beyond mid-thigh depth. Even there, a wave took her by surprise and before she could do anything about it, she'd been sucked off her feet by the undertow and dragged away from the beach. With only time for a yelp of surprise, she tumbled under the water, panicking because she couldn't seem to find her way up to the surface again.

When someone grabbed hold of her and hauled her out of the surf, she found herself clasped to Sam's bare, wet chest, gasping and spluttering.

'All right now?' he asked gently.

No, she wasn't all right. She was reacting to him again and her heart was pounding so hard, he must have been able to feel it. She just hoped he'd put it down to the scare. Water crashed around them and he steadied her carefully, moving them back to where the last eddies reached only to their ankles. He had a lovely, sun-tanned body and hers was as white as a fish's belly.

'I'm fine now, thanks. I'd – um – better get out of the sun.' She went back to sit under the beach umbrella, watching enviously as Sam plunged back into the sea with Penny, body surfing back to shore. The two of them seemed perfectly at home in the turbulent water.

Kirsty pulled her sarong round her shoulders because even at this time of day she was getting red.

'I wish I could swim like you two,' she said when they came back.

Penny laughed. 'We all learn to swim in primary school in Australia. And Sam is half fish anyway.' She studied

Kirsty's face. 'Better get you home out of the sun now. Oh look, here's Franco. Sam, will you take Kirsty back? I'll just stay on for a romantic sunset with my darling.' She went to fling herself in her husband's arms, lifting her face for a kiss.

Kirsty watched enviously. The two of them were very much in love. It showed in every gesture they made, the looks they exchanged. She suddenly remembered that Ed was the one who'd introduced them. If this was an example of his match-making . . . No, she wasn't going down that track.

She found herself sitting in the front seat of Sam's Honda next to his half-naked body. He was wearing only the board shorts he used for swimming and had put a towel across the back of the car seat, which was too hot for bare flesh. She felt very self-conscious, trying not to stare at his tanned, muscular chest.

At the house, he stopped the engine. 'Ed's got an outdoor shower for when you come back from the beach, so that you don't trail sand indoors. I'll show you where it is.'

Kirsty hadn't realised what the arrangement of pipes at the far side of the house was for. There was so much to learn about a new country. Before he switched it on, Sam pulled her back because the first water out of the pipes was hot from the sun, then she went to stand under it.

As he turned away, she called, 'You might as well use it too, then maybe you'd like a cold beer? I can show you what I've done to the embroidery.'

Still in his bathers, towel round his shoulders, he wandered into the house barefoot, accepted the beer with a smile then studied the embroidery, nodding approval.

'You're good at this.'

'I like doing it. Mending embroideries, I mean. I was in a group who did that for historic pieces, helping to preserve our heritage. I'll be another few days yet with this one, though. I'm waiting for some special embroidery silks to arrive.'

He smiled. 'Now, who's spending money on whom?'

She looked down at the vivid picture and stroked it with her fingertip. 'It's a pleasure. Your great-grandmother was really good, you know. This is well worth preserving.'

'Yes. I wish I'd known her.' He waved one hand in a sweeping gesture and changed the subject. 'You settling in all right?'

'Yes.'

'If there's anything you need to know, just give me a ring.'

'Thanks.'

He took a big swallow of his beer, closing his eyes in pleasure. 'Ah! That's so good on a hot day.'

After he'd left, Kirsty got angry with herself. She'd been about as interesting to talk to as a wood beetle. She didn't usually have trouble chatting, but thanks to Ed's suggestion, she always felt self-conscious when she was with Sam.

Then it occurred to her that he'd been struggling for words too, avoiding her eyes, coming out with platitudes. He'd finished his beer quite quickly as well. It was a pity. She'd like to have made friends with him, real friends – as she had with Penny.

She wandered round the house, unable to settle as the loneliness closed in again. She'd be glad of Ed's wake on Saturday and the chance to meet new people. It'd be her birthday a week after that. You ought to do something to celebrate a birthday. It wouldn't feel like a celebration if she was on her own. Even Rod took her out on her birthdays, though always to cheap little places.

She was even missing her brother, tetchy as he had been lately.

A year seemed a long time to live on your own, a very long time.

She shook her head, annoyed at herself. She was being stupid! What else could you expect in a new country? Strangers queuing up to say hello?

Two days later Kirsty went for a drive in her new car, buying a few bits and pieces, fresh fruit and vegetables, wonderful local cheeses and olives, a few bottles of white wine in case her guests didn't like Ed's red. She didn't drive fast, not on these twisty roads, but it was lovely to feel the wind in her hair. No wonder Ed had chosen to live here, no wonder tourists came here. It was a great place to live.

When she got back, she found Ellie lying on her veranda, about to deliver a pup.

'Oh, my goodness!' Kirsty rushed to phone Penny, but there was no answer. When she went back to check on the dog, a tiny pup was lying beside Ellie on the old, silver-grey wood and being thoroughly licked. There was only one other person to call: Sam.

He was there within minutes and together they watched three more puppies being born. Neither of them spoke as the miracle of new life unfolded before them.

'Aren't they beautiful?' Kirsty whispered. She bent down to slide some more clean newspaper under the dog, then sat beside Sam on the veranda swing.

He used his foot to set it swaying and she leaned back, enjoying the gentle movement. As she turned towards him, however, she felt that indefinable tug of attraction again and when she looked at him, she could see from the look in his eyes that he was feeling the same.

Then the look vanished, replaced by a guarded half-smile. As if getting more comfortable, he moved to the far end of the swing.

But even though they weren't touching, their silence was as telling as words would have been and in the end, she could bear it no longer and jumped to her feet. 'I'll go and make us a long, cool drink, shall I?'

He looked relieved. 'Yes. And you might try calling Penny again.'

This time they got her on the phone. 'I'm so glad Ellie's safe! I only popped out to buy a few things. I'll come straight over.'

By the time Penny arrived, the fifth and what seemed to be the last of the pups had been born.

'I wonder why she came round here to have them?' Kirsty asked.

'Didn't I tell you? She used to belong to Ed. We took her when he went to England. He'd not had her long when he was diagnosed with cancer.'

They all looked at the pups, who were now busily feeding.

'Well, no harm done.' Penny smiled at the new family. 'I'd better get them home, I suppose.'

Kirsty found a cardboard box and lined it with crumpled newspaper, then they placed the pups in it one at a time, with Ellie hovering nearby anxiously.

After the others had left, Kirsty sat on the veranda for a long time, wondering if Ed could have been right about her and Sam. The physical attraction was certainly there and Sam had seemed like a different person today as he helped out with the pups, with no sign of his previous grumpiness or hostility.

But the next day passed and the next, and she didn't see a sign of him, so maybe she'd been mistaken about him being attracted to her. He wasn't pottering around in his garden when she drove up the track. He certainly didn't come near her house. And he was never at Penny's when she went round to look at the pups.

He must be avoiding her. She'd betrayed her reaction to him and he was embarrassed by that.

Pity.

She told herself she was being silly. There had never been anything between them but a few glances and what her own imagination had supplied. If he didn't think of her in that way, it was his right.

It was Ed's wake the following day, so Sam would have to come here then. She'd make very sure she didn't embarrass him. In fact, she'd stay right away from him.

The phone rang just as Sam was leaving for Ed's wake.

'Yes?'

'I'm in the neighbourhood and I'd like to pop in and see you. I need to work out exactly what to bring for Tina.'

What a feeble excuse that was! Lorraine had some ulterior motive, she always did. 'Well, I'm just going out so it's not convenient, I'm afraid.'

'When will you be back?'

'How should I know? I'm going to a wake.' He realised he hadn't told her. 'Ed died a while ago in England and they're scattering his ashes today.'

'Did he leave you anything?'

'His old car.'

'Pity. A chunk of money would have made life a lot easier for Tina. Who got the money? He was loaded, wasn't he?'

'A woman from England. She's the one scattering his ashes today. Sorry. Must go. You can ring me some other time and discuss Tina's visit. There's no need to come here in person.' He put the phone down, wishing now that he hadn't picked it up. Lorraine always seemed to leave a bitterness behind her.

When he arrived, taking some beer along as his contribution, he found he was nearly an hour early, the first person there besides Kirsty, because he'd mistaken the starting time. 'Oh. Sorry. I'll come back.'

'No, do come in. I could actually use some help, if you don't mind. It's taken me longer than I expected to get ready.'

'All right. And could you do me a favour, do you think?'

As they worked he told her about his daughter's coming visit. 'Lorraine's forced her to come and visit me but as you've seen, I've not much to offer a guest.' His eyes took on a distant look, almost as if he was no longer aware that Kirsty was there, but was speaking his thoughts aloud. 'It's Lorraine's fault. She stripped me of an amazing percentage of my assets when we divorced. They've coined a term for it these days, "toxic wife syndrome". I was reading an article about it on line only the other day. Women like that marry for money and take as much in the divorce as they can.'

'Your ex's attitude must make things difficult.'

'Yeah. I'm not at all looking forward to Tina's visit, either. Lorraine's made sure she'll regard me as the villain of the piece. I hardly know my own daughter these days and Tina definitely wasn't impressed by my house.'

Kirsty tried not to smile and failed.

He pulled a wry face. 'All right, it's a tumbledown shack. But the land is actually a pretty good investment and I bought it for the peace and quiet. The house is weatherproof at least and it does me for the moment, but it only has one bedroom.'

'Where are you both going to sleep, then?'

'Tina can have my bedroom and I'll bunk down in the studio.' He hesitated. 'I was going to ask if I could borrow one of your single beds.'

'Of course. But wouldn't it be easier for Tina to come here? I've got five spare bedrooms and two bathrooms.'

He couldn't hide his surprise at this.

'What have I said?'

He grinned. 'You're going to fit in all right as an honorary Aussie, Kirsty Miller.'

'What do you mean?'

'Offering to put up a complete stranger for a neighbour.'

'Oh.'

'I may just accept once you've had time to think it over. I'd better warn you, though: Tina isn't easy to deal with. She still acts like a moody teenager, not a twenty-year old.'

'I don't need to think it over, Sam. The offer's there.'

There was the sound of a car outside just then and he wasn't sure whether to be glad or sorry that other guests were arriving. The more he got to know Kirsty, the better he liked her.

Which didn't mean he'd take up Ed's suggestion. No way was he hanging out for a rich wife. Or any sort of wife at all. Been there, done that, not going again.

Few of the guests were wearing mourning clothes, but there was no doubt they all regretted Ed's passing and the things they said about him were very touching.

When the time came for the little ceremony, Kirsty felt rather nervous, for all the friendliness of these strangers. She clapped her hands to gain their attention and when the dozen or so heads were turned in her direction, she said simply. 'I think we can lay Ed to rest with his wife now.'

She picked up the urn and carried it outside. When she stopped by the rose bed, the others formed a semi-circle round them. She waited till she had their attention then held up the piece of paper. 'Ed has made it clear what he wants. Sam, would you join me, please? Penny? Franco?' She waited till they were standing on either side of her, then smiled at everyone. 'Ed's actual words were, "No fuss. Just do it and wish me well".'

She turned her back and stepped towards the rose bed, taking the lid off the urn and saying, 'Be happy with your Mary, Ed. I miss you.' Then she scattered some of the ashes and stepped aside, holding out the urn to Sam.

He took it and said simply, 'I loved you like a grandfather, Ed. I miss you too.' He passed the urn to Franco.

'I'll miss your help with the wine making, old friend.'

Penny took the urn from her husband. 'You gave me Franco, Ed, as well as your friendship. I miss you like hell.' She emptied the rest of the ashes and turned to walk blindly into her husband's arms, wiping her eyes with the handkerchief he pressed into her hand.

'You all right?' Sam asked.

Kirsty looked at him through a mist of tears.

'Oh, hell.' He put an arm round her shoulders and guided her towards the house, calling over his shoulder, 'Food will be served in a few minutes, folks. I'll give you a yell.' He guided her into the kitchen and pulled her close.

She clung to him for a minute or two. 'I didn't know him for long, but I was very fond of him. He looked so like my grandfather, it was uncanny. It was as if I'd lost Pops twice.'

'I can see that you really were fond of him and I'm sorry for suggesting otherwise.'

She blew her nose and managed to stop crying, then turned to the display of food. 'I suppose we'd better take the cling film off and feed people. I've got some things warming in the oven.'

Just as they were about to invite people to eat, another car pulled up the drive. Sam cursed under his breath. 'What the hell is my ex doing here?'

Kirsty turned round to see a woman get out of a big silver car. She had to admit to herself that she'd been curious about Sam's ex. She saw an ultra-thin woman, ferociously smart, with short, spiky hair and very long earrings.

'Will you do me a favour?' Sam muttered.

'Yes, of course.'

'Will you pretend we're . . . together?'

In response, she slipped her arm in his and let him lead her across the grass.

'Sam, darling, I couldn't leave you to face this alone.' Lorraine held out her cheek for a kiss.

He made no move towards her. 'I'm not alone.' He smiled lovingly at Kirsty, then turned back to the newcomer. 'And you weren't invited today, Lorriane. This gathering is only for Ed's friends.'

'I'm sorry you've had a wasted journey,' Kirsty said quietly, 'but this whole event was arranged by Ed himself, so I'm afraid I can't invite any outsiders to join us.'

'Well!' Lorraine glared from one to the other, then snapped, 'I'm sorry to have to disturb it, but even if I can't stay, I need to use the bathroom before I set off again. I presume you won't deny me that?'

Sam glared at her. 'I'll take you down to my place.'

'She can use mine,' Kirsty began.

'She's only trying to poke her nose in and work out how much you've been left,' he said.

Spots of colour flared in Lorraine's cheeks. 'You have a nasty, suspicious mind, Sam Brady, and always did have. What possible business is it of mine what she has been left?'

'I know how you think.' He turned to Kirsty. 'I'll be back shortly.'

She reached up to kiss his cheek. 'Don't be long, then, darling.' She had the satisfaction of seeing the other woman scowl at this endearment.

Sam declined a ride in Lorraine's car and marched down the track to his house, leaving the gates closed so that she had to park outside them and teeter up to the house in her ridiculously high heels. He walked along in silence, but when he got there, he turned to see Lorraine still standing a few metres away, hands on hips, staring at his house.

'My god, Sam, couldn't you find something better than this? When Tina told me about it, I thought she was exaggerating.'

'I like it. Will you please hurry up and do what you must. I have a wake to attend.'

'Do you really have to go back? I want to have a little talk about Tina.'

'Use my bathroom then get the hell out of here. As I said earlier, if you want to talk about Tina, you can phone me.'

She moved forward, nearly overbalancing as the soft earth of his herb bed gave way. He made no effort to help her, didn't want to touch her. Inside, she looked round, making a scornful noise.

'The bathroom is over there.'

She took her time and he paced up and down the veranda, angry with her, not wanting her to invade his space.

When she came out, she said, 'I'm not leaving till we've had a talk. For Tina's sake, you need to reconsider, take out a second mortgage if necessary. I can't afford to continue subsidising her. I've enough trouble paying my own expenses.'

'I'm not discussing anything now. I'm attending the wake of a very dear friend and you are holding up proceedings. If you don't leave immediately, I'll pick you up and carry you back to your car.'

'You wouldn't dare!'

'Try me.'

Their eyes met for a moment, then she stepped off the veranda. 'You'll regret this.'

'I regret many things.' He escorted her down to her car and left her repairing her make-up in the mirror.

He waited at the gates of Whitegums till he heard her car engine start up, then he went to join the others. He didn't have much of an appetite, but he drank a beer or two and ate a couple of pieces of chicken, then found himself a seat in a corner.

Franco came over to join him, waving a bottle of Ed's wine. 'You all right, mate?'

'Oh, just a bit annoyed.'

'Was that play-acting with Kirsty, or are you two really together?'

'Play acting for my ex's benefit.'

'Shame. She's a nice woman, Kirsty.'

'She is, but the last thing I need at the moment is to get entangled with anyone.'

Franco gave him a pitying smile. 'It's not "entangled" when it's the right woman.'

Sam shrugged.

A short time later Penny started them off reminiscing about Ed. Stories about their friend flowed for about an hour, most of them humorous. He had, Sam thought, been a much liked man.

When the guests had all left, except for those who lived on Gulliver Road, Kirsty began to clear up and soon all four of them were in the kitchen together.

It didn't take long to put things away then she said, 'Would you fancy another glass of wine, or do you have to get back?'

'If Franco will nip across to check on the pups, I'll stay for a while,' Penny said.

'I'll come with you,' Sam said.

The two men walked off round the house.

'Getting on better with Sam now?' Penny asked.

'Not in the way you mean.'

'Pity. The two of you look good together.'

Only when the other three had left did Kirsty realise that she thought it was a pity too.

The strength of that wish surprised her.

Chapter Nine

That evening, just as Kirsty was getting ready for bed, there was a phone call.

'It's Marlene here, honey. I'm still in Australia.'

'I thought you'd have gone home by now.'

'No. I picked up some sort of lung infection and they won't let me fly for another two or three weeks. I was wondering if you'd like a visitor for a few days?'

'I'd love to see you. I'll come up to Perth and fetch you.'

'I can hire a car to bring me down. I'm not up to driving myself yet, still get tired easily.'

'Waste of money. Anyway, I'll enjoy a trip up to Perth.'

'You're sure I'm not imposing?'

'Marlene, I'd really, really love to have you. Where are you staying? I'll come and fetch you tomorrow.'

She spent the evening making one of the spare bedrooms as welcoming as possible, and packing an overnight case for herself.

In the morning she set off early, delighted at the thought of seeing Marlene again, and even more delighted at the thought of having some company.

* * *

Sam noticed the silver convertible go past the end of his driveway as he was watering his garden. Kirsty looked so happy and excited, he wondered what had caused it. He went into his studio, but wasn't able to settle to work.

Damn you, Ed! he thought. Why did you try to set me and Kirsty up together? I can't relax when I'm with her.

He set down the brush without getting the paint out. He needed a new computer and now was as good a time as any to get one.

He popped into the art gallery while he was in town. Rhys looked up from the tiny counter near the door.

'Sam! I was just going to phone you. We've sold another of your paintings. Do you have any more of those flowery ones?'

He stared at Rhys, as much shocked as pleased. He'd been struggling for two years and suddenly, it seemed, things were starting to happen. 'Yes. I have some, but they'll need framing.'

'Leave that to us. We won't overcharge you but we have a framer who has a particular knack for finding just the right frame or mounting. She's brilliant. We all benefit from maximising sales, you know.'

'I'll bring the paintings in tomorrow, then. How many do you want?'

'Would you have half a dozen?'

Sam did a quick calculation. 'I've only got five and one's quite big.'

'How big?'

'About two by one metres. And – um, it's very brightly coloured, bougainvillea mainly.'

Rhys shot an assessing glance round the gallery. 'We'll find a place for it, don't worry. Just bring what you've got and I'll have a cheque waiting for you from the other sales.'

'Great.'

Later, Sam picked up a bottle of champagne. Once home, he rang Penny and Marco to come and celebrate and, after a moment's hesitation, Kirsty. But there was no reply from Whitegums, though he tried several times.

When he and his neighbours were sitting on his veranda celebrating his sales, he asked casually, 'Have you seen Kirsty today?'

'No.'

'She drove out this morning and I thought she'd be back by now, but there was no answer when I called her.'

Penny shrugged. 'She may have gone up to Perth. It's not really any of our business if she wants to go away for the night.'

'She should have told us so we could keep an eye on her place.' He swirled his wine round his glass, watching the bubbles make trailing patterns. 'She doesn't know anyone in Western Australia, so where can she have gone?'

'No need to worry about her, I'm sure. She's a very capable woman.'

'No. I suppose she'll be OK.'

Penny's look was speculative, so he didn't mention Kirsty again.

But after they'd gone he couldn't stop worrying. He even strolled up the lane to see if that damned convertible was back, and it wasn't. She was probably all right, but he knew Ed would want him to keep an eye on her. Well, that's what neighbours did.

Dammit, she should have told them where she was going and how long she was going to be away for.

In Perth, Kirsty booked into the same hotel as Marlene. She found her friend looking wan and not at all like the robust woman who'd buzzed energetically round Perth shopping with her.

Marlene hugged her. 'Don't say it!'

'Say what?'

'How haggard I look. I've got a mirror. I'm not infectious or I wouldn't have called you, but the doctors have forbidden me to fly yet. There's not a high enough percentage of oxygen in planes, they reckon. Well, you must have felt how stuffy they are sometimes. Thank goodness for travel insurance or this would have cost me a fortune.'

'Well, we can have a nice meal together tonight and drive down tomorrow. There are all sorts of great places to visit near me and lovely restaurants – well, the menus look lovely and I've been dying to try some of them, only I don't like going out alone at night.'

Marlene smiled. 'Sounds great. Tonight's meal is on me. But if you don't mind, honey, I'd really appreciate some home-cooked food most of the time. I'm tired of restaurant meals. And I'd like to laze around with a good book or two till I feel better. Maybe we'll visit a bookshop this afternoon. If you don't mind, we'll postpone the sightseeing until after I've pulled myself together a bit.' She sighed. 'It was a nasty virus. Haven't had anything hit me like that for years.'

They didn't stay up late and didn't try to set off too early. Even so, Marlene's increasing pallor worried Kirsty.

Her friend slept for part of the journey, waking with a start as they turned into Gulliver Road. She winced as she straightened herself and gave a tired smile. 'Fine companion I am.'

'It doesn't matter. If you need to rest, then that's what you must do. You don't have to sing for your supper.' She pulled up outside Whitegums. 'Voilà!'

Marlene studied the house. 'I like it. And the vines we passed look very healthy. When's the harvest?'

'Towards the end of March. Whenever Franco says they're ready.'

'If I'm still here, I'll help out.'

Sam delivered the canvases to the gallery the following morning and went to deposit his cheque in the bank, feeling more satisfaction about earning this relatively small amount of money than he had about the hundreds of thousands he'd earned in his former life as a corporate planner, money his ex had spent all too lavishly.

Back at the block he decided to fit in a couple of hours' work before eating lunch, so grabbed a quick coffee then went across to the studio. He beamed at the sight of the huge canvas, which was standing on two easels he'd attached to one another with a couple of planks. The canvas had faint black lines all over it, two solid days' work of drawing out the design. He loved that moment when he'd outlined his design and the canvas seemed to invite him to step forward joyfully and create a thing of vivid beauty.

Humming, he got his paints out, squeezed some on to one of the old plates he picked up from the charity shop and used as palettes, then let it down with linseed oil. He was surprised to see that the bottle was half full. Surely it'd been nearly empty? The paint looked different when he'd mixed it, he couldn't work out how, but it didn't smell any different.

After staring at it for a minute or so, he dipped up a big brushful and tested it out on a piece of paper. It didn't flow quite as well as usual, but maybe that was because it was cooler today. The colour was exactly what he wanted, though, so he began to work carefully in the top right-hand corner.

After a couple of hours, hunger drove him across to the house. He ate quickly, yawning, then went to lie down for a few minutes on the sofa.

He woke a couple of hours later, feeling groggy, and got to his feet, angry that he'd wasted the best daylight hours. But he'd been working rather hard lately, driven by a furious need to translate his ideas on to canvas. Maybe he should slow down a bit now that he had Ed's money as backup.

He strolled across to the studio and stopped in consternation as he looked at the canvas. The corner he'd painted with such care was badly blistered.

'What the—!' He went across to examine it closely, then took a step backwards and looked at the canvas. Ruined. How could this have happened?

He picked up the tube of paint and shook his head. Surely not this? It had been brand new this morning and he'd broken the seal himself. He picked up the bottle of linseed oil. It looked all right. It wasn't until he set it down next to an unopened bottle that he noticed the slight colour difference. It was lighter than the oil in the new bottle. He opened it and sniffed, then opened the new bottle. Did the old one have a slightly different smell to it? Perhaps, but not very different, and not something he recognised or could identify. Just – different.

A memory struck him suddenly of setting this bottle down after he'd finished the last painting. It had been almost empty. Someone must have been tampering with his painting materials. Who would do such a thing? He lived in an isolated place and the few people nearby were his friends. Few others came near Gulliver Road.

He began to pace up and down, then went to the door and stared blindly across his block, still trying to puzzle out what could have happened. Who had been here? Suddenly he remembered his ex. Lorraine hadn't been near the studio, but she'd still been in her car as he walked back to Whitegums, fiddling with her make-up as usual. He'd heard the car start up, but hadn't waited for it to drive away.

And surely even Lorraine wouldn't do a thing like this to him?

He experienced a leaden, hollow feeling as he remembered the furious arguments that had led to their break up, the wild threats she'd made. She'd married him for his money, he'd realised that years ago. But by then they had Tina, so he'd tried to make it work. And most of the time Lorraine had been pleasant enough to live with, as long as she got the luxurious lifestyle she craved. She'd spent his money almost as fast as he earned it and had been outraged when he tried to talk to her about him stopping work for a while and trying to become an artist, because it would mean her reining in her lavish lifestyle.

But what benefit would she get from damaging his work now, years after they'd parted? Revenge? Surely people didn't go in for that sort of thing nowadays? It was something you read about in gothic novels.

Only . . . now he came to think of it, he'd known her play nasty tricks before on people who'd upset her. And Tina's art lecturer would have been expert enough to tell her what to use, though of course she'd not have asked outright, she was too clever for that. She'd been seen with him. Well, it sounded as if the man was him. He must have money, then, or she'd not bother with him.

No, he just couldn't believe this damage was down to her!

Then his gaze fell on the ground outside his studio. There, clearly showing to one side were a woman's footprints with deep tiny holes at the rear, the sort you'd get from stiletto heels.

Only one person had been here wearing stiletto heels: Lorraine. But she hadn't been across to his studio, just to the house to use his bathroom. He squatted to study the footprints more carefully, then walked across to his house. There, in the moister earth of the herb garden, where she'd teetered and nearly fallen, were more footprints with those telltale heel indentations.

Sick to the soul, he went back inside the studio and touched the big canvas. So many hours spent drawing out the design. Wasted now. And the canvas itself was ruined in that corner. He'd have to go and buy some more big canvases, then start this particular design from scratch again.

And while he was at it, he'd buy a big lock for the studio door and iron mesh for the windows. No one else was getting a chance to damage his work.

He briefly considered calling in the police, but for Tina's sake, he couldn't do it. And would they be able to prove anything? The studio hadn't been locked until now, not even at night. He'd felt so safe here in his cosy retreat.

Marlene fell asleep after tea and since Kirsty felt like stretching her legs, she decided to stroll down to Sam's and invite him to her birthday party. She was determined to mark the occasion and Ed's wake had given her the confidence to hold another function just for her immediate neighbours. People round here were very casual about parties and holding them out of doors made clearing up easy.

The little side gate to Sam's house was open and her sandaled feet made no noise on the dusty track, so he didn't hear her coming. He was sitting on the veranda, arms pulled tightly round himself. His whole body radiated unhappiness. She got close enough to see the misery in his face before he heard her. He raised his head and stared at her so owlishly she realised he'd been drinking, even before she saw the empty beer cans near his chair.

'What's wrong, Sam?'

He said nothing for a few seconds, then got to his feet, swaying a little. 'I'll show you.'

As he moved, he stumbled and she automatically reached out to steady him.

'Come and see what she's done.' He put one arm carelessly round her waist and drew her in the direction of his studio.

Once there, he let go of her to steady himself against the wall. It took him a minute to find the light switch. 'Where is the stupid thing?' he muttered. 'Ah, there it is.'

The room suddenly blazed with light and he pointed across the room. 'See.'

She turned to look in that direction. There was a huge canvas on an easel. It had drawing all over it, a big vine laden with flowers. It must have taken him ages to do that. He'd started painting in the top right-hand corner, but it was badly blistered, the vivid red marred by ugly brown streaks and bubbling. She went closer, horrified at the damage. It looked as if someone had taken a blow torch to it. 'What happened?'

'Someone tampered with my linseed oil. Don't know what they put in it, but that's what happened when the stuff was exposed to air.'

'Who would ever do anything as cruel as that?'

'There's only been one stranger round here lately. Think back to Ed's wake.'

It didn't take a second to make the connection. 'Your ex? Surely not?'

'She's the only one with the motive and the opportunity. Isn't that what detectives look for?' He laughed, but it was a harsh, bitter sound and his voice broke. Automatically Kirsty went to put her arms round him.

'Took me two whole days to draw that outline. I was really pleased with it,' he muttered against her shoulder.

'You'll do another one, just as good.'

'I rang the local supplier and he hasn't got any more of those huge canvases in stock, so I can't start on the remake for a few days. I was all geared up to do that painting.'

He didn't seem to have noticed that he was playing with her hair. But she noticed and the gentle touch made her catch her breath. If he'd been sober she'd not have tried to stop him, but he was very drunk.

'Shall we go and sit on your veranda?' She tried to pull him towards the door.

He stayed where he was, his arms still round her and his breath warm in her ear. 'I've run out of beer. Can't even drink myself senseless. Have you got any beer or wine at your place?'

She smiled. From what she could see, he seemed to have made a pretty good attempt at getting drunk. 'I'd much prefer a cup of tea or coffee.'

'I've only got coffee.'

'That'd be lovely.'

He kissed her gently on the cheek then his lips moved down to capture hers and the kiss seemed so right she couldn't help responding to him.

As they paused for air, he stared at her, then shook his head and kissed her cheek before pulling away. 'No. Mustn't. Pity.'

She was growing tired of people saying that word in connection with the two of them. But now wasn't the time to discuss with Sam why he thought he shouldn't kiss her. Under the influence of drink, he'd let his guard down, but she doubted he'd be as forthcoming when he was sober. 'Let's go and get that coffee.'

Inside the house, he insisted on filling the kettle, splashing water everywhere as his hand wavered underneath the tap. He put the kettle back into its cradle and switched it on, then sat down on the couch and smiled at her.

'You're very pretty. I'd like to sketch your face one day.' He yawned and leaned sideways with a weary sigh. Within seconds he was fast asleep.

Kirsty switched off the kettle and let herself out of the house, walking slowly back to Whitegums. She put up one hand to touch her cheek, where she could still feel Sam's last kiss, light as a butterfly, then she touched her lips, where his first kiss was much more strongly imprinted.

Only as she was getting into bed did she remember that she hadn't invited him to her birthday party. He'd been a charming drunk, so if the saying In vino, veritas held any truth, he had a nice nature. Well, no friend of Ed's could have been nasty. Look at the lovely people who'd come to the wake.

It took her a long time to get to sleep. She kept remembering the kiss, remembering Mike's kisses too. It had been a long time.

She missed the companionship and warmth of being a couple: doing things together, making plans, laughing over life's silly twists. And seeing how happy Penny and Franco were made it worse, somehow.

She definitely couldn't go back to living with Rod. Not now. Neris and Sue were right. She should have left him years ago, for both their sakes. Why had she not seen that for herself? Why had it taken Ed's bequest to shake her from retreat mode?

Rod waited impatiently. Linnie was late, which was unusual for her. When the door knocker went, he called 'Come in!' but it was only the postman with a parcel, a book he'd sent away for.

It was a full hour before Linnie turned up and he could see immediately that she'd been crying. He didn't know what to do about that. Should you pretend you hadn't noticed? Or should you ask what was wrong?

In the end he couldn't bear the unhappy silence. 'What's upset you, Linnie?'

She looked at him, clapped one hand to her mouth as if to hold something in, then let the hand drop and burst into tears. 'It's my ex. Glen came round to the flat last night and if my neighbour hadn't come to my help . . .' Her words trailed away and she drew up her sleeve to show him a big bruise on her arm. 'He's a violent man. We've been divorced for three years but he still tries to get money out of me for drugs when he's desperate. As if I have anything to spare!'

Rod looked at her arm in horror. He'd heard of wife beating but never seen its effects up close. 'What can you do?'

'Not much. A legal order means nothing to him when he's on drugs.' She tried to smile, but it was a poor attempt. 'Sorry. No need to unload my troubles on to you. You've enough of your own.'

'I don't mind. Only I'm not much use at the moment.' He gestured to his leg. 'I can hardly look after myself, let alone help you.'

'I wouldn't expect any help from you, Rod. A bruise is nothing. It'll soon get better. He broke my arm once. That seemed to take ages to heal, but it was only a few weeks. I left him after that.' She looked at the clock. 'Well, I must get on.'

'Are you eating your lunch here?'

'Can't. Sorry. I'm a bit behind.'

'Why don't you bring the boys for tea instead then? I can order in a take-away for us all.'

She hesitated. 'We couldn't impose.'

'I'd welcome the company. And Tommy can use the computer. Please . . .'

'All right, then. But I'll bring a cake for afters.'

She carried on working, more subdued than usual. He missed her bright cheerfulness, which had warmed something inside him.

He hoped he was doing the right thing by trying to help her and cheer her up. How did you know whether what you were doing was right? Other people seemed to have an instinct for this but he hadn't. To him, people were hugely difficult to understand and even harder to talk to. Numbers were much easier. They obeyed the rules. That's why he'd become an accountant.

He would, he decided, ring up his boss in the morning and ask if there was any work he could do at home. He was going mad sitting here alone day after day, thinking about things he'd avoided for a long time, like how different he was. And how lonely.

When Sam woke up the following morning, he groaned and went to drink a glass of cold water then forced a piece of dry toast down through the queasiness so that he could take a couple of headache tablets. After that, he made a cup of coffee and took it out on the veranda, sipping it slowly. His head was still thumping and he couldn't remember what exactly had happened last night. He'd lost his capacity to take much alcohol over these two abstemious years. Who'd have thought a few beers would make him legless? Frowning, he thought about the previous evening.

He remembered the damage to his painting only too well.

He also remembered kissing Kirsty, but he couldn't seem to sort out how that had happened. He hadn't forced himself on her, had he? No, surely not. She'd definitely returned his kiss, so it couldn't have been unwelcome.

He shouldn't have done it, though. Kirsty wasn't the sort of woman you took lightly. He'd have to go and apologise – and make it clear that he wasn't looking for any sort of long-term relationship. Only . . . he didn't want to upset her. And it wasn't the first time he'd wanted to kiss her. Wouldn't be the last, either. Pity.

Once his headache had settled into a dull throb, he walked grimly up the lane to Whitegums, automatically going round to the back. She was working in the kitchen, cooking something, looking happy and pretty. He hesitated at the kitchen door then rapped on it.

She turned, her face lighting up when she saw who it was. 'Come in!'

He took two steps inside and stopped, not daring to go any closer. 'I believe I owe you an apology.'

'What for?'

'I was drunk last night. I can't remember exactly how it happened, but I think I kissed you.'

'Are you apologising for it?'

'Yes, I suppose so. I was drunk and—'

'It was only a kiss. I quite enjoyed it, actually.'

'Oh. Well, that's all right. As long as I didn't – upset you.'

He was scowling so fiercely she deliberately kept her voice light. 'What, one kiss? Hardly.'

There was the sound of footsteps and an older woman came into the kitchen, looking from one to the other. 'Am I interrupting something?'

'No. This is Sam from just down the track. Sam, this is Marlene, a friend of mine. She's been ill, so she's come here to recuperate.'

Sam took the hand Marlene offered, then stepped back and studied at her. 'I feel as if I know you from somewhere.'

Marlene's face took on a shuttered expression. 'We've never met.'

'Strange. I felt. . . Anyway, I hope you get better soon.' He turned back to Kirsty. 'I'd better be going.'

'Why don't you stay for a coffee and a piece of my home-made fruit cake.'

He hesitated. 'Home made?'

'Yes.'

'I'd kill for a piece.'

'You and Marlene go and sit on the back veranda and I'll bring it out to you.'

He held the door open, took a seat and tried to think what to say.

'You're an artist, I gather, Sam?'

He realised his companion had spoken. 'Sorry. I was wool gathering.'

'Kirsty tells me you're an artist.'

'Yes. I do flowers mainly.'

'I'd like to see your paintings.'

'I've got no finished pieces left at home. The gallery in Margaret River took the lot.'

'Then I'll make a point of going in to look at them. Kirsty's going to drive me there this afternoon.'

He saw Kirsty pick up a big tray in the kitchen and hurried to hold the door open. The cake was even better than he remembered, so he accepted a second piece. 'Next time you go away, it'd be as well to let us know – me and Penny, I mean. We were a bit worried about you. We always look out for one another's houses.'

'I'll try to remember.'

He drained his beaker of coffee. 'That was great. Now, I'd better go and start clearing up.'

He walked slowly back. It wasn't as hot today, thank goodness. He wished he could remember the kiss more clearly. Kirsty wouldn't read more into it than he'd meant, would she?

What had he meant anyway?

Damned if he knew. He shook his head and went to find a smaller canvas to start another painting.

Marlene cocked one eyebrow at Kirsty. 'That's the guy Ed told you to marry, isn't it?'

She could feel herself blushing. 'Haven't we agreed that Ed was out of line there?'

'Now that I've seen his choice, I'm not so sure about that. Sam's rather attractive. I'd not dismiss the possibilities out of hand, if I were you.'

'Don't you start! People have been trying to set me up with men for the past few years and I'm simply not interested.'

'Tell me what happened between you yesterday?'

'There's nothing to tell.'

'I may be old but I'm not blind. The air hummed when you two were together today, yet you avoided each other's eyes. Why? You're both single and free, aren't you?'

So she told Marlene about Sam kissing her. 'I think he regrets it now.'

Her friend sat frowning in thought. 'Maybe Ed was right about the attraction between the two of you, but I don't know if it was wise or foolish of him to suggest you marry. Only time will tell, I suppose.' She chuckled. 'Stop blushing and let's make plans for the next few days. I'm feeling a lot better already.'

'I've invited Penny and Franco over for a barbecue on Saturday. It's my birthday, you see. I'd meant to invite Sam, but I keep forgetting.' Her brain had gone to mush when she saw him today.

'We'll stop on our way out to ask him.'

'All right.' She looked at Marlene, her brow wrinkled in confusion. 'I wonder why Sam thought he'd met you before?'

Marlene hesitated. 'Well . . . promise me you'll not tell anyone.'

'I won't, of course I won't.'

'I've been in a TV series that's been shown all over the world. I wasn't one of the major characters but I was in it for quite a few years.'

'I'm sorry. I don't watch much TV, so I didn't recognise you. I wouldn't have thought Sam watched much TV, either.'

'He must have seen an episode or two. I left the series last year, when they killed my character off. Very dramatic. I wear my hair differently these days and I've stopped colouring it, so people don't often recognise me. But I suppose Sam has an artist's eye for faces.'

'He said last night that he'd like to sketch me.'

'You should let him. There's something nice and intimate about an artist sketching a pretty woman. It could lead to all sorts of interesting situations.'

'Marlene!'

'Oh, all right. I won't press the point. But you shouldn't let a luscious man go to waste. Let's go and buy a few things for your birthday. I love organising parties.'

Chapter Ten

Saturday morning fulfilled the pessimistic forecast of the TV weather presenter, bringing a cloudy sky and winds that whipped the summer dust into a blur which stung bare ankles.

Kirsty watered a few special plants then stood sipping a cup of tea by the kitchen window, watching the fairy wrens again. They were almost Disney-esque (if there was such a word!) in their cuteness. The phone rang and when she picked it up, her sister was at the other end, wishing her a happy birthday, even though it was the day before her birthday still in England. They chatted for a while and Kirsty put the handset down with a sigh, wishing she could have her family here today.

A second phone call was from Neris, and they chatted for ages.

By the time Rod rang, Kirsty was near tears. They'd all sent cards so she hadn't expected phone calls as well. She turned as Marlene came into the kitchen. 'Did the phone calls wake you? I'm so sorry.'

'Nonsense. It's a lovely morning and I'm raring to go.'

'Raring to go?'

'Yes. I'm taking you out for lunch today.'

'You are?'

'Of course I am, birthday girl. We'll go into town and find somewhere that appeals, then choose the very best on the menu.'

'But I have tonight to get ready for.'

'There's not that much to do for a barbecue and there are two of us to do it. Besides, there's a lovely gourmet shop that does take-away food. We can get some stuff from there.'

In town, fate brought Sam walking towards them on the main street.

'The more the merrier. He can join us for lunch,' Marlene said at once.

Kirsty opened her mouth, but before she could protest, her friend had yoo-hooed and waved one hand to catch his attention, before beckoning vigorously.

He came across and nodded to Kirsty. 'Happy birthday.'

Marlene twined her arm in his. 'Are you busy for the next hour or two, Sam honey? We're going for a birthday lunch, my treat, and I'd like to invite you as well.'

His expression grew rather wary. 'I can't impose.'

'Dear boy, I can afford to buy lunch for twenty without even blinking at the cost. Surely you're not going to deny me one of the few pleasures left to an old woman? After all, it is Kirsty's birthday.'

He smiled reluctantly. 'I'd love to join you, then. Thanks.'

Marlene turned to thread her other arm in Kirsty's and pull them both up the street.

They found a café where they could sit outside, sheltered from the wind, and it was while they were ordering that Sam suddenly gaped at Marlene.

'You're not—'

She cocked one eyebrow at him.

'You are. You're the aunt, Seraphina Gold.'

She clapped one hand to her bosom. 'Alas! My dark secret is revealed. Yes, I am. Or rather – I was. I'm dead now, written out of the series.' She studied him. 'You don't look like the sort of man to watch TV soaps.'

'My colleague's wife is addicted to *Golden Pride*. I've been forced to watch it a few times over the years.'

'And didn't enjoy it.'

He flushed. 'I – um—'

She chuckled. 'It got very silly at times, made me wonder if the scriptwriters were off on a trip to la-la-land. But it paid so well, I stuck with it as long as they'd have me. At my age, with my husband dying young, it was a godsend. I shall be comfortable for life on the money I was paid for that series, and what I'm still getting for repeats.'

Marlene had a gift for keeping lively conversation going and the three of them talked and laughed until Kirsty suddenly realised it was after three o'clock. 'I can't believe it's so late! I have to get ready for tonight.'

'Need any help?' Sam asked as he escorted them back to her car.

'Oh, well. Yes, actually. The cooking. I've never done a barbecue before and I was going to ask you or Franco to do it.'

'I'd be happy to take charge of the cooking.'

They finished their shopping and as they were parking at Whitegums, Marlene said thoughtfully, 'I think Ed should have trusted in good old Mother Nature. When you two forget to be self-conscious with one another, the chemistry zings.'

Kirsty didn't reply, but the remark pleased her. Only she wasn't going to do anything to make Sam feel she was hunting him. She had too much pride for that.

But she could hope, couldn't she?

That evening Sam was the last to arrive, by which time Kirsty was worrying that she'd done something to upset him. Marlene sat chatting to Penny and Franco as if she'd known them all her life.

When Sam rounded the corner of the veranda, Kirsty waved to him from the kitchen window. He paused to say hello to the others, then came inside, holding out a small, square. 'Be careful. It's still a bit wet.'

She found herself holding a small painting of a beautiful white rose, just like the ones in Ed's garden.

'It's beautiful.' She gazed at the painting in delight. 'I shall always treasure it.'

'Um, I'm glad you like it.'

'I love your paintings.'

There was another of those tingling moments between them and she found it hard to breathe evenly. Then his expression became guarded, so she said hurriedly, 'Are you still going to do the barbecuing for me?'

'Yes.'

'Good. I've put out some cooking utensils. Tell me if anything is missing. I'll just show this to the others.'

She escaped outside, grateful that the dimmer lighting there would hide her flushed face. 'Look what Sam gave me.'

'You lucky thing.' Penny held it at arm's length. 'You'll

have to get it framed. Where are you going to put it?'

'Somewhere I can look at it often. I love it.'

Sam watched her showing off the painting. It was clear she really did like it, wasn't just pretending. He'd hesitated to do one, but she was alone in a strange country and he did want to mark her birthday. He'd only just had time to finish it.

While he cooked the food – steaks and fancy chicken sausages – he listened to the others chat, watching Kirsty till he realised what he was doing and forced himself to look away.

Later, they persuaded Marlene to tell them what it had been like being part of a TV soap for so long. He found her face fascinating and was definitely going to sketch her before she went back to the States. He wasn't good at painting faces, but he had a talent for sketching them and enjoyed doing it as light relief from his flowers.

When Marlene produced a birthday cake with half a dozen lit candles on it, he saw that Kirsty's eyes were over-brilliant. One tear escaped and she wiped it quickly away with one fingertip. She had lovely hands, long fingers which made the slightest gesture elegant.

Oh, hell, he was doing it again, watching her.

The following day Marlene sat studying the small painting, head on one side. 'I wonder if Sam's paintings are still for sale in town. This is really good.'

'He said he'd consigned his last few to one of the art galleries, didn't he?'

'Yes. So if you're going to get that one he gave you framed, I'll come with you and take a look at his others. I'd really love a memento of my visit here.'

'That'd be nice. I'll ring Penny. She'll know where to go.'

Rhys at the art gallery was very helpful about the framing. He was about Kirsty's age and had a gentle, friendly manner. She left the painting with him, rather reluctant to part with it, and he promised to phone her when it was ready.

Marlene bought two of Sam's larger paintings and arranged to have them shipped out to LA. 'They'll fit beautifully into my living room.'

As they walked away, she smiled at Kirsty. 'I have to go up to Perth next week for a medical check-up. If I'm all right to fly, I'll make arrangements to leave soon after that.'

'You know you're welcome to stay longer. You'll miss the wine harvest.'

'I know. But they say fish and guests go off after a few days. And anyway, I think Ed was right. You do need to learn to stand on your own feet.' She nudged Kirsty and grinned at her. 'Did you see the way that guy who owns the art gallery was looking at you?'

'What?'

Marlene rolled her eyes. 'Honestly, are you blind? Rhys was admiring you. He has your phone number. What are you going to do if he asks you for a date?'

'He won't.'

'Bet you ten dollars he will.'

'I'm not betting. He won't.'

'And if he does?'

It took her a moment or two to answer that, it seemed such a novel idea. She'd stopped thinking of herself as desirable, but now Sam had kissed her and Marlene thought Rhys fancied her. That all felt rather nice. 'I'll accept.'

'Good girl. Do Sam a world of good to see you going out with someone else.'

Kirsty sighed. 'Marlene, I won't be doing it for that reason but because I enjoyed Rhys's company. He's an intelligent man and interesting to talk to.'

Only he wouldn't ask, she was sure of that.

Geoff's wife, Lara, rang Sam up about the painting he was to do for them. 'I loved the one Geoff's using as bait for our corporate designers. I'd like something in rust or orange, not too garish but colourful enough to provide a focal point in my new silver, black and wooden décor. About this size.' She reeled off some measurements, which Sam jotted down.

'No worries, Lara. I can do that. Just let me have a quick look through my files and ring you back. I've been collecting flower photos for years and if I tell you the name of something suitable, you can either find it on line or go to a bookshop and get a book of native flowers. That way, if we already know you like the flower, I won't be making any false starts. Or I could scan the photo in and email it to you.'

'Good idea. This is my main email address.'

He went to the filing cabinet in his studio and picked through the red/orange files, settling on a *banksia menziesii*. He had a glorious photo of one of the candle-like flowers from the small tree, with the styles released on the lower part of the flower spike to make it look as if a six-inch candle was sitting in a cup of tiny spiky petals. He closed his eyes for a moment, visualising this on a painting, and decided it'd look best with two or three of the flowers and a small honeyeater hovering near the largest one. He loved the delicate little birds which fed mainly on nectar, and he often sat on his veranda watching them flutter in and out of the native flowering bushes he'd planted round his garden to attract birds.

He got on the phone to Lara to explain his suggestion. 'I've scanned it in and emailed it to you, but it won't be quite the same colours as my finished version.'

'I'll bear that in mind.'

Within half an hour Lara got back to him to approve his idea. 'But can Geoff and I come down to look at it once you've started on the colour, just to make sure it's exactly right and to get a dab of it to match other things with?'

'Of course.'

'How about next Saturday? Will you be far enough along with it by then?'

It'd be a rush, but worth it. He knew her reputation and really wanted her to handle his work. 'I can have one of the flowers done, not the whole painting. If you don't like it, I can sell it via our local art gallery instead. They've sold a few of my paintings lately.'

'How much do you want for it?'

He took a deep breath. 'You can have it for free if you'll agree to be my agent. I've no time to manage the business side of things and you have excellent contacts.'

'Geoff mentioned something about that. Look, Sam, I don't really want to take anyone else on board at the moment.'

'Just think about it and don't make a decision till you've seen the painting.'

Silence, then, 'All right. But I've got a pretty busy schedule and you know I only work part-time, so if I'm not going to represent you, we'll pay for the painting.'

'Seems fair to me.' He knew better than to press the point. He'd make sure the flower he did was glorious. He was still waiting for the huge canvases to be delivered, but he already had one the correct size for Lara's painting. The project appealed to him and before he knew it, he was sketching out the scene. It would be rather like a botanical painting, but with more character and life, not quite as detailed, though still very realistic. And the bird had to be placed just so . . .

Once started, he lost himself in his work and didn't emerge from his abstraction till he ran out of food. He opened the fridge and found only a couple of apples. The freezer section was completely empty. When had he taken the last item out? He couldn't even remember. Laughing at himself he went outside and only then did he realise how late it was. He stretched and yawned. Too late to go to the shops and anyway, he was exhausted.

He'd beg some food from Penny, he'd done that before. But no one answered the phone and he was ravenous. Should he beg a few slices of bread and cheese from Kirsty?

He'd not have hesitated to ask Ed. And Marlene was still there, so he wouldn't be on his own with Kirsty. He'd soon get over this attraction to her if he didn't act on it. Must do. This was not the time to become seriously involved with a woman, not when he had a chance to make some real progress with making a new career for himself.

And even if he did get involved with someone, it wasn't going to be someone as rich as Kirsty. He wasn't giving any woman reason to feel her money gave her the power to demand things of him that he wasn't prepared to give.

It occurred to him then that he didn't actually know how rich Kirsty was. But old Ed had been pretty comfortable and she'd bought a BMW convertible, hadn't she? That must mean serious money. No, she wasn't for him.

But he would borrow some food from her to put him on till morning. Tomorrow he'd do some shopping. And he'd better have a bottle of decent wine in the house, in case Lara wanted a drink.

'Hello! Anyone there?'

'We're out at the back.' Kirsty swung round in time to see Sam walk round the corner of the house. He was wearing disgraceful, ragged clothes stiff with paint, and there were splashes of colour on his fingers and one smear of bright orange down his right cheek. His eyes were rimmed with dark circles and he looked almost grey with fatigue.

'Sorry to trouble you, Kirsty, but could you lend me some bread and cheese, please? I've completely run out of food.'

Marlene stood up. 'You look like you need a proper meal, Sam. You get him a drink, Kirsty, and I'll heat up some of our leftovers.'

'Let me—' Kirsty was beginning when Marlene fixed her with a firm look.

'I made the casserole, honey, and I know how best to heat it up.'

Kirsty bit back a protest, well aware that her friend was arranging a way for them to be together. 'Beer or wine, Sam?'

'I'd kill for a beer. I've run out of that, too, and I'm really thirsty.'

She looked at him, worried about his pallor. 'When did you last eat?'

He shrugged and ran one hand through his hair. 'This morning . . . I think.'

The two women exchanged glances and went into the kitchen.

Inside, Kirsty grabbed the container of olives, a chunk of cheese and some biscuits and set them out on a tray, together with two cans of beer.

'I'm doing him some vegetables as well as the casserole,' Marlene announced. 'That man has lost weight visibly this week.'

Kirsty set the tray down between herself and Sam, then popped the can of beer and gave it to him. He took a swig then looked at the food, licking his lips. She cut a piece of cheese for herself and set it on a biscuit, then waved a hand at the platter. 'Join me.'

He ate like a man who'd not seen food for days. The olives vanished, then the cheese. Suddenly he realised he'd been eating steadily and looked at the nearly empty platter in consternation. 'Why didn't you stop me?'

'You looked as if you needed it.'

He leaned back and tipped up the can of beer with a sigh of delight. 'Thanks. I'll pay you back.'

'What did you say when I tried to pay you back for the food you left me?'

He grinned.

'I've heard about artists losing themselves in their work, but a person still has to eat. You look dreadful, Sam.'

He spread his hands deprecatingly. 'It's a special piece I'm working on for a woman I hope is going to become my agent and help me sell my work for big money in Perth. One of the flowers has to be finished quickly because she's coming down to inspect it. Heaven help me, it has to match her décor and she's a bit of a perfectionist. Actually, she's the one who loves 'Golden Pride'.'

Marlene joined them just then. 'When is she coming down?'

'Saturday.'

'Why don't you bring her up to meet me? That'll put her in a good mood.'

'I couldn't use you like that.'

She chuckled. 'Then you're the only person I've met who couldn't. Besides, I volunteered to help.'

'No, definitely not. It wouldn't be right.'

She studied him, but didn't argue. 'Eat my good food while it's hot. You'll do that for me, at least, surely?'

He ate steadily, making little murmuring noises of appreciation. Kirsty went and opened a bottle of Ed's wine, pouring glasses for herself and Marlene as well.

When he'd cleared the plate, Sam leaned back in his chair and looked at them. 'You're wonderful. I'll find a way of paying you back.'

Marlene leaned back too. 'You can keep Kirsty company occasionally. She'll be very quiet here after I've gone.'

'You're leaving soon?'

'In a week or so.' As he started to get up, she put one hand on his arm. 'Please stay and chat for a while. We've been very quiet and lazy today. I'm going up to Perth on Sunday to see the doctors the next day about flying again. Kirsty's insisting on driving me up, though I could easily have hired a car.'

'You'll keep an eye on Whitegums for me while I'm gone, Sam?' Kirsty asked.

'Of course.'

When he'd left, she looked at Marlene and didn't try to hide her feelings. 'I do like him. I've tried not to, but I do.'

'Give him time. He likes you as well, but he's fighting himself at the moment. Now, how can we keep watch on Sam's house on Saturday so that we know when his guests arrive? I'm going to make a sudden appearance, asking to see his paintings. I'm sure I can help woo this Lara woman for him.'

'But he said he didn't want to use you like that.'

Marlene made a rude noise and waved one hand dismissively. 'Since when do I let someone else dictate what I do?'

'You're a terror.' Kirsty could feel her smile wavering. 'I'm going to miss you dreadfully when you go back.'

'Before I leave, I want your promise that you'll start wooing Sam.'

'Marlene, I've told you I can't do that.'

'Kirsty, you can and you must. If you want him and he wants you, the other stuff that keeps you apart is nothing. Life's far too short to waste opportunities. Surely you've learned by now to carpe diem? You lost your first husband, honey. Don't lose your second before you've even got together.'

* * *

On the Saturday Sam dressed as smartly as he could, clean jeans and top, his better pair of sneakers.

But when he went out to check the studio, he couldn't help picking up a brush just to improve on a couple of details. He didn't even hear the car draw up and jumped in shock when someone spoke behind him.

'I guessed you'd be here.' Geoff was standing in the doorway, smiling. He stood aside to let his wife come inside.

'Sorry.' Sam looked round for a cloth to wipe his hands, but they were still stained. 'Great to see you, but I'd better not shake hands.' He gestured to the easel. 'This is it, Lara.'

She walked forward in silence and studied the painting, looking at the photograph sitting on its own small easel to one side. 'Is that going to be the finished colour?'

'I can vary the shade a little, if you want.'

'No, no! I want it exactly as it is in the painting. Could you dab some on a piece of card for me? Thanks. And what's that?'

'A honeyeater about to take a sip of nectar.'

Her rather sharp expression softened. 'Nice touch.' She looked round the studio. 'You're certainly giving your all to your art, Sam. I can't believe you live in that hovel.'

'It's quite comfy, actually. I—' He broke off as he heard voices from outside.

Kirsty peeped into the studio. 'He's in here, Marlene. Are we interrupting anything, Sam?'

'Well, actually—'

Marlene came into the studio and he heard a gasp from Lara.

'Aunt Seraphina!'

'Yes, honey. I'm a friend of Kirsty, which is how I met Sam. Do you watch the show?'

'I'm addicted. I've been watching it for years. I was so sorry when they killed off your character.'

'She'd had a good run. And I was ready for a rest. Fancy me meeting a fan out here in the wilds of Australia!' She winked at Sam. 'I came to look at your paintings. Is that all right?' She walked over to join Lara.

He resigned himself to accepting Marlene's help and waited.

Kirsty came to stand next to him and whisper, 'I couldn't stop her.'

'She's a feisty dame.'

The two women were studying the painting. They went from it to the photograph and back, gesturing and chatting. Geoff had gone outside again and was sitting on one of the rough, home-made benches, basking in the sun.

Sam jerked to attention at Marlene's next words.

'I've bought two of his paintings myself.'

'You didn't need to do that,' he said fiercely. 'I don't want anyone's charity.'

Marlene turned to look at him in surprise. 'I didn't buy them out of charity, but because I loved them. As far as I'm concerned, when you have to sit and look at a painting for years, you'd better be sure you're going to enjoy it. I'm not an art investor, honey.'

He looked at her doubtfully, not sure whether to believe this or not.

Kirsty tugged at his arm. 'She really did love them, Sam.'

'Oh. Sorry.'

Marlene rolled her eyes and turned to Lara. 'He's useless at the business side, isn't he? If I weren't going home to the States soon, I'd take him in hand myself but I've been away for long enough. Kirsty's driving me up to Perth tomorrow to see a doctor and check that I'm all right to fly. I picked up a virus, you see, and she's let me come and recover from it here.'

'We could drive you up to Perth, if you like,' Lara said eagerly. 'And you could stay with us instead of a hotel.'

'I couldn't impose,' Marlene said, winking at Kirsty.

'Impose! It'll be an honour. Think of all the pleasure you've given me.'

'Well, if you put it like that . . .'

Sam had the feeling he'd got on a train that was running downhill without a driver.

'Let's all go out to lunch now,' Lara said. 'We were going to take Sam anyway. You two could join us if you're free. Geoff's heard of this super new restaurant just outside Margaret River. They've got a reputation for gourmet dining round here, you know. And we've a room booked overnight, haven't we, darling?'

Geoff blinked in shock, made a quick recovery, then said, 'Um – yes, we have.'

Sam hid a smile. The humour of the situation was beginning to dispel his annoyance at Marlene's intervention. He'd wanted to use his corporate contacts, hadn't he? And his new friend was doing a brilliant job on Lara. 'I'd better go and wash this paint off properly, then.'

'You go and help him, Kirsty,' Marlene ordered. 'He's got some in his hair, just where he can't see it.'

* * *

That evening Sam went up to the house, marched up to Marlene and pulled her into his arms, giving her a smacking kiss on each cheek. 'You're a manipulative witch.'

She gave him an urchin's grin. 'I am, aren't I? What's the betting that by the time I've stayed with them a day or two she'll agree to handle your sales?'

'I'm grateful, truly I am.'

She nodded, serious now. 'You have talent, Sam. I'd not be doing this otherwise, I promise you.'

He concentrated on the can of beer Kirsty had slipped into his hand. He felt perilously close to tears at this kindness.

After two years of privation and hard work, he was starting to find his way, he really was. But he found it harder to cope with the prospect of success than he'd expected. He'd lost the hard carapace he'd developed in his old life and was so much more vulnerable, because the paintings came from his soul not his brain. What they brought into his wallet was less important than that the new owners loved them.

Chapter Eleven

The house felt strangely quiet after Marlene had left. Even the phone didn't ring. Kirsty kept busy but the silence seemed to echo around her and when it started to rain, just a gentle sprinkling of moisture, she went to stand by the window and watch it. It didn't feel at all cold, though.

She hadn't seen a drop of rain since her arrival, but Penny said it would start raining regularly soon, as they got most of their rainfall in the winter half of the year. Before then, they'd bring in the grapes.

The first raindrops were fat and sparse, plopping down on the silver-grey wood of the veranda and drying before the surface was completely dampened. Gradually the wood became wet, however, and it rained enough to darken the soil and drip off the trees. She'd never welcomed rain before, but here it felt good, made the air seem fresher.

By nine o'clock she was tired and since there was nothing she wanted to watch on the television, she decided to have an early night.

The old nervousness she'd felt when she first arrived seemed to have resurfaced and for all her tiredness, she had trouble falling asleep.

A couple of hours later she woke suddenly, staring into the darkness. Had there been a sound, or had she been dreaming?

Just as she was about to snuggle down in bed again, she heard something. Definitely not a natural sound. Senses alert, pulse racing, she sat up again.

It sounded like . . . No. It must be an animal of some sort. Only, there weren't any large animals here, except for kangaroos, and they didn't shuffle.

Her heart was pounding and she clapped one hand to her mouth to hold back a scream. She'd never felt so alone in her whole life.

The footsteps came closer and closer, and she saw a shadow pass her window. It was a man's shadow, not her imagination.

What was she going to do?

She waited, nerves taut. The footsteps went past, moving away slowly, then came back. The shadow passed again, but this time it stopped and someone called, 'Kirsty! Where are you?'

She didn't answer, couldn't have formed a word for sheer terror. Was this man going to break in? How would she defend herself?

He laughed a second time and called in a throaty voice, 'Get back to where you belong, Kirsty Miller.'

The footsteps went slowly away again.

She waited . . . and waited. But there were no more sounds.

In the end she gave herself a talking-to. You can't stay here. You have to check the house. It's a moonlit night so you'll be able to see if there's anyone still around if you don't switch on any lights inside.

Shivering, she slid out of bed. All she could find to defend herself with was a high-heeled shoe. She went barefoot, making no sound as she walked.

Opening the bedroom door was an act of bravery that had her heart pounding. She opened it a crack, ready to slam it shut again, but the corridor was filled only with moonlight and slivers of shadow too small to hide a man. Gradually she opened the door fully, standing with the shoe held up, ready to hit out.

But there was no sound, no shadows moving, only her own breath sounding all too loud in the silence.

She crept along to the kitchen, where she unhooked the heavy steel bar used for sharpening knives. It felt better to have something that would really damage anyone attacking her, but her heart was still pounding as she walked round the house, checking each room, each door and window. But they were all locked. No one had tried to break in.

What had the intruder been doing here, then? Was it someone who got his kicks out of frightening people? He'd certainly frightened her. Only he couldn't have seen that.

She went back to bed, pulling a chest of drawers across behind the door and sitting up in bed, listening. . . listening.

For over an hour she stayed awake, all her senses stretched as tightly as elastic bands. After the first few minutes she allowed herself to slide down in the bed. But she kept the steel next to her.

When she did fall asleep, it was to doze uneasily. She kept waking up, starting in shock, thinking she'd heard something.

As the sky grew lighter, she groaned in relief.

Once it was fully light, she went round the inside of the house again, after which, holding the steel at the ready, she went outside. She walked along the grass, not disturbing the dust of the veranda near her bedroom window. The light rain hadn't penetrated far on this side of the house and there were definitely footprints in the dust that had been scattered everywhere by the wind. The footprints were large, could only have been made by a man – and not a small man, either.

None of her visitors had walked round this side. Neither had she for a few days. She mainly used the wider veranda and decking outside the kitchen.

When she went back inside, she locked the door carefully behind her and sat down with a cup of tea to think it through. She didn't want to face another night unprotected, still felt shuddery and tired.

What she needed was some sort of alarm system so that she could call her neighbours if she felt threatened. Surely there would be someone in town who installed them? Would they come and do it quickly if she told them how urgent it was? They must.

Should she call the police? She didn't know, couldn't make up her mind.

If it happened again, she certainly would.

As soon as she thought he'd be awake, Kirsty walked down to Sam's to ask his advice. When she told him what had happened, he gaped at her.

'What?'

'I'm not imagining it. There are footprints on the veranda.'

He tossed his paint-stained rag aside and stretched, easing his shoulders. 'Show me.'

When they got there, the veranda had been swept clean of footprints, which frightened Kirsty more than anything else. She clutched Sam's arm. 'I'm not imagining it. I'm not! Someone's been back since I left the house.'

'Stay there.' He walked slowly along the edge of the veranda, stopping once or twice, then made his way back. 'There was enough rain to dampen the soil and show footprints. Look at this.'

She followed him and gazed down at the indentations.

Sam put his own foot next to one particularly clear footprint. 'A bit bigger than mine. Size 11, I'd say.'

She tried not to show her fear, but it shivered through her veins like ice.

'I'm going back for some plaster of paris.'

This was the last thing she'd expected to hear and she looked at him in bewilderment.

'I want to take a cast of that print.' Then he stopped and frowned. 'I'd better get another witness though. Let's go and ring Penny.'

They went inside and she rang Penny, explaining what had happened.

Within ten minutes their neighbour had joined them. Sam fetched the plaster of paris powder and mixed it, then started taking an impression.

'You'd better come and sleep at our house tonight, Kirsty,' Penny said. 'And why haven't you called the police?'

'What can I prove?'

'Are you crazy? It's for them to prove things, not you. But they can't do anything if they don't know about your intruder. Anyway, he must still be around if he came back and wiped away the footprints.'

Kirsty had been trying not to think about that.

Penny looked at her watch. 'I've got an appointment at the hairdresser's, but I'll cancel it if you need me to stay with you.'

'No, you go now.' Sam turned to Kirsty. 'When's Marlene coming back?'

'Tomorrow, I think.'

'Then I'll sleep on your veranda tonight.'

'I've five spare bedrooms. You can sleep inside.'

'If there's a prowler, I want to catch him. It'll be easier if I'm outside. It's still warm enough to make sleeping out quite pleasant. I do it voluntarily sometimes during hot spells.'

She couldn't help it, she flung her arms round his neck and hugged him. 'Thank you.' When she pulled away they stared at one another, not saying anything, and the moment seemed to go on for a long time. Then he took a step backwards and she said, 'If you're doing that for me, I'm insisting on cooking tea for you.'

He nodded, face unsmiling. 'Will you be all right if I go into town and buy what you need for an alarm you can use to summon me.'

'You might not be at home.'

'I mostly am. But it's only in case. This is probably only a single incident.'

'I'll give you some money,' Kirsty said.

He nodded.

She looked at him, feeling a lump come into her throat. 'If this is how Aussie neighbours help one another, I continue to be impressed. And grateful.'

At that he gave her one of his lovely smiles.

His and Penny's support meant a lot to her. She was not only alone in a foreign country, she was living in an isolated spot. If she hadn't had her neighbours to turn to, she didn't know what she'd have done, how she'd have faced being alone here with an intruder prowling round.

'Why did he do it, though?' she wondered. 'He said, "Get back where you belong, Kirsty Miller". That means he knows my name.'

She gestured to the open land around the house. 'Why would an intruder come all the way out here and make no attempt to break in and steal something? Why did he call out and make sure I knew he was there?'

'Beats me.'

She couldn't come up with any good reason, either.

'I've changed my mind,' Sam said. 'Come into town with me and we'll call in at the police station.'

'All right.'

The police took careful notes and promised to send someone out later in the day. 'It's probably some young hoons passing through,' the officer said reassuringly. 'Holiday makers do some stupid things sometimes, especially if they get drunk. I don't think you'll have any more trouble.'

But she didn't think it was youngsters. It had been one man, not a group, and he hadn't acted stupidly, but in a way calculated to upset her.

The thought that kept nagging her for the rest of the day was why. Unless it was a madman on the loose, there had to be some reason for him targeting her.

As it turned out, Rod's boss rang him before he got round to contacting her. After a polite enquiry about how he was getting on, Melissa suggested sending some work home to him.

'I was going to phone you and ask about that,' he admitted. 'It's boring being stuck in the house all day.'

'That'd be a big help. There's no one who can sort out the tricky cases like you and until Jenny starts, we're very short-handed.'

He glared at the phone and before he could prevent himself, the words burst out. 'Then why can't I get a promotion? I've been on the courses you suggested, done everything you asked.'

There was a long silence at the other end, then she said, 'Look, I'll bring some work round myself tomorrow morning and we'll have a chat about that. Oh, and there's a holiday spot coming up for a month from now, if you're still interested. Someone wants to change their dates.'

'All right. I'll see you tomorrow. And I'm very interested in taking leave next month.'

He hung up the phone and sighed. It was, he supposed, going to be another of those little chats about getting on with people, being more tactful, all that sort of rubbish. They didn't care how well he did the tasks he was set. The talk wouldn't change anything, it never did. Afterwards other people would continue to get promoted over his head.

It must be wonderful to be in Kirsty's position and not have to work for anyone. Only – what would you do with yourself all day? Even if you didn't have one leg in a plaster cast, looking after a house and reading wouldn't occupy all your time.

He liked to use his brain. It was a good one for thinking, in spite of his communication difficulties. If only he'd been born like everyone else, life would have been so much easier. However hard he tried, he just couldn't relate to other people properly. He knew that, could see it happening and was still powerless to prevent it. Sighing, he went to find something to read, settling eventually on one of Kirsty's romances because he'd read all his own books and once he'd read them, he just about knew them by heart.

He stared at the couple embracing on the cover, moving his arms to imitate the way the man was holding the woman. He'd never held a woman like that, but he'd wanted to sometimes.

Sitting with his plastered leg raised, he opened the book and began to read it with his usual methodical care. But this time he kept stopping to consider what he'd read, trying desperately hard to understand love and how couples got together.

It was like looking into a lighted window from outside.

Kirsty was also wondering how to fill her time. After she got back from shopping, she put a casserole on and made a cake, but it was still only mid-afternoon. She wandered round the house, frowning at the faded wallpaper or yellowed paint in the various rooms. After this new problem of the intruder was sorted out, she'd do some decorating. The whole house was dingy.

Of course, she could afford to bring in some decorators and have the whole place painted or papered in whatever style she chose. But it'd make it more hers if she did most of the jobs herself. And it'd give her something to do. She already knew she'd have to find a new purpose in life, even if it wasn't a paid job, couldn't just live idly.

Sam, who'd had a phone call to make, arrived to install the electronic equipment for a rudimentary alarm system that you just plugged in. 'It's a lot easier these days to fit your own place out,' he said cheerfully.

'I didn't know you were good at electrics.'

'Anyone can do this. It's made for idiots.' He tapped himself on the chest as he said that and grinned at her.

She didn't make the mistake of offering to pay him for today's work, didn't want to do anything to destroy the comfortable mood. 'Marlene rang. She's coming back tomorrow and leaving next week.'

'Good. You'll not be on your own while she's here. But I will sleep on the veranda tonight to see if that sod comes back. It must just have been a one-off, surely?'

She shook her head in bafflement. 'How can we tell? If it was a one-off, I can't understand why someone would come so far off the beaten track to frighten a complete stranger. Only – he knew my name. How? I've racked my brain, but can't figure it out.'

They ate tea quite late, because it took longer than he'd expected to finish setting up the alarm system. After that, they watched a couple of TV programmes together then he stood up. 'I'll go home now, in case he's watching, and creep back a few minutes later. Tomorrow I'll scout round further afield and see if there's any trace of him. I should have done that today, really, but I wanted to get your alarm system set up to make sure you could call for help.'

'I'm grateful.' She frowned. 'He could only have come along Gulliver Road, surely?'

'We'd have heard him if he'd come up the road in a vehicle. But there are other blocks of land adjoining yours at the rear and a rough road a bit like ours leads to them. I think there are six properties there, smaller places than this, but I'm not sure. He could have come across via one of those. Two of them are weekenders that are unoccupied most of the time.'

Her heart sank. 'It's not possible to keep an eye on all that.'

'No. But I've fitted you up with an alarm system and I'll tie it into a car battery tomorrow so that if he cuts off your electricity, it'll still work.'

She stared at him in horror, that thought sending shivers down her spine. 'Might he do that?'

'He might or might not. He might never appear again. But better safe than sorry, eh?'

She felt nervous once she'd said goodbye to him and didn't bother to clear up the kitchen properly because there were no blinds at the windows. She scribbled the words kitchen blinds down on her list of things to do.

In her bedroom she decided to go to bed fully dressed, in case she had to run out to help Sam. If anyone attacked him she wasn't leaving him to struggle alone.

Three taps on her bedroom window, as agreed, let her know that Sam was back, after which she felt better – well, more or less.

She hadn't intended to sleep, but after a poor night she was exhausted and the first thing she knew, it was dawn.

She went outside and found Sam rolled up in a sleeping bag, breathing deeply and peacefully. He looked younger when he was asleep. She wished – She didn't let herself pursue that line of thought and went quietly back to the kitchen to wait for him to wake up.

Had the intruder been a one-off occurrence? She hoped so.

Marlene endured a lot of fussing from Lara, who loved the soap she'd starred in so much that she couldn't stop talking about it. Using reminiscences of things that had happened behind the scenes, not nasty things but amusing or charming incidents, Marlene kept Lara fascinated and was able to use the time to push for support for Sam.

She refused to allow her hostess to drive her back, however, and got into the chauffeur driven vehicle with a sigh of relief.

'You sound tired,' the driver said cheerfully.

'I am. Lovely people, but very talkative. You won't be upset if I don't chat, will you?' This man didn't seem to have recognised her, thank goodness.

'Not at all. I'd rather drive in silence. Some of them like to talk, though, so I try to oblige.'

'Well, you'll oblige me by keeping silent.'

They stopped part-way down, by which time Marlene was feeling more herself. She bought herself and her driver a meal, then they carried on.

When she arrived at Whitegums, she got out and stretched, looking at the place with regret, already anticipating her final departure. She'd really enjoyed being here, would miss Kirsty's company when she flew back, but when she'd called her daughter in the States, it had sounded as if Sandy's second marriage was in trouble, so she'd be needed there.

Life never stood still.

Kirsty came out to give her a big hug and help carry her luggage inside. Marlene turned to the driver. 'I'll see you next week.'

'Sure thing. A pleasure to drive you, ma'am.' He got in and drove away.

'Have you enjoyed some peace and quiet?' Marlene asked as they walked inside.

'Not exactly.' Kirsty explained what had happened.

'I can postpone my departure if it'll help.'

'No. You've been very kind but you have your own life to lead. And anyway, Sam's been helping me.'

'Good. Every cloud has a silver lining. Keep asking him for help. None of this British stiff upper lip.'

'You're incorrigible.'

Marlene winked at her. 'I am, rather. Only way to be at my age. You can do and say things people would never put up with if you were younger.'

Sam went exploring that afternoon and found signs that someone had been camping out on the veranda of one of the weekenders. There were also recent wheel marks made by a smallish car in the sandy drive. He investigated further and found cigarette stubs and the wrapper from a bar of chocolate, which he stowed away as evidence.

This didn't give any indication of whether the man would return, but it seemed to indicate that someone had been watching Whitegums as well as trying to frighten its occupant. Why?

He heard the sound of a car on Gulliver Road and walked back through the bush, relieved to find that Marlene had returned with Kirsty.

'What did you find out, Sam honey?'

'Signs of someone spending at least one night on the veranda of the nearest weekender.'

'But they've left now?' Kirsty asked.

'Yes, though for how long I can't say. I don't know the owners, but I'll ask around and if someone has a contact number, I'll let them know someone's been camping out on their property.' He looked at her face, rather pale and worried today. 'Marlene's back now and you've got an alarm system. Remember, I'll only be five minutes away.'

'I can't impose on you like this.'

'Of course you can. I'd have done exactly the same for Ed.' But he'd not have worried about Ed in the same way.

He refused to share their meal and made his way back to the studio. But his thoughts kept returning to Kirsty. She was putting a brave face on it, but he could tell she was scared.

And if anything happened to her . . . he was surprised how much he hated the thought of that.

Chapter Twelve

Rod's manager, Melissa, turned up the next day with a box full of files and a determined smile on her thin face. He didn't like her, so didn't offer her a cup of tea, wanting to get this over with. He swung himself along the hallway on his crutches and led her into the kitchen, which was also their dining room and the only place with a decent sized table.

'You seem to be coping all right on the home front,' she said brightly.

'I've got help and she's very efficient.'

'Good, good.' Melissa fiddled with a folder, then looked at him as if trying to work out how to say something.

'Just tell me.' The words came out more harshly than he'd intended.

'All right. First, let me make it very plain that we have no complaint about your work. On the contrary, you're the best we have at untangling figures and sorting out dodgy accounts. However . . . you're not good with people and you haven't improved much, in spite of the courses we've sent you on. You could never manage other people successfully, Rod. That's why we can't promote you up the normal tracks.'

'I'd better look for another job, then. It's embarrassing to be on this level after so many years' service. I could get more money in a private company, even if I can't manage people for them.'

'Yes. I can see that. And we do want to keep you. So I've been discussing it with the director of our area. We feel that your special skills should be recognised, so we're going to set up a job that you can apply for. However, we have to do things according to the rules so others will be able to apply as well.'

'And they'll have better interview skills, so one of them will get the job.' He shoved the papers away, not caring that some of them went flying. He couldn't pick them up, didn't care anyway.

'Not necessarily.' Melissa took a deep breath. 'If you quote me on this, I'll deny I ever said it, but I do appreciate how well you do your work, Rod, so if necessary, I'll coach you myself in interview techniques. If you can just – you know, speak more gently and carefully, stick to the facts – your skills and experience will speak for themselves. I doubt there's anyone else who can match you there.'

He blinked. They'd said similar things to him before, but it'd not led anywhere so he hadn't believed they meant it. Did they mean it now?

'The only trouble is, if I coach you, I can't be on the interview panel and I could probably do more good there. Is there anyone else who could coach you, do you think? Or else . . .' she hesitated, 'I can give you the name of a coach, if you can afford to pay him.'

He sat thinking this over, then looked at her. Only when he started to speak did he catch sight of his face in the mirror opposite and realise that he'd scrunched up his mouth in a frown. Kirsty sometimes teased him about the way he looked when he was thinking hard, and Linnie had noticed it too. That'd go down brilliantly at an interview . . . *not*. 'I can afford to pay someone. I'm very careful with my money, practise what I preach.'

Melissa let out a long breath and it suddenly occurred to him that she'd been nervous. He stared at her, surprised by this thought. 'I can't do small talk, though. I just can't.'

She smiled. 'No. We had noticed.'

'I'll do my best.'

'You always do, Rod. Now, about these files . . . Here, let me pick those up for you. And do you want me to make you a cup of coffee or something? It must be hard to do that on crutches.'

When she'd left, Rod sat thinking hard. He saw his scowling face at the mirror. Well, with no one there it wouldn't matter if he scrunched up his mouth. In the end, he decided he needed someone to talk it over with. Someone who'd not be scornful.

Dare he? Yes.

Picking up the phone he dialled Linnie's mobile number and when she answered, he invited her and the boys to tea.

'We can't keep imposing on you.'

'I need to talk to someone about . . . this thing that's cropped up. I need . . . help. Besides, I like your boys. They don't pussy-foot around, they say what they think.' When she didn't speak, he added, 'Please?'

'All right, love. We'll be there at the usual time.'

It was almost like a date. Not quite, but as near as he'd managed for a good few years. He was no good at chatting up women. He'd proved that in a few disastrous encounters when he was younger. But he didn't need to try with Linnie. She did enough chatting for the two of them. And he liked showing Tommy how to do things on the computer.

When he looked at the mirror he was smiling. He studied his face. It looked better smiling. He'd have to practise that – maybe find something to think about that made him smile.

But the smile faded as he thought about the interview. He was dreading it, absolutely dreading it, even before he'd applied for the job.

He picked up the romance book. It was bewildering, but he intended to finish it and see if he could learn something, and from others like it. You could learn so much from books and that was all he had to entertain him now his sister was away.

Since Kirsty was safe with Marlene for the next few days, Sam worked hard on Lara's painting, and if he said so himself, it was a good one. On the final day before Marlene left, he invited his neighbours round to look at it, and have cheese and wine as a farewell. He didn't intend to be the sort of person who only accepted other people's invitations, not now he could afford to extend a little hospitality in return.

He also invited the people from the next road, well, those who lived there permanently. While everyone was milling around and chatting, looking at his painting, which he'd hung out of their reach, and examining the drawing and sketches, he managed to get some information from one of the guys about the owner of the weekender and a promise of a phone number.

After the party had wound down, he walked Kirsty and Marlene up to her house.

'The lights are on!' Kirsty exclaimed as they turned the corner of the track. 'Did you leave them on, Marlene?'

'No, honey.'

'I'm coming in with you,' Sam said.

They found that someone had forced the lock on one of the sliding glass doors at the rear. No damage had been done, but lights had been switched on everywhere. When he looked at Kirsty, her face was white and her lips a tight line. He saw both fear and anger in her expression.

Marlene was furious. 'I can't leave you on your own like this, honey. I'll postpone my flight.'

'Yes, you can. I can always press my emergency button and call Sam for help.'

'What about when you go shopping? You'll never know whether anyone is waiting for you inside.'

Kirsty couldn't hide a shudder.

'Marlene's right. You'll have to install a full security system,' Sam said abruptly.

Kirsty nodded. She had a hollow feeling inside at the thought of someone coming into her house with the sole purpose of upsetting her and succeeding, damn him! She'd pay whatever it took to make her house more secure.

But you couldn't make anywhere completely secure, not as long as there were windows that broke so easily. And she didn't want to live in a fortress under the shadow of fear.

* * *

Linnie turned up with a carton of ice cream. Rod liked the way she always made some contribution.

He found himself even more tongue-tied than usual, but she kept the conversation going over tea, which was take-away from the local Chinese restaurant, the dishes chosen after much debate with the boys.

After the meal Rod settled Tommy upstairs with the computer and Linnie let Jem watch television in the front room while she washed up.

By the time Rod had made his painful way down the stairs, she had the kettle boiling and the kitchen immaculate. She turned to greet him with her usual warm smile. 'Sit down and tell me what's upsetting you. We've hardly had a word out of you tonight.'

He sat down gratefully and she plonked a cup of coffee in front of him and joined him with one of her own.

He told her about Melissa's visit, trying to remember exactly what had been said. He didn't look at Linnie as he spoke or the words would have dried up. When his tale had been told, he felt her hand cover his.

'Oh, Rod, you poor love! You are bad with words, aren't you?'

He nodded.

'And I've got too many. I wish I could share mine with you. I've been in trouble all my life for talking too much.'

'I like it when you talk.' He tried to tell her he liked her as well, but couldn't force the words out. 'Thanks for coming round.'

'You're going to see this interview coach, right?'

He nodded.

'And in the meantime, I'll teach you a few tricks for getting on better with people. I've taught them to my lads and it does help, I promise you.'

He reached out and took hold of her hand, watching her carefully in case this upset her. But it didn't seem to. She turned her hand in his, so that she was holding him of her own accord. It was a warm little hand, reddened from a lot of housework, but the nails were well cared for. A nice little hand. He summoned up his courage and gave it a quick squeeze. She didn't say anything, but the smile she gave him was softer than usual, made him feel strange inside. Unless it was the food they'd eaten.

No, he knew it wasn't that. The restaurant was known for its excellent food.

Then Jem came in to ask for something and the rapport was broken. Rod hoped he wasn't imagining it as a special moment but he thought, he really did think, that perhaps Linnie liked him.

Who knew where that might lead?

But would he have the courage to follow that path? Women liked fancy words and he didn't even have enough ordinary words.

Then he remembered the romance novels. There was a whole shelf of them in Kirsty's room. Surely he could learn something from them?

'You're scrunching your face up again, Rod. What are you worrying about?'

He looked up to see that Linnie had come back and Jem was no longer there, so greatly daring, he said, 'You. And me.'

She grew very still and now it was her turn to frown.

He didn't know what to say now, so waited.

'Give it time, love,' she said at last. 'We're only just starting to know one another.'

That made sense. He nodded.

But when he went to bed he remembered how her hand had felt in his. He'd liked it. Very much. And she hadn't pulled away.

There were no more intruder incidents during the next few days, but after Marlene left, Kirsty admitted to herself that she felt nervous and exposed. She didn't admit that to anyone else, though. She wasn't going to let this drive her away from Whitegums or . . . she stood stock still as that thought sank in.

Drive her away! It couldn't be Ed's great-nephew, could it? No, he lived in England. What was his name? Had she ever known it? If she had, it was lost. Surely the fellow wouldn't come all this way to harass her? Only. . . if she did leave, she'd forfeit the house, not to mention the rest of the money and investments, which were being held in trust for her. And half of that would give the nephew quite a substantial sum.

She wanted very much to go and talk it over with Sam, see if he felt she was being silly or whether she might be on the right track. But she'd promised herself not to go pestering him once Marlene had left and she didn't intend to break that vow.

No one was going to accuse her of chasing after a man, especially a man who didn't want any involvements.

Whatever Marlene said.

* * *

When Kirsty's water pump that serviced the reticulation stopped working, Penny said immediately, 'You'd better ask Sam to look at it. He's mended it a few times. If it could speak, it'd call him "Daddy".'

'I can't presume.'

Penny rolled her eyes. 'Oh, you're so English sometimes! Here, I'll give him a call.'

'No, don't!'

But Penny fended her off and made the call anyway.

Sam turned up at Whitegums late that afternoon. 'I'll have a look at the water pump for you.'

'Thank you. But only if you'll let me pay you for your time.'

His lips tightened. 'I thought we'd already agreed about neighbours helping one another. You mended that embroidery for me, after all.'

'Yes, but . . .' He was already walking down the garden.

He spent an hour fiddling with the pump and it worked perfectly the first time he tried it. The flower beds were suddenly misted with spray as the reticulation kicked in. He turned to her with a triumphant grin. 'There you are. I haven't lost my old touch. But we'll soon be into the rainy season, so you won't be using this for much longer anyway. If it lasts till next autumn, the next owner of Whitegums can replace it.'

She stared at him. 'The next owner! What do you mean by that?'

'You've got to stay here for a year. I can't see a Pom settling on a bush block like this one, so I figure you'll be selling it once your time is up.'

'I don't know yet what I'll be doing. I may decide to stay in Australia. And I like living at Whitegums very much, actually.'

'Oh. I'd just assumed.'

'Well, don't. Now, I've got plenty of food and you surely won't mind that way of me saying thank you?'

He pursed his lips then looked ruefully down at himself. 'I'd love to, but I'm filthy.'

'You can take a shower. There are still some of Ed's old clothes here. The trousers might be a bit short for you, but they're clean at least.'

'OK. Thanks.'

He was walking down the corridor and had stopped outside her bedroom before she could gather her wits together and call, 'They're in the second bedroom along. I'm in Ed's old room now.'

Just as he came back, the phone rang and Franco said, 'The merlot grapes are ready and I've got a couple of days off work. We'll harvest them tomorrow, if that's all right with you. I'll ring Sam in a minute and ask him to help. Between the four of us, we should manage easily.'

'Sam's here. I'll tell him.'

'Put him on, would you? I need a word about something else.'

When Sam put the phone down, he smiled. 'I like helping Franco make the wine.'

'I don't know how much use I'll be, but I'll do my best.'

'Oh, you'll do all right. It won't be too hard with only the merlot grapes to do. It'll be much more tiring when we get the cabernet grapes in. And Franco will keep an eye on you. That small vineyard is his as much as Ed's, because he loves it. The two of them used to spend hours testing things and fiddling with the wines.' He gazed into space for a minute or two. 'Ed's left a big hole in all our lives, you know.'

'In mine too. I grew very fond of him in a short time.'

They ate on the veranda – steaks with her special mushroom sauce, jacket potatoes and a mixed salad, followed by parkin she'd baked the day before and hadn't got round to freezing yet. She loved the dark sticky cake. It reminded her of her grandma.

They didn't talk much but he made appreciative remarks about her cooking and ate two pieces of parkin.

During the meal he kept looking at her with a slight frown and she could guess what he was thinking about, so she made the situation even clearer. She might not want to chase him, but she didn't mind making sure he knew she wasn't a fly-by-night. 'I really do like living here, you know. I can't imagine going back to an English town again, or living in a small terraced house like Rod's. There's something about all this space.'

She waved one hand, unable to find the exact words to describe her feelings, then fell silent. She hadn't realised until she put it into words that she'd fallen into the habit of thinking of this place as home. Her own place, where Rod didn't rule the roost. She felt guilty about how much she enjoyed being free of him.

'Ed was right about one thing, if not about others,' she said at last.

'Oh?'

'I did need to get out of a rut. So I'm grateful to him for pushing me into coming here, very grateful indeed.'

'And how is your brother taking all this?' he asked.

'I haven't told him how I fell about Whitegums. Rod's still talking about coming out here to see if I'm all right once he's better, by which he means he'll come and try to organise me again. His leg is improving, but he'll have to wait until he can get time off work, so I should be all right for a few months. And then, well, I'll have to think of some other excuse to put him off.'

'Just tell him no, for heaven's sake!'

'It's not that easy with Rod. He just goes ahead and does things anyway.' She thought it time to change the subject. 'Once I've got the house in order, I'll find something worthwhile to occupy my time.' She had an idea or two for using her genealogy skills, which went well with her understanding as a librarian of how to research. Indeed, she'd been going through Ed's papers and out of curiosity she'd started making a family tree for him. How sad to be the last of your family, to see a name die out!

Sam stood up. 'That was great food. Thank you.'

'Thank you for your help.'

He moved towards the door. 'Let me know if you have any more trouble with the pump, or – or anything else. I'll – um – wash these clothes and bring them back.'

'Don't bother. Just throw them away, or use them to paint in. And thank you for helping me.'

She went round, checking that all the doors and windows were locked, then settled down to watch television. But she didn't take in much of the programme. She kept worrying about how attracted she was to Sam. And wondering how attracted he was to her.

Marlene was right. Ed should have left things alone, allowed a relationship to develop naturally between the two of them. Their old friend had probably done the opposite of what he'd intended and made sure nothing would ever come of it.

The next morning Kirsty was up before it was light, feeling excited. She went out to the wine shed that stood on the border between Whitegums and the Calliones' block. It was brightly lit and Franco was there already. He paused to greet her then continued working.

'We need to get everything ready first.'

'Just tell me what to do.'

Penny came round the corner, smiling and carrying some equipment. 'It'll only take a couple of hours today to get the merlot grapes in. It'll be much harder next week with the cabernet. We didn't really need all four of us today, but we always do the grape picking together.' Her smile faded. 'Ed could only watch last year, but he was still there. It feels wrong not to have him with us today.'

'Maybe he's with us in spirit,' Kirsty said gently.

'I like to think so.'

A short time later Franco led the way out into a world turned pink by the dawn sky. He waved Sam and Penny towards the end rows then took Kirsty to another row and gave her a lesson, showing her how to snip off the bunches and put them gently into the wheeled trolley, which would be emptied into the cart attached to the tractor, standing at the end of the rows.

They worked hard for a couple of hours and when all the grapes were picked, went back to help Franco process the fruit. He put them through the crusher-destemmer, then they went into a fermenting vat, where they'd sit for two or three weeks, skins and all, before being pressed.

The whole day passed very quickly and Kirsty was surprised when it began to grow dark.

'I've got a casserole cooking gently at home,' Penny said, 'and we're all going into our hot tub or we'll be too stiff to move tomorrow.'

'But—'

She fixed Kirsty with a firm glance. 'No arguments. We'll leave the men to clear up, then collect your bathers and night things. After the hot tub and meal, I guarantee you'll not have the energy to struggle back along the lane.'

Kirsty slept well that night in Penny's spare bed, better than she had for a while, dreaming of rows of wine bottles and tunnels of vines hung with fat bunches of grapes.

Chapter Thirteen

Two mornings later Rhys from the art gallery rang, apologising profusely for the delay in getting her little painting framed. 'The framer's mother died and she had to rush over to Sydney to sort things out. It's come out nicely now, though. Well worth the wait.'

'I'll come in and collect it next time I'm in town.'

'Why don't I bring it out to you? And then, if you like, we could go out for dinner. I know a nice little restaurant on your side of town.'

'Oh. I'm not sure. I—'

'Just say no if you're not interested.'

She suddenly had the thought that it'd do her good to see other men, put her feelings for Sam into perspective. And Rhys seemed a really nice guy. 'I am interested.'

'That's great.'

When she put the phone down she walked out into the garden and cut a couple of roses for the bud vase she kept in the living room. But her thoughts were on the date she'd just made and she scratched herself on a thorn. Needing to talk to someone, she rang Penny and invited her over for a coffee.

'You come here instead. The pups are so adorable. You hardly got a chance to see them the other day. You are still interested in taking one, aren't you? Well, come over then. We have other people interested, so you'd better choose yours now.'

'All right.'

The world suddenly felt brighter. She'd always wanted a dog of her own.

She walked across to the next block, stopping at the wine shed on the way. But Franco was busy and there was nothing she could do to help, so she carried on to the house.

Penny took her out to a kennel where the pups were kept, which had a fenced run round it. They were at a delightful stage, tumbling over one another, playing. Their mother sighed and looked at the two women as if to say she'd had enough of motherhood now. One of the pups took Kirsty's attention more than the others, a female with a lovely golden coat. She was the smallest, but didn't let that stop her pushing her brothers and sisters aside to get a good share of milk.

'Can I pick her up?'

'I'll pass her to you.'

Kirsty held the warm little creature close to her chest. It wriggled, sniffed her hand and give it a tentative lick before abruptly falling asleep. At that minute Kirsty lost her heart to it.

'I'll have this one. And I'll call her Taffy, because of her colour. It's just like the soft toffee we used to make with our grandma when we were kids.'

'Good choice. We'd better put her back with her mother now. Ellie's rather watchful when people handle them, though she trusts me, of course.'

When they were sitting down, Kirsty took a deep breath and shared her dilemma with Penny.

'Sam's an idiot. Everyone can see the attraction between you two. You go on this date, Kirsty. Everyone needs a social life. It'll do Sam good to know you're going out with other men. I'll make sure he's aware of it.' She chuckled.

So why was Kirsty not feeling happy and excited as she walked back? Why did she wish Rhys hadn't asked her out?

Kirsty felt ridiculously nervous on the day of the date. She had felt the same with every man she'd dated since Mike's death – reluctant.

Rhys turned up with the painting and that got them over the first few minutes. It was indeed beautifully framed and would look good on the wall once that was painted.

'I shall start decorating soon,' she explained. 'In the meantime it can hang there anyway.'

'Big house.'

'Yes. It was left to me by an old friend.'

'Lucky you. I had to work hard to afford a partnership in my aunt's art gallery. It's going well now, though.' He looked at his watch. 'I've booked a table for seven. I hope that's not too early for you, but by the time I've driven you back and then driven home, it'll be quite late.'

'I could come in my own car.'

He smiled and shook his head. 'When I take someone out, I do the driving. Do you need to get anything?'

'No. And actually, I'll be glad to have you drive me home

because I've had an intruder and I'm a bit nervous. I'm getting a full security system installed, but in the meantime, it's a bit nerve-racking coming back to the house.'

They had a delicious meal at a very elegant and expensive Chinese restaurant. The food was better than any she'd had in England, and came one small course at a time: prawns in a delicate sauce, chicken with bok choy, stir-fried vegetables, sang choy bow with the pork mince in little lettuce cups, and finally szechuan beef with crispy rice noodles, a more robust dish.

'I can't believe I ate that much!' she said two hours later.

'You didn't. They were quite small servings.'

'I ate more than I usually do, though. And the wine was lovely.'

'A friend of mine has a vineyard in the district. He's won one or two medals for his chardonnay. You need a robust wine to go with food like that, but I think whites are better than reds.'

'I must give you a couple of bottles of Ed's wine. If you like it, I'll give you a case, because they mounted up while he was ill and Franco wants some space made.'

'I'd like that.'

The conversation never flagged, thanks mainly to Rhys's conversation skills, but as they got nearer her house, the more tense she grew.

When he stopped, she braced herself to let him kiss her, but he didn't. Instead he leaned back and smiled at her.

'The spark isn't there, is it?'

'Pardon?'

'You and me. We could be friends, but we couldn't be lovers.'

She could feel her whole body sag in relief. 'You're right. I did enjoy your company and it was a lovely meal, but as you say, the spark isn't there.'

'I enjoyed your company too. Friends, then.' He offered her his hand and they shook on that. 'Now, let's go and check out your house.'

The intruder had visited her again. This time he'd emptied out her kitchen cupboards and spread flour, coffee and butter all over the floor.

Kirsty stared at it in horror, then swallowed hard. 'Good thing I have an alarm to call my neighbours if I need help.'

'An alarm won't stop this sort of thing happening while you're out. And by the time they get here, he could have murdered you. It isn't some former boyfriend stalking you, is it?'

'I don't even know who it is.' Her voice wobbled on the last words. 'I haven't got a former boyfriend and even if I had, he'd be in England.'

Rhys looked at her, his head on one side. His voice was very gentle. 'You can't sleep here on your own after that, Kirsty. I'm staying the night. I presume you have a spare bedroom?'

'I can't ask you to—'

'You didn't ask, I volunteered. And I'm not letting you refuse my offer. We did say we'd be friends, after all, didn't we?'

'Yes. And thanks.'

'How did he get in?'

'I don't know. Last time he forced a door.'

'Let's take a walk round the house together before we do anything else.'

She went to take the sharpening steel from the drawer. 'My trusty sword.'

'Very sensible.'

This time the intruder had broken a window in one of the spare bedrooms and put his hand through to undo the catch.

'New window needed here tomorrow, and keyed locks needed on all the windows,' Rhys commented.

'Yes.' She continued but they found nothing else amiss. When they got back to the kitchen she looked at the floor, feeling disgusted that someone would do this. 'I'd better clear up then I'll make up a bed for you. With five spare bedrooms and two spare bathrooms, I dare say I'll find you a corner.'

'It's a bit of a hovel, isn't it?' he agreed with one of his gentle smiles. 'Give me the sheets and I'll make up the bed and I'll sleep in the room with the broken window. I'm a very light sleeper and no one will get in without waking me, I promise you.'

Why couldn't she fall for someone like Rhys? she wondered as she cleaned the mess from the floor.

Why did she have to fall for a grumpy artist with hang-ups about steady relationships?

Kirsty got up early in the morning. She found Rhys standing by the kitchen window drinking a cup of coffee. For some reason she didn't feel embarrassed. It was as if he was an old friend or a cousin. She'd always wanted a cousin. 'What would you like for breakfast?'

He hesitated. 'Well . . .'

'I've got bacon and eggs, if that's what you usually have. And it's no trouble to cook.'

'Fine. I do like a hearty breakfast, I must admit.'

They were sitting at the kitchen table, chatting easily, when Sam came along the back veranda. He stopped outside the door and stared at the two of them in shock, then his expression became grim and he half-turned away. But after one step, he swung back, scowling.

She opened the door. 'Hi, Sam. You're just in time to join us for coffee.'

'I don't want to interrupt anything.'

That insinuation made her angry. 'You're not interrupting anything, though it'd be my own business if you were.'

Sam turned to Rhys. 'We don't usually see you out of town.'

'I took Kirsty out for dinner last night, and when we got back—'

Sam flung up one hand to stop him. 'None of my business, as the lady said.'

Rhys rolled his eyes at Kirsty then overrode what Sam was trying to say next. 'She had an intruder last night. Someone vandalised her kitchen. I wasn't leaving her on her own after that.'

Sam turned to her in shock. 'How did he get in this time?'

'He broke one of the spare bedroom windows.'

'You can't go on living here on your own.'

'I refuse to be driven away. If I don't last out the year, I lose my inheritance.'

There was dead silence, both men staring at her, then Rhys asked, 'Who to?'

'Ed's great-nephew, whom he didn't like. If I bow out, he gets half of everything and a charity gets the rest.'

'You have to tell the police about that. There must be some connection.'

'What can they do unless they catch him?'

'They can find out if he entered Australia from the passport records.'

'I don't even know his name.'

'Who does?'

'The English lawyer.'

'Write to him. Better still, ring him up. Now, I'll just go round the outside of the house to look for traces of his visit. And after that, I want to board up that broken window.'

Rhys stood up. 'I'll come with you.'

Kirsty was left on her own. 'Whose house is it?' she asked. But they were out of hearing by then. 'Men!'

They were talking earnestly, seeming in much better accord with one another. Well, they'd known each other for longer than she'd known either of them. By the time she'd brewed another pot of coffee they were back. They'd found signs that once again the intruder had been using the veranda of the empty house.

She saw Rhys studying Sam with a faint smile, then he looked at her and gave a quick wink, as if to say he'd picked up the vibes.

Which was more than she had. She never knew where she stood with Sam. One minute he was acting as if she was poisonous, the next he was going out of his way to help her and behaving as if he was totally responsible for her safety.

* * *

After Rhys had left, Sam asked, 'What I came round to ask was, is it all right for me to borrow Ed's tools sometimes? He didn't mind and I've got to do a few repairs before my daughter comes to stay next week.'

'Of course it's all right.'

He glanced past her and saw the cans of paint, which she'd left in a corner. 'Doing some decorating?'

'Yes. Well, I was about to start till Franco rang up and said we'd be picking grapes.'

'I'd have thought you'd get someone in to do that sort of thing.'

'I like doing it myself.'

He picked up a paint tin and studied the colour label as if there was nothing more interesting in the world. 'Are you and Rhys an item now?'

'As if it's any of your business, but no. We went out for dinner together last night for the first time and agreed that we're just friends, because that certain spark isn't there between us. He slept in another bedroom.'

'Oh. Well, it isn't any of my business. But if you're going out at night again, let me know and I'll stroll up a couple of times and check the house.'

'Thanks. That's very kind of you.' She'd rather have gone out on a date with Sam, and to hell with the house. 'The contractors can't start work for a few days to install the security system, and I still haven't found anyone to monitor it. But they're going to fit window and door locks everywhere, at least.'

'I'll continue to monitor it, with Penny and Franco as backup. We're not likely to all be away at the same time.

The contractors can set that up quite easily and it'll be better than having a siren, because the intruder won't know someone's heard him. If we're lucky, we might even catch him.'

'I couldn't impose on you like that.'

'We've had this discussion before, Kirsty.'

'Right. Neighbours help one another. Thank you very much. But in return, I'll continue to make tea for you at least one night a week, plus I'll bake you a cake every week.' He was silent for so long she thought he was going to turn her down, then he grinned.

'Fine. I like your cooking.'

When he'd left she went into her bedroom and thumped her pillow good and hard – several times. 'Men!' But it was only one man she was referring to, really.

Outside, the kookaburra started laughing again.

She locked the house up and went to see what Franco was doing in the wine shed, but she didn't take in a word of his careful explanation because her thoughts were still on Sam.

Chapter Fourteen

Five days after the merlot harvest another call from Franco took them all out picking the cabernet grapes. Kirsty felt more use this time but it took over four hours' hard work to get the grapes in this time.

When it was done, she walked slowly back to the receiving area of the shed with Penny, stopping to breathe in the pungent odour of ripe grapes.

There was more to do this time and Franco was a hard taskmaster.

'He's a perfectionist where making wine is concerned,' Penny muttered to Kirsty as they took a short break. 'How are you holding up?'

'My back is killing me,' Kirsty admitted. 'But I'm loving it.'

Sam came to join them for a break, but a few minutes later Franco shouted out an order and they were working again.

This time Kirsty was ready with one of her cakes to add to the casserole Penny had made. Sitting in the hot tub she sighed happily as she let the warm water bubble against her aching back.

She hadn't been so truly happy for many years.

* * *

The electrical contractors arrived at Whitegums at seven o'clock the following morning, as arranged. Penny set an alarm for six o'clock and Kirsty rushed home to wait for the workmen, still yawning. She'd been surprised at how early Aussie tradespeople started work.

They finished everything in one long, hard day's work. She asked Sam to come up before they left and they explained the settings to him as well as her.

When their van had rumbled off down the track, she turned to him. 'Let's hope that keeps him out.'

'If someone's determined to get in, you can't really keep them out. But at least this will bring me rushing up to your aid.'

'You know, you're a bit of a Galahad underneath that grumpy exterior.'

'Grumpy?'

'Mmm.'

He stared at her for a minute. 'I'm not grumpy, I'm—' He clamped his mouth shut and walked away without another word.

Smiling at his reaction, she went inside, wishing it didn't get dark so much earlier now and praying that the intruder wouldn't come and pester her tonight.

In the middle of the night her phone rang. Heart pounding, sure this was bad news from the UK, she picked up the receiver.

Whoever it was hung up on her.

An hour later it rang again. She unplugged the phone in her bedroom, and although a faint ringing sound from the kitchen woke her an hour later, she ignored it and turned over. She had a very solid door on the bedroom in this old-fashioned house, and the security people had fitted an internal bolt to it. She wasn't going outside the bedroom during the night for anything. The phone rang again a few minutes later, then once more.

She'd have to unplug the kitchen phone before she came to bed next time, she decided, and rely on her mobile phone. But she didn't want to face twelve months of harassment like this, so maybe they could find some way of flushing out the intruder. Or perhaps he'd make a mistake. Or Sam would catch him.

No, that wouldn't be a good thing because she didn't want Sam to get hurt and the footprints suggested the man was quite big.

What did she know about this sort of harassment? Her life had been very peaceful until she came to Australia. She smiled wryly. She'd certainly been shaken out of her rut.

Kirsty went outside early the next afternoon to find Sam working on her garage doors. 'What are you doing? You should be painting.'

'I was, but this section needs to dry a bit before I can continue. In the meantime I'm making sure you can lock the car up safely. We don't want your intruder damaging such a valuable vehicle. I have to go and buy a few bits and pieces to finish off the side window, though.'

'Why don't you take my car? And I'll give you some money. You're not paying.'

He looked at her, then back at the convertible, clearly tempted.

She didn't wait for his agreement, but fetched her keys and some money, slapping the notes into his hand.

'All right. I can't resist. I'll be very careful with it.'

'It's only a car.'

When Sam came back she was out on the veranda, struggling to open a can of paint.

'Let me,' he said.

Their hands touched. They both leapt backwards and the can of paint went flying. Of course, the lid flew off as it hit the floor.

With a wail of dismay she leapt forward to grab it. She and Sam collided in mid-air, ending up sprawling in the paint.

The veranda was covered in white puddles and splashes. So were they. She looked at him and burst out laughing. He did, too.

They scraped up what they could of the paint, then hosed the veranda down, each using one of the two rear garden hoses.

'Good thing it's water-soluble paint,' he said. 'I think we've got most of it off.'

'Could you hose me down next?' she joked.

'Certainly.' He turned his hose on her, so of course she retaliated in kind, which developed into a water fight. In the end, she cried pax, but as she turned from putting her hose away she found him behind her. He was standing much too close. She couldn't breathe properly.

He seemed to be having the trouble moving too. Then, with an inarticulate murmur he pulled her into his arms and kissed her. That was fine by her and she twined her arms round his neck.

When the kiss ended, they stayed where they were, pressed against one another. She could tell the minute he changed his mind, as his whole body went stiff.

He pushed away from her. 'This isn't meant to happen.'

'Why not?' she demanded. 'What's wrong with enjoying a kiss or two?'

'Kisses lead to other things,' he said darkly.

'I'm well aware of that. I was married once.'

'I was married too. And I'm never, ever getting married again.'

She set her hands on her hips and met that one full on. 'So? Does that mean you're never going to date anyone again, either?'

'Well . . . no.'

'So come out for dinner with me tonight and let's slay the demons you keep conjuring up.'

'Are you inviting me to sleep with you?'

'Certainly not! I'm inviting you to come out for dinner – my treat – as a thank you for fixing the garage door.' When he didn't reply, she set her arms on her hips and added, 'I double dare you!'

He relaxed visibly. 'Very logical and persuasive argument. Oh, all right. I'll drive. I know a great little Italian restaurant.'

It was a great evening. They talked and ate, then talked some more. Plastic tables and elderly chairs, crockery that didn't quite match. It was so different from her outing with Rhys they might have been on another planet, but the food was just as delicious.

That undercurrent of attraction was still there, but they managed to keep it in the background. Well, she hoped she had and if Sam felt anything, he was concealing his feelings brilliantly.

She got him to talk about art and his fascination with painting flowers. It turned out he was also an amateur botanist who helped save endangered species of plants by growing them and distributing the seeds.

When they got back, he came in for coffee.

The phone began to ring. She hesitated, not wanting to pick it up. 'Could be my brother Rod, or the intruder. He rang several times last night.'

'You'll only find out if you answer it. If it's the intruder, pass it straight to me.'

Reluctantly she picked up the phone and relaxed, mouthing, 'My brother'.

Rod never bothered with small talk. 'Where have you been? I've been calling for ages. I wanted to discuss your money. I've been thinking what's the best thing to do.'

She tried to be patient, but when she let slip what sort of car she'd bought, he began haranguing her about wasting her inheritance. In the end she snapped, 'It's my money and I shall spend it how I please.' Then she put the phone down.

It began to ring again and she turned to Sam. 'Let's take our coffees out on the veranda, shall we?'

The phone rang several times over the next half-hour.

She didn't answer.

Sam didn't comment.

After he'd gone home, she told herself it was a good thing he hadn't kissed her again, then the new Kirsty sighed and admitted it was not at all a good thing. She had wanted him to kiss her, hoped for it, longed for it. And if he didn't do it again of his own accord, she was going to kiss him.

She slept badly – again.

Dreamed of him – again.

But at least it wasn't the intruder disturbing her sleep. Well, only indirectly. She kept wondering why he hadn't continued his telephone harassment, hoped he wasn't planning anything horrible, but felt somehow that he must be.

Rod was worried. It wasn't like Kirsty to put the phone down on him and refuse to answer. He'd only been thinking of her welfare, after all.

When Linnie came round the next day, he confided in her.

'Your sister's right,' she said at once. 'It is her money.'

'But it's me who's good with finances.'

She studied him for a moment, head on one side, then came and sat on a chair opposite him. 'Rod, please don't let what I'm going to say spoil our friendship. You're probably brilliant with money, but you're terrible with people. If I didn't chat to you, you'd sit there silent, except for coming out with blunt remarks every now and then.'

He thought about this, then sighed. 'I know. And you're the easiest person I've ever met to talk to.'

She reached out to clasp his hand. 'You have to let go of your sister and move on. She's making a new life for herself. So must you.'

It was a while before he could gather his thoughts and put them into words. He was grateful that Linnie waited patiently, not rushing him. 'I have to be sure Kirsty's all right. She was in a bad way after her husband died. I care about her.'

'Then go out to Australia and see for yourself. You're getting the plaster off next week, aren't you?'

He nodded. 'But I'm not due to start my holidays yet.'

'Tell your boss it's an emergency and go to visit Kirsty. That will settle things one way or the other.'

When he looked up, Linnie had gone back into the kitchen and was humming away as she mopped the floor. The sound was very soothing.

The more he thought about it, the better her idea seemed.

He had time now, whereas later on, he might not have. Though he wasn't getting his hopes up. He'd filled in the application form for the job, seen an interview trainer and worked out what to say. Only they might not ask the right questions and what was he to do then? He was to go back to the trainer after he'd read a particular book and done some practice. Why not go to Australia in the meantime? He could read the book and think about the exercises in it while he was on the plane.

Of course it was a waste of money to go for a short time, but sometimes you had to spend to preserve what you'd got. He could squeeze in two weeks before the job interview?

He'd do it. He'd go to Australia.

But he wasn't going to tell Kirsty he was coming in case she tried to stop him. It'd be better to surprise her then she wouldn't be able to turn him away.

It was only as he was settling down for the night that Linnie's words came back to him: don't let this spoil our friendship.

He had a friend! He hadn't had a friend since he'd attended special classes as a lad with other misfits like himself. Oh, they all knew they were misfits, whatever words people used to dress up the programme.

He wondered how his former friend Matthew was getting on. They'd kept in touch for a while after school. After he got back from Australia, he'd see if he could find Matthew again.

He smiled in the darkness. He preferred Linnie, though. She was the best friend he'd ever had, and she might not be well educated, but she was really good at dealing with people.

Sam's daughter arrived at the block a day early, driven down by her mother, who hadn't bothered to warn Sam. He saw the two women scowl at each other as they got out of the car and his heart sank.

'Here she is, and you're welcome to her,' Lorraine said.

Tina shot a disgusted glance round. 'It's worse than I remembered. How you can live in a dump like this, Dad, I don't know.'

'I like it,' Sam said.

'Where am I sleeping?'

'In the house. I've borrowed a bed from a friend and I'll sleep in the studio.'

Lorraine waited till Tina had taken her luggage inside. 'Keep her here while I'm away. I'm having my house decorated because I need to sell it, so I don't want her getting in the painters' way. She won't be able to come home till I get back.'

'How did you force her to come down here?'

'Threatened you'd cut off her allowance unless she visited you.'

'Thanks for dumping the blame on me.' He hesitated, then asked, 'Why did you damage my painting?'

'I don't know what you mean.'

'You do.'

She flushed and began to fiddle with a bracelet. 'I was angry about something. I'm sorry. Did it make a mess?'

'It completely ruined one of my big canvases. I'd spent several days drawing out the picture and had to abandon the lot.'

'Oh.' She stared at the ground for a moment or two, then looked up at him. 'I'm sorry. I don't always think things through when I'm angry.'

'Maybe it's about time you started. You are, after all, forty-two, not sixteen.'

'Well, I don't feel it! And people tell me I don't look it.'

He studied her dispassionately. 'Your body doesn't show your age, but your eyes do. They've got an old, jaded expression.'

'Thank you very much. I can always trust you to make me feel good.'

He shrugged. 'What's wrong with being forty? I'm enjoying my life more now than I have for a long time.'

She opened her mouth to say something then stopped and breathed in slowly and deeply, before fumbling in her pocket. 'This is my mobile number, in case there's an emergency.'

He stuffed the piece of paper in his pocket. 'Enjoy your holiday. Where are you going, by the way? Just in case I need to contact you.'

Her colour deepened. 'I'm staying with a friend, not going anywhere. We're seeing if we're compatible. Tina doesn't make it easy for him to come round to my place.'

Inside the house, Tina was shamelessly eavesdropping. She'd guessed there was a man involved, but hadn't known it was so serious. Did that mean her mother was going to chuck her out? She felt tears fill her eyes. Neither of her parents wanted her now, and she was twenty, so she should be living alone. Only, she was really struggling with her studies and couldn't afford to spend any more time working for money, and truth be told, she didn't feel capable of making a life of her own. It wasn't fair. Life had sucked ever since her mother and father split up. And if she didn't get her degree, what sort of job would she get? A lousy one, that's what. It was hard enough to get jobs even with a degree.

She found the only bedroom and stared round, open-mouthed. It was small, with faded greenish paint on the walls. There was a creaky old bed, a huge old-fashioned free-standing wardrobe and a chest of drawers. She pulled a drawer out. It was stuffed full of his socks. Where was she supposed to put her things?

She wandered out again into the main room, peering into the bathroom and pulling a face at it. Just as horrible. Old-fashioned shower with plastic curtain, faded, multi-coloured tiles. New toilet in a pinkish colour that didn't match anything. He must have picked it up in a junkyard. The shower head was dripping and had a rust streak across it. The sink had coppery green stains under each tap, while the mirror was tiny and speckled. How was she to see to do her hair or put her make-up on?

In the living room-cum-kitchen she made another horrifying discovery. There was no television. She looked round and found no stereo system, either. What did he do for entertainment? At least he had a computer. Well, he must have because he'd emailed her and her mother sometimes. But where was it?

When he came in, she heard her mother driving away. The bitch hadn't even bothered to say goodbye. She glared at her father and told him just what she thought of the place and its lack of amenities.

'Do you watch much television?' he asked. 'You never used to.'

'No, but what else is there to do here?'

'Talk, read, have barbecues with the neighbours. And I thought we'd have a trip round the vineyards one day. There's even a small vineyard just up the track.'

'Yeah, right, and I bet your neighbours are as old and weird as you. I'll go mad here.' She couldn't hold back the tears – well, it was that time of month – and took refuge in the bedroom, slamming the door behind her.

Sam hesitated, then went across to his studio. He wasn't running after her, petting and cajoling her. Tina was twenty, for heaven's sake, not a child.

She was only here for a fortnight, but it was going to seem a very long time!

Chapter Fifteen

Kirsty went into town to stock up on fruit and vegetables, stopping at Sam's on the way to let him know she was going out and ask if he needed anything fetching from the shops.

When she went into the studio, he was drawing the design for another large painting, so lost in his work he didn't even hear her come in. She hated to disturb him, but didn't want to upset him again, either. 'I thought I'd better let you know I'm going into town for the afternoon.'

He spun round. 'What? Oh, it's you. Good. Very sensible. I'll be up there like a shot if I hear anything. I'd better tell Tina – oh, there you are. Kirsty, this is my daughter. Tina, this is my neighbour. She's having trouble with intruders so don't use the phone till she gets back. It's connected to her security system and rings me when she's out if anyone breaks into her place.'

'Does that mean I can't use the computer at all?'

''Fraid so. I'm only on dial-up here.'

Tina rolled her eyes. 'What is there for me to do, then?'

'I've told you. There's a whole shelf of books. Give me today to finish this, then I'll take you out.'

Kirsty could sense the anger crackling from the girl and felt a bit sorry for her. 'You can come into town with me, if you like, Tina. I'm only doing the grocery shopping, but it'll be an outing, at least.'

Sam's expression betrayed his gratitude.

His daughter shrugged. 'Thanks. Anything's better than hanging around here. I'll just get my things.'

When she'd gone, Sam said, 'She's only been here since yesterday and already I'm counting the hours till she leaves. She's done nothing but complain.'

'Well, it is a bit spartan here. She can come up and use my computer, if she wants. Are you redoing the design that was destroyed?'

'Yes. It's going a lot quicker this time, thank goodness. I'm dying to get started on the painting.'

Outside, Tina had turned round to ask her father something, but heard him say he was counting the hours till she left. Tears welled in her eyes.

At least his neighbour understood how boring this place was. She seemed a nice woman. And how had one of his paintings got damaged? Had there been an intruder here as well?

She went into the house and got her bag. She'd not dare buy anything today because she was a bit short of money, had celebrated the end of term too many times with meals out and drinks. She'd needed to work during the Easter holidays, but her mother and father had put paid to that by forcing her to come down here.

When she saw the silver convertible parked at the end of the drive, she stopped to stare in awe. 'This is yours?'

'Yes. It was an extravagance but I love it.'

The car was unreal and Tina enjoyed the ride into town. 'How fast does it go?'

'As fast as the speed limit.'

'Isn't there somewhere you could open it up?'

'I don't want to go any faster. I enjoy living too much.'

Tina would have gone faster on the open road. Much faster. But when people got older they lost their sense of adventure. From what her mother said, Kirsty was rich because she'd had the sense to con the old man out of his fortune, unlike her stupid father. Her mother said Dad didn't even have the sense to chat up the heiress. Tina looked sideways. Trouble was, she couldn't see this woman putting up with anyone who sucked up to her.

All Tina wanted was to pass her exams and get a job, so that she could enjoy life while she was young. Her mother said as soon as you got married and had a baby, the fun stopped. Tina realised her companion was talking and turned her head sideways again. 'Sorry. What did you say?'

'I want to go to the gallery first and see Rhys, who sells your father's paintings. You might like to see how good they look.'

As if she was interested in her father's daubs. Her mother said they were rubbish and Dad would never make a living from them.

'Maybe we can look in the dress shop windows on the way there. Me and my mother are into retail therapy. Don't you love looking at clothes?'

'When I need something, yes.'

'Don't you ever just wander round the shops?'

'No. I'd rather read a good book any time.'

Tina stifled a sigh but didn't argue. If she kept on the good side of Kirsty, maybe she'd get out and about a bit. She'd have to tread a bit carefully.

The gallery was just off the main street. It looked like an old house on the outside and was all pale, airy spaces inside. She was impressed, though she didn't say so. The owner wasn't bad looking either – for an older man. He seemed on very good terms with Kirsty. Perhaps they were an item.

When he realised who Tina was, he led the way to a side room. 'This is one of your father's paintings.'

She was gob-smacked, as her English friend always said. It was definitely the best way to describe how she felt and it was a moment or two before she could speak. 'My dad did that?'

'Don't you like it?'

'Yes, I do.' She walked closer, marvelling at the intricate work that had gone into it, and how real the flowers looked. Then she stepped backwards a couple of steps at a time.

'I love it,' Kirsty said. 'I've not seen that one before.' She too went up to it, then moved away, before going up to it again.

'There are two other paintings by your dad in the next room, Tina.'

She nodded to Rhys and went to look at them. And they were just as gorgeous. She couldn't believe her dad had done them, just . . . couldn't believe it. Her mother was wrong. He was good, seriously good.

She stayed in the room with the paintings, hearing the others talking next door without being close enough to understand what they were saying. She was trying to get her head round this new side to her dad.

An elderly couple came in, stopped dead and went across to examine the painting Tina liked best.

'It's beautiful,' the woman said. 'Just what I want.'

'Well, take your time and look at the rest, but if you like that one best, we'll buy it.'

The wandered round the room then went out into the next.

When Kirsty came to fetch her, Tina was still studying her dad's paintings.

The two of them went back to the owner, who was putting the phone down.

'Something wrong?' Kirsty asked.

'Sally has the flu badly and can't come in for a week or more. I've some important people coming down from Perth later today, so I really need someone to watch the door – and after that to help out generally till Sally's better. I don't suppose you'd like a few days' work, would you, Kirsty? It's going to be busy over Easter.'

She shook her head. 'No thanks.'

Tina took a deep breath. 'I would.'

He looked at her in surprise.

'I need to earn some money to help me through uni. I don't know anything about selling paintings, though I've been doing art appreciation.'

He studied her. 'Do you have anything smarter than that to wear?'

Her heart sank and she looked down at herself. 'Not very. Mum said I only needed to bring casual stuff.'

'I can lend you something,' Kirsty said. 'And I can bring you in to work in the mornings if your dad will fetch you back at night.'

Tina had to wonder what was in it for Kirsty. Was she interested in Rhys or her dad? No, it must be Rhys. Who'd ever fancy her dad? He was as scruffy as they came these days, and there was more grey in his hair every time she saw him, while Rhys might be older, he was elegant and very attractive. She held her breath as he studied her.

'I'll give you a day's try-out,' he said. 'Tomorrow. Come about eight so I can brief you.'

As they walked through the streets, Kirsty studied her with a knowing expression on her face. What was it about older women that they seemed to understand more about you than you did about yourself?

'What?' Tina asked in the end, unable to bear the scrutiny for much longer.

'You didn't know how good your father was, did you?'

'No. Mum said he was rubbish.'

'She was wrong.'

'Yeah. She was.'

They bought some groceries, had a coffee then drove back. They stopped to let her father know she was back and was going up to Kirsty's to look at clothes. He hardly heard Tina come in and she wasn't even sure he'd taken in what she said.

No wonder he didn't want her around. He was too wrapped up in his painting. He'd never wanted her around, had often cancelled his visits when she was younger, till in the end she told him to stop coming.

She kept wondering how her mother had persuaded him to have her for these two weeks. And what exactly was her mother doing? Who was this new guy? Her mother had been very careful to keep him away from Tina. Hadn't told him she had a twenty-year-old daughter, probably.

Kirsty had noticed the droop in Tina's mouth and the way Sam just about ignored her. 'It's not you, you know. Your father's always like that when he's painting. He'll be quite sociable by tonight, once the light fades.'

Tina shrugged. 'I don't need him. I only came down here because Mum said Dad would cut off my allowance otherwise. But I know it was really her who organised it because she wanted to spend time with her new guy.'

Kirsty pulled up in front of the house.

'This is much bigger than Dad's place. It's pretty too. His hovel ought to be knocked down. Give me a bobcat and I'd do it in a flash.'

'It's pretty basic, but he doesn't care about that. Come round this way. I usually go in via the back. Let's grab some lunch then we'll go through my clothes and see if I have anything suitable. You may think they're all too old for you, though.'

'I'd wear sacking if it meant I could earn some money.'

Kirsty smiled. 'I remember those times. Mike and I were permanently skint when we were students.'

'Mike?'

'My husband. He died a few years ago.'

'Oh. I'm sorry.'

They found two outfits that looked good yet business-like on Tina.

'This one hasn't even been worn yet. How can you bear to lend it to me?'

'It's only a skirt and top, not a family heirloom.' Kirsty felt sorry for the girl, who seemed rather immature for twenty and not the brightest button in the jar either, from the way she prattled about clothes and her uni friends. 'I'll pick you up at eight in the morning. I've got to paint some walls now.'

Tina walked to the door, then turned and looked back. 'Could I help you paint? I've never done any but it can't be that hard. I've got nothing else to do.'

Kirsty could hear the desperation in the girl's voice and felt very angry with Sam. 'It's fiddly at times, but not difficult. Are you sure you want to help me, though? You'll get messy.'

'If you've got some old clothes I can borrow, I'll be all right. No one's going to see me, after all.'

Kirsty hid a smile. She counted as no one, did she? She wished there was a young guy in the neighbourhood to cheer the girl up. In the meantime, she'd accept Tina's help, not only because she felt sorry for her, but because she was lonely too. It'd be nice to have someone to chat to while she worked.

There was a knock on Kirsty's front door around nine o'clock that night. Picking up the sharpening steel, she went to see who it was. No one round here used the front door.

There was no one there. Instinctively she pressed the electronic pendant round her neck that would connect her to Sam's phone, then went and switched off the internal lights, so that he wouldn't be able to see in.

She stood in the hall, listening hard. The place stank of paint. If it wasn't for the intruder, she'd have had the doors wide open to air it.

Footsteps sounded on the bare boards of the veranda and she saw a face press briefly against the window of the sitting room. She saw her digital camera on a side table and snatched it up. Switching it on, she peered cautiously through the kitchen doorway. For long seconds she waited, then a shadowy outline appeared at the window, peering in again.

Before he could move on along the back of the house, she crept down the corridor to the end bedroom at the rear. When the man reached it, she was waiting with the camera. She didn't know if it'd work through the glass pane, but pressed the button. As the light flashed she got an impression of longish dark hair and a squashy nose, then the after-image half-blinded her.

They both stood still for a moment then there was a muttered curse from outside, followed by footsteps moving quickly away. As she looked out of the billiard room window, she saw a figure running across her block towards the empty weekender.

Sam hammered on the kitchen door almost immediately, calling her name, and she ran to open it and tell him what she'd seen.

'Lock up again!' He ran off after her intruder.

More footsteps sounded on the side veranda and Kirsty swung round again. But it was only Tina. 'Come inside quickly.'

'Was it your intruder again?'

'Yes.'

'Oh, wow! I can't believe this. It's like something out of a horror movie. Wait till I tell my friends.'

'It something I could do without.'

It was a while before Sam returned, panting slightly. 'I didn't catch him but I saw his car. It was an old wreck, a Falcon, light coloured, maybe even white. He had the number plate covered with rags, though.'

'Why can't the police do something?' Tina enquired.

Kirsty sighed. 'They've only got my word that there is an intruder, and they can't be everywhere. Even if I called them, by the time they got out here he'd be long gone and they'd have missed a couple of other incidents. They did approve what I'd done about security systems and linking it to my neighbours' phones, but they're helpless unless I get some more concrete evidence. I took a photo of him with my digital camera, but it was through the window. Shall we have a quick look?'

They stared at the muddy image, but though it showed a man's shape, the details were poor and he could have been anyone.

'Pity,' Sam said. 'You'd better come down and sleep at my place for the rest of the night.'

'He won't be back tonight.' Kirsty tried to sound confident, wasn't sure she'd succeeded.

'Why don't I come and sleep here with you?' Tina offered. 'If you don't mind, that is, Kirsty? He'd find it hard to overpower two of us.'

'I can't ask you to do that.'

'You didn't. I volunteered.'

'Your father won't want to put you in danger.'

'As if he cares,' Tina muttered.

Sam stared at her in shock. 'Of course I care! Whatever gave you that idea?'

She shrugged.

Kirsty didn't know what to say because she didn't want to make the situation between them worse. But there was an edgy atmosphere every time they were together.

Tina laughed suddenly. 'It'd be worth the risk to have a proper bedroom and bathroom again. And I bet you've got a television here, haven't you?'

Kirsty nodded, trying to work out from Sam's expression what he was thinking. 'If you don't mind, Sam?'

'It's the first time I've regretted having nothing to offer a guest.' His eyes were sad as he looked at his daughter. 'But I do care about your safety, Tina, very much.'

She shrugged, her expression becoming hostile again.

'You could stay here too, Sam,' Kirsty offered tentatively.

'I think, with this intruder around, I'd better keep an eye on my own property. The paintings are suddenly of some value. They sold another today.'

'That's wonderful.'

He nodded. But Kirsty could see that his eyes were still sad and his brow was wrinkled. He was watching his daughter as if he was puzzled.

'Let's get to bed, then. This young woman has an early start in the morning.'

'Which bedroom am I sleeping in?'

Kirsty saw Sam out but couldn't think what to say to him. She felt as if she was navigating through terrain planted with landmines. She didn't want to alienate Tina from her father, but she wished he'd be more positive about his daughter, show her he loved her, do things with her.

The trouble was, she supposed, he had a chance to make something of his painting and the visit had come at the worst possible time as far as he was concerned.

But why was Tina so sure Sam didn't care about her? It was obvious to Kirsty that he cared very much. Had his wife been dropping insinuations about him? Kirsty wouldn't put it past her. Anyone who'd destroy one of Sam's paintings had to have a very nasty streak.

The next morning Sam was out in his garden early, watering. He watched Kirsty drive past with Tina laughing beside her. His daughter didn't even turn her head to look at him.

He heard a car coming up the track about an hour later and walked to the gate. It was Kirsty. She slowed down, her hair tangled, her eyes sparkling and her cheeks flushed. What an attractive woman she was! 'Everything go all right?'

'Yes. Tina was very excited. She took some waking up this morning, though.'

'It's very kind of you to do this. I should have taken her into town.'

She looked at him. 'I think it's best if I do. I don't know what's going on between you two, but she's hurting and you should do something to fix it. She really is worried about her studies, you know.'

'She was never an A student, didn't care about studying, and I didn't think she should go to university, but Lorraine was set on it.'

'Tina told me she'll be thankful if she scrapes through.'

'I'll pick her up this evening from work.'

'Will you remember to collect her once you start painting?' Penny had joked that Sam wouldn't even notice an earthquake when he was working.

He grinned. 'I have an alarm clock with a very annoying, loud tone. I'll notice it, believe me. We'll buy some take-away in town so you won't have to feed her.'

'It's no trouble.'

'I can't go on accepting from you, Kirsty. I have to stand on my own feet, and I can afford to look after my daughter in a modest way. I'll bring her over later this evening.'

'Right.' She drove on.

But her expression made him feel as if he'd kicked a puppy. And why the hell did Tina feel he didn't care about her? Of course he did.

When Linnie turned up with another bruise on her face, Rod looked at her in horror. 'Did your ex do that?'

She nodded.

'But I thought you'd taken out an order against him?'

'The law isn't there to enforce it when he comes round.'

'Have you reported this to the police?' He touched the bruised skin gently. It felt as soft as it looked. She had lovely skin.

'What's the use? I can't prove anything.'

'Didn't your neighbours see anything?'

'If they did, they're not going to admit it. No one wants to get involved with another person's troubles round where we live. Now, I—'

Rod put out his crutch to bar her way. 'We'll go and report it to the police now. My car needs an outing, so you can drive me.'

'It'll only make Ken worse next time. And you won't be here for a while if you're going to Australia, so I have to manage the best I can.'

It was then that the idea struck him. 'Wait.' He swung himself slowly back to the kitchen, with Linnie trailing behind.

She didn't say anything, just put the kettle on. Only when she'd put a mug of coffee in front of him did he gesture to the other seat. He waited till she'd brought her own mug across. 'Why don't you stay here while I'm away? We have a police station just down the road. I'll tell all my neighbours and they'll keep their eyes and ears open, so you can yell for help if there's any trouble. He won't frighten them. Phyllis is ex-Army and George hates criminals and violence. Jenny and Jonathon across the road are into self-defence. They tried to get me to go to one of their classes once.' He ran out of words and blinked in shock. He didn't often make such a long speech.

'But . . . I can't do that!'

'Why not?'

She was clutching her mug to her chest, her knuckles white against it. 'What if Glen broke in and damaged your house? He does that sort of thing, you know.'

'He'd be caught, I know he would. No, you should do it. It makes good sense.'

'Oh, Rod, you're so kind to us.' She picked up his hand and cradled it against her face.

That drove any other persuasive speeches right out of his head. He could feel his face growing warm, didn't know what to say except, 'You'll do it, then? Move in while I'm away.'

'Yes, I will. I know I shouldn't, but I'm so worried about the boys. What if he starts on them next? They love coming here, so they'll be over the moon. And I'll look after the house properly, you can be sure of that. When are you leaving?'

'Next week.'

'I bet your sister's excited.'

'She doesn't know. I'm going to surprise her.' He wasn't telling Sue or their mother, either.

And he wasn't going to admit that Kirsty had put the phone down on him a couple of times. If he told her he was going to Australia, she might even forbid him to come. He wouldn't put anything past her at the moment. The inheritance had gone to her head.

No, the only thing to do was surprise her.

She'd be glad to see him . . . wouldn't she?

Chapter Sixteen

Nearly three months after her arrival, Kirsty was weeding the front garden when she heard a car coming up the track. She stood up, easing her back, and to her surprise saw a taxi pull up in front of her house. When her brother Rod got out of it, she let out a low groan. Oh, no! Why could he not leave her alone as she'd asked? And how had he got holiday leave so soon?

He was beaming at her so she tried to smile back, but couldn't quite manage it. As she went out to greet him, she noticed he was moving stiffly. 'Rod! What a surprise! Why didn't you tell me you were coming? How's your leg?'

'All right. I was worried about you having to deal with all that money, so I took two weeks' emergency leave. That'll give us enough time to sort out the financial side of things and make sure you're not being cheated.'

Typical of him to talk about money instead of asking how she was and looking round at her house and garden, as others would have done. 'I don't see why you were so worried about me.'

'You kept putting the phone down on me, so I knew something must be wrong.'

'Well, it isn't. I just didn't want to talk to you about the money. And I still don't.'

He didn't even seem to hear her last remark. She'd make sure she repeated it later, though it might take several times to get past that bizarre personal filter of his. 'You'd better come inside.'

'I'll just pay the driver.'

'You didn't take a taxi all the way from Perth, surely?'

'Of course not. I found out how far away from Perth your house was before I left England. I came by coach to Margaret River, then took a taxi out here because there doesn't seem to be any public transport.'

'There isn't.'

As the taxi left, Rod stared round for the first time. 'Don't you have any neighbours?'

'Yes. Good ones, too. You passed Sam's house as you came up Gulliver Road.'

'You mean someone lives in that rusty heap of tin?' He began moving towards the house, walking inside without waiting for her.

'Let me come past, Rod, and I'll show you the way.'

He stopped just inside, peering into the living room. 'Good, solid furniture. It lasts a long time, that sort does.'

She tried to keep her tone cheerful. 'Come this way. I'll put you in the bedroom at the far end. There are six bedrooms and three bathrooms, so you can have your own bathroom, too.'

She pushed open each door to show him the layout of the house and at one stage he muttered, 'I don't know what anyone needs all this space for. It must be very costly to heat.'

'It's keeping cool that people worry about here, not heating. We're well into autumn now and I've not needed any heating yet – just a cardigan in the early mornings and evenings.'

In the bedroom she checked the drawers, because she hadn't got round to clearing out this room yet. They were full, of course. This time they were women's clothes. Had Ed ever thrown anything away? She pulled the drawers out, one by one, emptying their contents on to the bed in the next room. 'There. Do you want any help with the unpacking?'

'Of course not.'

'Come and get a cup of tea when you're ready.'

She escaped to the kitchen and stood for a moment, open palms pressed to each cheek, wondering how to deal with him. She wasn't going to let Rod run her life again.

But how was she to get that through to him?

The vow not to let her brother run her life was even harder to carry out than she'd expected.

By teatime he had rearranged her living room. He did this while she nipped round to Penny's to tell her what had happened and look at the pups, who were nearly ready to leave their mother.

Kirsty stared at the room in shock when she got back. 'What have you done that for?'

'This way is more efficient.'

'But it's not how I want it.'

She started to put things back and when he asked to see her accounts, she carried on shoving the chairs back to where she wanted them.

'I don't seem to be suffering from jetlag, Kirsty, so we may as well make a start tonight.'

'How many times do I have to say that I don't need your help, Rod? I have an accountant here in Australia.'

'Of course you need me. It's my job. It'd be silly for you to pay someone else to do what I can do for free. You'll only need this accountant to check that I've not infringed any Australian laws this year. Next year, when you're back in England . . . there's a car coming.' He swung round, looking as if he was expecting invaders.

Kirsty went to the window and saw Sam drop Tina off. He drove away without coming in to say hello.

'Hi, Kirsty! I had the greatest day and—' Tina broke off at the sight of Rod.

'This is my brother. He came out from England to surprise me.'

Instead of pursuing her argument with Rod, she explained quickly about Tina being her house guest. His disapproval was obvious, so she took advantage of him visiting the bathroom to beg Tina not to leave her alone with him.

'Are you sure? I was going to ask you if you wanted me to move back to Dad's.'

'On no account. In fact, if you do I'll come after you with a stick and beat you good and hard for deserting me. I didn't want Rod to come and he'll try to interfere in everything. It'll be easier with a guest here. He, um, says exactly what he's thinking and has tunnel vision when he wants something.'

Tina grinned. 'It's like that sometimes with Mum. She goes on and on until she wears you down.'

'So does Rod. Did you have a good day?'

'It was way cool. So interesting, so laid back, too. Rhys is going to teach me about paintings. He thinks very highly of Dad's pieces. Mum was so wrong about them. Did she really damage one of them?'

'You'll have to ask your father.'

'He won't talk about it, which means she did. That sucks big time.'

Rod came back to join them and fixed Tina with one of his looks. 'I'm afraid we don't have time to gossip because I'm only here for two weeks, so if you could find something to do and leave us in peace . . . ?' He held the door open.

She stared at him open-mouthed.

Unable to believe that even he could be so rude, Kirsty went to put her arm round her guest's shoulders. 'We are not going over my accounts, Rod, so there's absolutely no reason for Tina to leave us alone. After all, she's living here too at the moment.'

'But I need to talk to you. Privately.'

'Not tonight you don't.'

He glared at her. 'Look, it makes sense to—'

There were footsteps on the veranda and Kirsty saw Sam approaching the back door with a bowl of tomatoes, presumably more largesse from Franco. 'Let your dad in, Tina, will you please?' She hoped the girl would have the sense to tell him what had happened and when the two of them held a low-voiced conversation, she relaxed a little – only to find that Rod had moved his chair closer to hers and was saying, 'Why didn't you tell her to go away? We've a lot to get through while I'm here.'

'How many times do I have to tell you—'

Sam came in and she bounced to her feet. 'This is my brother. Rod, meet Sam, Tina's father, the neighbour whose house you passed.'

'You need to get that roof of yours fixed properly,' Rod said by way of greeting. 'It's badly rusted.'

'It still keeps the water out.'

'Beer?' Kirsty opened the fridge and thrust a can at Sam, mouthing 'please stay' as she did so.

He grinned and offered her the bowl of tomatoes. 'Penny just brought these round and I thought you'd like some. The cherry tomatoes are still fruiting madly. Franco's had some amazing crops this year.'

'He says the wine will be good, too.'

Sam nodded his thanks as he took the can of chilled beer.

She offered one to Tina, then looked at Rod, who didn't waste his money on drink.

'I'll have—' A sudden yawn overtook him and he blinked, looking surprised. 'I must be more tired than I'd realised. I think I'll go to bed.'

Without a word he left the room.

'He's very . . . direct,' Sam said.

'Yes. Let's go and sit on the front veranda, then we won't disturb him.' More importantly, Rod wouldn't hear what they were saying unless he eavesdropped in the front room, which wasn't the sort of thing that usually occurred to him.

The other two followed her outside, carrying some outdoor chairs round from the back.

By the time they were seated, Kirsty had downed half her beer. 'What am I going to do?'

Sam took the chair next to hers. 'You didn't want him to come?'

'No.' She lowered her voice. 'He's a dear, in his own way, believe it or not, but he's obsessive where money is concerned.'

Tina leaned back, looking more relaxed than she had since her arrival. 'He'd drive me round the bend in two minutes flat.'

'Me too, when he's in one of his moods,' Kirsty said. 'Don't you dare leave me alone with him in the evenings. And you're both invited to tea tomorrow. You will come, won't you?'

'Wouldn't miss this show for world.' Sam raised his beer in a salute to her then took a drink. 'What are you going to do with him all day, though? Tina and I will both be working.'

'I don't know.' Kirsty stared down at her can, tracing a pattern in the condensation on the outside and taking a sudden decision to be honest. 'Perhaps I'd better explain that Rod has a communication disorder. Please don't be offended by him. He simply doesn't understand how to be tactful or – or even what other people want, half the time. He's brilliant with figures, honest and well-meaning, but totally hopeless with people.' She realised her can was empty and was about to stand up when Sam took it out of her hand.

'Shall I get you another one?'

'Please. And get one for yourself too. Tina, how about you?'

'I'm a bit tired. If you feel safe with Dad around, I think I'll go to bed.'

When she'd gone, Kirsty leaned back with a sigh. 'Thanks for staying.'

'My pleasure.'

They didn't say much, but even the silences were comfortable tonight. Unlike her brother, Sam was sensitive enough to realise how distressed she was about Rod's arrival. He didn't offer her any solutions but let her talk. She couldn't find any answers to the problem, though.

After Sam had left, she went straight to bed, only to lie awake half the night worrying.

Rod was up early because he'd set an old alarm clock of Ed's, which was loud enough to wake the whole household.

The sound brought Kirsty out of the mists of sleep. Realising it was nearly time to get up anyway, she went to check that Tina was awake. She showered and dressed rapidly, then found her brother in the kitchen with a pot of tea brewing. 'You'll have to get your own breakfast, I'm afraid, Rod. I'm taking Tina into town before I eat. She's got a temporary job there.'

'Why should you have to do that?'

'Because I want to.'

'But think of all the petrol it's costing you.'

'I'm happy to do it. Ah, there you are Tina. Grab some breakfast quickly and then we'll be off.'

On the way into town, Tina said quietly. 'Are you sure you don't want me to move back to Dad's?'

'Don't you dare!'

'He's a bit overpowering, your brother I mean. Far worse than Dad.'

Kirsty looked at her in surprise. 'Sam's not overpowering.'

'He keeps trying to boss me around, barking out orders like a sergeant major.'

'That's because he cares about you.'

'He doesn't really.'

'Whatever gave you that idea? Of course he does.'

'I overheard him saying to someone that he was counting the days till I left. And that was the first day, before I'd even settled in.'

'You must have misunderstood him.'

Tina shook her head. 'No, I didn't. I do recognise my own name. And anyway, I knew it before I got here. When I was younger, he was always cancelling his visits to me. He did that at least half the time.'

A quick glance showed Kirsty that the girl was blinking furiously and her eyes were overly bright. She debated whether to interfere, but the memory of Tina's unhappiness about her relationship with her father wouldn't go away. On the way back, she stopped off at Sam's and marched into the studio to confront him about what Tina had said, speaking almost as bluntly as Rod would have done, too upset to be tactful.

He stared at her in horror. 'I didn't mean it that way.'

'But you did say it.'

'I suppose so.'

'Well, she overheard you. And she says you were always cancelling your visits when she was younger. She's obviously still hurting about that. What gives, Sam?'

He put down the paintbrush and rubbed his hands on a rag, frowning. 'It's not true that I cancelled the visits. Lorraine was always ringing me up and saying Tina didn't want to see me . . .' He froze. 'She wouldn't!' A minute later he said, 'She would. Lorraine would do anything if it suited her purpose. Look at the way she damaged my painting.'

Kirsty waited, glad Sam wasn't an uncaring father.

He rubbed his hand over his brow, leaving a smear of lilac paint behind. 'Oh, hell, and I never even guessed. All those years!' He looked at Kirsty, anguish written on his face, pain echoing in his voice. 'How do I ever get over that with Tina? I missed so much of her childhood.'

'I don't know. I'm a fine one to advise anyone when I can't even deal with my own brother.'

'Coffee?'

'Please.'

They sat on Sam's rickety little veranda for a while, not saying much, then she stood up. 'I'd better go back and face Rod.'

'Good luck.'

'Thanks.' She needed it.

In England, Linnie came home from work and set about preparing a meal for her sons. She felt safe and happy here in Rod's house, which was carefully protected against burglars with a good deadlock on the door and locks on every single window.

It was obvious he looked after the place carefully, but she itched to do something about the décor. Except for his sister's bedroom, it was full of dark practical colours and patterns that clashed. She could just imagine him in a shop, choosing sensibly for wear and tear, without a thought to how items would look next to one another. Poor love, he had such trouble relating to the world. And the things he came out with! So blunt, no tact whatsoever.

But give her someone like Rod any day, after what she'd had with her lying, cheating ex. Rod was honest and caring, at least, and look how kind he'd been to her boys.

Someone knocked on the front door and she stiffened. Who could that be? No one knew she was here. She went into the front room and peered outside through the bay window, shocked rigid to see her ex-husband standing there, his face mottled and red with anger.

'It's Dad!' Tommy shouted from upstairs. 'You said he couldn't find us here.'

'I don't know how he did. Stay where you are. Don't let him see you.'

Glen thumped on the door. 'I know you're in there, Linnie! Open this door at once!' He started thumping again, on and on, and for a moment or two she froze, terrified he'd get inside. Then she rushed to pick up the phone in the kitchen and call the police.

But before she could start dialling, there was the sound of a siren outside. Still holding the phone, she ran back into the front room and saw a police car drawn up outside, its light still flashing. 'Oh, thank goodness,' she whispered. 'Thank goodness.'

Two officers got out and approached Glen.

He glanced round once when they asked him to move away, but ignored them and began thumping on the door again, yelling, 'Come out this minute! Come out, Linnie!'

She shivered. From the slurred way he was speaking, he must be bladdered, always had been a nasty drunk. Or else he was using again.

One officer tapped him on the shoulder, and he turned, fist swinging, as she'd seen it swing so many times.

It connected with the officer's shoulder, not face, because the man was taller than him. Before Glen could do anything else, they had him turned round and pressed against the wall next to the front door, one arm twisted behind him. While the male officer held him, the female officer quickly handcuffed him.

He struggled all the way, but they managed to shove him into the back of the car, then the female officer came back to knock on the door.

This time Linnie opened it.

'Excuse me, ma'am, but do you know that man?'

'Yes. He's my ex-husband. There's an order out against him to keep him away from us, but he keeps breaking it.' She pointed at the bruise on her cheek. 'He did this a few days ago, so a friend lent me this house while he was away. I don't know how Glen found out where I was.'

'Are you willing to prosecute him?'

'Yes. And don't worry, I won't back out of it. Though I doubt it'll do any good.' She couldn't go on like this, felt near to tears and she didn't usually let things get her down. But she'd felt so safe here.

The officer's expression was sympathetic. 'Are you going to be all right, do you think?'

'Yes. Only – I think you should keep an eye on him after you let him go. He'll come back here again, I know he will.'

'I doubt they'll let him go till he's sobered up. You ring us straight away if he does come back. I'll tell my sergeant and he'll get someone to drive past every now and then. Is anyone else living here?'

'Just my sons. They're only nine and seven.'

'No other adults?'

'I'm afraid not.'

'Then be sure to keep your doors and windows locked, ma'am.'

'I will. How did you know Glen was annoying me?'

The officer smiled. 'One of the neighbours phoned us and luckily, we happened to be nearby.'

There was a shout from the car and they saw Glen trying in vain to break the window with his shoe. He was quite stupid with drink, though not too far gone to not thump Linnie if he got near her, never too drunk for that.

'I have to go. We'll come back later for a statement, if that's all right, ma'am? I'd like to get him safely locked up without delay.'

'It's fine with me. I'm not going anywhere.'

Linnie shut the door and locked it carefully. She was quite sure Glen would be back. He always was. If not tonight, then another time. She'd have to be even more careful than usual, because she didn't want this house or Rod's belongings damaging.

Or herself.

But where she'd go when Rod came back from Australia, she didn't know. She'd always avoided women's refuges, but she might not have a choice now. A tear rolled down her cheek, then another, but she scrubbed them away and went to cook the boys' tea, trying to speak cheerfully.

An arm went round her waist as she stood by the sink and she turned her head to smile at Tommy, who was nearly

as big as her now. Then Jem pressed against her from the
other side, so they all had a cuddle.

'If Dad comes back again,' Tommy said, 'I'm going to
find a big stick and hit him.'

'If he gets into this house, you'll do as you promised and
barricade yourselves in that bedroom.'

But he shook his head obstinately, which gave her
something else to worry about. If Glen hurt one of her
boys, she wouldn't be answerable for her actions.

When Kirsty got back to the house, she found Rod pacing
up and down, waiting for her.

'Ah, there you are. Look, just fetch me the information
the accountant gave you and let me have a quick glance at
it.'

'I want my breakfast before I do anything else.'

He followed her into the kitchen. 'I can't believe you're
taking a stranger into town every day. And do you pick her
up at night as well?'

'No, her father does that.'

'He should be taking her as well. Why isn't she sleeping
at his place?'

Kirsty hesitated, then decided to see if she could divert
Rod's attention. 'Because I've got an intruder. He's turned
up several times now. I've had a security system put in, but
it's better to have someone living here as well.'

He gaped at her. 'An intruder? Here? In the middle of
nowhere?'

'Yes. And he made a mess of my kitchen last time,
trampled food all over the floor. Trouble is, I'm too far out

of town to have the security system monitored, so it's linked to Sam's phone and he comes running if it goes off. That's why I'm happy to do him a favour and take Tina to work at a time when he's very busy himself.'

Of course Rod ignored her final sentence. 'I'll give up work and come and live with you.'

'No.'

'I can send in my resignation from here and—'

She was so terrified Rod would do this and then be out of work that she went up to him and shook him by the shoulders to get his full attention. 'I said no. I don't want it and anyway, if you do that, it breaks the conditions of the inheritance and I'll lose everything. No relatives to stay for more than a month. Remember?'

'I'd forgotten that.'

She didn't move away. 'Listen to me, Rod. It's time I made a life for myself. Even if I come back to England, I won't be living with you again.'

He blinked and stepped rapidly away from her, his face twisting as if he was in pain.

She could see he was upset and was sorry for it, but her wishes had to be spelled out once and for all. 'I've been grateful for your help, but I must stand on my own feet from now on.'

He said nothing, just went to put the kettle on, shoulders hunched. Had he accepted what she'd told him? She couldn't tell. He sat in the kitchen drinking a cup of tea while she ate her breakfast, his eyes and mouth scrunched up in thought.

What was going on inside his head? she wondered. Surely he wasn't going to try to make her change her mind about him going through her business accounts? Surely she'd got through to him now about what she really wanted?

The trouble was, with Rod you could never quite be sure how he'd take things. Or what he'd do.

Chapter Seventeen

When Sam went to pick up his daughter, he found her in animated conversation with Rhys, gesticulating, cheeks rosy with enthusiasm, eyes sparkling.

He'd not seen Tina look so happy for years. He stood by the door, waiting for the conversation to finish, his thoughts going to Kirsty, as they did all too often these days, try as he may to distance himself from her. And now he'd promised to eat his evening meals at her place while her brother was there. That wasn't wise. Only, she needed him. And he enjoyed being with her.

'Earth to Dad! Come in, please.'

He jumped in shock as someone touched his arm and realised Tina had come across to join him and was trying to get his attention. He returned Rhys's farewell wave, then said hesitantly, feeling as if he was treading on eggshells, 'Sorry. I was lost in thought. Look, do you want to grab a coffee somewhere before we head off home? I didn't have time to get one before I left.'

'Been painting all day?'

He smiled. 'Yes.'

'Something orange?'

'What?'

She smiled as she pointed to a dab of paint on his forearm, but her voice had a sharp edge to it as she added, 'However did you manage to drag yourself away in time?'

'When it's something important, I use an alarm clock, a very loud one, and put it outside so that I can't switch it off without leaving my painting.' He thought he heard her mutter 'important' scornfully, but pretended he hadn't heard. 'Coffee, then?'

'Whatever.'

Her face had lost the lively look now and the only word for her expression was guarded. That upset him. His daughter shouldn't need to be guarded with him.

As soon as they were seated, he took the bull by the horns. 'About my visits to you during the past few years—'

'I'm over all that stuff now.'

'Well, I'm not. Why did you keep sending word you didn't want to see me?'

She gaped at him.

'At least half the time Lorraine rang me to say you didn't want to see me.'

There was dead silence, then Tina carefully tore the end off a tube of sugar, emptied it into her coffee and began stirring, moving the spoon round and round as if it was the only thing she cared about in the world.

He didn't say anything, sensed that it was important to wait until she was ready to look up.

'I didn't say that.' A tear rolled down her cheek, then another one.

He laid his hand on hers and they sat for a minute or two.

'Mum can be a real bitch sometimes, can't she?'

'Yes.' His voice was thick with emotion. 'And all those years we lost – nothing can bring them back.'

Tina fumbled for a tissue. 'I thought it was you backing out. I've hated you. For years I've thought you didn't care about me.'

He nodded. 'It showed, and that baffled me. Why did you see me at all when you thought that?'

'Mum said if I didn't, you'd withdraw the maintenance payments.'

He shook his head. 'I'd never have stopped paying. She knew I wanted to support you, even after you turned eighteen. You were the main reason I went on working at a job I hated, because I wanted to see you safely through school and university.'

Tina pushed the coffee away from her, untasted. Another tear ran down her cheek, then others followed. 'Can we go back to the car now, please?' she asked in a choked voice and rushed outside.

He paid for their untouched drinks then followed her.

She didn't say a word until they were sitting in the car. He put his arm round her and patted her shoulder. There were tears in his eyes as well. All those years, stolen from him!

She pulled away from him after a moment or two, blew her nose and said in a thickened voice, 'That settles it. I'm not going back to uni.'

'You're too close to graduating to quit now, Tina.'

'I'm going to fail anyway. I'm no good at academic stuff. I've learned more from Rhys in a few days about the history of art than I've ever learned from books or lectures. And what's more, I like selling stuff, helping people find just what they want, making sure the place looks its best.'

'You can't make a career out of part-time work in art galleries.'

'I know. But there must be something I can do, something similar perhaps. I hate studying, Dad, and I hate working in that café, too.' She took a deep breath. 'I'll never forgive Mum, never!'

Then she was crying again, this time sobbing in a loud, gusty way, as a child sobs, her mouth square with years of unleashed anguish. She made no attempt to hide her face or keep her voice down. He took her in his arms, his tears mingling with hers as he rocked her and made soothing noises in her ear.

When they'd both stopped weeping, she looked at him shamefacedly. 'I can't face that horrible brother of Kirsty's. Not yet.'

'No.' He pulled his mobile phone out. 'I'll give her a ring, tell her we're going out for a meal.'

'I can't go into a café looking like this, either.'

'I know. We'll get a takeaway.'

'Pizza?'

He gave her a smile. 'It was always your favourite comfort food, wasn't it?' He held up one hand to stop her speaking. 'Ah, Kirsty. Sam here. Look, something's come up and we'll not be there for a couple of hours. We'll grab something to eat and I'll bring Tina back later. I'm sorry to let you down, but this is important, family stuff from way back that Tina and I had to clear up. Bye.'

He turned back to give his daughter his fullest attention. It was, he felt, his big chance to get on better terms with her, perhaps his only chance now. It was the most important thing in his life at the moment, even more important than his painting. Lara would just have to wait for her damned accent piece. And his own life would have to wait, too. Especially Kirsty. The last thing he needed was complications about a relationship.

The day seemed interminable to Kirsty. In spite of what she'd told him, Rod kept trying to talk her into 'just showing' him her accounts. She doubted he'd go through the drawers in her bedroom. She'd made it clear when she went to live with him that she would never, ever stand for that.

But in case he didn't draw the line at going through her desk, she put all her financial papers in a plastic dustbin liner and stuffed it away at the back of her wardrobe, draping an old blanket over it.

She took him to see her vineyard and he studied the rows of vines, then the equipment inside the wine shed in silence. He asked how much all the bottles of wine were worth, but didn't want to taste any of it.

As they walked back to the house, he said, 'That vineyard should add value and attraction to your property when you sell it.'

In the afternoon she took him out for a drive. He agreed to visit one vineyard for comparison with hers, but wasn't interested in seeing any others. She insisted he go with her into the chocolate factory and cheese factory, but they left him cold.

Let's face it, he wasn't interested in anything except figures and making an orderly life. She knew that, really, but at least going round tourist attractions got them out of the house and passed a few hours.

'Where shall we go tomorrow?' she asked as they returned. 'You can look through the brochures and tell me.'

'I don't want to go anywhere.'

'You mustn't waste this opportunity, Rod. You've spent a lot of money coming here, so you should see something of Western Australia while you're here. Maybe we could go away for a couple of days as well? There's an old whaling port called Albany on the south coast, and on the way there we could look at the Valley of the Giants. The brochure says the karri trees there are so big you could drive a car through one of the hollow trunks, and people did in the old days, only they've been fenced off from traffic now.'

'I'm not interested in being a tourist. I came out here solely to help you and you won't let me even glance at the figures. It's so stupid. I could at least check them, make sure you're getting the best return on your investments.'

'I know. But as I keep telling you, I have to do things myself now to prove that I've moved on.' She tried again to explain, but without much hope that he'd understand. 'After Mike died, you were wonderful to me, Rod. I can never thank you enough for that. I was frozen with grief. And as I started to recover, I went into a sort of human safety mode, I think, not taking any risks. That wasn't living properly.'

'I enjoyed having you. We've been so happy together. Never a cross word and—'

She looked at him in astonishment, amazed he could believe this. 'Of course we've had cross words! And we lived together peacefully only because I could escape to my bedroom, or into books, not because we were doing anything worthwhile. We weren't. Either of us.'

Silence for quite a long time, then he gave her one of his stubborn looks. 'I'm not giving up. You can't handle that much money on your own.'

'I've got help.'

'But that accountant may be cheating you!'

'I trust Ed's judgement. He'd not employ a cheat.'

They ate the evening meal in silence, then he said, 'There's a lot of garden for one person. I could help you set the vegetable garden out for the winter plantings. You were talking about that last night to your neighbour.'

'Penny's husband Franco is going to do that with me. He's got green fingers – luminously green. You've eaten his wonderful tomatoes. You wouldn't understand the growing conditions here any more than I would. And you've never been into gardening.'

'I'm pretty strong. I could dig over the ground for you.'

'Not necessary.' And actually, she didn't think Rod was particularly strong. He led a very sedentary life. He'd learned to defend himself as a lad because he'd had to, and he'd defended her and Sue a couple of times too when they were children, but that wasn't the same thing as being physically strong.

She spent the rest of the evening sitting in front of the television with him, pretending to watch a programme which didn't interest her.

In the middle of it, Rod said suddenly, 'That Sam fellow is taking advantage of you.'

'What? No, he isn't. Here in the country neighbours always help one another.'

'This business with his daughter is a ploy to worm his way into your good books.'

'I tell you, it isn't! If it were, don't you think I'd have enough sense to realise that? I'm not stupid. Anyway, how can you judge him when you hardly know him?'

'You're a rich woman. Why else would he be hanging round?'

'Talk about insults! I'm not exactly Mrs Ugly, you know. Some people think I'm quite attractive, even without knowing about the money. Another man has asked me for a date, too, since I've been here.'

Rod stopped talking to stare at her as if he'd never seen her before, then shook his head. 'You're all right, but you're nothing special in looks. No, it's got to be your money he's after.'

No wonder her brother had never married! No woman would put up with his tactlessness.

It was a huge relief when she heard Sam's vehicle and saw him and Tina go past the window towards the kitchen entrance.

She got up without a word and went to greet them.

'I'm tired,' Tina said, avoiding her eyes. 'I think I'll have an early night.' She ran down the corridor to her room.

Kirsty turned to Sam, hoping he'd explain.

'We had a talk about the way her mother has been keeping us apart for the past few years. It was traumatic, as well as cathartic. Would you mind if I didn't stay?'

'No, of course not.'

She was glad he and his daughter were beginning to sort out their differences, of course she was. But she could have done with some comfort herself tonight. She had to force herself to go back and join Rod. As she locked the back door, she thought she saw a figure at the end of the garden, but Rod came in to get a drink just then and when she looked back at the moonlit scene, the figure had vanished.

She wasn't sure if she'd really seen someone or just imagined it, but she felt safer with Rod and Tina there.

He didn't say much, just continued to watch an Australian current affairs programme on the television with the solemn expression of an alien studying the natives on a strange planet.

In the end, Kirsty went to bed early with another of Ed's romances, pleading exhaustion.

The next day Sam's mobile phone rang while he was working. He decided not to answer it, then changed his mind at the last minute and snatched it up, remembering that it might be Kirsty's security system.

'Geoff here.'

'Oh, hi.' Stupid of him to feel disappointed!

'How's Lara's painting going?'

Sam looked across at it. 'Almost finished.'

'She wants to show it off to someone ASAP. You know what she's like. Has to do things the minute she thinks of them.'

'I can have it finished by the weekend, if you like. It's going well. But it'll need careful handling because the paint won't have dried properly. I can get it framed here, but it'll add a few days extra.'

'I'll check with Lara. She may want to have it framed herself. On another subject, that big painting of yours is now hanging in the foyer at work and people really like it. They stop to stare at it. They were even talking about it over coffee at a management meeting the other day. They're all surprised it's yours.'

'Maybe we shouldn't have told them that.'

'Are you crazy? It gives it an added interest. Lara's going to show her painting to the chairman when he comes round to dinner, to make sure he gets the message that you're a hot item on the art scene.'

'That's great, really kind of her.' Well, Sam assumed it was either kind or good business. He could think of no ulterior motive for her doing that. He smiled. His paintings were selling in the local art gallery and ironically, as soon as he'd got Ed's money, he hadn't needed it, which was a good thing with Tina needing extra help. Not that the paintings were bringing in a fortune, but he'd grown used to living frugally. 'Sorry. Got some interference on the line there. What did you say?'

'I said, Lara asked me to remind you of the other painting you've promised to do for her charity.'

'I haven't forgotten. Has she said anything about taking me on as a client?'

'Not exactly, but reading between the lines, if the one you've done for us pleases her, I think she might take you on. She's good at PR and all the other stuff you need to make good sales.'

'I know.'

Sam felt a lifting of his spirits as he put the phone down. When it rang a short time later he didn't even hear it, he was so immersed in his work.

Rod set his travel alarm to wake him when Linnie was at home during the English evening, which meant he had to ring in the middle of the night. He woke at once and shut if off, then padded along to the kitchen barefoot to make his call. He'd asked Kirsty if she minded and promised to keep it short, not wanting to waste her money. She'd just waved a hand as if that didn't matter. But it did. Money always mattered.

He let the phone ring four times, then cut it off before dialling again, as he'd agreed with Linnie before he left.

'Hello?'

He liked her breathy voice, which always sounded as if she'd been hurrying. 'It's me, Rod.'

'I didn't think you'd ring.'

'I said I would, didn't I? How are things going?'

'We're looking after your house very carefully.'

He frowned. Something about her voice didn't sound right, not as bouncy as usual.

'Rod? Are you still there?'

'Sorry. Yes. Just thinking.'

'I bet you're scrunching up your face.'

He stared at his reflection in a glass door. 'How did you know?'

'I guessed from your tone of voice. You always do when you're thinking.'

'Never mind that now. Linnie, are you sure you're all right? You don't sound . . . like you usually do.'

'Oh. Well, we had an incident. Glen must have followed me and he tried to get in. It was a bit hairy, but that nice neighbour of yours across the road called the police and they took him away.'

Rod felt suddenly afraid for her. 'You're all right, though, you and the boys?'

'Yes. But I'm being careful, keeping my eyes open.'

He heard her voice wobble. That meant she was still upset. Didn't it? 'Have you told me everything?' He heard a sob. 'Linnie?'

'He came back in the night and smashed a window. I've got it repaired, don't worry, but I'm a bit nervous. I think after you get back I'll have to go to a women's refuge and let them find me somewhere to live in another town. They do that, you know. But it'd mean taking the boys away from their school and . . . Listen to me, going on about my troubles. You don't want to know that.'

'I do.'

'Well, you know it now. Cheer me up. Tell me about your holiday.'

'Kirsty won't let me help her.'

'Well, if you've done your best . . .'

'But she's got all that money to look after and she's already wasted a huge chunk of it on a fancy BMW convertible.'

'Rod, love, she's a grown-up. If she can afford a convertible and wants one, good luck to her, I say. I wish I could have one. It must be wonderful to drive a car like that in a warmer climate.'

'Yes, but—'

'Rod, you have to let her deal with her own life.' She sighed. 'I want to deal with my own life as well, only I can't. I'm too frightened of Glen.'

'Don't do anything till I get back. You can stay on with me for a few days and I'll help you sort something out.'

'I'm not your responsibility, Rod love.'

'But I want to help you. And I don't want you to leave town.' He breathed deeply and looked at the clock. He was about to run over time. 'Look. I'll ring in a couple of days. You take care.'

He put the light off but stood in the kitchen staring blindly out at the blurry darkness. Nothing was going right. Kirsty didn't want his help and Linnie needed his help, only he wasn't there to give it.

He didn't know what to do, but he definitely didn't intend to waste any more time going round vineyards. People frittered away too much of their money on wine. No wonder they were short of cash or went bankrupt.

What was Kirsty's accountant like? How did she know he was a good one?

Rod went back to bed but couldn't get to sleep for a long time.

After she got back from taking Tina to work the next morning, Kirsty rang Penny to invite her and Franco round for a barbecue that evening. 'It won't be much fun, I'm afraid. My brother's not, um, very good socially. But I'd really appreciate your help and I will feed you nicely.'

'Things not going well?' Penny asked.

'Oh, you know what it's like with big brothers. They never admit you've grown up and keep trying to boss you around. And now that I've got some money, Rod thinks men are after that, not me.'

'I know which man you're referring to, and I'd say your money has had the opposite effect on him.'

'Yes. I realise that, but Rod doesn't believe me.'

'Persevere. With Sam, I mean.'

'Mmm.' But did she want to chase a man who was so determined not to be caught? Well, inviting him to a neighbourhood barbecue wasn't chasing him, was it? And she needed as much help as she could get with Rod.

Sam turned up that evening in his usual faded jeans, which she could tell he'd washed and ironed in honour of the occasion. Tina went across to give her father a hug, which brought a smile to his face, at least.

It faded when he was forced to chat to Rod. The two men were excruciatingly polite to one another, making stilted conversation about cricket, which she knew neither of them gave two hoots about, and then the latest troubles in the Middle East, about which they had very different views. They abandoned that topic abruptly.

Franco then started a discussion about this season's wine, but as he was the only one who knew anything about it, that didn't last long, either. The evening, Kirsty thought ruefully, would win a gold medal for the most boring barbecue ever.

'He's definitely a fortune hunter,' said Rod scornfully when he came into the kitchen to help her carry the food out.

He was speaking so loudly, she looked round in panic, hoping no one had heard. 'Shh! He's not.'

'You're too trusting. You always have been.'

She didn't let herself get into an argument, but snatched a plate of food and walked out with it.

Sam was standing by himself, hands thrust deep in his pockets, staring up at the sky. She looked at Penny, but her friend was laughing quietly with Franco and Tina, so Kirsty walked over to join Sam. 'Fancy something to nibble?'

He picked up a piece of cheese and popped it into his mouth, chewing slowly. When he'd swallowed it, he said, 'I don't like your brother. And if I come to tea again, I'll end up being rude to him. I'll still come if you want, but I can't guarantee to keep my temper.'

'He's only here for another week. I'll . . . manage. And anyway, Tina will be around part of the time. I really like your daughter, Sam.'

'Yes. I do, too.' He hesitated, then said quietly, 'Thanks for giving me the heads-up about Lorraine keeping us apart for years. It's not going to be easy, I know that, but I think Tina and I now have a good chance of growing closer. She's only got a few months to live with her mother, then she's moving out.'

'Good. How's the current painting going?'

'Really well. I'm taking it up to Perth next weekend when I drive Tina back.'

Rod called out for her from the kitchen and with a sigh, she excused herself to Sam.

A little later she found herself alone with Penny near the rose garden. The perfume wafted through the still night air and just for a short time, there was a feeling of peace.

'Ed loved this part of the garden,' Penny said softly. 'His wife planted these roses.'

'I like it, too.'

'The pups are ready to go to their new homes. Do you want me to keep yours till your brother's gone back?'

Kirsty thought about that. 'No. It'll give me something to do, training a pup, and Rod quite likes dogs, though he prefers certain breeds, especially Labradors. He even talked of getting one, but with us being out at work all day, he decided against it.'

The gathering broke up earlier than usual and Kirsty didn't protest as her guests began preparations for leaving. They'd stood by her nobly.

Sam hugged his daughter, thanked his hostess formally for having him, nodded to Rod then strode off down the track.

Penny gave Kirsty a hug and whispered, 'Bear up. You can take refuge with us any time you're desperate.'

Tina joined Kirsty in the kitchen as she was clearing the things away and whispered, 'I know I should be polite to your brother, but I can't hold my tongue for much longer. What's he got against my dad?'

Rod came in just then, ready to do the washing up.

'Tina and I can do this,' Kirsty said. 'You get off to bed. You're still suffering from jetlag.'

'I like to take my share of chores and I always do the washing up.'

Kirsty stepped back. 'Right. Go for it.'

Tina rolled her eyes. 'Can I use your computer then, Kirsty?'

'Yes, of course.' She turned to see Rod rearranging her crockery cupboard and bit back a sharp remark. Only one more week, she reminded herself and went to bed with a book, leaving him to it.

Chapter Eighteen

The next morning Penny called round to hand over the puppy. Tina was still in bed, having a long lie-in on her day off.

Kirsty held out her arms for the pretty little creature, holding Taffy close to her and murmuring endearments.

Rod looked at it, wrinkling his nose in disgust then scowling at Penny. 'She doesn't want a mongrel like that! If she has to have a dog – and I think it's a big waste of money – she can afford to buy a pedigree dog, one whose nature we can be sure of.'

'But Rod, I—'

He took the puppy out of Kirsty's arms before she could stop him, picking it up carelessly by the scruff of its neck and making it yelp in fright as he thrust it into Penny's arms.

With a glare, she cuddled the whimpering puppy against her chest.

At that moment something snapped within Kirsty. 'Don't take her away, Penny! I do want her. Come here, Taffy.'

As she handed the puppy back, Penny murmured, 'Go get him, girl!'

Kirsty turned to her brother who was already opening his mouth to protest. 'Don't touch Taffy again! And don't interfere in what I'm doing.'

He stepped back, but she knew he'd not let the matter drop.

The feel of the warm wriggling body boosted her courage and she smiled at her friend. 'Thanks, Penny. She's lovely. Sorry, would you mind if I didn't invite you in? My brother and I have something important to discuss.'

'Not at all.' Penny winked as she got into the car and drove away.

Kirsty turned to Rod, braced herself and said, 'Come into the house. We need to talk.'

'We certainly do!' He went to hold the door open for her, looking down at Taffy in disgust. 'It'll wee all over your floor and chew things. Do you really need the trouble of taking care of a puppy when you're only here for a year?'

'I've always wanted a dog, as you well know. Sit down there. I'll just pop Taffy into her box.' She did that and went to sit opposite him at the table. It was hard to say it, but she did. 'This visit isn't working out, Rod. You really should have checked with me that it was a convenient time for you to come.'

'I didn't think I had to wait for an invitation to visit my own sister.'

'No. I suppose you didn't, and that's partly my fault because I've let you walk all over me for years.' She let that sink in for a moment, then added quietly and firmly, 'But not any more.'

'Now you've got money, I suppose you're—'

She held up one hand. 'Don't say something you'll regret, Rod. I don't want to fall out with you, so I think it'd be better if you either booked an earlier flight home or went sightseeing in Perth for the rest of your stay. I'm still sorting out my life here and I need my space.'

He gaped at her.

'I'll come to England for a holiday next year and in the meantime I think you should get out and make a few friends. Build a new life for yourself, as I'm doing.'

'You don't mean it. That man has been brainwashing you. All he wants is your money.'

She smiled at that thought. 'No, it isn't Sam, it's me – though I'm hoping very much that he does want me.'

'I think you'd—'

'No more, Rod! When you get home, I'd be grateful if you'd pack up my personal things and freight them out to me – I'll pay for that – but you can keep the household equipment and crockery. I've more than enough furniture here for my needs.'

When he started to argue, she snatched up the car keys and pup, and fled, shouting, 'I mean it! Start packing!' over her shoulder.

Sam was working in his garden. He scowled as the car screeched to a halt and she got out. 'Isn't your dear brother with you to protect you from a fortune hunter like me?'

'Get me a cup of coffee and stop talking rubbish! Rod can think what he likes, but I know you're not a fortune hunter.' As Sam continued to stare at her, she added, 'Aren't I welcome? If I'm not, I'll go to Penny's, but I'm not going home.'

His frown vanished. 'Escaping?'

'Just for a while. Tina's still in bed and I've told Rod to pack up and go home early.'

He whistled. 'Drastic measures.'

She sighed. 'It was either that or murder him.'

Sam gestured to a chair. 'Sit down, then. This corner is a sun trap. I often sit here in winter.'

He came back a short time later with two mugs of coffee. 'Will your brother leave?'

'He'd better.'

'You won't soften and let him stay?'

'No. Definitely not.' She looked down at the puppy, which had fallen asleep in her lap. 'He told Penny to take Taffy back and shoved the poor dear into her arms so roughly he hurt her. That was it. I suddenly saw red.'

She took a sip of coffee and smiled down at the little dog. 'The whole family has always made allowances for Rod, but I'm beginning to agree with my sister. I think we were too lenient with him. He should have been forced to adjust better than this, even if he only learned by rote how to get on with people.' She took another sip and added, 'How could I have let him boss me around for the past four years?'

'You were probably upset after you lost your husband.'

She nodded. 'Very. Mike was a great guy and I loved him to pieces. I've always been a bit shy, but with him beside me, I could have conquered the world. Mind, he wasn't very good with money, which fretted Rod, but we had a wonderful time together.'

Sam didn't look at her as he said, 'And now you're on your own.'

'Yes.' She guessed he was warning her off. Well, she wasn't going from being dependent on one man to being dependent on another, so she'd let that remark pass for the moment.

She was sure now that Ed had known what he was talking about when he said she and Sam would make a good pair. She felt so comfortable with him. It was more than just enjoying his company, he turned her on in a way only one other man had, so that she wanted Sam in every way a woman could.

But she couldn't slay all the dragons in one day. First she had to deal with her brother. And anyway, she wanted to take it slowly with Sam, build up a good relationship, give things time to develop naturally. So she sat and talked of other things, her plans for the house, how best to train Taffy.

And busy as he was, he gave her that time unstintingly, seeming to sense she desperately needed relief from Rod's company.

When she left, she felt calmer and ready for the fray again.

She found her brother sitting in the kitchen but could see his suitcase standing in the hallway. He looked so unhappy she nearly weakened, then pulled herself together. 'I'm sorry if I said it badly.' She went and gave him a quick hug. 'You shouldn't have come here and tried to take everything over.'

'If caring for you is taking over, then I have to say that—'

She put one finger across his mouth. 'Rod, you always try to take over the people you care about. I think you need to see a counsellor and get your act together before you're too old to marry. If you don't, you'll have a very lonely life. I'm already sure that I'm never coming back to live in England permanently. And it wouldn't work for you to come and live here with me. You need to figure out what you are going to do with yourself.'

He was silent for a minute or two, then surprised her by saying, 'I don't want to leave with a quarrel between us, Kirsty. Let me stay as planned and—'

'Not this time, Rod. My life here is too fragile.'

'It's that man, isn't it? The Sam Brady fellow? You're in love with him.'

'Am I?'

'Yes. I've seen how you look at him. That's why you've got his daughter sleeping here, so that he'll be grateful, so that he'll have to come round.'

'Rod, I like Sam and I think he likes me, but I wouldn't play tricks to get his attention. He and I are not involved in that way – not yet, anyway. I think we're both old enough not to rush into things.'

'He's only after your money.'

Of course that was the main thing Rod would care about. She gave up trying to be kind and picked up her car keys. 'I'll drive you up to Perth now. There's just time to get there before dark. There are some excellent hotels.'

'And you? Will you drive back in the dark? That isn't sensible.'

'I don't always feel like being sensible.' She smiled at her car. That shiny silver convertible was another case of not being sensible and she so enjoyed driving it, hadn't regretted buying it for a minute.

She went along to Tina's room and found her guest sprawled on the bed reading. The look Tina gave her was rather hostile, but she didn't have time to find out what was wrong. 'I'm driving Rod up to Perth. Will you be all right?'

'Yes.'

'And can you look after Taffy for me?'

'Of course. Where is she?'

'Sleeping in her box, but she'll want letting out as soon as she wakens. And feeding.'

'I'll do it. I shall enjoy playing with her.'

'Thanks. And Tina – lock up carefully.'

Tina shrugged. 'I think it's you the intruder's after, not me.'

'I hope you're right. Maybe we should ask your father to sleep here too.'

'No. I'll be glad of some quiet thinking time.'

Kirsty hesitated. What did that mean? Then she gave a mental shrug and went off to drive her brother to Perth.

Kirsty drove up to the city mainly in silence. She pulled up outside the nice hotel she'd stayed at, saw Rod look at it and hesitate. 'It's a great place to stay. Give yourself a treat for a change.'

He got out of the car and turned to look at her. 'Be careful.'

'I will. And Rod, make a few changes to your life. Get some good counselling.'

He said nothing, just stood watching her drive away.

She felt guilty for sending him away, of course she did, but relieved too, as if a burden had been lifted from her shoulders.

Humming along to the radio, she headed south down the freeway into a clear, star-filled night. She stopped at a service station and filled the car with petrol, then bought some food, suddenly ravenous. She enjoyed every single one of the chips, even if they were full of fat and covered in salt. Sometimes you needed comfort food.

Gradually the feeling of euphoria faded and she grew tired. The last part of the drive back seemed longer than usual and she was exhausted by the time she got home. But she'd done the right thing. Definitely.

It occurred to her as she drove past Sam's gateway that if she could deal with Rod, she could cope with Sam as well. That made her smile. He wasn't a man you dealt with easily, though, and he had a lot of things on his plate at the moment. But when did life ever wait till a convenient time before tossing something at you, even something as important as love?

And how could she compete with his painting and his newly improved good relations with his daughter?

She couldn't at the moment, would have to wait her turn. And perhaps it was better that way.

Perhaps.

She remembered suddenly how she'd rushed into the relationship with Mike, the joy and excitement of being together. Did you get that in a second relationship or was it bound to be more sedate?

No, Penny and Franco were anything but sedate. They were always touching, kissing and exchanging smiles.

And she didn't intend to have a placid relationship. If she had one at all, it was going to be rich and full.

Kirsty had been so late getting back from Perth she'd had to set her alarm and was feeling bone-tired as she got up, not in the mood for arguments. But it gradually became obvious that something had deeply upset her remaining guest.

Tina got up early without needing to be called. She was polite but didn't smile once, and didn't initiate any conversation when normally she'd have been chattering away.

'What's wrong?' Kirsty asked after a few minutes of this.

'Nothing.'

'I'm not a fool, Tina. Tell me what's wrong.'

The girl hesitated, then said, 'I overheard what your brother was saying yesterday – about you and my dad. I thought you were helping me out of friendship for me, as well as him. But you weren't, were you? You were helping me because you fancy him, as a way of getting him into your bed. Using me!'

'I was not!'

'I don't believe you, so I'm moving out when I get back from work. If I have to sleep on the floor at Dad's place, I'll do it, because I'm not going to be used like that by anyone.' She glanced at her watch. 'If you don't mind, could we please leave now? I don't want to be late for work. I'm grateful for the lifts and sorry to trouble you for one this morning. I'll give you some petrol money before I leave.'

Kirsty closed her eyes for a moment, her head spinning with tiredness. She didn't need this. 'We'll talk tonight. But I won't accept petrol money from you under any circumstances.'

'It's only fair.'

'Tell me about it tonight.'

When she got back from the shops, Kirsty fed Taffy, cleared up a mess and once the puppy was asleep again, locked up carefully then took the pup's box into her bedroom with her. Even though it was full daylight, she didn't forget to put the alarm system on, leaving only her bedroom unarmed.

She woke with a shock some time later as the alarm began to scream. She didn't dare go outside to investigate, could only hope that Sam would respond to it.

To her relief, a couple of minutes later there was the sound of a car coming up the track and she waited till footsteps came along the veranda before leaving her room.

'Kirsty? Are you all right?'

She unlocked her bedroom door and hurried outside. Sam had already used the key she'd given him to come in through the kitchen door and switch off the alarm.

His eyes raked her from head to toe. 'You're all right?'

'Yes. I was asleep, but luckily I'd put the alarm on. Has he broken anything?'

'I don't think so. Let's check.'

The house was all right but one of the flyscreens had been ripped out of its channel in an attempt to get to the door lock. When they'd finished checking, Kirsty put the kettle on and made Sam a sandwich.

'Sorry about that. I hate to interrupt your painting.'

'I'd hate it even more if you got hurt.' He drank a mouthful, then put his mug down and looked at her. 'What happened between you and Tina? She rang to say she was moving back to my place tonight after work.'

'She overheard Rod saying something about you and me, and got it into her head that I'm only using her to get at you.'

'Oh.'

'I'm not. But Tina's very insecure about her relationship with you, so maybe it's for the best that you spend a day or two living together. I'll miss her, though. She's good company.'

'There is no me and you. There can't be at this stage of my life. I thought you understood that. I'll make sure Tina understands it too.'

Kirsty looked at him, suddenly tired of this refusal to face facts. 'There is something between us, however much you deny it. And it's your choice not to do anything about it, not mine.'

'Well, if you want to know the main sticking point, I'm not latching on to a rich woman. I don't want your money.'

'Who said I'd give it to you? Funny, isn't it? Rod was quite wrong about you. Rather than attracting your interest, my money is preventing you from even giving me a fair go.'

Sam was silent, then sighed. 'I'm sorry. Maybe it's the wrong time in my life as well. The painting is pretty consuming at the moment. Anyway, I have to take Tina up to Perth in a day or two. We'll talk after I get back. You'll be careful while I'm away? I'll let Franco know I'm going.'

She tried not to let her feelings show, because now was definitely the wrong time for a showdown. 'I'm always careful these days.'

He hesitated. 'I'm still worried about you being here on your own.'

Suddenly something inside her seemed to snap. 'Actually, I'm getting fed up to the teeth of that damned prowler. Maybe you should start worrying about him. I'm not putting up with this any longer. I'm sick and tired of being afraid, living behind closed doors and I'm going to do something about it.'

'Don't let that make you do anything rash.' There was silence for a moment or two, then he said, 'Tina's packed her things and I said I'd fetch them.'

'They'll be in her bedroom, I suppose.' Kirsty sighed. 'I wanted to talk to her tonight, try to persuade her she's wrong about why I've been helping her, but I suppose she's not in a mood to listen.'

'No, definitely not. And to add to the problems, I think she's started to get nervous about going back to live with her mother, not to mention the studying.'

He paused again on the way out, looking embarrassed. 'I'd like to thank you on Tina's behalf for your kindness. You've been wonderful to her.'

After Sam left, the day seemed to drag. Kirsty washed the bedding and towels from her two guests, annoyed that after the weeks of fine weather, it chose to rain just as she had several loads of washing to dry.

She thought of ringing Marlene for a chat, but didn't want to sound too miserable so decided to wait. She half expected to be woken during the night by the prowler, but she wasn't. That didn't mean she slept well, however.

When Kirsty drove down the lane the following morning, she was going shopping more to be with people than because she needed anything desperately. She drew to a halt at the end of Sam's drive. The place looked deserted. She'd heard his car earlier. He'd probably left already.

It was threatening rain again, so there'd be no worry about watering his garden, but he hadn't even asked her to keep an eye on his house.

Naturally she gravitated towards the gallery, staying for a coffee with Rhys, who looked at her thoughtfully but said nothing. What had Tina told him?

'Are you missing your assistant?'

'Yes, I am. She's really good with people, even the amateurs who try to get me to offer their paintings for sale. She picked out a couple who seem quite promising. That was sheer instinct. She must get that sensitivity from her father.'

'It's in the genes, I suppose.' Kirsty forced herself to talk cheerfully about the book she was reading and a film she wanted to see, then took her leave.

Back at the house, she checked carefully, but no one had broken in, nor had the threads of black sewing cotton that she'd placed strategically across parts of the veranda been disturbed. So the intruder couldn't have been prowling round today.

She didn't feel like decorating, didn't feel like doing anything, really, but she wasn't going to sit and feel sorry for herself, so she sorted through Ed's stuff that she'd taken out of the drawers in the room Rod used and piled anything useful ready to take to the charity shop.

Keep busy, that was the thing to do. And she'd go into town tomorrow and find something to join, a health club, or . . . something.

In Perth, Sam and Tina went to her mother's house. There were two cars outside and she looked at one in surprise.

'That's Darren's car. I'm not with him any more, so I can't understand why he'd come round. I doubt he'd want us to get back together. He made it pretty plain I was too young for him. And I didn't expect Mum to be back from work yet.' She tried the front door, but it was locked, so she took out her key. 'Mum hates having to answer the door. Come in, Dad. The least I can do is make you a cup of coffee and something to eat.'

Inside there was no sign of anyone in the lounge room, but there were sounds coming from her mother's bedroom, sounds that were quite unmistakably the sort made by two people making love.

Sam looked at Tina in consternation, watched as the realisation sank in of what Darren was doing in the house. He couldn't believe Lorraine had sunk so low she'd pinch her daughter's boyfriend. 'Should we slip away and come back later?' He saw tears well and pulled her into his arms. 'Oh, darling.'

Tina leaned against him for a minute or two, then smeared the trails of moisture away with the back of one hand and said in a low voice, 'I can't come back to live here, Dad. Not now. I'll leave university and get a job, finish studying part-time.'

'You'll finish the course now. I'll pay for a flat for you.'

'You've not got enough money.'

'I didn't have, but Ed left me some, certainly enough to pay for a flat for a few months, though I'd be grateful if you'd go carefully with your spending.'

'Are you sure?' She hugged him. 'Thank you. You're the best dad ever.'

At that moment Lorraine came out of her bedroom, stark naked. She looked at Tina. 'Oh, hell!'

'Go and pack,' Sam told his daughter.

Ignoring her mother she ran along the corridor to her room.

Lorraine fumbled inside the door and tugged a dressing gown round herself, scowling at Sam. 'This could have been avoided if you'd let me know you were bringing her back today.'

Trust her to put blame on him. Nothing was ever her fault. 'You disgust me. I thought you'd reached rock bottom when you ruined my painting, but this is another level of nastiness. I'll wait here while Tina packs in case she needs me. She's moving out and I'm going to find her a flat.'

'Suit yourself. I knew you'd been lying and you had some money tucked away. It'll be nice not to have the expense of keeping her, I must admit, not to mention having the house to myself. I'm too young to be celibate.' She stretched lazily, letting the front of her dressing gown slip open deliberately.

Her lean, well-toned body had once pleased Sam, now it disgusted him, the flesh too hard and tanned, more like a man's. He liked softer women, with shoulder-length hair, not a short, spiky crop like Lorraine's. Folding his arms, he ignored her. From down the corridor came the sound of drawers and cupboard doors slamming – and a girl sobbing.

'She's too soft for her own good,' Lorraine muttered.

He didn't bother to argue.

Darren came to stand by the door of her bedroom, a towel wrapped round his lower body. 'You all right, Lorraine?'

'Yes, darling. But I think it'd be more . . . tactful if we waited in my bedroom till they've left.'

Sam helped pack all Tina's gear into his car. 'Don't cry!' he said as he saw tears roll down her cheeks. 'We've got too much to do today. He's not worth it anyway.'

She nodded and blew her nose vigorously. 'It's her I'm upset about most.'

They went flat hunting. There wasn't much to choose from and places were horrendously expensive, rents having risen a lot lately. Eventually they found a furnished unit with two bedrooms that she could move into the next day.

'I'll put up a notice and get someone to share with me, then it won't cost you as much, Dad.'

'You're going to be all right?'

'I was over Darren, really. But it's humiliating, Dad, that's the worst thing about it. Mum always makes you feel a failure if you haven't got a guy, says you can pull anyone if you really want to and now she's pulled mine. He's a bit young for her, though, isn't he?'

'Yes. Far too young.'

'I used to dream you two had got back together again. Now, I'm really glad you didn't.' She tried to force a smile, but it wasn't very successful. 'I'm going to study really hard, no partying at all, for the rest of the year. I'm not a shoe-in for a pass, but I'll do my very best, Dad, I promise.'

'That's all anyone can expect from you. And let me know when you need more money.'

'I'll try not to.'

After that they hit the op shops where they could buy her second-hand crockery and other items for the flat very cheaply. It turned out to be fun as well as benefiting the various charities who ran the shops.

That night they found a cheap Chinese restaurant, but Tina fiddled with her food so much he said, 'What's bugging you?'

'You aren't going back to make it up with her, are you?'

'Kirsty? That's my business, don't you think?'

'I thought she really liked me.'

'She did – does.'

Tina shook her head. 'It was you she was after. She was just using me.'

'She wasn't. Kirsty's not like that.'

'Dad, you're so naïve about women. Of course she was.'

'Why would a rich woman like her go to that length to chase after a poor guy like me?'

'Because she's got the hots for you. You're not bad looking, for a wrinklie.'

He put one fingertip to his daughter's lips. 'End of discussion. When you've calmed down, you'll realise how wrong you are about Kirsty. Now, I've got an early start in the morning, so let's go back to the hotel. We'll get the waiter to pack up what's left of this meal and you can take it to your new flat for your dinner tomorrow.'

'First lesson in frugality,' she joked. 'Before, I'd have thrown it away.'

When Sam dropped his daughter off the following morning, she gave him a big hug and didn't seem to want to let go. 'You will come and visit me sometimes, Dad?'

'If I'm up in Perth, I definitely will. I can't afford to come up often, but that doesn't mean I don't care about you. I'll phone regularly and of course you're welcome to spend the next holidays with me. In fact, let's agree to do that, eh? In the meantime, work hard and take care of yourself.'

He hesitated and turned back. 'Do you think you'll have any trouble with your mother?'

'No. I'm not giving her my address, so how can she find me? As if she'd want to anyway! And I'm still too angry to go near her.'

'With reason.' He glanced at his watch. 'Now, I really must go. I have an important meeting scheduled.' He kissed his daughter's cheek, gave her a quick hug and left.

He hoped this wouldn't scar Tina too badly.

It might even make her grow up a little.

Lara was waiting for him at her luxurious, ultra-modern house, which always looked like a pile of white boxes haphazardly thrown together to Sam, though it had won an architectural award. He carried the painting inside and stood it on the kitchen bench as she indicated, before uncovering it. She was going to have it framed herself, luckily, which would save him some money and effort.

She stood and considered the beautiful, glowing banksia flowers, not saying a word. He waited, confident that it was good. If she didn't like it, Rhys would easily be able to sell this one for him.

'Gorgeous,' she said at last.

'So you want it?'

'Yes. How much do you charge for paintings like these, Sam?'

'The gallery charges about three to five hundred dollars, depending on size. I have to pay them thirty per cent of that.'

'They're not charging nearly enough. We'll start at a thousand from now on for one this size, and the gallery must do the same if it wants to continue selling your work. But after they've sold the ones they've got, you're to consult me about what you do with any others.'

'I don't think I can afford to tell Rhys that yet.' He saw her expression tighten and added hastily, 'Look, Lara, the truth is, I'm a bit short of money at the moment.'

'I thought that old man you were friendly with left you enough to live on for a year.'

'There's been a family crisis – yesterday in fact. My daughter's had to move out from her mother's, so I'm paying for a flat till she's finished her studies. This is her last year and I don't want anything to rock the boat.' To his relief Lara didn't ask what had happened.

'You're too soft for your own good, Sam. Tell the gallery to up its prices a bit, but we won't insist on a thousand dollars this time. I'll be charging you thirty per cent on all sales I make, too. As for the corporate pieces, we'll be charging several thousand dollars for each of those, I haven't decided exactly how much yet.' She laughed at his expression of shock and her voice softened. 'You're good, Sam. Really good. Or I'd not be acting as your agent.'

He looked at her, not speaking, trying not to grin like an idiot, then he said simply, 'I'm glad'.

'Now, you must let me pay you for this gorgeous painting.'

'No. I said it would be a gift and I meant it.'

'But Sam—'

'No. And I'll send up another for your charity bash once it's finished.'

'Thank you. But you must let me frame that one as well. I'm rather good with frames.'

He'd passed some paintings in the hall and went back to study them. She followed quietly, not interrupting him.

'Did you choose these frames?'

'Yes, of course. I oversaw every detail of my house. It matters to me.'

'You've got a brilliant eye for what's right. I'm happy to leave my paintings in your hands.'

'Thank you.' She couldn't conceal her pleasure at this compliment.

They settled down for a business discussion about her plans then she fed him a lunch which was as beautiful and minimalist as her house, before sending him on his way. He still felt a bit hungry.

He smiled as he drove, remembering the way she'd said simply, 'Gorgeous', when she saw his painting. This was a high compliment from Lara, who was a hard-headed businesswoman and offered praise sparingly. She was very suitable as a corporate wife for Geoff, but was still doing her own thing part-time and he'd guess that even so she made a good living in her own right. She and Geoff exuded affluence.

Before he left Perth, Sam went to a supplier he particularly liked and bought the biggest canvases he could fit into his vehicle, together with a lot more art materials, arranging for three even larger canvases to be delivered to him.

He was glad to leave the city behind. He'd come back to Perth again whenever Lara wanted him to appear at functions or meet people, and make sure he saw Tina every time. But until then he had a lot of work to do, getting together a collection of paintings and doing a couple more of the huge corporate ones.

If they really did bring in a few thousand each, life would be so much easier. Maybe then . . . He allowed himself to daydream for a few moments about Kirsty's soft body and gentle smile. Unfortunately that made him worry about how she was coping on her own and whether the intruder had bothered her again. He felt he'd left her in the lurch.

He swiped the air with one hand, trying to dismiss that thought, but it still hovered at the edges of his mind. There seemed to be so many balls in the air. Could he risk dropping one at such a crucial stage of his life, not only his painting and all that went with it, but his daughter's love and need for support?

He knew Kirsty wasn't like Lorraine and surely wouldn't be so demanding, but how could you ever tell for sure? And it still stuck in his gullet that she was rich. He didn't want to be the poor husband of a wealthy wife.

Wife! Where did that come from?

'No way!' he said aloud. 'You were wrong about that, Ed.'

Chapter Nineteen

Rod took the first available flight back to England and arrived on a grey April afternoon, with a chill wind whistling round his ears.

By the time he got out of the airport, it was evening and the streets were quiet. He studied them with pleasure, happier than he'd expected at being back home in England again.

As the taxi turned the final corner, he saw a man standing in the doorway of the little shop, staying half-hidden while starring down the street. The shop was closed, so it seemed a strange thing for anyone to do.

Rod forgot that, however, in his delight at seeing his house. He was even happier when he saw that the coloured glass panels in the top of the door were it up. The light was coming down the hallway from the kitchen and that meant Linnie was there, Linnie and the boys. He hadn't realised how lonely he was until Kirsty came to live with him and now, he hated living alone. But he wouldn't be alone tonight.

Pulling the key from his pocket, he tried to open the door, but something prevented it from moving more than a crack. He peered at the gap and scowled as he saw a chain stretched across it. His door hadn't had one of those safety chains on it when he left. Linnie's ex must have been bothering her again. This had to stop.

He rang the doorbell, saw an indistinct figure through the coloured glass panels and waited for her to open the door.

Instead she came along the hall and stopped a couple of paces away, calling in a voice quavering with fear, 'Go away, Glen! Don't make me have to call the police again.'

'It's me, Rod.'

Silence, then she peered through the gap, let out an audible sigh of relief and reached up to unlock the chain.

She looked over his shoulder as she pulled him inside, shutting the door quickly, not only locking it but sliding the security chain back into its socket. She had dark circles under her eyes and looked exhausted.

'You look awful, Linnie. What's been happening?'

'Come and have a cup of tea first. Are you hungry? I'll—'

He put out one hand to stop her walking away from him and she flinched. 'I'm not going to hurt you.' He saw tears in her eyes, didn't like that, so pulled her into his arms. He'd seen people hug one another when they needed comforting and holding Linnie felt to be the right thing to do now. He loved the soft feel of her.

She shuddered and pressed herself against him, weeping quietly. He dared to stroke her hair, such lovely curly hair she had, then heard the boys come to the doorway of the kitchen at the other end of the hall so half-turned. Tommy had the rolling pin in his hand.

'Go and sit down again,' he told them. 'Your mother and I need to have a talk.'

'Yes, you do that, boys.' Her voice was husky. 'You know I'll be all right with Rod.'

He guided her into the front room and she sat on the couch. He was going to sit on a chair opposite, but she pulled him down beside her, keeping hold of his hand, tears still rolling down her cheeks.

Greatly daring, he took her into his arms again. She didn't pull away. He hoped desperately he wouldn't make a mess of this.

The important thing was to find out the facts, he decided after holding her for a minute or two. You were much safer if you knew what was going on. 'Stop crying and tell me exactly what he's been doing or I can't help you.' He fumbled in his pocket and found a handkerchief, which he shook out and pressed it into Linnie's hand. Fabric handkerchiefs were old-fashioned, Kirsty had often told him, but he didn't like the feel of paper ones.

Linnie blew her nose and wiped her eyes, keeping hold of the handkerchief as she cuddled up to him again.

How small and warm she felt against him! It was a moment before he got back on track. 'Tell me.'

Haltingly she explained about Glen, how the police said if her ex annoyed her again, they'd arrest him and keep him locked up. Only, every time she called them, he slipped away before they could catch him.

After she'd finished speaking, Rod sat thinking hard, wondering now if the man at the end of the street had been her ex.

He was amazed that this was happening to her as well as to his sister. He didn't understand a lot of things people did, but normal people didn't usually hurt one another, he knew that. So men who did this sort of thing were warped in a nasty way. Kirsty seemed to be coping much better with her problems than Linnie, though.

In the end he decided on one thing. 'If he comes when I'm here, I'll thump him.'

Linnie tried to smile, but her face was all wobbly. 'I don't think you're the macho type, Rod, even though you're quite a big man.'

'Is your ex a big man?'

'No. But he's strong and wiry, and he fights dirty.'

'Well, I'm still going to thump him if he upsets you. I don't like it when you cry.' Something occurred to him. 'You are legally divorced from him, aren't you?'

'Yes, of course.'

'That's good. I think you'd better marry me, then I can look after you and the boys properly.'

Her mouth fell open and she didn't seem able to speak, which worried him. Had it been the wrong thing to say? He watched her anxiously, not at all sure what to say or do next.

'You don't mean it.'

'I do. I don't like living alone. Kirsty doesn't want me. And I enjoy being with you.'

She smiled but still looked sad. 'People usually marry because they love one another, Rod.'

'I don't understand about love. I don't understand a lot of what people do and feel.' He took a deep breath and told her his secret. 'The doctors say I have a communication disorder. I'm always saying the wrong thing to people. But I did mean it when I asked you to marry me, Linnie. I really, really like being with you. And I like the boys, too. I like showing them the computer and – and seeing them eat a good hearty meal.'

'I didn't realise you had this problem. I thought you'd never married because you didn't – um, like women.'

It took him a minute or two to work out what she meant. 'I'm not gay. I'm just not good with people, men or women. You must have noticed that.'

She smiled. 'Yes. But I've also noticed that your heart is in the right place and you're kind.'

He reached out to tuck a strand of hair behind her ear. 'Well then, perhaps you could consider marrying me.'

'But if you don't love me—'

She broke off and chuckled suddenly, reaching up to trace one finger across his forehead. 'You're scrunching up your face again.'

He was going to brush her finger away but then decided he liked her touching him. 'I can't help it when I'm thinking hard. It's very important to get this right, you see.'

'Why is it important, Rod?'

Her voice was gentle and she didn't seem angry. 'Because . . . it's what I want most in the world.'

'Now you've got me puzzled. I don't know what to say – and that's not like me. I usually say too much.'

He smiled at that. 'Maybe you've got all the words I can't find.' Then he yawned. 'Sorry. I didn't sleep much on the plane. I'd better go to bed, I think.' He stood up, but she didn't move so he stopped to study her anxiously. 'I haven't upset you?'

'No. You've paid me a very big compliment and you've given me a lot to think about.'

'Oh. Well, that's all right, then. I'll see you in the morning. Wake me up before you go and I'll make sure you get off to work safely.'

Linnie watched him leave, then sank down on the couch again. He was such a strange man, but nice. Well, he was always nice to her and the boys. He did say some surprising things, though, just came right out with them. Now she understood why, it made her feel protective about him. She smiled. What a way to propose!

She wondered if he had any other friends apart from her and his sisters. She'd seen no sign of it while he was on crutches. If she hadn't been here, she didn't know how he'd have managed.

Kirsty must have sent him home early from Australia. Well, it'd been silly to go there unannounced.

Marry him! Fancy him asking her that.

It had been quite touching, really. Poor lamb, he did struggle with people. She enjoyed his company, though. He was a clever man in his own way and he'd really helped Tommy. Rod didn't mean to be rude when he said exactly what he was thinking, she understood that. And after all those years with her lying ex, she much preferred a man like him.

Enough to marry him?

As if she'd take advantage of him like that. She wasn't educated and she had the boys. Only, they liked him too, for some reason. Strange, that.

She looked round. If she did marry him, she'd have to change the house a bit. It was so dreary inside.

No, what was she thinking of?

If there was one thing she was certain of, it was that he'd meant his proposal. It wasn't in Rod to tell anything but the truth.

Lost in thought, she went back to the kitchen to see to the boys. But she couldn't sort things out in her mind. Like a lot of people with an unhappy experience, she'd sworn she'd never marry again. And she'd meant it.

Only, she really liked Rod. And trusted him. Felt safe with him.

Kirsty found an advert in the library about a reading group starting up. She'd dealt with a lot of these groups over the years, but from the other side. Rashly, she put her name down and went to buy the book they were to read before the first meeting.

It was a heavy literary novel and she didn't like it from the word go. Weird characters and a plot that seemed to consist mainly of them agonising about life or arguing with one another. When she couldn't stand another turgid page, she turned to a romance she'd bought at the same time, delighted to meet more normal people and to be sure it'd have a happy ending that would leave her feeling good.

But that only emphasised her own lack of a happy ending. Sometimes you couldn't win.

What do you think I should do, Ed? she wondered that evening. But there wasn't even a hint of an answer in her head.

Sam popped in to see her a couple of times, just to check that everything was all right, that there'd been no sign of the intruder, that her reticulation system was working properly. The latter seemed a rather lame excuse for a visit and she took a little comfort from it.

The trouble was, he spent most of each visit standing several paces away from her, and each time refused a cup of coffee and piece of cake, though normally he'd have jumped at the offer, because he was a sucker for home-made cakes.

She went to see Penny. 'I'm a bit worried about Sam and . . .'

Penny held up one hand. 'He made me promise not to discuss your relationship with him.'

'Oh.' What relationship?

'You'll have to work it out between you.' She grinned. 'I wish you luck, though. Apart from the fact that he's working long hours at the moment and is deep down tired, Sam can be just a tad stubborn when he's settled something in his own mind.'

Kirsty couldn't return the smile. 'Tell me about it. I'm going to need all the luck I can get. His stupid pride is such a barrier.'

'Well, I am going to say one thing: I'm on your side. You go for it, girl.'

All very well for Penny to say that. How did you persuade a man that money didn't matter? And from things he'd said, she suspected Sam had no idea how much Ed had left her. He'd throw an even bigger fit when he found out.

She walked slowly home, warmed by the greeting Taffy gave her until she realised that several of her threads of cotton across the veranda had vanished. That meant someone had been walking round her house, even if they hadn't tried to break in. Shivering, she went inside and locked the door. She hated living like this, shut in like a prisoner, was getting very angry about it – and about a lot of other things too.

But what could she actually do about any of them?

The following evening Kirsty let Taffy out for a run in the fenced part of the garden. When she went to call her back, the pup didn't come. Kirsty walked the perimeter and found a hole in the fence, not a big one, but big enough for a small body to push through. The hole looked as if it'd been made recently and the ends of the wires seemed to have been cut. No dog could have done that, not with such thick wire and a newish fence. If the intruder had done it – she pushed that thought aside. She'd deal with that later. The main thing now was to find Taffy.

She called again, but still there was no answer. Nearby in the bush, a mob of kangaroos was grazing peacefully, one with a joey standing next to it. At the sight of her, the little creature jumped head first into its mother's pouch, its limbs folding up like little bundles of sticks.

But though she checked the whole garden, there was no sign of the pup. She didn't think she could bear it if anything happened to Taffy. She'd grown to love the little dog so quickly.

She phoned Penny but there was no answer.

She put the phone down, picked it up, then put it down again. 'Oh, heavens, don't be a fool!' she told herself and dialled Sam's number, getting only his voicemail.

'Sam, I've lost Taffy.' Her voice wobbled and she had to pause for a moment to calm herself. 'I wondered if you'd seen her.'

She put the phone down and did another tour of the garden, then set off down the lane, calling to the little dog as she went. She stopped by the rows of vines, able to see between them at this time of year, and got right to the road before she found Taffy, who was lying on the dusty verge, very still and covered with blood. With a sob she rushed forward to kneel by the puppy.

When she saw that Taffy was still breathing, she couldn't hold back a groan of sheer relief.

Footsteps crunched along the gravelled edge of the road behind her.

Kirsty looked round, relief shuddering through her at the sight of Sam.

'I heard you calling out and saw you going past. Is she alive?'

'Just. She's been hit by a car, I think. Can you take us to a vet?'

'Of course. I'll get my car.' He ran off up the track and when he came back with the vehicle, jumped out with an old blanket. 'Get in and hold that on your lap. I'll pick her up and give her to you.'

A minute later they were driving along the main road, with Kirsty holding the precious bundle, tears dripping down her face.

'Is she still breathing?' he asked as they stopped at a junction.

'Yes.'

'Then there's hope. I don't think the car could have run right over her. She's too small to survive that.'

'Mmm. Is it far to the vet's?'

'A few more minutes.'

It seemed more like a few hours, but at last they got there and carried the little animal into the surgery. As Taffy was taken away, reaction set in and Kirsty suddenly felt shaky.

Sam's arm went round her. 'Come and sit down. It must have been a dreadful shock to find her like that.'

He guided her to a chair and sat beside her, his arm still round her shoulders. It felt so right. When she looked up, his expression was tender and concerned. 'You're a kind man underneath that sharp talk.'

'I told you before. In the country, neighbours help one another.' When the tears stopped flowing, he drew his arm away and pointed. 'There's a coffee machine. Would you like a cup?'

'Yes, please.' She watched him stride across the room, his long, rangy body easy in his shabby clothes. Another woman was looking at him in open admiration and Kirsty experienced a twinge of jealously and a very strong desire to tell the woman he was taken.

That's when she realised how much she had grown to love Sam Brady. Truly love him.

He turned and their eyes met across the room. She couldn't help smiling at him. He smiled back, then suddenly his smile faded and he pressed his lips together as if holding something tightly inside him.

The old Kirsty would have given up. The new Kirsty decided to do something about this once Taffy was all right.

His face was expressionless as he handed her the plastic cup. They might have been strangers. He went back to get one for himself then left a chair empty between them as he sat down again.

Oh, no, Sam Brady! Kirsty thought. You're not getting away with it. Your stupid pride isn't going to stand between us. I lost my happiness once, and there was nothing I could do to bring Mike back, but you're not dead, just stubborn. This time I'm going to fight for what we could have. I don't know yet what I'm going to do but I'll think of something.

The young veterinary nurse called to them. 'Could you come through, please, Mrs Miller?'

Kirsty stood up. Sam stayed where he was.

'Please come with me,' she begged, suddenly terrified it was going to be bad news.

He got up, but made sure he didn't get too close to her as they walked.

The vet smiled at them. 'It's not as bad as it could have been, Mrs Miller. We need to operate on your dog, however. She has a broken leg and we may need to pin it. It won't be cheap, I'm afraid.'

'The money doesn't matter,' Kirsty said at once. But that response brought a deepening of the scowl on Sam's face. Nothing she said seemed to suit him today.

'You may as well go home, then, and leave her to us, Mrs Miller. Ring about seven tonight and we'll tell you how she is.'

They drove home in silence. Kirsty suddenly remembered the hole in the fence and told him about it. When they got back she took him to see it.

'Made deliberately, and recently too. If I get my hands on that—'

'Join the queue. I'm first in line.'

They walked back to the house.

'Will you be all right?' he asked in a cool tone as they reached it.

'Of course. Thanks for your help today, Sam.' Then she remembered. 'Oh, no! I didn't lock up.'

He turned back again. 'I'd better come in and check that everything's all right.'

It wasn't. Her newly painted hall had the words GO BACK TO ENGLAND painted in huge letters along the wall. Her make-up was ground into the bathroom floor. Her clothes were scattered all over the bedroom.

'Stand at your bedroom door and I'll check the rooms further along the hallway,' Sam said.

Something inside her snapped. 'No, you stand there and I'll check. I'll feel better if I do it myself, and after all, it is my house.' Anger fuelled her as she searched every walk-in cupboard and wardrobe, even peering under one high, old-fashioned bed.

When she got back to Sam, she said crisply, 'Stay at the corner of the hall and I'll check the rest of the house.'

'Yell if you need me.'

But she didn't. The intruder had been and gone. He seemed to have a second sense about when they were coming back.

'I'd expected you to be more afraid.' Sam gave her a puzzled glance sideways.

'I'm beyond that. What I am now is angry, very angry indeed. If that man ever comes near me, he's in for trouble.'

'Don't do anything rash.'

'Why not? I've been careful all my life and what good did that do me?' She marched to the front door and held it open. 'Thank you for your help. I'll be fine now.'

Later, when Kirsty rang the vet's, they told her Taffy was recovering well from the operation. Returning to the kitchen, she poured herself a glass of Ed's wine and raised it in a silent toast to her dog's recovery.

She suddenly remembered her old friend's other comment. She went to find his letter. Yes, there it was.

> But dear Kirsty, if you've the courage to go to Australia, I'm sure you'll also have the courage to deal with Sam should things turn out as I expect between you.

The Kirsty functioning in safe mode wouldn't have had the courage, but the new one might, once she'd figured out what to do.

On that thought she went to bed and slept more soundly than she had for a long time.

The following morning Kirsty checked again with the vet, delighted that Taffy was doing well and could come home later that afternoon. After that she went shopping. She indulged herself in a few books and a new dress, one which showed her figure to good advantage. Her reflection made her realise that the more active life she'd been leading since coming to Australia had tightened her muscles. She looked good, really good, even if she did say so herself.

On the way back to the car she popped into the art gallery and found herself face to face with a huge canvas covered in flowers in hot pinks and reds, a surrealist jungle that seemed as full of joy as of flowers. She didn't need to be told the artist's name. Sam's work was entirely his own. She hadn't seen this one before, though.

Rhys came up to her. 'It's beautiful, isn't it? He's had it for a while, apparently. Don't know why he didn't give it to me before.'

'How much is it? You haven't got a price on it.'

He grimaced. 'Didn't want to scare away the punters. It's a thousand dollars. His new manager has insisted we put up the prices. She could be right.'

Kirsty bought it without hesitation because it spoke to her, reinforcing the fact that life was to be enjoyed, not feared.

She paid extra for them to deliver the painting later that afternoon, because she wanted it as soon as she could. Then she went on to the police station to consult them about buying herself a pepper spray in self-defence, only they called it OC, not pepper spray.

The same detective who'd come to inspect her house after the first break-in saw her standing at the desk and came across to speak to her.

She explained about recent events and he scolded her for not keeping them informed. After that, he gave her a lecture about when it would be reasonable to use the spray. 'I think in your case we can invoke Regulation 7(2) and let you have one, as you'd be using the OC for lawful defence of your own person.'

She sagged against the counter in relief.

She had to drive to the nearby city of Bunbury to buy a can of the spray, but it was well worth it. She felt better already for having it to hand. She'd never want to use a gun, but she was quite comfortable with the idea of inflicting a little pain on her intruder. He was in for a big surprise if he came near her again. She had had e-nough.

She got back in time to pick up poor little Taffy and take her home.

Once she'd fed the dog, rearranged the living room and taken delivery of her painting she was exhausted.

'Tomorrow,' she told her reflection. 'I'll dress up like a movie star and then . . .'

Then she would confront Sam.

The next morning Sam received an early phone call.

'Sam? Lara here. Can you get up to Perth this afternoon and come to dinner tonight? The chairman's noticed your painting in the foyer and wants to talk to you about it, so I'm arranging a little gathering.'

'I suppose I could.'

'Don't get all enthusiastic. I'm not doing this for me, you know.'

'Sorry, Lara. I am grateful, truly, and of course I'll be there.'

'Where will you be staying?'

'Nowhere. I'll drive straight home afterwards.'

She clicked her tongue in exasperation. 'Money saving again?'

'Yes.' He'd just had a couple of bills to pay for Tina and didn't intend to waste money on hotel rooms.

'You'd better stay with us, then. I want to take you to lunch with a couple of people tomorrow. You do have some decent clothes, don't you? Very smart for the dinner party and smart casual for the lunch.'

What was he, an artist or a clothes hanger? He bit back an impatient response. 'All right.'

'Good. See you just before seven.'

He put the phone down and went hunting among the boxes stacked in a lean-to shed for lack of proper storage space, finding a suit, a pair of casual slacks and a couple of shirts. They all needed pressing, of course. He hated ironing, but this was too important, so he got out the necessary equipment out and set to work. Afterwards he tried the clothes on, just to be sure they still fitted. They were a little loose, but not too bad. He grimaced at his reflection. How he'd agonised over his appearance in the old days. How little he cared now.

'Sam? Are you there?'

'Penny. Come in.'

She stopped dead in the doorway, letting out a peal of laughter. 'I wish I had my camera. I've never seen you smartly dressed before. You look so . . . well, not you any more.'

He pretended to take a huff, then grinned at her. 'I can dress smartly when I want to. Look, I'm going up to Perth this afternoon. I'll have to switch Kirsty's security system over to Franco. Is that all right?'

'Yes, of course. What's up? Tina's OK, isn't she?'

'Yes. It's business I'm going for, to do with my paintings.'

'I thought Rhys handled that sort of thing.'

'These are the bigger ones, corporate art for foyers. I've got myself an agent in Perth.'

'Sounds impressive.'

'She is impressive. It's a nuisance having to go up there, but necessary.'

'Has this woman sold your big one, then?'

'Not yet, but I'm hoping she will soon. She's going to ask a fat chunk of money for it.'

'Good luck, then.'

It was still early and he didn't want to wake Kirsty, so he walked up to Whitegums to leave a note stuck on her front door, saying where he was going. He was on the road an hour later.

Chapter Twenty

Rod was woken by someone shaking his shoulder. He jerked awake and saw Linnie standing beside the bed with a cup of tea in her hand.

'Sorry to wake you, love, but you said you'd see us off safely this morning.'

'Yes. Thank you.' He sat up, took the tea and sipped it gratefully.

'How did you sleep?'

'Really well.' He took another sip, wondering why her tea always tasted nicer than other people's. He reached for his glasses. 'What time is it? Oh. I'd meant to wake up sooner.'

'We've half an hour before we have to go. Do you want me to make you some breakfast?'

'No. I'll get a proper meal after I come home.'

He went down to find the kitchen warm and full of light. Then he realised why. 'It looks better with the blind fully up like that.'

'I hope you don't mind.'

'Not at all.' It was lovely to come down and have people to talk to. He smiled at the boys, who were eating bowls of cereal.

Linnie finished wiping a plate she'd just rinsed. 'Hurry up, boys.'

When they'd gone up to get their school things, Rod asked, 'Will you be coming home for lunch?'

She hesitated. 'Won't you want a bit of peace?'

'No.'

'All right, then.'

'Good. I'll drive my car behind yours, make sure he's not following you.'

He watched the boys go into their school, followed Linnie to her first job, saw her safely inside then went home again. He thought he saw the man who'd been watching the house nip into the corner shop as he turned into the street, but wasn't sure so he went up to the bedroom and watched. A few minutes later he saw the man walking along the street, hands in pockets, shoulders hunched, and it was definitely the same one.

Rod was worried about Linnie's safety. He'd learned to defend himself when he was at school – he'd had to because of being different – but that was a long time ago. Would he still remember enough to get the better of this Glen person?

He must. He wasn't letting someone hurt her. He sat down to make a few plans, just in case. When he was at school he'd always done that, had plans ready for every eventuality, in case someone tried to bully or hurt him. He still made plans sometimes for dealing with things at work, but they didn't seem to work very well.

Sam arrived in Perth a little before the agreed time and parked near the river till it was just before seven o'clock.

He was quite sure Lara wouldn't want him arriving early and Geoff would only just be getting home from work.

When he thought about it, Sam wasn't looking forward to meeting the chairman again. Malcolm Foster had made a big fuss when he'd given notice and hadn't been happy to lose someone so experienced. Sam hadn't missed working for the company at all. Smiling wryly, he parked and walked up to the double front doors of the huge white house with river views.

Lara opened the door. 'Ah, there you are.' She scanned him from head to toe and pulled a face. 'You did bring some decent clothes for tonight, I hope?'

'Yes. But I didn't want to drive up in them or they'd have been crumpled.'

'Very sensible. Bring them in and get changed quickly. I want to have a chat before they arrive.'

'Who's coming?'

'The Fosters and the Versteegans, with Maura from personnel to make up the numbers.'

'Should make for a docile group.'

She grabbed his arm. 'I hope you're not going to make comments like that in public, because if so, I'm not representing you.'

He'd forgotten how lacking a sense of humour she was. 'Just joking, between you and me.'

'Don't do it again. You never know who might be listening. This is your room, your en suite is through that door.'

'Elegant décor. I like the touches of burgundy.' In that, at least, he could be sincere. She had impeccable taste.

She smiled. 'It has come out rather well, hasn't it? Now, put those clothes down on the bed and listen to me.'

He did as ordered and waited.

'No discussing finance tonight or at any time. Refer all that sort of thing to me.'

'What am I here for, then?'

'The chairman wants to see the painting you did for me. It's perfect in that room, by the way. And it's simply good tactics to have you here as well. There's nothing like the personal touch.'

'I've been looking forward to seeing the painting in situ.'

'You can see it after you've showered and changed.' She looked at her watch. 'Must just check that the caterers are on the ball. Come downstairs as soon as you can. People are arriving at eight.'

The evening passed in a blur. From somewhere, Sam dredged up his former conversational skills. The fact that he still had paint on the outside of one wrist seemed to amuse them all. He always had streaks of paint somewhere and didn't care, couldn't be bothered to inspect himself in a mirror every time he took a shower. He bore the teasing with resignation and humour. That was easy enough. Not being a company slave any more made him feel rather relaxed, while all the others were clearly on their toes, watching the chairman covertly, choosing their words carefully. He remembered those days.

His painting of the banksias dominated the living room and he was secretly impressed by how good it looked there.

Of course the chairman cornered him at one stage and everyone else moved away and started chatting earnestly.

'Not regretting your move, Brady?'

'No, sir. I needed to paint.'

'Damned good, that painting you've loaned us.'

'Thank you. I thought of the company first, of course.'

'Good, good. How much do you want for it?'

'Ask Lara. She's my agent now.'

The chairman pulled a face. 'She'll charge me twice as much as you would.'

'I don't think so. I'm well aware of what people pay for corporate art. And that one turned out particularly well.'

'It's generated a lot of interest. People seem to like it.'

He couldn't help asking, 'Do you like it, sir?'

Foster pursed his lips, then nodded. 'Yes. Cheers you up. I hated that miserable daub they had there before. They told me it was the in thing, but it didn't appeal. And no one ever commented on it. Had some Japanese visitors the other day and they stopped to look at your painting, stood there for a damned long time, actually.'

'I'm pleased.'

'Always paint flowers, do you?'

'Yes. I love them.'

The chairman nodded. 'The wife wants a painting for our house. Can you do one for us?'

'Of course.' He didn't want to, but he knew better than to refuse.

Lara came across to join them, slid her arm into Sam's and smiled at the chairman. 'He hasn't really got the time to do you a painting, because I have a contract pending for another corporate piece. However, I'll see he gives you priority, for old times' sake, Malcolm. We must ask your wife about colour schemes. Maybe I can drive Sam round in the morning before he goes back to his rural retreat? And now, if you'd like to come and sit down, we'll serve the meal.'

Nothing else was said about money or commissions, but before Sam went to bed, Lara told him to be ready for a quick trip out at eight o'clock in the morning. 'Prue Foster has an appointment at nine, but she's very keen to be one of the first to buy a Brady painting. We'll come back here afterwards and talk business, then do lunch with these other people who may be useful to us. You didn't talk about prices to anyone tonight, did you?'

'No, Lara. I'm more than happy to leave that side of things to you.' He wished he could leave the socialising to her, too, but he knew how important it was to be seen, especially when your appearances were rare.

Just before lunch Kirsty put on the new dress, let herself out of the back door and sauntered down the lane to Sam's house, determined to speak her mind about the way he wasn't even giving their relationship a chance.

His car was missing and everything was locked up. She could have wept in frustration and disappointment.

She walked slowly home and only then did she see the note he'd stuck to the front door. If they had letter boxes in front doors in Australia instead of at the street edges of their gardens, she'd have seen it before. With a sigh for her bad timing, she read it then changed out of the dress, choosing a pair of shorts with a pocket in which to carry pepper spray before she went to sit out on her veranda. She was unable to settle to reading, however, still struggling with the miserable story the book club had decreed everyone should read.

In the end she tossed it aside and went to find something more enjoyable. She'd take her name off the book club list next time she went into town if this was typical of what they chose.

She went to fiddle with the computer and clear out another of Ed's cupboards. This one held old family photographs and to her delight they were all carefully labelled. She decided to go through them later and see if they'd help her finish putting together the family tree she was doing for him.

All evening she kept listening for the sound of a car on the track. But it didn't come. So Sam must be staying in Perth.

When Penny rang to see if she was all right, Kirsty asked, 'Do you know when Sam will be back? His note only said he had to nip up to Perth.'

'Tomorrow, I think.' Penny chuckled suddenly. 'He'd been ironing some clothes and trying them on. I nearly died laughing at the sight of him in a suit, though actually, he looked rather good except for his hair which needs a trim. He was really grumpy about having to get dressed up. I'd love to have taken a photo.'

'I can't imagine him in a suit.' After turning down an offer of a glass of wine at their house, Kirsty made herself a salad. Then she went into the living room, not switching on the television, but getting her book again. Only, she spent more time staring at the beautiful painting on the wall than reading and kept wondering what Sam was doing.

* * *

When it was time for Linnie to come home for lunch, Rod went to the window of the front room, where he was hidden behind some net curtains but had a clear view of the street. He saw her car draw up in a space halfway down the street, then stiffened as he saw another car draw up further down the street and recognised the man who got out.

Glen didn't rush forward but stood watching Linnie as she got some shopping bags out. When one fell and things spilled on to the pavement, Rod figured he'd have enough time for Plan 3. He snatched his mobile phone and ran out of the back door, intending to come up behind her ex and take him by surprise rather than confronting him head on. He remembered from his school days how useful surprise could be.

He ran along the narrow strip of waste ground between the two rows of back yards, coming out on to the street through the narrow passageway between numbers 15 and 17. To his relief, both Linnie and her ex had passed the end of this and were between it and his house now. Most important of all, Linnie was still all right. He stayed where he was, not wanting to give his presence away, then swung round as he heard footsteps behind him.

The old man walking down the little passageway towards him was a neighbour Rod knew by sight. He put one finger to his lips and said in a low voice, 'Could you please watch what's happening for a minute or two, Mr Pettins? My girlfriend's ex is stalking her and we have to prove it's him before he can be prosecuted.'

'Eh, there are some nasty beggers around these days. I'm happy to do that for you, lad, but I'd not be much good in a fight, so don't count on my help there.'

'I'll do the fighting if I have to.' Rod shoved his mobile phone into the man's hand. 'Do you know how these work? Good. Call the police if you think we need help.'

He didn't wait for a reply but went back to peep out down the street. Linnie was nearly at his front door and even as he watched, Glen ran forward, took hold of her arm and tried to pull her away. She shook him off, but he grabbed her again, shaking her violently.

Sorry he'd been delayed, Rod ran along the street, not bothering to hide now. Just as he got near, Linnie kicked her ex and he thumped her.

That made Rod see red. Rushing forward, he grabbed the man from behind, dragging him away from her and roaring, 'Stop that!'

Glen staggered backwards, recovered quickly then bunched up his right fist and let fly.

Rod kept light on his feet, swaying to the side so the fist missed him. He moved away from Linnie because he didn't want her getting hurt. Glen came at him again and Rod chose his moment carefully to step aside. Her ex, who smelled of booze, kept going, bumping into a lamppost, letting out a yelp of pain and grabbing it to steady himself.

'You just stay away from her from now on!' Rod shouted.

'She's mine and she's coming back to me!' Glen yelled back, raising both his fists.

'We've been divorced for years and I'm not yours.' Linnie moved forward to stand beside Rod. 'Why will you not accept that and leave me alone?'

'Stay back, Linnie love,' Rod ordered.

She hesitated and moved into the doorway again.

That distracted him for a moment and Glen managed to land a punch, then kicked him on the bad leg.

Furious, with pain stabbing through him, Rod picked the smaller man up and slammed him against the nearest car, quickly twisting his arm behind him. They did it on police shows all the time to stop people getting away. To his relief, it worked.

The old man was now hovering nearby and shouted, 'I've called the police, lad.'

Linnie called, 'Be careful, Rod.'

But he didn't need telling that. He was always careful. Keeping tight hold of the other man's arm, he waited for the police to come. He didn't know where his glasses were, didn't care, because he'd done what he wanted, which was to protect Linnie.

It seemed a long time until there was the sound of a siren in the distance. At the sound of that, Glen tried once more to get away, but cried out in pain and stopped moving as he hurt himself by pushing against the arm lock.

A car screeched to a halt and a policeman got out and ran up to them.

'Let him go now, sir.'

Rod did so, stepping quickly back.

'He attacked me!' Glen yelled. 'You saw it. Charge him with assault.'

One of the officers went to stand beside him, the other came up to Rod.

Linnie came to link her arm in Rod's, recognising the female officer. 'It's my ex again. He tried to drag me to his car, said he was taking me away from here. My boyfriend saved me.'

Mr Pettins came forward to join them. 'I was the one who called you. I saw it all. That one,' he pointed to Glen, 'attacked this lass and this chap came to her rescue.' He pointed at Rod.

But Rod was looking at Linnie, squinting because it was hard to see clearly without his glasses.

She held them out to him. 'Here you are, love. I don't think they're damaged. I picked them up so you wouldn't tread on them.'

He took them off her and put them on, studying her carefully. 'Are you all right? He didn't hurt you? He did! That's another bruise on your cheek. It wasn't there this morning.'

The female officer was listening and looked hard at Linnie. 'That's a new one since last time we met. Did your ex do it just now?'

Linnie touched it gently and winced. 'Is it a big one?'

'I'm afraid so.'

'Glen likes hitting me.'

'Do you want to press assault charges?'

Linnie nodded. 'Yes, I do.'

'How about you, sir?'

Rod nodded. 'Definitely.'

'Could you follow us down to the police station and give statements, then? All three of you, if possible.'

'Yes. Just as soon as I've locked my house up.' He looked at his neighbour. 'Do you want a lift down there with us, Mr Pettins?'

'Aye, lad.'

'We might as well go in my car,' Linnie said.

Her smile was so warm and beautiful that Rod couldn't stop smiling all the time he was locking his house up, or while she was driving them into town.

When she got out, she gave him a big hug. 'You saved me, Rod. I can't thank you enough.'

Words failed him totally, so he hugged her back. He really liked hugging her. It was much easier than saying fancy words.

It had all been very interesting, Rod thought as Linnie drove him and Mr Pettins home afterwards. Just like the TV police shows.

When they were alone in the house, he turned to Linnie. 'I still want to marry you. You'll be much safer with me.'

'Oh, Rod.' She gazed at him as if waiting for him to say something else.

He frowned, wondering what else she wanted from him, then suddenly remembered a film he'd seen on the plane coming back from Australia. The hero hadn't said he loved the heroine, so she hadn't believed he really cared about her. It had all seemed very silly at the time, but now he could see Linnie felt the same. Well, he did care about her. Very much. And if that was what they meant by love, it was all right by him, so he said it. 'I do love you, Linnie. And I don't want anyone to hurt you ever again.' He waited, watching her face, trying to work out whether he'd said the right thing.

When she started to cry, he was worried, then he realised she was smiling through the tears. As she put her arms round his neck, he held her close and risked a kiss.

'Yes, love, I will marry you,' she said softly in his ear.

'Oh, good. Now that's settled, can we get some dinner? I'm starving hungry.' He couldn't understand why she started laughing. But he often couldn't understand why people laughed, so he didn't worry about it. She was still holding his hand, after all.

Kirsty was woken in the middle of the following night by the unmistakable sound of Sam's car chugging along the track. Sounds carried so clearly in the still air. 'Welcome back, Mr Brady,' she muttered and got little more sleep that night. She lay there listening to the frogs droning away, thinking about Sam.

All the next day she waited for him to call round, but he didn't. She tried to summon up the courage that had sent her down to his house the previous day and couldn't, so decided to find something to occupy herself with instead of moping around.

In a sudden spurt of energy she moved all the sagging furniture out of one of the spare bedrooms and piled it outside on the veranda, though she couldn't move the huge old wardrobe, only drag it away from the wall. Taffy had recovered enough to limp clumsily beside her, treating this like a game, which made it take twice as long, but was double the fun.

Having worked out a colour scheme, she went to buy some paint. Of course she had to pass Sam's house. The car was there and the door of his studio was open. She hesitated, then drove past without stopping.

Penny rang later to ask her round for a drink the next day. 'Sam's back and it's the anniversary of when Franco and I met, so I thought I'd invite a few people round tomorrow to celebrate. It'll be too cold to have it outside, but we use the garage as a party room in winter. It'll be very casual.'

'That'd be nice. What shall I bring?'

'How about one of your gorgeous cakes?'

'Fine. Chocolate do?'

'Wonderful.'

Kirsty decided to wear the special dress. She looked in the mirror and saw that her hair was dull and full of dust from working on the bedroom, so went to have a shower and wash it.

There was a knock on the front door just as she was about to start blow-drying her wet hair. With a sigh she put down the hairdryer, wrapped the towel round her head and went to answer it. It wouldn't be Sam, because he always went round the back.

But it was him!

They stared at one another for a few moments then she gestured to him to come in. 'So you're back.' Great conversation starter, she thought angrily. State the obvious, why don't you, Kirsty Miller? And show him you're flustered while you're at it. She'd intended to look special next time she saw him, not like a dripping water rat. 'Want a coffee? Or a beer?'

'No, thank you. I just came to see how Taffy was.'

'She's a lot better, thank you. I keep her shut up in the kitchen in the daytime. If I give her free run of the house, she gets on to the beds and makes a nest in the covers. How did you go in Perth?'

His face lit up. 'Brilliantly. Lara's acting as my agent now and the chairman wants to buy the huge painting for the foyer, plus he's ordered a smaller one for his house. And this morning I heard that Rhys had sold another painting down here.'

'Oh, er, yes.' Would he mind that she'd bought it? Kirsty wondered. You never knew with Sam's touchy pride. 'Why don't you come through and see Taffy for yourself?' She led the way to the kitchen and to her relief, he didn't glance sideways into the living room. He knelt down and spent a moment or two petting the little dog. Kirsty wished he'd lavish that much attention on her. She felt in need of a bit of petting.

Sam stood up. 'No more incidents with the intruder?'

'No. But he's been around. I bought some pepper spray, so if he tries anything on, he'll be in for a nasty surprise.'

'Good. Oh, just let me switch the security system back to my place.' He turned to leave and as he walked back towards the front entrance, he did glance sideways.

To her dismay he stopped dead and stared at the painting, then glared at her. 'I didn't need your charity. Tell me how much you paid for that and I'll buy it back.'

'I didn't buy it out of charity, but because I loved it on sight.'

'Oh, per-lease! You've barely started to redecorate, let alone got round to choosing colour schemes and art accessories.'

Hands on hips, she glared at him. 'You get more tactful every time I meet you, Sam Brady! But you're not having my painting back. If you think I'd spend that much money out of pity, or buy a painting I didn't like for any reason, you've got rocks in your head.'

'Oh.' He took an uncertain step towards the door.

'I really do love it,' she said more quietly. 'It seems to tell me to enjoy life.'

That remark made him swing round and stare at her as if he had never seen her before. 'You think it says that?'

She wasn't backing off. 'Yes. I don't care what you meant it to say, that's what it tells me.'

'But that's exactly what I wanted when I painted it.' He gave a short laugh. 'I'd not have thought you'd understand that.'

Her anger flared up again at this gratuitous insult and she gave him a push. 'Get out of here, Sam, and don't come back till you can do it without insulting me!'

At the edge of the veranda, he stopped, opened and shut his mouth, then walked away.

She was glad she'd got rid of him. Well, no, she wasn't glad, couldn't lie to herself. But she was glad she'd kept her self-respect.

He need never know she'd been planning to propose to him the day he went to Perth.

Going back into the bathroom, she glared at her damp hair, then her face crumpled. She put the hairdryer down and went to get herself some tea. Why bother to style her hair? What did it matter now what she looked like?

Sam was still setting up barriers between them.

Out of sheer pride, Kirsty went to Penny's celebration the next day. She dressed in the new outfit, took care with her hair and if she said so herself, she looked really good.

She arrived early, using the car because she wouldn't have felt safe walking home on her own, not with the intruder around. Sam wasn't there when she arrived, but she saw Rhys and went across to speak to him. 'Small world. I didn't realise you knew Penny.'

'She and I went to school together in Perth. I lost touch with her for a while, but caught up again when she moved down here. How are things?'

'Fine,' Kirsty said brightly – well, she hoped she sounded cheerful. Only she didn't think she'd quite managed it.

'I know we've only recently become friends, but I know you well enough to tell when you're putting on a mask. Things aren't fine, are they?'

'No.'

'Is it because Sam's gone away again?'

She stared at Rhys in shock. 'Gone away again?'

'You didn't know?'

'He never said a word. I heard his car earlier on but thought he was just nipping out to buy some beer for the party.'

Rhys's eyes were full of concern. 'He's gone down south on a photography trip, says he needs some inspiration.'

She bent her head for a minute or two. 'I think Sam's doing it to put distance between us. Does he think how we react to one another will go away?' She gave Rhys a wry smile, not trying to hide her sadness. 'Maybe it will for him. Anyway, I'm not going to mope all evening. Tell me how things are going at the gallery? Selling a nice lot of pictures?'

'Quite a few. Sam's go more quickly than most, but I've a couple of other artists whose work is doing well.

Tina discovered one of them, actually. This woman does fantasy art, glorious females who look as if they've come from another universe. Her work reminds me a bit of the pre-Raphaelites, only with a modern twist.'

'I must come in and look at them. I couldn't get beyond Sam's picture last time.'

'Have you heard from Tina?'

'No. She decided I was using her to get into her father's good books and that was it.'

'Ungrateful child. I shall have to have words with her. But she has so little self-esteem and her ego is even more tender at the moment. Did you know her mother is now shacked up with the guy Tina used to go out with?'

'That's terrible. How did you find that out?'

'I phone Tina once or twice a week.'

'You do? That sounds suspiciously like—'

He held up one hand in a stop sign. 'I'm only a friend. I'm a bit old for Tina. I have to go up to Perth now and then, and I got her number from Sam so I could keep in touch. I'm thinking of offering her a job in a new gallery I'm opening in the city. She loved working for me and did amazingly well for a beginner, though of course she still has a lot to learn, stuff they don't teach you on art appreciation and history courses.'

'That'd be so good for her.'

'Good for me, too. I'd be doing myself a favour as well as her.'

The evening passed pleasantly enough, Kirsty supposed. She chatted to people, listened to advice she didn't want on managing a big block and waited for someone to leave because it would look rude to be the first to go.

When Rhys started saying his goodbyes, she went to ask him a favour. 'Could you please drive home behind me, just to check that things are all right?'

'You could stay here if you're nervous,' Penny offered.

'I've got Taffy to see to.'

'I'll not only come with you, I'll stay until you've checked out the house,' Rhys said.

'I'm sorry to trouble you.'

'It's no trouble.'

Whitegums lay bathed serenely in moonlight as they drew up in front.

'It's a grand old place,' Rhys said as he walked inside with Penny. 'Go and have a careful check, then I'll leave you in peace.'

Noel saw them go inside together and turned away, scowling. That fellow again. He'd stayed the night last time. Well, it was getting colder and he didn't intend to hang around just in case the fellow left her warm bed in the middle of the night. This whole venture wasn't going nearly as well as he'd hoped because that damned woman refused to be scared away.

He needed to increase the pressure. Only how? He was working long hours in a lousy, menial job, clearing up in a café kitchen, stacking dishwashers and scrubbing pans to earn his keep. He was living in his car half the time, staying the occasional night in a motel to get clean again, or else staying on the veranda of this dump, the floor of which seemed to get harder each time.

Was it worth it? His wife insisted it was.

What if the Miller woman didn't go back to England before the year was up? His wife would go mad at him and would probably leave him and clean him out of what property he did have left. Brenda was a prime bitch, but she did bring in a steady income and his job was often chancy, so he didn't want to split up with her. Besides, better the devil you knew. No woman was to be trusted.

He trudged through the damned bush, which was full of nasty creepy-crawlies and insects. As he passed some tall gum trees, a bird hooted just above him, making him jump. Something rustled in the foliage and he hurried on quickly, hoping it wasn't a snake – or did snakes not move about during the night? Who the hell knew? Or cared? He was fed up to the teeth of Australia, that was the only thing he was certain about.

He was exhausted tonight. It'd been extra busy at the café with a big birthday party for some stupid young bimbo. He sighed.

Next time he went to Whitegums he'd make sure he scared the hell out of the Miller woman. He drew the line at rape, didn't think he could do it. And he didn't want to murder her, either. But he was angry enough to hurt her a bit, and anyway, she deserved a good thumping for pinching his uncle's money.

He got into his car and started it up, wondering if there was something wrong with the motor, because he seemed to hear a faint echo in the engine. Or was that another car in the distance? He listened. Just someone passing through on the main road. Sounds carried a long way in the still night air.

Driving slowly, he rolled down the track to the road, where he stopped to pull off the rags covering his number plates. He wasn't having anyone near Whitegums tracing him through the car. The neighbours didn't seem interested in what went on at the shack, thank goodness, and there hadn't been any sign of the owner. Bit of luck that. Only bit of luck he'd had since he got here.

He hated sleeping rough. What did Brenda think he could do with so little money and time, because of the need to work? But she'd refused to send him any more, the bitch.

Tonight he was going to break into one of the holiday rental homes he'd found and sleep in a comfortable bed, for a change. He'd done that once or twice now.

Chapter Twenty-One

Kirsty woke up early. Her dreams had been of Ed. He'd been standing in front of her, shaking his head sadly, looking disappointed. He hadn't said anything, but she knew why he felt she'd let him down.

She couldn't stop thinking about that dream. Ed had been so like her grandfather, both in looks and in being wise about people. She'd gone down to try to talk sense to Sam once, but it had taken a lot of courage. Maybe she'd summon up every last ounce of courage and give it one last go after he returned.

'Will that suit you, Ed?'

When the kookaburra started laughing, she could almost believe that was his answer.

But days passed and with no sign of Sam, her courage faded and doubts crept in.

On the following Saturday she heard a car on the track, but it didn't sound like Sam's. She went to stand on the front veranda, listening. The car stopped. It hadn't come up the track to Penny's or she'd have seen it, so it must have gone to Sam's.

Who could it be?

She was annoyed with herself for sticky-beaking, she didn't like nosy people, but she couldn't help wondering who it was and lingered to see what would happen next.

A few minutes later, the car engine started up again. It didn't go back towards the main road, but came further up the track, turning off towards Penny's. She caught a glimpse of it, yellow, medium-sized, not new. She didn't know Australian car makes well enough to recognise what sort it was.

Shortly afterwards she heard the engine again and this time it came to Whitegums. Tina got out, hesitated then came towards her. The driver, a young man, stayed inside the vehicle.

'I'm sorry to trouble you, Kirsty,' Tina said stiffly, 'but I wondered if you knew where my dad was. I've not heard from him all week and I'm a bit worried, so Danny – this is my flatmate – said we'd have a day out and call to see Dad or at least find out if anyone knew where he was.'

'Sam went away a few days ago on a photographic trip. No one knows when he'll be coming back, I'm afraid. Won't you come in and have a coffee?'

'No, we—'

Danny got out of the car. 'To tell you the truth, Tina, I need to use the john.' He was tall and lanky, with an American accent and a fresh, open face.

'Be my guest.' Kirsty led the way round to the back entrance.

'Nice place to live,' he commented. 'My parents have a cabin in the woods back home and you can really chill out there. Your place has the same feel to it.'

She showed him where to go and went back to Tina, who was standing by the kitchen door. Fed up of this unwarranted hostility, she said bluntly, 'I wasn't using you to get at your father, you know. I was actually enjoying your company.'

Silence.

Kirsty put the kettle on. 'You found me guilty without a trial. Don't judge me by your mother's standards.'

Tina flushed. 'How do you know about her?'

'From Rhys. We've become good friends. *Just* friends. He speaks very well of you.'

For the first time Tina's expression brightened. 'What does he say?'

'That you have a good eye for paintings.' She hesitated. 'Has he said anything else to you?'

Tina shook her head.

'Then I'd better not betray a confidence. But it's all good news, I promise you.' She got out three mugs. 'You can't go without a drink. Do stay.'

Tina nodded, then said in a rush, 'I'm sorry if I misjudged you, Kirsty. I was just so upset about – oh, all sorts of things. Rhys says I was being stupid.' She blinked her eyes and sniffed, hunting in her bag.

Kirsty snatched up a tissue and handed it to her, then gave her a quick hug, smiling at her. 'How are the studies going?'

'Better this time. Danny's so easy to live with that I feel more relaxed about everything. I hadn't realised what a difference that makes. Mum was so difficult. Danny and I aren't dating or anything. We're just friends, you know.'

'I do remember the difference.' Kirsty sighed at the memories which poured back suddenly. 'I met my husband when I was studying. We moved in together almost immediately and he was easy to live with, too – especially after my brother. At least Mike and I had a few years together.'

'Did you stop loving him as much after the first year or so?'

Kirsty turned from getting out a cake, puzzled. 'No, of course not.'

'Mum says everyone cools off after they've been married a while.'

'Mike and I didn't. We grew closer – and happier.'

Tina bowed her head, fiddling with the strap of her back pack. 'It's my mother's fault,' she said eventually.

Kirsty waited.

Tina looked across at her desperately. 'She's trained me to think badly of people, to expect them to let me down. And they mostly have.'

'Your father hasn't. I didn't. Rhys didn't either. Oh, Tina.' The girl was crying even harder, so Kirsty went across and took her in her arms. Over Tina's shoulder she saw Danny come to the doorway, then give her a half-smile and back away again.

'I always mess things up,' Tina sobbed. 'I'm sorry, Kirsty.'

'If you're sorry, we can mend our bridges and carry on being friends.'

'Won't you always remember what I did?'

'You didn't really do anything.'

'I did. I told Dad it was you or me, said he couldn't have both of us.'

'Ah.' Which explained a lot about Sam's erratic behaviour. 'Well, now you can tell him you've changed your mind, can't you?'

'Do you . . . are you and he together?'

'Not yet, but I'm hoping. He's a bit stubborn, though. I think your mother left him rather wary of relationships.'

'Tell me about it.'

When Tina was calmer, Kirsty sent her to wash her face and made some coffee for Danny.

'She's one screwed-up kid,' he said quietly. 'I'm glad you two have made up.'

'Let me know if she needs any help in any way.'

He smiled. 'Or I could even try to help her myself. She reminds me so much of my kid sister – needy and unsure of herself. Mom brought me up, Dad and his sister brought Cindy up. I think I got the better deal.'

Impossible not to like him. Tina seemed to have been lucky with her flatmate.

In the end, since her two visitors didn't have any definite plans, Kirsty persuaded them to stay overnight and leave early the next morning, not surprised when they chose separate bedrooms. You could usually tell if there was an attraction between two people, and there were no sparks flying between them, no warm glances or touches.

She rang to invite Rhys and her neighbours round that evening and noticed Tina's eyes following Rhys everywhere. For a time the two of them sat in earnest conversation in one corner and afterwards Tina was glowing with happiness. He must have told her about the prospective job.

All in all, it was a very pleasant evening.

If only Sam had been there, it'd have been perfect. Why had he stayed away so long?

How would he react when he came back and she confronted him?

Penny rang Kirsty the next afternoon. 'Franco's mother is ill. We need to go to her. She's nearly eighty.'

'Do you want me to look after Ellie for you?'

'Would you?'

'Of course. Good job this happened after the pups had left home, eh?'

'Yes. But we're worried about leaving you on your own. We were thinking – maybe you should come up to our house. What do you think? You'd be a lot safer here.'

Kirsty nearly said yes. Then pride stiffened her spine. She'd vowed not to be driven out of Whitegums and she wasn't going to let the intruder do it. 'No. Bring Ellie round here. The three of us will be all right. Taffy will enjoy seeing her mother again. They love playing together.'

'Are you sure?'

'Yes.'

When they'd left, Kirsty admitted to herself that she wasn't at all sure she was doing the right thing. Only she was tired of letting the prowler goad her and damage her possessions. Somehow she had to fight back. And you didn't do that by running away.

Sam was lying in a motel room, wondering the same thing: was he doing the right thing staying away from home? He'd taken enough photographs of foliage to last him for a long time, trying hard not to think about his many-horned dilemma. But it kept coming back to him in the dark reaches of the night.

His choices were to upset his daughter, with whom he was newly reconciled, by getting together with Kirsty – supposing Kirsty would even have him after the way he'd mucked her about. Or he could upset both himself and Kirsty by not following through on the feelings they had for one another, not only the physical attraction, but the fact that he liked her, enjoyed her company, admired her bravery in sticking it out against the intruder.

But the other thing he still found it hard to get past was the thought of marrying a rich woman. He really balked at that.

Marrying! That word again. Only he wasn't the sort of man to play around with a woman for a few months and then move on to another relationship. If he had a wish list, he'd put a secure emotional base at the head of it, way ahead of anything else. A marriage like those of his parents and grandparents. Even Lorraine hadn't destroyed his belief that such a thing was possible, though his relationship with her had made him vow to be extremely careful if he ever chose a life partner again.

He smiled. Impossible to think of Kirsty playing the silly mind games Lorraine had, impossible to think of her being anything but honest and loving.

He groaned and turned over, seeking in vain to lie comfortably on this bumpy bed.

Today for some reason, he was worried about Kirsty's safety, he couldn't understand why.

What if the intruder came one day while Franco and Penny were out? How would Kirsty cope then? There would be no one to hear her if she called for help.

He fell asleep at last, only to dream of her, and in that dream Ed told him to go straight away and help her. Sam sat bolt upright in bed, still hearing the screams that had echoed through his nightmares, still seeing Ed's worried face. He glanced at the clock. Half past midnight. He felt wide awake and however hard he tried to reason with himself, he couldn't banish the feeling of anxiety, the sense that Kirsty was in danger.

Making a sudden decision, he threw off the covers, stuffed his clothes and toiletries into his backpack, carried his sketching and photographic equipment out to the car and wrote a cheque for the nights he'd stayed at this motel, shoving it and his room key into the reception area letterbox.

He set off, staring down the tunnel of light from the car's headlights as he travelled through the dark, moonless night. He felt as if he was the only person alive on the planet.

And it was good to be going home.

Surely Kirsty would be all right? Surely it had just been his imagination playing tricks?

Only one way to find out.

Kirsty woke with a start as glass smashed somewhere in the dark house. She pressed the emergency button, then remembered that Penny and Franco were away for the night. Her heart started pounding and fear froze her for a minute.

Then she picked up the phone. There was no dial tone. But she had her mobile in her handbag, so she found that and dialled 000. She whispered a plea for help, explaining that the police already knew about the intruder's other break-ins. A voice spoke reassuringly, but they couldn't give her a clear idea of their arrival time.

Getting out of bed, feeling very shaky, she slipped on her trousers and shoes. She didn't switch on the light, wanted to show no sign of being here. Ellie and Taffy, who were in the room with her, had woken up and she'd tried to shush them. She saw them in the moonlight, looking at her as if for guidance as to what they were to do at this hour of the night.

She picked up the sharpening steel and made sure the pepper spray was in her pocket with the lid off. Then she waited, sure he hadn't finished with her.

There was the noise of more glass smashing, sounding closer this time.

'Go home to England!' a man's voice yelled. 'Damned well go home, you stupid bitch! Don't make me hurt you.'

She didn't answer, but was quite sure by now that it was Ed's great-nephew. Who else would be so keen to get her out of the country? What was he like? From his footprints he'd seemed a big man. Could she deal with him on her own, or would he overcome her? And if he did, what then?

Her breath caught in her throat. Surely he didn't intend to murder her?

The noise of smashing glass came from very close at hand this time, the next bedroom, from the sound of it. Ellie whined in her throat and Taffy echoed her mother.

Suddenly afraid for the puppy, Kirsty scooped her up and shut her in the en suite. Ellie might be of use, but Taffy would probably get in the way. The pup at once began whimpering, distracting Kirsty for a few moments.

She missed the approach of a man's shadow against the window and jumped in shock as the sliding door was smashed. She caught a glimpse of the head of a sledge hammer withdrawing, then it thudded back and more glass shattered. Fear nearly paralysed her and she couldn't move, could hardly breathe.

Sam drove on through the night, swerving suddenly and cursing as he realised he had a flat tyre. He slowed the car down and pulled over to the side of the road, swearing under his breath as he got out. The moon was now rising, but it didn't provide enough light for a rapid wheel change.

He grimly set to work to change the tyre, which had a dirty nail sticking out of it. Everything seemed to take twice as long as usual.

No other cars passed, there was just him and the night – and that strange, nagging anxiety for Kirsty's safety.

'Tonight I'm going to teach you a lesson you won't forget, Kirsty Miller.' The intruder laughed and wielded the sledgehammer again.

Ironically, it was the laughter that did it, made her so angry she lost the paralysis of extreme fear.

'Or maybe I'm going to teach you a lesson,' she muttered. 'Laugh at me, would you?' She went to stand in the shadows to the side of the window, waiting for him to come in. She could have run away, but didn't want to. She was armed and wouldn't hesitate to hit him with the steel bar or spray him.

He cleared the worst of the jagged shards of glass from the frame with the hammer and stepped inside. For a moment he stood there, staring round the room.

Kirsty raised the steel bar and swung it at him. But in lifting it, her arm knocked a picture on the wall behind her, sending it crashing to the ground and giving him enough warning to duck. She managed to land a blow on his shoulder, but not with the force she needed to disable him.

He grabbed hold of the steel and laughed again.

Furiously she fought him for possession of it because if she lost it, she didn't know what to do. The pepper spray was in her pocket, but she didn't dare let go of the steel to fish it out. When she tried to bring her knee up as the self-defence books told you to do, she couldn't hit the spot and he laughed again.

And then he managed to take away the steel, flinging it across the room, where it smashed into the dressing table.

Ellie was growling and barking, circling them as if trying to find a way to help, but when he kicked out at her, she dodged backwards.

Sobbing with anger rather than fear, Kirsty fumbled for the pepper spray, but before she could pull it out of her pocket, he grabbed hold of her in a gorilla-like embrace, trying to pull her arms behind her. And he was succeeding, because he was so much bigger than she was.

Suddenly he yelled in pain and let go of her, turning to kick out at Ellie, who must have bitten him. His foot connected and the dog went flying across the room towards the sliding door that opened on to the veranda.

'Stay!' Kirsty roared, terrified for the dog.

As the intruder moved towards her, she backed away, holding up the small can of pepper spray, and jerking up her pyjama top to cover her lower face because the policeman had told her it could affect bystanders too. Holding her breath she sprayed it over the intruder's face and backed quickly over to the open door as he screamed and stumbled backwards. Her own eyes were stinging but she sucked in mouthfuls of fresh air and blinked quickly, and the discomfort eased.

Ellie pressed against her, whimpering, and she said 'Sit!' firmly.

What would the intruder do next? Should she run away? She didn't know what to do. And anyway, she'd left poor Taffy shut in the en suite bathroom. He might take his anger out on the puppy.

As he got out of his car, Sam heard the scream and it sounded horribly like the one in his dream. He ran round to the back of the house, horrified as his feet crunched over broken glass that seemed to litter the whole veranda. What the hell had happened here?

'Kirsty! Where are you?'

She ran into his arms. 'Sam. Oh, Sam!'

'Are you all right?'

'Yes.' She pulled herself together. 'I've sprayed him with pepper spray, but we ought to tie him up, I think, till the police get here.'

He moved forward and found the intruder rolling to and fro on the bed, moaning and rubbing his eyes.

'I don't think he's going to try to get away.'

'Should we do something about his eyes?' she whispered.

'No. Serves him right.'

'I can't leave him like that. What if his sight is damaged?' She held her breath and covered her mouth with her top again then dashed into the en suite, dampening a washcloth and hand towel.

Sam took them from her and held the towel over his own face. 'You hold the steel.' He had to shout to get the intruder's attention and the man sobbed as Sam gave him the damp washcloth. He held it to his eyes, still rolling his head to and fro in agony.

While that was happening, Kirsty checked Ellie, but the dog didn't seem to have anything broken from being kicked. Taffy was now pressed against her mother on the veranda, shivering.

The intruder stopped rolling round and made a sudden dash for the door. But Sam sprayed the air in front of him and he jerked back, subsiding on the bed with the cloth held across his face again.

'I'll sue you for this,' he yelled.

'I don't think so,' Sam said, back at the open door again.

There was the reflection of a flashing blue light in the track. 'I'll bring them round.' Kirsty rushed out to show the police where to go, explaining quickly what had happened.

It was some time before they left again, taking the intruder with them, under arrest and facing a string of charges.

After all the noise and fuss, the house seemed unnaturally quiet. Kirsty walked back along the veranda, staring down at the glass crunching beneath her feet. 'I think that's the last time he'll come visiting.'

'Yes. Sounds like it'll be the last time he comes to Australia, as well. He wasn't very good at hassling you, was he?'

'Good enough to frighten me for a while.'

Sam kicked some of the glass to one side. 'Are you . . . all right?'

'Yes. Thank you for your help. You came just in time.'

'It looked to me as if you'd have managed without me.'

She shuddered. 'I was never as glad to see anyone. I hope I never have to fight off another intruder as long as I live. It was horrible.' She began to shake as reality set in.

Sam muttered something under his breath and put his arms round her, holding her close. 'You'd manage. You're a strong woman in all the ways that count.'

'How did you know I needed you tonight? Or was it just a coincidence?'

'I had a dream.'

She looked up at him in puzzlement. 'A dream?'

'Yes. Ed. And you, screaming.'

'Oh. Well, if I'm ever in trouble, I hope you get another dream.'

He released her and took a step backwards, looking at his watch. 'It's nearly six o'clock. Just getting light. How about a cup of tea?'

She'd been expecting his hug to last longer, but clearly the barriers were being put firmly into place between them again. She was too drained to do anything about that now, so made the tea, welcoming its warmth.

When she'd finished her cup, she stood up. 'I'll find a brush to clean up the veranda.'

Sam took it out of her hands. 'I'll do that.'

She snatched it back. 'I'm perfectly capable of sweeping up glass. I only want a path for Ellie and Taffy to get to the garden safely. I'll do the rest later.' When he didn't say anything, she snapped, 'Go home now, Sam. I'll be all right. You don't want to get involved, after all.'

He hesitated, moved away a couple of steps, opened his mouth, then shut it again. 'You're sure you'll be all right?'

'Yes.'

When he'd gone she didn't let herself cry, but continued sweeping up the glass with short, vicious strokes, muttering to herself about stupid, pig-headed men.

As soon as it turned eight o'clock, she reckoned tradesmen would be at work and managed to find a glazier who could send some men out straight away to measure up and fit new glass, it being an emergency.

For a while she watched the two men work, then she left them to it and drove into town to make a statement at the police station.

Noel Porter was locked up safely and had admitted what he'd been doing to her.

That nightmare was over.

The other nightmare, the one in which Sam always turned away from her, was still ongoing.

Rod's boss Melissa rang up to arrange a time for the job interview.

He put the phone down and began to worry.

Linnie put her hand on his arm. 'What's the matter, love?'

He reminded her about the special job and how terrible he was at interviews. 'There's the man who coaches me, but I never seem to do it right when I go to see him. You wouldn't – come with me, would you?'

'I don't know anything about interviews.'

'No, but you'll be there. That'll make me feel better.'

Her face softened. 'All right.'

She sat by Rod's side as the coach went over some simple techniques and made him practise answering. When the session was over, they drove home.

'I reckon I can remember enough to practise it with you,' Linnie said.

'You can?'

'Yes. It's simple, really.'

They went over it again and again, and she said he was getting quite good at it.

When he went for the interview Rod felt better than he'd expected to. The main thing was to say as little as possible and only to answer their questions, not tell them how to set the world of accounting right.

When he came home, Linnie was waiting for him. 'How did it go?'

He shrugged. 'I don't know. I think I did what we'd practised but how can you tell how well it went down with them? I won't find out till tomorrow morning. Melissa is going to ring me.'

'Then I'll stay home from work tomorrow and be with you.'

'Thanks.' He smiled at her for a moment, then said briskly, 'I'm hungry now. I wasn't hungry this morning, but I am now.'

When he'd finished eating, he said firmly, 'How soon can we be married?'

'As soon as you like.'

He pulled up a notepad and began making a list of what needed doing.

'Hoy!'

He looked up.

'There are two of us,' she said. 'When we make lists about our life as man and wife, we make them together.'

He looked down with a frown.

She took the pencil out of his hand. 'Together,' she repeated firmly. 'And it's about time you kissed me again. You don't do it often enough.'

He smiled. He liked kissing her. He hadn't understood before how nice it could be. But then, he'd never been in love before. He'd have to find a book that told you more about making love. That was worrying him a bit, he had to admit. He'd never done it before and she had.

Kirsty sat in the living room thinking hard. If Sam hadn't come rushing to her rescue, hadn't held her so tenderly, hadn't hesitated at the end before turning away, she'd be telling herself to forget him. But he'd given all the appearance of a man torn in two.

Was that because of Tina?

Or because of the money?

Ed had been right. She would definitely have to make the running. She straightened her spine. Was she going to let Sam go on denying the feelings they had for one another? No, she damned well wasn't.

She remembered the book she'd bought from the motivational speaker. It said you had to be proactive.

Heavens, it seemed like a lifetime ago now since she'd read it! She went to stare at herself in the mirror. She didn't even look like the same woman and she didn't feel like it, either.

So, she decided, she wasn't going to let Sam get away without a fight. A battle, even.

Chapter Twenty-Two

Kirsty woke up early next morning to find it raining heavily. Before she could change her mind about confronting Sam, she set off down the track with her umbrella. She didn't put on her fancy clothes this time. It was herself she was offering, not her clothes. And she didn't take the convertible either, because that simply shrieked of wealth and her money was one of the things standing between them.

There were lights on inside the cottage, because it was a dull sort of day. She didn't knock on the door, but pushed it open and marched inside.

Sam turned round, looking surprised.

'We need to talk!' she said. 'About us.'

'I'll put the kettle on.'

'Never mind the kettle.' She marched forward and grabbed him by the front of his paint-stained sweatshirt.

He stiffened and she was afraid he was going to pull away, so she locked her arms round his neck and when he opened his mouth, she stood on tiptoe and kissed him before he could speak.

He tried to push her away, but only feebly, and then his arms went round her and he began kissing her back.

When she risked moving away, she saw love in his eyes, unmistakable. But then she saw those shutters click down again. 'Don't do that!' she yelled. 'Stop hiding behind your damned pride!'

Taking a deep breath she said very rapidly, 'Ed knew what he was talking about. You and I, we're right for one another. And you may be stubborn but I'm more stubborn. I love you, Sam, and I think you love me. Our feelings aren't going away and neither am I.'

His hands went round her waist, then slid up her back as if they had a life of their own.

'We could – have an affair?' he said. 'See how we go for a while.'

'I'm not into affairs. I'm into love and marriage, the whole damned shebang. Oh, Sam—' Her voice broke and she couldn't think what else to say or do to convince him to give their relationship a chance.

The phone rang and they both stared at it. When the answering machine clicked on, they heard Tina's voice and Sam went to pick up the handset.

'I'm here, darling. Is something wrong?'

Tina's voice echoed from the speaker so Kirsty heard every word.

'No, Dad. Nothing's wrong. I've been a bit worried about you, that's all. I came down but no one knew where you were.'

'I was off on a photographic trip.'

'Did Kirsty tell you we were there? We stayed over with her.'

He turned to stare across the room. 'No, she didn't. She was a bit busy fighting off the intruder last night.'

There was a gasp, then, 'He came back again? Is she all right, Dad?'

'Yes, she's fine. She had a pepper spray and used it to hold him till the police arrived.'

'I'm so glad you were there for her.'

'She'd already disabled him by the time I arrived home. She's a very capable woman.'

Kirsty turned towards the door, thinking to move out on to the veranda and give them privacy. Sam waved one hand at her to stop her and mouthed, 'Don't go.'

Was that a good sign? Oh, she hoped it was.

'Thank goodness for that. Dad, look, Kirsty and I made things right between us. I was way out of line telling you to choose between her and me. I'm sorry about that. I really like her.'

'I'm sorry I missed seeing you.'

'Well, next time you come up to Perth, we can meet.'

'It's a date. Look, Tina, I've just got something important to attend to at the moment. I'll phone you back this evening. All right?' He set the phone down and turned to Kirsty. 'I can barely support myself, let alone a wife or family. It's no use trying to pretend, I do care about you, but I hate the thought of being dependent on you.'

'Then I'll give the money away.'

'That would be stupid.'

'Not as stupid as both of us living separately a few hundred yards from one another, wanting one another, kept apart by your stupid pride. So I'm telling you now, Sam Brady, the sensible thing is for you to marry me – and soon. I've had more than enough of this messing around.'

His mouth set in a line.

How could she make him understand? She had to try. 'Sam, I wasted years mourning Mike, afraid of falling in love again and getting hurt. Well, I did eventually fall in love – with you – and I did get hurt. But I still want you.'

He took a step towards her. 'I'm sorry. I never meant to hurt you.'

'I felt dreadful when you went away. Without even saying goodbye. That's as cowardly as anything I've ever done. Far worse!'

His voice was low, his eyes full of pain. 'I knew if I saw you again I'd lose control.'

She glared at him. 'Well, why aren't you losing control now? Sam, if you tell me you don't love me, I'll go away and not bother you again. I'll be miserable, but that won't be your problem. Can you tell me that, Sam?'

He shook his head. 'No. I can't lie to you, Kirsty. And – I've been miserable, too.'

'You have?' She beamed at him. Taking him by surprise, she pushed him down on the nearby sofa and sat on his knee. 'Then you must marry me.'

A smile tugged at the corner of his mouth. 'Why must I?'

'Because I say so, and I can be as much of a bully as my brother if I let myself. And since you've admitted you love me, I'm not going to give up on you.'

'I'm terrified.' He began to kiss her, then stopped and sighed against her neck. 'How much money did Ed leave you?'

'A lot.'

He looked at her, then growled something under his breath and pulled her to him. As he kissed her, she forgot everything except the touch and feel of him.

When he stopped she demanded, 'When are we getting married?'

'Let's just take this easy?'

Was he backing off? 'No. I won't accept half-measures.' She stood up and stumbled towards the door. Before she had reached it, however, he was there, one arm across it, barring her way.

'I want marriage, children, commitment, Sam. I'm not into affairs or compromises. If you won't give me all that, I'll walk away from here, even if it means giving up my house and inheritance.'

'I was gathering my courage together.' He pulled her into his arms. 'I can't bear to lose you. Oh, hell, Kirsty, I love you so much, I could only think of dark, gloomy paintings while I was away. Dead flowers, rotting greenery.'

'I think your flower paintings are brilliant, Sam.' A thought occurred to her. 'In fact, you'll probably end up rich and famous in your own right and then my money will matter even less.'

'You really don't care about it, do you?' he said wonderingly.

'No. It's you I care about.'

'I care about you, too. I was determined not to, tried to be rational, but it's not rational to deny something so obvious. Will you forgive me?'

Joy flooded through her. 'Oh, yes.'

He took her hands and raised them to his lips one after the other. 'In that case, Kirsty Miller, will you please do me the honour of becoming my wife?'

She couldn't speak for a moment, only nod as joy blossomed inside her.

'What, no words?' he teased as he drew her into his arms. 'No bullying?' He kissed one corner of her mouth. 'No more demands?'

'I'd love to marry you.'

This time Sam's smile didn't falter. 'Good,' he said softly.

Kirsty could imagine their old friend watching them and smiling. Thank you, Ed, she thought as she took back the initiative and kissed Sam good and hard.

The following day they went to ask Penny's advice about a good local marriage celebrant.

'Does that mean what I think it does?' she asked.

'Yes. We're going to get married.' Sam grinned at her. 'She's trapped and tamed me.'

Kirsty let out a snort and poked one finger into his chest. 'You, my friend, are completely untameable.'

'It was Ed who married me and Franco,' Penny said, smiling reminiscently. 'He made it such a lovely event.'

'He was a marriage celebrant?' Kirsty asked in surprise.

'Yes. Didn't you know?'

'No.'

Then Kirsty remembered something she'd found out recently. 'He was also a distant relative of mine, which must be why he reminded me so much of my granddad. I've been going through his papers and old family photographs doing a family tree for him. He came back to the same part of England our family has lived in for generations. I wonder if he knew?'

'He can't have known or he'd surely have said something.'

'We'll have a big party to celebrate your wedding,' Penny said. 'Franco and I will host it as our wedding present to you.'

'I can't let you spend your money like that,' Kirsty protested.

'If you'd rather have a fancy, formal event—'

'No!' They both said together.

'Then we'll do it our way and everyone will bring a plate.'

'We'll discuss the details later,' Kirsty said. 'Where are the yellow pages? We need to find a marriage celebrant.'

That evening Rod rang her up from England. 'I've got two pieces of news for you,' he began, as usual not bothering with preliminaries or asking how she was.

Before Kirsty could reply, there was a murmur of voices and she wondered who was with him.

'Linnie says I should ask how you are first.' He waited and when she didn't reply, said, 'Well, how are you?'

'I'm fine. Um – who's Linnie?'

'The woman I'm going to marry.'

'You're getting married?'

'Yes. She knows what I'm like and she doesn't mind. She's divorced and she has two sons and I like them, so we're getting married.'

'Well, congratulations.'

There was more muttering and a woman's voice came on. 'I'm Linnie. Pleased to meet you, Kirsty. I hope you don't mind us getting married?'

'I'm delighted. Actually, I'm going to get married myself soon.'

'To the artist?'

'Yes. What did Rod say about him?'

'He was very suspicious but I said he should credit you with a bit of sense.'

'Thank you.'

There was some clattering and Rod came back on the phone. 'Are you marrying that Sam fellow?'

'Yes. I love him and he loves me.'

'You're sure of that?'

'Yes. And what's more, his paintings are starting to sell. He's going to be a very famous and successful artist and I'm going to be his home business manager.'

'Well, if he's successful, that does make a difference. I still don't like him, though.'

She chuckled. 'What's your other piece of news, Rod?'

'I got a promotion to a special job they set up for me. Linnie practised interview questions with me and – well, I did it.'

'I'm so glad for you. Have you told Sue yet that you're getting married?'

'No. I suppose I'd better. She might not approve, but whether she does or not, I'm still marrying Linnie. Goodbye.'

The line went dead and Kirsty chuckled again as she put the phone down and told Sam her brother's news. 'Whoever this Linnie is, she deserves a medal.'

'So we have his blessing?' Sam asked.

'Sort of. He says it's better if you're successful but he still doesn't like you.'

Sam threw back his head and roared with laughter. 'Come here and cuddle me, woman. We have only a month and a day of freedom before we tie the knot.' Then he frowned as he remembered something. 'What did you mean about being my home business manager?'

'Well, I have to do something with my time, so I thought I'd handle the everyday details and the money side of things and leave you free to paint.'

He pulled her to him for another kiss. 'Not only beautiful but intelligent, too.'

'I'm not beautiful.'

'You are to me.'

This reduced her to happy tears, but Taffy jumped up and began to lick her ear, and she was soon smiling again.

Later, Sam found a bottle of champagne and the first toast was, of course, 'To Ed.'

Acknowledgements

THANK YOU! Several people with far more expertise than me went out of their way to help me with information about winemaking on a small scale. My thanks go to: George Geris, Senior Winemaker at Villa Maria Estate, Marlborough, New Zealand, and his wife Barb Jeffcott Geris, Margaret Boski from New South Wales, Andrew Watt from Winequip, Victoria and Ron Macfarlane from Margaret River, Western Australia.

ANNA JACOBS was born in Lancashire at the beginning of the Second World War. She has lived in different parts of England as well as Australia and has enjoyed setting her modern and historical novels in both countries. She is addicted to telling stories and hopes to celebrate the publication of her one hundredth novel in 2022, as well as sixty years of marriage.

annajacobs.com

ALSO BY ANNA JACOBS

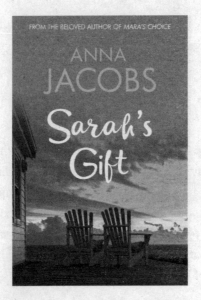

Sarah Blakemere has been married and widowed and seen great success in her business life. Now at the age of ninety-five, she signs her will, pleased with how it will throw the cat among the family pigeons. She has left her luxurious home in Western Australia, to two female relatives in the UK, on the condition that they live in the house together for a year. After that they can sell it and split the money between them, but if either of them doesn't last the full year, another relative will be invited to try for the inheritance, but will still have to last a full year before the house can be sold.

Will the experience do as Sarah had hoped and shake Portia and Fleur out of their ruts? And when they find another surprise bequest from Sarah, what will they do with it?

FROM THE MUCH-LOVED AUTHOR
OF THE PENNY LAKE SERIES

*The Best
Valentine's
Day
Ever*
and other stories

ANNA JACOBS

Romance can be found in every corner of the world and has changed the lives of people in every period of history. In this collection of sixteen stand-alone short stories, including a brand-new tale, Anna Jacobs encapsulates the spark of first love and the glow of second chances in her inimitable style.

'The Best Valentine's Day Ever': Heartbreak prompts Chrissie to seek comfort with her gran, Nancy. But unhappiness and misunderstandings turn into a celebration across generations.

'The Group Settler's Wife': Western Australia, 1924. Maggie is forging a new life for her family, the chance for a fresh start after the lingering effects of war. While unaccustomed to the rough conditions of pioneer life, Maggie discovers a strength to herself and will find happiness where she did not expect it.